YO-CCP-544

UNIVERSAL REMOTE

Michael Hartnett

neshui publishing

Published by Neshui Publishing, Inc.
1345 Bellevue Ave.; St. Louis, MO 63117
www.neshui.com

Copyright © 1999 by Michael Hartnett
All rights reserved. No part of this book may be reproduced
without written consent of the author.

ISBN 0-9652528-6-8
Distributed by Book Source
1230 Macklind Ave.; St. Louis, MO 63110

to
Jerry, Bridget, Donna, Brittany and Patrick

Channel 1:
Encore! Encore!

One year after old man Miller cut off his left ring finger in front of his Regents Chemistry class, I returned to the wealthy Long Island high school where he taught, where he had been given what the administration had hoped was permanent leave, and where he was subsequently returned, pronounced healthy in every way. Education had never been my beat, but old man Miller was certainly within the purview of my territory.

The administration was happy to have me there to report on the heartwarming return of its once very loved and then very much ignored brilliant lab man. Farmingville's own Mr. Wizard here to prove that one little aberration — a severed digit, grossed out, repulsed, hypnotized kids, and blood all over his lab coat — would not recur the way most aberrations seem to transform overnight into unrecognizable harbingers. Yet from the talk in the faculty room (whatever that type of talk is worth), Miller might not have put all his cutlery back in the cabinet.

"What do you think, Cochrane? Will it be a repeat performance?" laughed Dolores Sterns, a ninth grade social studies teacher who didn't brush her hair because her three uncontrollable children never left her the time for such matters.

"I've got ten bucks with Plummer on it," said Cochrane, neater and shorter than Dolores. "In fact, Plummer told me he'd throw in an extra ten bucks if I pick the right finger."

"Well, that's easy enough," piped in Jones, the phys ed. teacher in his sweat pants, "it's gotta be the pinky."

"Why the pinky?"

"Well, it's next to the ring finger, so he might as well make a set; plus, with the ring finger gone, he's got room on both sides of the digit to get at it, and the pinky's smaller too, so it makes easy cutting."

"That all sounds good," said Cochrane, "but I've worked with the man for thirty years, and I know him. If he's going to be cutting, he's going to one-up himself from last time and unless he goes for his big toe or his whole hand the only amputation I see him doing is the thumb."

"Hey," I interrupted, weighing whether this conversation would be the sidebar to a feature —Headline: *Colleague Had Expected Encore* — or some perverse elements to a front page story. "You don't think he is really going to do it?"

"Well, I'll tell you one thing," Cochrane began to me in his lecture tone, something teachers seem unable to resist, "I don't even think Miller knows what he's going to do today. All the kids have been talking about is that they can't wait for the old man's last lecture. Now that might just seem like they want to get Chemistry over with, but I've heard kids from other classes are trying to get into the lecture too. Maybe he won't do anything, but a lot of kids are expecting him to do something. I know when I'm teaching a physics class and lots of students are expecting me to do a special experiment, I make damn sure I can find something to fly across the room."

A true professional, Cochrane finished just as the bell rang and each teacher mumbled some groaning curse, picked up his books and left the sanctuary. I took off too, down to Miller's room; finding him there in his angelically white lab coat, fiddling around with the test tubes.

"Russell!" he greeted me, after squinting a few seconds through his doubled pane glasses that could also serve for goggles. Doc Miller always greeted me that way. To old man Miller, I wasn't the typical reporter, for I spent most of my days writing of technology, all types of heady stuff about the biotech, aerospace, sewage treatment, hyperconductors, microchips, cryptology, stereolithography ... you know, everything that could make its way into a column that didn't deal with crime or sex. Nothing really sordid, unless of course, you call the Miller story sordid, and I'm just on *this* case because Doc only wants to speak to me. He had been army buddies with my father, serving at the veterans hospital after the war. "How are you doing, old bean? Read your pieces on non-lethal weaponry. I knew there was nothing humanitarian about those things. It's about time somebody told the public those weapons are only being developed to immobilize an enemy long enough so that it can be annihilated."

Conspiratorial in nature, Doc Miller would have had this conversation linked fast enough to the Kennedy assassination if I let it happen... I had to get a few quick quotes out of him right away if I were going to run to Prometheus Technologies, return for his lecture, and slap out this story before I yoked together the technology column I should have finished two days ago.

"How's it feel to be back in the classroom?"

"Oh good, good, as well as can be expected. The kids don't listen to me of course, but no one has tried to sue me."

"What is it like one year after the incident?"

"Oh fine, I can only count to nine instead of ten. But otherwise, no different. I just wish the kids would listen."

"What?"

"I wish they would listen to me."

"Listen to you about what?"

"Listen to me about anything. They are either talking to each other while I'm speaking or they are not paying attention to anyone."

"How can you deal with that type of crap?"

"Well, I keep telling myself I only have a few more years to retirement and it'll all be over. If they would just listen, this teaching would be bearable."

"Well," trying not to act like one of his students, "I hate to disappear right now, but I just wanted to stop in. I've got to run out to cover a story, but I'll be back for your lecture. Tonight, if you'd like, you can meet me at Tara's and we can put down a few."

Miller said he'd like that and then returned to his beakers. From behind, with his crew-cut, his big back and his stumbly, brute manner of setting up a room, he reminded of my old man, but he wasn't the first lost and maimed fellow to make me think of Dad since he died. That didn't mean I was any more inclined to actually follow through on that drink I seemed to offer Doc. But the paternal reminder did make me feel a little more weaselly about scooting over to Prometheus Technologies, a place I had no business going to, especially when Miller needed someone to listen to him. Listening to Miller, after all, was supposed to be part of my job for the afternoon.

Channel 2:
Breakthrough at Prometheus Laboratories

"Where the hell have you been?"

Geoffrey Sphere, dressed like a congressman about to appear on C-Span, didn't wait for me to explain. He sat in his chair and picked up his unwieldy remote control looking around his laboratory, one modeled after a futuristic house.

"Watch this," he told me and pointed at the television screen, clicking on. I started watching, thinking he was going to show me a news report, when he tells me, "No, I mean watch this," and he points and clicks again and the stereo goes on. "And this," he points and on goes the microwave, then he continues to point and click as the oven, the washing machine, the faucet, the computer, various lights, vacuum cleaners and steamers, until everything in the lab operates off the remote.

"Now watch," and Geoffrey proceeded to adjust the appliances, switching television stations, lowering the stereo and shifting it into CD mode, turning up the microwave to high heat and the stove to broil, throwing the washer into spin cycle and the water from hot to cold. He even clicked at the hard drive of the computer, opening software and sending messages to the printer.

"You did it, huh," the old bastard was much further along on his invention than he had led me to believe.

"Well Carmen came up with the missing element," he explained with generous mortification. For the first time since I walked in I noticed Carmen's presence in the room. Before then, she didn't seem essential because she couldn't be turned on and off by the remote. She looked a little frazzled in the corner, like she had been doing much more than pointing and clicking. Her dark hair and eyes were a bit wild, neither had rested on a pillow for a few days. There would be time to hear her story and his, I could already see me using their contrasting personalities, her strange Latin coolness, his WASPish ticks, not to mention their physical polarities, he with the neat, snappy, short, bald white fire and she somehow sloppy and statuesque, you know, languid and slovenly... Christ, always writing this copy in my head when I should be doing something else.

"Let me take a look at that," I told Geoffrey, signaling for the remote.

"Sure, you can even have my chair."

What a soft chair it was and that clumsy remote somehow felt good in the hand. I clicked the control first at the washing machine, and then I was off. I could describe to you what happened next, but using a remote is a highly personal experience — more a man's private property than his land, his house, his barbecue, and God help me, even his wheels — so I prefer not to share the ensuing minutes with you. Anyway, describing these remote moments has a masturbatory quality that I can't deal with quite yet. Suffice to say, that well over half an hour passed before Sphere could get me out of the chair and back to listening to him.

"So, I see you are impressed," Geoffrey crowed.

I tried to hide my sheepish embarrassment. He couldn't understand the guilt I was feeling right now, guilt that even I hadn't expected. I accepted his offer for a PR man in an offhand way, while I was interviewing him on the Island's technology boom. I'm sure he didn't know and certainly didn't care that working for Prometheus while I'm the technology columnist for the paper was more than a little conflict of interest. But I had grown sick of my exalted position in the community — as the esteem for technology has risen, so have I. Even I started taking my position too seriously. To be a PR writer for Prometheus had just a healthy enough level of impropriety and corruption that it appealed to me.

Besides, I wanted to work with Carmen. A few years ago, I had interviewed her, her husband Frederique dropping by with their six kids, and I heard their grand immigrant tale of how Frederique put Carmen through universities and years of degrees so she could be the woman she is today. "Hey, I knew she had more brains than I did," Freddie told me with noble self-effacement. Meanwhile, the children bawled, so Carmen changed Aldo's diaper while Frederique changed Leslie's. Carmen's whole story *had* to be a scam, yet the six kids were there clamoring about Frederique, he in his janitor's fatigues, as Carmen managed to look smart and motherly — a hard trick for any human to manage. She played the role so well that I was tempted to kiss her even with that grand presence of the family. Now Geoffrey, he was another piece of work. Yet I can't get into talking about him right now.

Suffice to say, that filled with a sense of fatalism, I well understood after the first interview that taking this position had all the feel of a bad movie plot. I was being drawn into a situation of absurdist tendencies where people were acting and reacting to adhere to some structure that had been branded into them by the multitude of screens they gazed upon, mesmerized long ago, reinstilled these so many years.

Geoffrey told me: "I just knew a breakthrough would come any day now. That is why I hired you to do PR." ·You would believe him too if you heard Sphere next. He looked down at a piece of paper and started talking:

"This remote will change the way we all live. Everyone talks about how the Internet brings the world into your home, but you still have to move around your home, trudging from appliance to appliance, opening and shutting doors, turning knobs, twisting hands, moving from one machine to another like some automaton. Well, what kind of control is that? What kind of freedom can a man have if he spends his days from pillar to post, clicking switches, never able to get settled? The very best he can hope for is to twist around in his swivel chair, scooting along on his rollers like some baby in a walker. What kind of control is that?"

I was writing feverishly. Fucking nut-jobs make good copy.

"What are you doing?" he asked.

"Taking down notes."

"Don't bother. I've got it all down here on transcript," he said, smacking the paper with the back of his hand. I wanted to ask why is he reading it to me if he's already got it printed out, but evidently he was paying me right now to be his television audience. I became a willing, pliable consumer for his infomercial.

"No longer will we have to move to get to the world. Now the world will be in our laps. The universe will flash across eyes. We just have to point to it and turn it on. All signals, all channels, all codes, all messages can be read by this remote. Perhaps it can't look into a man's soul or read a man's mind, but when have those abilities cleaned your shirts and cooked you a warm meal? ..."

He went on and on. Carmen smoked a cigarette, looking daffy and spent, a gentle grin responding to something well beyond the reach of his words. Ten minutes later, he was talking about his family. Since I couldn't listen to his drivel, I thought instead. Perhaps I took this job because I had long been fascinated by the impact of the remote control. It had been my companion for many a sleepless night. I had theorized this advancement would ultimately take the technology where it had long been heading. The invention of this remote meant that talk would become short, trivial and endless. I didn't realize until Sphere droned on with his press release that the effect would come so quickly. I was beyond thankful that Miller's lecture called me away from Sphere's monologue. I took his press release and promised a call later.

As I was leaving, he had already clicked me off his channel and was mumbling something to Carmen about a glitch, pressing buttons, making his way 360 degrees around the room,· fiddling with every modulation on every machine until the revolution found him back pointing at me, beaming out parting words.

"The world will be in our laps," he repeated triumphantly.

Channel 3:
Short Cuts Through the Development

Now that I was outside, I could finally start asking myself real questions like how much use is a remote on a washing machine or a microwave if you still have to bring the clothes and food to them?

How much reprogramming would have to be done in people's households and at what expense?

What would happen after a power outage?

Would the appliances all have to be reprogrammed?

So what if there were surge protectors and battery backups, isn't this still more of a fad luxury item?

Yet as I hopped into the car and thought about how that remote might unlock the door, turn over the ignition and start the air conditioner, I could see its appeal. Christ, I had been toying around with that awkward looking thing for thirty minutes at the lab, and I hadn't even realized it. Undeniably, something was here. Practical? Perhaps not. Powerful? Shit yeah.

A gadget to command all gadgets.

When I closed the car door, I shut out all further thoughts of the remote. Remembering what an incredible rush I was in — could I jam any more into this afternoon? — I got into the car, turned on the radio and stopped thinking. The sports show host was talking about a trade between two teams and two players that everyone knew wasn't ever going to happen, but it was worth fantasizing about anyway. If I wanted to get into Miller's lecture hall before the students did, I had to arrive there in eight minutes. There was no way I was going to breeze past the nine traffic lights of Route 26, so I took a short cut through the developments, whipping along, making time, time time, cheating on stop signs, shifting through the ways and lanes.

I neared the end of making my last left and rights through this planned circuitousness, when in front of me stood a minivan, turned and halted short. I applied the brakes, listened to the announcer's take on the NBA playoffs and got out. Around the other side of the van, I spotted a small crowd of mothers and children, some crying. One of those toy battery-operated jeeps that toddlers drive was crushed up in front of them. They couldn't be crying over the jeep, could they? No, I had been to too many of these scenes. I could hear the wail of the EMS vehicle heading around the corner.

A little dark haired boy lay motionless on the pavement. He was scraped up from a tumble, blood on his thick mats of hair, his mother seemingly afraid to move him. She held his hand and rubbed his forehead, sobbing quietly; a cute little kid. They are all cute little kids: it could have been Zach. The EMS workers were already gently moving her aside to do CPR on him. I did what I hadn't done in years at one of these scenes. I got the hell out of there. Out of the way, out of the absurdity. As I returned to my car, I could see her crying, crying loudly, uncontrollably, not the mother, no... the neighbor up the block who smacked into the little boy. Inside of her van, she seemed to have a thousand groceries; still in the back was an infant screaming its fucking lungs out. I had written this story too many times before. She was trying to get home, the kid in the back has been yelling all the way, she turns around to tell her precious little one that "we are almost there," and bam, an unattended boy is driving his jeep out in the road, an advanced and spirited, admirable and lovable youth beyond recognition, he's riding his jeep and she's riding her van and the infant wants out and...

Before I became the *Herald's* technology columnist — actually how I became the *Herald's* technical columnist — I covered car accidents, covered them like no one before me. They were my obsession. Rarely were these accidents malicious, though sometimes reckless, they were most often just stupid and inevitable. So many big machines, so much volume, considerable speeds. *More people are killed in car crashes than in wars.* That was the type of copy I would write. I jumped on every safety proposal from air bags, to anti-lock brakes, to stronger bumpers, you name it... they helped, but with more fucking cars and .drivers... you get fatalistic. I can't remember the last time I wore a seat belt. I had become such a cult figure that I sponsored bereavement groups, not just for the victims families, but for the drivers.

A couple years of that, and I tell you I was becoming a wreck myself. Now I am just waiting my turn, like every other patriotic citizen. This time it was a woman with a van full of groceries and a screaming child; next time, perhaps, it'll be a man taking a short cut listening to a sports radio station. There was a story to be written about the boy, a fine, sad story, I suspected his soft dark eyes were shut for good inside the ambulance. It would be a cautionary tale. *Be careful out there. Look sharp.* Even now, back in the car, I wasn't wearing my seatbelt. No, my obsession with car accidents had clearly ended. What more proof could I need than to drive away from this one. You know what struck me strange here was the almost total absence of liquid — except for the blood on the boy's head, and even that was minor. The liquid whether it was oil, radiator fluid, vomit or blood always gave a human quality to all those twisted cars and bodies — the fallen bumpers, decapitated heads, mangled arms and torn grills. The liquid always lent a reality to it, even more than woeful lamentations of loved ones. No, I was still in a hurry, and had no time for this daily ritual. Old man Miller was probably already starting.

I listened back to the sports radio and forgot the boy, his mother, the driver, Miller, and even the remote. A caller was telling the host that Greg Maddux was the most likely present day player to be a Hall-of-Fame candidate. All there was left to do was to listen and rush. Perhaps tonight I won't have that recurring dream of my parents pressed inside their Nissan after a car crash, a dream which makes even less sense now that they're both dead. I can't tell you what happened in the next five minutes because I don't remember. I do know that when I got out of the car, I was back thinking about the remote and not about Miller.

As I stepped outside again to the warm, sunny day, the shadow of maple trees cast toward the school, I decided that encryption was key to the whole Prometheus remote plan. You'll soon figure out that I know nothing about technology, but I sure know how to explain technological advances to others. Follow me on this one. If this universal remote were security coded, you could carry it around like a wallet because it would be at least as valuable and necessary as money or a credit card. It could operate your alarm systems, garage doors, house locks... it could be the essential element in a man's life.

Of course, a dozen movie plot ideas came into my head, of burglars with decoding remotes, decrypting computers sending criminal messages across the internet and, naturally, the tale of a man who loses his remote and thereby loses his identity. Yes, when I took the role of Prometheus' PR man, I entered into a movie plot all right, but that might be a hell of a lot better than reliving pathetic little tragedies of kids in toy cars getting a head start on the collisions of the bumper-to-bumper world and of old men with missing fingers whom nobody will listen to.

It used to be my job to write of the former; now walking into the school, I resigned myself to the latter.

Channel 4:
How Many Years Was That Till Miller's Retirement?

Miller was already talking in the jam-packed lecture hall by the time I had gotten there. He seemed to be concluding a discussion about Nikola Tesla.

"Even though Edison did manage to gyp him out of so many of his major advancements, Tesla still left us with the induction, synchronous and split-phase motors and new forms of generators and transformers. And let us not forget of course the high frequency resonant transformer. You know, the old Tesla coil. But I talked about Tesla last year around this time. I don't want to do that again.

"Hell maybe I'll talk about the Krebs cycle for awhile."

A student was whispering in the back.

"Son," Miller pointed. "You're going to have to leave now."

"I'm sorry, can't I stay?" the young man asked, pleadingly.

"I'm sorry, I won't talk again."

"No you won't because you are leaving."

The boy trudged out like he had left his liver back on the seat. Begging to stay in Miller's class? Cochrane may well win his bet after all. They were all listening to Miller alright, not a cross conversation, no hand signals, no passed notes, no hushed tones, there was Miller and silence. And he made full use of it, leapfrogging from topic to topic, he moved from the Phragians to the Hittites to the Big Bang in single bound, and then he jumped ahead.

"Today in the *Times*, scientists reported that they have managed to create antimatter. Now granted the substance fizzled out in a few billionth of a second. But if they can hold onto that stuff long enough so it can take a good whack into matter, then we'll have something, huh? That'll give us some rocket fuel to warp us to another galaxy. Now that is where the magic of science is taking us. Jesus, when I was your age, I remember them detonating the first atomic bombs, the Manhattan Project, Los Alamos, all that crap..."

On he went, a little bit of science, two parts preaching, two parts reminiscing. After awhile, I could hardly listen, only trying to grab a quote or two in his winding, windy speech. The memorable lines would come, if I could just stay with him. Ultimately, he must have known of my short attention span, or at least that of the students, for he signaled his conclusion.

"For all of us to survive in the next millennium — and I'm talking to you now, cause I can't see me being there for long — we are going to have to deal with separation. Not just a physical separation from others with the fax lines and the internets and the fiber optics and the digital satellites. Yes, we will relate via conduits, electric portals and sliding mice clicking billions of pads away from one another. We must learn not only to separate from others, but to separate from ourselves. This is no time for the faint and the weak-hearted."

Here he picked up a nice kitchen knife. He did not seem angry or crazy or anything else. He just seemed to be lecturing. Still, a couple of his closer colleagues moved toward the podium.

"No, we must separate, willingly and efficiently, with surgical precision." And with that, wanting to say much more but seeing Cochrane almost in reach of him, old Doc Miller made one short deft movement, snapping down with the blade on his left pinky. The knife sliced through with the sound it might make cutting a thick carrot.

"Christ!" yelled out Cochrane.

Miller did wince, throwing a handkerchief over the stump. And then most considerately — especially for the students who felt they got gypped because of their teacher's rapidity and understatement in the amputation — Miller raised the severed digit to the audience, woozily triumphant.

"BOOOOOOOOOOOOP," the bell had rung. Damn fine pacing by old man Miller. Cochrane hoisted his arm around a now very pale and dizzy looking Miller, leading him in a stagger out of the room. Meanwhile a nervous and repulsed lab assistant placed the finger in an ice pack trying to preserve it.

Out of their trance, the movie over, the kids starting talking.

"Oh sick man."

"That's disgusting."

"Did you see that, it snapped right off. How could he do that?"

"Did you see him flinch? I didn't see him. You'd think he'd yell or something."

"Fuckin' eh."

"How could he do that to himself?"

"I wonder what he'll do next year."

"Probably more Tesla coils and fingers."

"Fuckin' eh."

As Cochrane headed out the door, he had enough presence of mind to squeeze tight on Miller's wound with one hand and to pocket ten bucks owed to him in the other.

"How many years till you retire?" asked Cochrane.

Miller lifted his bloody paw and raised the fingers left on it. "Three," he giggled.

Channel 5:
Cleaning House

Let's see how much shit can be piled into one day. With all this activity, maybe I'll get my first decent night's sleep since winter.

I had some copy to write about what was undoubtedly Miller's final lecture — second chances must been considered the limit when dealing with amputations. The administrators might not have been there for the lecture — pretty amazing they picked that period for a committee meeting huh? — but they would most certainly find the time to oversee his competency hearing. I confess for however overwhelming the day's pace, this story kindly wrote itself. All I had to do was type on my laptop at the bar, send it over to the newsroom, and see if old man Miller would be released from the hospital early enough to come on down. Even though his finger has gotta hurt, I figured the odds were pretty good of him getting out of his dinky apartment and crawling on over here; he knew better than anyone how poorly antibiotics and alcohol mix, but I suspected at this point he couldn't have cared. We had met at Tara's before because it was just the kind of hole in the wall that both of us appreciated — two pool tables, no lighting, little air, a dart board, no ties, much warmth, talk and hostility, low prices.

With the story to bed, an eight ounce burger in the belly and three beers past, Miller didn't show, but... well she'll tell you.

"Are you Russell Pines?"

"Yes."

"I figured. Not many guys come in this place with laptops. I'm Dave Miller's daughter, Angelica. He told me to come down and tell you he couldn't make it."

"How's he doing? Still pretty woozy?"

"He's doing alright. But the hospital wanted to keep him overnight for observation. You know, check his finger, feed him Jell-O· and send him home. Some guy talked about psychiatric treatment, but I don't think anything will come of it."

"Wanna drink?"

"Sure."

I signaled the bartender, "Can I get another beer and a —"

"Give me a bottle of Poland Spring water and a bottle of white wine."

"We don't sell bottles here lady."

"Here's two twenties. If you give me that $4 bottle of wine you've got in the cooler over there and that liter of water, I think you are in for a tidy little profit."

Silently, the bartender brought over the two bottles, uncorking the wine and Angelica unveiled a bright, white cloth from her pocketbook, poured some spring water on the bar and washed it off. As the bartender turned away shaking his head, she splashed water into the wine glass, swirled it about, and tossed the water out behind the bar.

"Everything O.K.?" I asked, eyeing from the bar, to the glass, and then to her perpetually dancing fingers.

"Fine," she said. "I just like things clean,". drying out the glass with another spotless cloth from her purse, "very clean."

She was prettily efficient like my first editor˙on the daily, who to my chagrin caught and corrected every one of my novice errors. Attracted and amused, I changed the subject for fear I would otherwise observe her too closely.

"So why'd he do it?"

"He told me he did it for his own personal amusement, get that. I think it's because amputations some way or another make him feel more aligned with one of those brilliant, primitive tribes of the past he's so fond of."

"Amputations make him feel whole then?"

She smiled a little, but I don't think in response to my comment. When she finally poured her wine, she was satisfied with the clarity and crispness of its appearance. Sipping, she explained, "He gets further into these tribes and rituals as his time in the classroom gets more and more miserable. All he does is talk to me about how things were different. That the students now seem unable to concentrate for more than thirty seconds. He's obsessed with talking about the year 2000."

"Your Dad's not one of these guys who keeps thinking the world's coming to an end is he?"

"No."

"I didn't think so."

"No, he envisions a great dark age coming... a bunch of zombies on computers playing video games." Now she drew out a third cloth, sliding it over her mouth and nose, the smoke apparently getting to her, even though she intimated no disturbance and disgust. Angelica, on first meeting, might just be the calmest compulsive I've ever met.

"Not your type of establishment is it?" I asked, though not ready to apologize to her for being here in the first place.

"It's disgusting," she managed to say without repulsion. "But it's got atmosphere. And I feel I've made a nice little oasis here. There's something attractive about dirt. It reminds me of Satan."

"Reminds you of Satan?" a sick little thought.

"Sure, Satan has always been depicted as the filthiest creature, and what soils purity but dirt..." now that conversation went on and on, somehow I got wrapped up in it as she spoke of how priests so carefully clean the chalice and she stretched her long, strong legs that were very smooth and very clean. I became convinced that she kept her hair so short so she would find fewer strands lying around. She somehow shifted from Satan to her job, in what my increasingly conspiratorial outlook saw as a neat and calculated manner.

"I search out artifacts for the Tesla Institute. i search and still have my fingers." The Tesla Institute collected all type of late

Twentieth Century crap, what they dubbed "Gems from the End of the Millennium," and when the millennium ends and they don't, the Institute will call it "Gems from the Bend in the Millennium."

"Right now I'm collecting remotes. You don't know where I can get my hands on the Sphere prototype?"

The Sphere prototype, how did she know about it, and how did she know I knew? Angelica was becoming increasingly attractive.

"No," I told her looking sincere, even though that is often the appearance I give off when people trust me least. "I wish I knew. Geoffrey has been hush-hush about it, ever since I wrote my first story about it." Now, perhaps she was only a faithful reader, that would be nice... but of all the articles she had to pick —

"I'd really like to get my hands on it. I got a feeling it might be worth something, especially since I've heard through the grapevine that Paddy Dangus wants the remote bad."

"Paddy Dangus?" I questioned with restraint, for she looked too intelligent to mock so early in a relationship. "We don't even know what or who Paddy Dangus is? How can you know he wants a remote?"

"We know Paddy Dangus blew up the plant for the microchip system that would have completely automated our military weaponry, and that he killed the three technicians who knew how to assemble it."

"Do we? That was just a cover-up. I'm surprised you're so naive," I couldn't help myself, although she took the comment like a smudge of dirt on my shirt. "Only Little Augie down at the morgue came up with anything about explosive traces, but they were sketchy at best and could have been generated through the chemicals torched in the blaze. Better to create some Luddite technoterrorist bogeyman than admit the microchip was inadequate and that the whole thing blew up right in their hands," and then I ended smiling, "You're conspiratorial."

"Microchip plants don't blow up from any combustion within the plant."

"Rather than admit they failed and face their investors, they made it blow up."

"Now who's conspiratorial."

She took a white cloth and cleaned my glasses. "At least you should be able to see better."

We talked of Sphere's remote and talked Paddy Dangus myths — even the one about his unhinging the super collider, wrecking the Eastwood laboratory for months — and I saw stories written all over them, but I was much more interested in listening than writing, as my beeper went off three times. Twice from my editor and then little Augie. My column *could* come out of the morgue. Shit, so many others had, but not tonight. Tonight just might be the column in which I transform into Technoman. An idea long simmering in my skull, becoming Technoman would change my very existence. I had been afraid to write the column because, once I did, the next year of my life would be dedicated to its edicts. Yet with each hour passing, I grow charged and determined for that grand life change.

At one point I thought Angelica with all her intense, paranoid nuttiness was looking deeply into my eyes. But when she said excitedly, "Oh a T63841," spying the bar's remote covetously, I figured I was mistaken. "They don't make those anymore. I must have it." Drawing a small spray from her purse — with all the cleaning materials in there I doubt she had room for make-up — she spritzed the filthy control, sliding her fingers swiftly among and about the channel slots, wiping away kegs of grime. Did she attend so carefully to the remote for my benefit or hers?

As she nailed the remote with an even heavier dose of liquid and rubbed with a vengeance, Angelica unknowingly switched the station from boxing to a wildlife show. A great cry swelled up from the barstools and as she grabbed the remote to correct her slip, the viscous instrument squirted from her hand and slid down the bar, kicking up drops of wine and caroming off drinks.

"Hey!" was the collective yell.

"What the fuck."

"Shit."

Grizzly ate salmon as the dying fish leaped waterfalls, trying to find their way home. A bowling ball of a man clicked the remote back to boxing. I was disappointed that order was restored so quickly. Thank goodness for a Hee Haw man, suspenders and all who got in bowling ball's face yelling, "I like the bears, put them back on."

"Fuck off."

Hee Haw went with one hand for the throat, the other for the remote, and there were bears on TV and a brawl in the bar. Bowling ball's friends were on Hee Haw in a minute, and there were guys with pool sticks who seemed interested in seeing *The Godfather* suddenly involved. Angelica drew closer to the group than her hygienic tendencies normally would have permitted, her quest for the trophy the greater force within her.

Now at any normal suburban bar this fight would have ended with the second punch, so the clientele could get back to the peaceful drinking and ass grabbing they so truly loved. But this was Tara's where every bad Western and biker flick was wondrously remembered and pathetically relived on a nightly basis. So the fight would go on, in slow motion perhaps, for a few deep breaths, smokers hacks, and flemmy wheezes were in order before a head would be smashed against the bar, while others played kill the guy with the remote. I continued drinking my beer, bemused. Every hairy gent who grabbed hold of the prize would get off one shot, a notch up or down, sending the television with tragically spastic fingers from porno channels to.family channels, before he would be squashed and send the instrument clattering across the room. The crushing got so great that some of the later possessors had to relinquish the remote before they even got to squeeze it. Pandemonium really broke out when C-Span made its way to the screen. The fighting grew to such Professional Wrestling proportions beneath the smoke and spilt drink that the remote had spurted unnoticed in a quiet corner as more and more customers piled on to the previous holders.

I looked for Angelica, but she was distracted because a half pitcher of beer had spilt on her shirt. I confess I too became absorbed by the display. Deciding any further observation was a particularly dangerous occupation, I returned my attention to the remote just as Angelica started rubbing her chest dry.

I confess I hadn't expected this gift. So looking like I was snatching up something much less important from the floor — my wallet, perhaps — I picked the remote up unnoticed. I slipped the instrument in my pocket, signaled Angelica and headed out with her.

"I guess the T63841 will have to wait."

"Yeah, there's no way you can get your hands on it now."

"I'm going to check out my old man, wanna come?"

"I'd like to, but I still gotta write a column tonight. Tell your dad I'll see him in a day or two." I didn't ask for her number, but we both know I'd find out if I wanted to.

"O.K., I'll tell him, see ya." She walked away, arms across her chest, bracing herself in the chilling night air. She seemed beautifully incomplete, not having collected anything in particular this evening.

Alone with my remote, I pointed and clicked at the air, at the nothingness. A big part of me wanted to take it home and place it atop my mantle in an absurdist gesture. My sense of honor or at least common decency made me want to return it to the bartender's hand and to its rightful place behind the bar. Perhaps I should have caught up with Angelica and with grand courtly flourishes bestowed it upon her. Yet I thought I would be sending the wrong message. My sense of cruelty had other ideas, so I threw it in the dumpster while the drunken men at Tara's battled for something that wasn't there anymore.

Channel 6:
The Birth of Technoman

It wasn't the alcohol that kept my fingers on the remote from the time I got home, 9:30, until now, twenty minutes before I had to send my story. Let's go make one more trip around the channels, deluding myself that it would be any more fruitful than the previous journeys; perhaps in my search, in my pushing buttons, something would appear on the screen that hadn't before.

And then for the fourth time tonight, I listened to my messages:

"It's getting late. I'm getting concerned. This is not like you. Are you O.K.? Call me when you are done screening your calls."

"Russell, Stan. Have I got a story for you. You won't bel
where they are talking about slating the permanent home for
nuclear waste fuel now. But you've got to get to me tonight ∠
8294."

"Russell? Fuck you. Call me back."

"Stop in tomorrow. We are ready to unveil
remote. Feel free to write a preview story on it bef
we have the press conference."

"Rus? Susan here. You remember the high speed microwave I
telling about at the convention down in Lancaster. Well, it's up. A r
in ten minutes. Call me at 212-874-3232. I'll give you first dibs on

"Call me Russell. I think I'm dying."

"Hey, it's Phil. I think you had something wrong
your aerospace retrofitting story. Stop into the off
tomorrow."

"Hey Rus, sorry I couldn't make it. When you get a chance,
me a call. Me and my three remaining fingers know some stuff ak
Paddy Dangus that might interest you. It looks like they are goin
keep me here a few days. The number is 722-4103."

"I'm returning your call. Sorry, can't
Tuesday night. I have to work late. Talk to
soon."

"Hey, what's up, it's little Augie. I've got the m
intriguing body chilling out for you. This is better ev
than the chemical accident and the Pequa Spring se
killer. There's alot to it, so call me as soon as you c
Use the private office number."

"Hello Mr., uh, Pins, this is Wayne from Chemical Bank,
have a great new credit card for you with 4.9 % financing an
$30,000 cash line. Call us. This card is made for you. 1-888-C
4600."

There was no column in those messages. The loneliness of
apartment lay there, slumped over in a few empty sweatshirt
was out of time.

Quickly I slide over to the computer and switch it on, calm
myself upon seeing the extension icons surface and the flash
pulsing light, a bright yet somehow fuzzy and dull light. No
click keys instead of buttons. Clearly, Technoman must com

life. A couple of years ago the idea dawned on me that perhaps I should spend a year immersed in technology the way Thoreau spent a year or two at one with nature. Needless to say I liked the idea much more than I desired to be the embodiment of it. So I promised myself that I would only write this Technoman column if I had no other. And to write now means I must commit for a year to such a life that I would not have dared even last week. Hey, Thoreau wandered alone out at Walden Pond; I can surely take on this lifestyle. Anyhow, I have nothing else to offer but this one idea. I am an empty vessel, and for better or worse, I must fill this vessel and this column with technology. So I write.

Pines Tar: Call Me Technoman

Why I Went Into the Net

Don't call me Russell Pines no more. As of 10:30 p.m. June 27, 1998, I am Technoman. Frankly, I didn't want to become Technoman. I have been waiting for two decades for someone to put on that cape and mask. I cannot wait any longer. For the next year, I will live the life that needs to be led. Here are the ten essential precepts of my manifesto:

1. Eat only food packaged in plastic, aluminum or any other appropriate unnatural substance. If heaven forbid, any of this food requires warming, then it can only go in the microwave, appropriately wrapped of course.

2. Employ no natural lighting in any room. Fluorescent, neons preferred.

3. Read only on a screen; all texts and material must be on electronics; no hard copy of books, magazines, journals, mail, etc. Even read the *Herald* off the Net.

4. Wear no natural fibers. No cotton, wool or leather. Put on plastic and fiberglass, or, in a pinch, rayon or polyester.

5. No nights with unaltered women. Some sort of plastic surgery is required.

6. All foods must contain preservatives and chemical additives.

7. Engage only in activities that require machines. To exercise, that means no running, except on a treadmill; no weight lifting, except with a soloflex, nautilus or universal. To work, obviously

that means computers, phones and faxes. To play, that means video games, laser fights, baseball with pitching machines, indoors of course.

8. Avoid the outdoors at all cost. Ten minutes outside, unprotected by a car, is the maximum. Never open windows in the car, house or office. Live by climate control and air pumped through distant vents.

9. Use credit cards only; except of course when it is impossible to do so, but even then, use a debit card.

10. Never talk to a person if the capability of talking to a machine is possible.

Twice a week I will wire you about my life as Technoman. For years I have been reporting about the cutting edge of technology; now I will speak from the inside of the mother board. Farewell my friends.

Channel 7:
Plastic Wrap

I forwarded my column and the machine picked up calls from Darlene at the *Herald*, old man Miller, little Augie and Angelica. Later that night I began to fulfill my manifesto at a night club, dancing to music that could only be described as post deconstructionist techno, where the mechanical elements of the synthesized rhythms are emphasized instead of being smoothed over. Wearing my only plastic clothes — a birthday sweatsuit from a colleague who felt obligated to buy me something three years ago (he hasn't gotten me anything else since) — my skin grew cold from the layer of perspiration swimming about the lining. It took me hours to find a girl who wore plastic pants and a rayon/polyester blend halter top inside of which were silicon breasts. Such women are rarer than I had imagined. Fortunately she seemed to be waiting at least two or three dance songs for me to appear in her life. Now that she had found me, she had no plans of letting me go until morning. When she said her name was Laser, I knew this girl was just insincere enough to qualify.

Life does not imitate art, but it does imitate bad television shows. Most of my conversations find their way in twenty minute sitcom formats punctuated by commercial breaks. That night we talked to each other like two bad actors in reruns who undeservedly still get royalty checks.

"I'm glad you could finally make it."

"So am I."

"Now we won't have to sell the farm."

"Or the children."

"Perhaps you can leave NASA now."

"When I'm done coloring my hair."

"Oh, so we have to wait another six months."

"How can we call it waiting when we're together."

"You have lovely eyes; are they real or are they the shade of your contact lenses?"

"I'm afraid they are my lenses, but if you'd like they can be my real eyes."

"Don't be afraid, I love that they are lenses. I was hoping they weren't real, but I'm kind of disappointed you are telling me the truth about them."

"I'm sorry, I promise I won't ever tell the truth again."

"How about those? Are they real?"

"Of course they are silly, what self-respecting girl would fake those?"

"Now we're talking..."

And when we exhausted our conversation, and you could imagine how long that must have taken us, we retired to my place and put on the television, to let someone else talk for a change. It didn't take long when I was softly kissing the nape of her neck before I tried to figure out whether it had been I or Gilligan who had been talking about being free. For hours I rubbed up against her plastic pants, hurling off the halter top, implanting my face into those implanted breasts. As we wrestled about, I tinkered with the remote control, going from channel to channel. Sadly neither of us came close to orgasm as the channels shifting from one to another involved us at least momentarily in a new show.

And then suddenly, Laser became enthralled by a rerun of a bad remake of the second part of a soap opera saga; I couldn't get

her to switch the channel and I grew very soft in the process
tried to grab the remote, but she held on tight and before we kne
it we were twisting around on the bed, switching hands a
turning channels, we wrestled and clicked, heaving bosoms a
flashing stations, neck nibbles and sound bites, heavy breathi
and phone sex lines, hip thrusts and butt workouts, they all sp
around, until we collapsed completely released of our burder
our inhibitions, our bodily fluids, and our remote as the nation
anthem came on and the station signed off for another broadca
day.

Channel 8:
Food To Preserve the Gods

Pines Tar: In My Grocer's Freezer

To be Technoman has not been as easy as anticipate
especially when it comes to eating right. The wondrously steri
supermarket was only a tease; its insincere appearance belied a
uncontrollable passion for produce grown out on actual farms.

Do you know how hard it is to live on a completely unnatur
diet? I thought it would be easy, but when I started reading th
ingredients... Boy was I in for a shock. Even the fine products
had every right to believe were completely artificial betrayed m
with their reliance on natural foods. Imagine my chagrin when
picked up the Pasteurized Processed Cheese Spread only t
discover that it was ignominiously conceived with "real cheese."

Much more disconcerting was my encounter with Spam,
hopelessly wholesome product. How could such a product s
recognized in pop culture, so endlessly satirized as a shinin
cliché of unnatural food be so genuine? It was a betrayal of
betrayal. Good fortune in all her randomness, however, brougl
me to Cathy, a punky college kid who obviously knew too muc
to stay in her supermarket job for long. I called her over to th
Spam can.

"Will you look at this?"

"What?"

"Look at these ingredients. They use real meat in here. What is this? Practically all the ingredients come straight from Mother Nature."

"So…"

"So where can a guy get his daily dose of chemicals and preservatives if he can't even rely on trusty old Spam?"

Kathy snickered at me for my innocence and naiveté, like I had been transported from the 50s. "Well if that's what you are looking for, then you're not going to have a problem; you're just grabbing the wrong can of Spam."

"Huh?"

"You need Spam Lite."

She pointed and I saw. I instantly had a good feeling about it… beginning with the artificial spelling of light. "Ohhhhh," I was impressed by its Day-Glo colors and its post-structuralist print.

"If you take this home, you not only have Spam's Sodium Nitrate, but have Sodium Phosphates, Potassium Chloride, and Sodium Ascorbate, not to mention the fact that the chicken is mechanically separated."

"Isn't all chicken mechanically separated?"

"Obviously not the way Spam Lite is, or why else would they bother writing it in the ingredients — See," she grabbed my finger and drew it across the line, "when else have you read mechanically separated on an ingredients list?"

"Never."

"There you go. I think you've found dinner."

"That's a start. But I am here in the middle of my life lost in the midst of supermarket lanes without a clue of where to shop for all the finest artificial products and ingredients. And as you know, when you shop the way I do, your meals are always the freshest, even the leftovers."

My appeal was not in vain. "Follow me," Kathy said, grabbing my hand, sweetly, assuredly. Before I knew it, I was zipping past terribly phony bacon bits and imitation extracts of all kinds, from vanilla to rum to strawberry to pineapple to black walnut. At the maple syrup department, Kathy taught me to seek out the NutraSweet label, and from there she made me squirt the no-stick cooking spray into my palm just to assure no oil inveigled its way unceremoniously into the aerosol can.

"You never can tell," bristled Kathy, who I was beginning to notice, seemed to lack a chemical imbalance. "The whole store is going to pot with all these twisted health crazes. Overpriced organics everywhere, natural foods with short shelf lives, a green tide of algae sucking the life blood out of good old American manufacturing. They keep this up and there won't be a factory open in America."

"What could possibly be done about it?"

She gave me an arch glance as if I were not the first to ask her such a question. "I know this sounds completely contradictory and absurd, but the only way is to buy diet goods."

"Diet goods?"

"Diet Goods, preferably the aggressively lowfat stuff," I was rapidly losing faith in my guide.

"What are you having for dinner tonight?"

I looked down in my pathetic cart of imitation bits of flavor and artificial condiments: "Spam Lite."

"Then you have begun. Now you must continue." She held my hand assuredly. I could truly have fallen in love with this girl if she hadn't known so much more than me. Before I even realized it, in my cart were links of Diet Polska Kielbasa and breasts of something known as Diet Turkey product; there were fat free TV dinners, all vegetable byproduct protein patties, twice processed, intensely reduced cholesterol sausage, skim pasteurized process cheese sauce (NOT made with real cheese), and fat free grated topping (most assuredly NOT real cheese). And as I found my way to the Fat Free Whipped Topping (I learn to love the word Topping, for a product can't be real if they have to call it Topping as opposed to what it is supposed to be), I knew the world was not such a bad place after all. You see man was still aping nature, with a little more shame since we ate the forbidden organic fruit, but with enough inherent dishonesty in packaging to make it all so... digestible.

"Don't get too giddy," Kathy warned as I scooped a half dozen of those fat free whipped topping beauties into my cart. "Try to remember that all foods are chemicals at heart. And look at these ingredients on the can. Look, sucrose, dextrose — just sugars really, and corn syrup, that's not something to put on the space shuttle and ship across the universe, and this imulin is just a polyfructose."

"So what are you telling me?"

"That even the most purely artificial foods have their natural impurities." I guess I looked a bit devastated because she rallied me. "It's not all that bad. Hey look! Non-fat dry milk solids, now that doesn't sound real at all, does it?"

I agreed, but as she started rattling off much more palatable ingredients, I was drafting a   larger personal policy: as Technoman, I would make a conscious effort of never knowing too much about the magical manufactured goods that I would embrace for the next year. I would live this year in blissful ignorance, for how else can a man embrace the mystery of technology, that old mystery destroyer itself? I could not, I would not, destroy technology's aura by trying to pull off its mask. Instead I listened to my high-priestess Kathy as if she were chanting a spell that would transport me into the very machinery that lies beyond the self. "Cellulose Gum, Mono- & Diglycerides, Artificial Color, Artificial Flavors (Hey more than one, this must be good stuff), Disodium Phosphate, Polysorbate 80, Lecithin, Carrageenan, Guar Gum."

"Guar Gum." I said it low and slow as part of a Gregorian Chant. "Guar Gum." Ohhh, I like that.

"What?"

"Guuuaaaar Guuummmmm."

"Oh."

"Say it again?"

"What?"

"The ingredients, say them again."

And she was off, no nightingale could record more saccharine notes. "... Diglycerides... Disodium Phosphate, Polysorbate 80," until finally, "Guar Gum."

I didn't have the strength to ask Kathy whether Guar Gum was predominately artificial or natural — I had my suspicions — but the avoidance did not inhibit me from muttering "Guar Gum" through the aisles in my most bloodless, computer-generated voice-mail tones. I was a purring engine and Kathy just kept tapping at the pedal. "I forgot to mention that Whipped Topping also includes a nitrous oxide propellant."

"Hey, that's a special bonus prize." My day wasn't complete until I paid a visit to the fat free non dairy creamer shelf where I was introduced to Polysorbate 80's cousin, Polysorbate 60 and his good buddy Titanium oxide.

I was feeling whole for the first time in my life when Kathy showed me I could be even more. I could be Whole Plus, New and Improved Whole, Extra Strength Whole, Whole with Fast Acting Agents. I don't know how I got there but Kathy had me down the cleaning fluid aisle and we were sampling products with our increasingly dilating nasal passages.

"Try this carpet spot remover. It's like no other smell in the world. You know it's the good stuff when the warning label says: **Avoid Breathing of Vapor**. Take a hit of that."

Nostril hairs were dropping to the floor, but I stayed faithful to the carpet cleaner, becoming one with its emissions, my head growing like an air bag. That last thing I remember was giving a go at the thick wicked liquid toilet bowl cleaner that ridiculously claimed it featured a new country scent.

"Honey, pace yourself. We haven't even gotten to the Dow chemical section yet."

But it was too late. Kathy had enough trouble reviving me with a newly manufactured ammonia compound and then dragging me to the check-out line.

I marched stiffly out to the car with my plastic packages, everything was encased for the ages... I would have to allow more time in my life for opening product packaging. Funny, I felt I had eaten a seven course meal already. At that moment I knew that for the next year I would have nourishment I never dreamed of. I could do no better than if I suckled at the rim of a test tube.

nnel 9:
ɔtiating a Little Space

ɔ *Tar: Intrafacing with the Universe*
Maybe I had the tone wrong, but I didn't believe that my
noman manifesto was a cry for help. Yet I have received an
nbly line of advice from counseling and rehab programs.
ɪ well-intentioned correspondents were not interested in
g me of my condition, they generally thought of me not as
noman, but Gadgetman, sending me scads of equipment.
t get me wrong... I don't mind owning the soup-to-nuts food
ɔssor with its bread machine, pasta maker and coffee urn, or
narvelous cell phone with the video monitor that amazingly
ɔrts to a hair dryer, or the James Bond spy style wristwatch
microprocessor tape recorder and baby laser beam, or the
ɔ blue electric suit with 2,727 small bulbs, or even the
ination electric shaver, walkman and smoke alarm. They can
ɔnhance my Technoman status.
ɔet none of these perpetually vibrating devices has changed
utlook on life more than the ·one the good folks.·at MIT
ɔd me when they heard of my mission. I forget what they call
t essentially the equipment turned me into a walking and
g. transmitting and receiving computer. I like to call it the
acer, since it creates both a permanent screen and a
anent connection between myself and the universe. The guts
nputer's hard drive goes on my left shoulder in a specially
factured sack as a one-hand keyboard sits in my right pants
t. The thin monitor hangs off my Microsoft baseball cap, so
look at the larger world of the screen rather than the small
about me. When I meet others in the newsroom or on the
, I calmly and superficially engage them as I idly read from
ɔreen, punching in commands from my pocket. A wall of
are confronts my colleagues if they choose to converse.
don't choose. I don't really talk in the conversations. I only
— that is the easiest form for ignoring.
he Intrafacer already saved me $2,800 at the autodealer. I
uying one of those new CompuCars, you know the ones in
lvertisements that are supposed to be the smartest, most

automated vehicles on the road. Here I was with Joey Bari
eyeing up a champagne LX model, and Joey says: "Look I
knock $25 off the lease price so it drops down to an even $69
month, but that's all I can do."

"How about the one that's Screensaver Blue? Isn't t
cheaper?"

"Screensaver Blue? Sorry we're all out of those."

I punched in some keys. "No you're not. You have two left
the lot."

"What?"

"It says here you have two left on the lot?"

"What's here?"

"On your inventory files."

"Well that might not have been updated."

"Says it was updated two in the afternoon today."

"We might have sold them since then. I tell you, you ca
believe the way these babies are flying out of the lot. We ca
even stock the showroom. It's terrible."

"Can you check if you have any left."

"Hold on."

About ten minutes later he returns, "Oh, we do have one l
I tell you what: I can let you have it for an even $699 a mo
just like the other. No additional charge for the very hot colo
the screen saver."

"I want it for $499 a month."

"What? That's ridiculous."

"Don't tell me that. It says right here," pointing up to
visor, "that you can go down bottom line $499 a month."

"What? That must be wrong."

"Your own inventory and budgetary codes say it. You wan
look."

"No, I want to talk to my manager. Maybe he can explai
to you."

He never did look.

"Don't get your manager. You know, after you waste my t
a little while, you are just going to give it to me. Look, I can o
this myself and you can go without your commission. I almost
that, but I thought this would be better. I guess I was wrong."

I started out, my Intrafacer always a step ahead of me, Joey called.

"Come back, come back, because I'm a nice guy and as a customer courtesy I'll give you the $499, but only this time O.K."

"Yes, yes, only this time, most certainly."

I drove my Screensaver Blue Compucar, or should I say my Compucar drove me to the Mall. By then I broke human contact as I shopped. That was the easiest thing I've done since I became Technoman. The paging beeps in the department store pulsed above the scraping racks of clothes, aluminum hangers screeched across stainless steel pipes, above the machine-like march of heels on imitation tile, above the registers rattling out humming line prints. How distant can one get?

"Try our new scent for men, Lawn."

I said nothing, she sprayed anyway. Like a bug hit with pesticide, I recoiled, limbs tightening and curling. I took out vials and dropped compounds on the cologne, punched in a few findings on the keyboard.   ·   ·

"What are you doing with the scent?"

I kept punching in and reading away, the hard drive jumping and reeling like it was spitting out a top-secret code for renegade chemical weapons. "What are you punching in? What does it say?"

She was still talking to me even when I moved two departments down. I have much more to say about my trip, especially about my relationship with a particularly lurid and uninhibited mannequin, but that will have to wait because I must tell you what happened when I was leaving the mall.

I took off into an exit lane, waiting for my Smart Car to give the go ahead to make a right. I wisely didn't take the exit by the light for that was backed up half the length of the mall lot. As I inched up to turn, cars kept passing in front of me, some speeding up, some tapping the brakes as I looked for a little pocket of space. After about a minute, I thought I spotted an opening, but my Smart Car vetoed me:

"Don't Proceed! Danger! Danger!"

Another thirty seconds passed before I got a second chance, and then -

"Not safe! Don't Proceed! Danger! Danger!"

This time I ignored, slamming on the accelerator. After a tiny surge, the car shutdown. "Hey, let me go!"

"Danger! Danger!"

"What?"

"And put on your seatbelt."

"When can I go?"

"When it is safe."

Small openings came my way and then bigger ones; and every time I stepped on the pedal, my Smart Car denied me, like I was a homeless man applying for a mortgage loan. So I waited for a half hour, playing video games and typing this column, biding time for my car's approval. When another car foolishly decided to crawl up behind me in the exit lane, I put on my hazards and waved him by. After waiting and waving a few more cars past, I discovered something funny about my Smart Car. The hazard lights seemed to work as a danger and safety override. The car no longer prevented me from moving.

Inexplicably, with the Smart Car no longer stopping me, I was having problems getting going. The pockets between the cars seemed to shrink. Anyway I now knew the dangers of the road. What was I, suicidal? I might have been, but Technoman certainly wasn't. I snapped on my seatbelt and returned to the tiered, enclosed parking lot, finding a nice, quiet, insulated and isolated spot. Inside that shrouded lot, inside my comfort-controlled Smart Car, inside my ever conversant, companionable Intrafacer, I whiled away the hours, watching the intersection off my screen, zooming in and out with my camera, coveting vehicles, calculating speeds and distances, calmly waiting for late night to cast its blanket about all but the halogen street lights, waiting for the roads to be safe.

When that hour came, I attained an inner serenity. My Smart Car and my Intrafacer guided me. I decided they had adopted me as their son — they would provide for me and protect me. They threw randomness in the microwave and turned it into alphabet soup. I wasn't serving technology; technology was serving me.

What could be more hypnotizing, more seductive, more reassuring. The Devil himself could have offered no better.

Channel 10:
Death in the Evening

Angelica must have read my column because among my evening's E-Mail sat her message:

"Get down to the resource recovery plant at midnight tonight and look for the white knight. There's a column in it for you. If it wastes your time, I will buy you a year's supply of processed, ready-whipped topping."

The road to the resource recovery plant was by design noisy. If by chance a huge truck did not come rumbling down, smacking into more potholes than pavement, the back of the compactor slamming hard against the latches, then the train trestle above would begin its rattling in anticipation of the night car, tooting and scraping, notifying no one special. The bugs chewed at me, the only living things except for the night watchman who had long learned to cover his skin with enough chemicals to dispel even these jaded, hardy, mutant gnats.

The resource recover plant gave steady furnace, plumes of pasty, pale smoke emitted, only halted by the buzzing and the feeding of more metal. Flaming blue methane gas rose from the landfill's base, obscuring the night's full moon. Finally, after an hour of indulging my senses, I spied trucks stuffed to the gills with dead machinery, appearing just below the flickering aircraft warning lights of the big stack. Old appliances, refrigerators and VCRs, toasters and dehumidifiers, blow dryers and answering machines crushed together in an orgy of transistors. A train passes and a truck approaches at the same time, the two combining to sound like a jet simultaneously taking off and crashing.

At a particularly nasty pothole, the truck coughs out a dying microwave from its ass, a hollow carcass of fading convections. Was this what Angelica meant... a graveyard of hardware?

Not until five minutes later, after the fumes of broiling plastics stewed about my nostrils leaving me intoxicated, lost in the humming of the feeding conveyor belt, did a raggedy old white pick-up break the trance. It headed into the landfill gates as if it belonged even though, with rusting holes rotting out its sides, I knew this was a one-time exceptional delivery. As it waited at the gate, I quietly strolled — Technoman does not sneak — up behind it and looked into the decaying flatbed. Stuffed black plastic trash bags were everywhere. Just as I considered ripping one open, fortune smiled upon me, for I saw a bag was unsealed. I knew I was too much of a coward to tear one myself.

The light from the tower flashed down upon the open bag, and shit if tumbling out of it weren't a pile of remotes.

The truck rattled in, and since the gate did not fully close, I followed the truck on foot up the long landing. No one else was around. The voice on the intercom must have been sitting in the tower. I came close enough to see the black bags thrown into the destruction bins, but I couldn't see their contents. It didn't matter though... I knew they were remotes. What else could make that hard clattering but a gaggle of those plastic instruments with the soft buttons rubbing and jostling against the tough, resilient shells?

Who was throwing away thousands of remotes? Where the hell were they coming from?

A stench wafted up from the leachate pond and I grew scared, so I left the facility, hovering out beyond the gates. The moon rose through the smoke again and the white truck soon rattled back out.

The driver wore a cap and was laughing. His beard seemed to cover all his face. He was the first living thing I saw all night, except for the bugs that gnawed at me. A terrible grating and grinding rose from the facility as the old white truck bounced out of sight. I jumped in my car and tried to follow him, but he drove fast through the back roads and when I thought I caught up with him, I only found myself at the end of a court with nowhere to turn.

Channel 11:
The Record of a Lost Soccer Game

As always when I was lost, I wrote a story, pretending I knew the perpetrator at the landfill who squandered our valuable, technological resources. And I waited for someone to turn up. Meantime, I stalled Geoffrey Sphere who seemed increasingly and singularly desperate to get out his product. I couldn't let his desire cramp my Technoman needs.

More than ever I had trouble focusing on one thing. Checking my e-mail was no help. One Rafter Simpkins, a clairvoyant who sends me creepy, usually inaccurate, missives, dropped one on me.

TECHNOMAN: I WANT TO TELL YOU THIS JUST IN CASE SOMETHING COMES OF IT. AFTER I TURNED OFF MY TV JUST NOW, I FELT THE STRANGEST, MOST INTENSE CRY OF MY LIFE. IT FELT LIKE THE WAILS OF A THOUSAND TV SETS WHIRRING FURIOUSLY THROUGH THEIR CHANNELS IN AN INSANE CRESCENDO THAT MADE MY EYELIDS BLINK UNCONTROLLABLY AND THEN, COMPLETE SILENCE. IT FELT LIKE THE WORLD WAS COMING TO AN END. YOU'VE BEEN WARNED.

— RAFTER

The time of the e-mail delivery was 10:43 last night, a little more than an hour before the drop-off. I was trying to figure out what the hell to make out of his message when the next letter caught my eye. It was from my ex-wife who I thought hated e-mail more than she hated me. Apparently I've moved up a notch. Yes, I get lost enough in these messages without Alice joining the fray. Somehow her last dozen phone messages I had dismissed with a touch of the rewind button didn't sneak up on me like this e-mail, catching me as I expected to read about remote control hijackers.

Dear Russell,

I figured since Technoman does not answer his phone (such an antiquated device), I would try a medium more on-line with your state of mind. I would not even bother if Zach didn't ask me every day about when you are going to come over. I tell him that Daddy says Hello with every check (He doesn't have to know that you are a much better father with your wallet than with your heart). Well ever since you've become this Techno-man (Mid-life crisis so early, Russell?), Zach's been bothered at school by his teacher. His teacher keeps talking about you, and Zach pretends we aren't divorced. It would make it a little easier on him if he could at least say he spoke to you. Russell, I know you don't care any more, but how would you feel if you were him?

Love despite all,
Alice

She always left with one of the galling questions — you don't fall in love with anybody unless she gets to you — so that I unfortunately would memorize the message even as I deleted it.

I looked into and beyond the blank screen. The last day at the house I was staring at no blank. I had been logging in, as I had for the previous nine months, every last fact and piece of information about my life as it was happening. I recorded all my bills and checks, my phone calls and faxes, my purchases... not a dime was spent by me without writing down where and why. I catalogued all my CDs and video and books, even Zach's toys were duly recorded. I inventoried tooth paste and tampons, counting rolls of toilet paper (11 a week, believe it or not), cans of soda and beer, the number of times the floor was swept, the ice cubes were filled, the lights were turned on. I barely had time to produce my column or anything else. I told Alice I wanted to record for a day or two, explaining that such information might be valuable for a time capsule or something. But the job was far too big. There were all those trips to the bathroom and those items in the trash, the types of bills I had in my pocket, the use of Q-tips, band aids and cotton balls, the turning of the microwave, the frequency of junk mail, the vicissitudes of gas miles and the 1/10¢ shift in petroleum, the number of rainy days, the collection of times the president's name appears in the paper. The problem was never where should I begin, beginnings were everywhere, but how could I end. Alice came down to the basement just as I was recording the water levels that the dehumidifier drew from the air.

"Russell, I thought you were done."

"I will be in just a few more minutes."

"You said that ten minutes ago. Zach is already late for soccer."

"In a minute, I'll stop in a minute and then I will take him to soccer."

"No, you won't. You have to take him to soccer now. Otherwise he can't go at all."

"What are you talking about, he can wait."

"The game started at 1:00."

"So, what time is it now?"

"1:20."

"Oh. Well, I'll be done in a minute."

"Not a minute. You have to go now. Look, I've done everything for you. I work the same as you do, but I do all the cooking, cleaning, shopping, planning, financing, and what do you do?"

"I write it all down."

"And what does that do?"

"That's what I'm trying to find out?"

"Look, I've tried to be good to you. You wanted to record everything that happens around here. I told you from Day 1 what a stupid idea it was, but you had to do it, so I let you like I've done with all your Phases. I took up the slack, took up more burden, acted as mother and father to Zach, kept a roof over our heads. But you have to stop now. I can't take it anymore."

"I can take it, so you better be able to take it. This is too important to me to stop now."

"Russell, I'm telling you for the last time — "

"Just shut the fuck up and let me get this stuff down so I can drive the kid to soccer."

And shut up she did. Now I was making progress. I had finished the dehumidifier and moved onto the number of staples used in the past month. I didn't even hear Alice until she had the mouse chord about my neck and was pummeling me on the head with the mouse itself.

"You cruel, sick, ungrateful bastard!"

Crack went the mouse across my temple.

"A lousy game of soccer even, you son-of-a-bitch." Possessed, she picked up the printer, that heavy, awkward printer, and hurled it at me. I was too surprised to duck (I was trying to finish one last sentence, you see), so it whacked me flush on the right shoulder, dropping me to the ground. By some stroke of luck she missed with the monitor — I think she should have unplugged it first since the outstretched chord held it a foot short of me. I was looking at the wavering notes on the screen that were somehow still alive when I felt what must have been the now cracked printer smash into my back. My spine has never been the same since that blow ... I couldn't even cry out as she kicked the monitor to death. Nine months of creation wasted, lost, aborted, eight years of marriage ended. We both spotted Zach standing but shrunken in the corner of the room.

My back hunched and turned.

As I now see myself there, broken, trying to gather up some old printouts of the records even while I limped out the door, I knew what I now must do. If nothing else, I would kick the soccer ball around with Zach for a few hours. I knew she timed the letter in hopes that I would impulsively make my way over before they took their Sunday trip to Grandma's house. Alice still tried to fit me in.

I put on my jacket and got ready to shut down the terminal when an e-mail delivery clanged. As I read the note, I strangely forgot about going anywhere.

Channel 12:
Paddy Dangus

Hey Technoman,

Well you got a better view of Paddy Dangus than anybody I know. If you've seen the beard, you've seen everything. Even without the white truck, who else would

```
have the balls to swipe those remotes?
Congratulations, you've seen a ghost.
Don't expect it to happen again.
         Three-Fingered Mordicai Miller
```

I shot him back an e-mail.

```
Three-Finger,
This won't do at all. Get in the chat room, #4753.
I've got much more to ask you.
                         Technoman
```

I waited in the lounge chair of the chat room until Old Man Miller logged himself in.

```
"Hey, late nights in the landfill giving
you the jeebee?"
```

"No, but your daughter dropping obscure Paddy Dangus leads in my lap certainly does."

```
"I didn't think you were so sheepish."
```

"How did she know about the Dangus dumping?"

```
"Well, I think she mainly guessed you
see. I mean there was a full moon and
everybody knows Dangus only works on full
moons."
```

"What is he a fuckin' werewolf?"

```
"No, but he only works by natural
light."
```

Under my flashing fluorescents and bleeding, pulsing monitor, I could relate in an inverted, paradoxical kind of way.

"Why did he do it? I mean thousands of remotes destroyed for what?"

```
"Why does Paddy Dangus do anything?
Revenge."
```

"Not the old land story again. Not everyone responds like he has when screwed out of property."

```
"And not everyone has had his virgin
property - land from his Irish ancestors
mind you - designated as a toxic waste
dump. And not everyone has the ability to
disappear into a landscape as if he had
never been part of a place, never been
```

part of a tradition at all. For years we
just thought he was buried underground
like one of his rotting potatoes, stinking
and wasting, returning to the worms. But
he rises out of the earth like Hades from
his chariot. Angelica tells me he even
came to her bedroom one night, although I
don't think I believe her. But she
believes."

Angelica & Dangus. They both collect, but Angelica to
preserve, Dangus to destroy. I could see it, yeah, just like I could
fall in love with Angelica if you give me enough time to be
bewitched and to get over the hurdle that she is hopelessly human.
I saw her in the night wearing all black and big earrings, smart
and talkative, she bends to thoughts twisting around the roller of
the first FAX machine, her eyes glaring through a translucent
food processor across the room to Dangus, a hologram of a man;
real only to a woman comfortable with the artificial. Yes, I could
see her with Dangus and I could see her with me.

I asked, "Why don't you believe Angelica?"

"Well, if I believe, I have to believe
the rest about Dangus out to neutralize
Geoffrey Sphere before his universal
encryption remote surfaces."

How does everyone know my fucking Geoffrey Sphere
connection? The whole Miller family must be in on this.

"Geoffrey Sphere? What is Dangus bothering him
for? Doesn't he know that Smart Houses will make
Sphere obsolete before he even gets his product out?"

"That's only if the Smart Houses are
stupid enough not to incorporate Sphere's
remote in the design, which surprisingly
isn't the case."

"Huh?" I couldn't follow Miller. He wasn't speaking too
clearly and Angelica returned to my mind. After all, what was
Technoman but an artifact Angelica should collect. I could see
myself strangely happy to be collected, roped off and glass
encased in a humble pavilion of my own. I felt the tremendous
desire to be a commodity.

"Nothing Paddy Dangus hates more than a Smart House, except ..."

"Except — "

"Except an even smarter remote."

Sphere's anxiety-laden, rushed proposal began to make sense. Has a white truck driven through Geoffrey Sphere's dreams? Fucking Paddy Dangus?

"What's up with Paddy Dangus and all these assaults anyway?"

"If you had to endure a skin-eating virus after losing your farm... Christ he sounds like Job! What do you mean what's up? He's found a better way for folks to listen than slicing off a few fingers."

I should have found out more, but these visions of Angelica soothing Dangus's wounds, his wicked scars and burns and psoriasis, forever cleaning the skin, overwhelmed my thoughts.

"Sorry, but I have to go; will get back to you soon," I abruptly signed off. I took some window cleaner and washed my eyes and face. For the rest of the night, I could see clearly, but not well.

Channel 13:
Too Scary Not To Share

I was just about asleep when the phone rang at 2 a.m. In a moment of confusion and weakness, I actually picked up the receiver.

"Hello? Russell, hello?" Fucking Geoffrey Sphere... no pay is worth this. As a way of either concealing or revealing, my annoyance, I switched my computer-generated voice on my Intrafacer and typed out my conversation.

"What do you want at this uncorporate hour in the morning?"

"I've got to talk to you about Paddy Dangus before it's too late."

"Dangus? You too?"

"He's after my remote."

"Where'd you get that idea?" Were old man Miller and Angelica somehow connected to him?

"He's been in the office."

"How do you know?"

"Well someone broke into the office, didn't take anything, and hardly made any mess. If I weren't so smart, I wouldn't even know he appeared. But he wiped his feet on the rug."

"It could have been a janitor."

"No janitor wears boots like these."

"So it must be Paddy Dangus's of all the possibilities of boots out there."

"Hey, it's still a full moon."

"Well, not for long. The full moon's got to be over by now."

"There's one more night Russell. And Paddy didn't visit just to wipe his feet on the rug."

"So what do you want from me?"

"To come down here."

"What?"

"To come down here now."

"At two in the morning?"

"Hey, I know how little you sleep. I need someone besides Carmen and me to see this place. I'm starting to get a little paranoid and neither of us feels that we can leave."

"So you want me to come down there to look at the boot marks of a phantom."

"Hey, Pines, we may be dead tomorrow. How can you take Dangus so lightly? Haven't you seen what the universal remote can do? You yourself wrote of the remote dumping and the white truck two nights ago. Why are you avoiding the danger of this? Even through that mechanical voice I can hear your fear."

And then he paused, a dramatic pause that only summer action movies use: "You possess a reluctance not worthy of Technoman."

The comment was just ridiculous enough for me to be moved. "O.K. I'll be down in a few minutes."

"Hurry."

Hurry? I had to be properly dressed. What would I be without a superhero suit of bright yellow plastic accessorized by all types of velcro straps and hardware gadgetry that made the Intrafacer look like a pocket knife? "I'm on my way," which was just a firm enough lie to hang up the phone on.

No sooner was I free of his pleading than the phone rang again.

"What now Sphere?"

"Sphere? No Sphere? Little Augie."

"Little Augie? What the hell are you calling me at... 2:07 in the morning?"

"Instinct. I felt now you might be picking up your phone. I lost your e-mail address. I got something for you... "

She waited.

"The corpse of a lifetime."

"Huh," my response mechanism seemed a little off.

"You heard me: a corpse you would kill yourself if you ever missed."

"Why? Is it a dead robot or something?"

"Oh yeah, the Technoman pose. How could I forget! No it's not a robot. It's as far away from a robot as you could get in fact, but, believe me, Technoman would be interested in such a corpse as the one I have stiffening up on my table right now."

"Then Technoman is interested."

"I knew it wouldn't be long before Technoman would refer to himself in the third person."

I punched the keys harder. Little Augustina struck a short in my wires. One thing I promised I would not do is resort to third person — I somehow felt I would be retro 60s and 70s. I didn't mind staying in place as Technoman, but going backwards was another story. "Let me rephrase, *I* am interested. What is it a saint or something?" Little Augie is obsessed with finding the bodies of not-so-living saints — she seems to have a relic fetish.

"Not quite a saint, I would say, but I would say just as good, maybe better."

"Better than a saint? What is it?"

"You'll have to come down to find out."

"When do you want to show me the body?"

"Now."

"I can't right now."

"Why?"

"I've got to look at some footprint... It's not worth explaining."

"What time are you working to?"

"Six."

"I'll make it there by five."

"See you then. But remember if you don't see the body this morning you never will, and you will regret it for the rest of your life."

"Alright, alright, don't be so damn dramatic. I'll see you later."

God, I was more charged up than ever. I wrapped myself in the plastic, which made me instantly sweat. I took some Demerol to calm my nerves and headed out the door.

Channel 14:
Dirty Propositions

In the dead of night, every light was on in Prometheus Laboratories. Paddy Dangus would not be sneaking in here in the small hours of the morning. If I weren't expected, I could not be recognized, so much gear I wore, a resin armor no humanity could penetrate. I appeared to be a hazardous site worker scraping a mere innocuous dirt imprint off the rug.

"What do you think?" asked Geoffrey.

What did I think, how the fuck did I know? It looked to be the type of dried mud found in every corner of the globe with the exception of a couple of particularly small, sandy Polynesian islands. There was nothing else to do therefore than confirm his fears.

"Dangus," I said.

"I knew it. What do we do?"

Why is he asking me? "You wait it out. Stay here tonight and tomorrow night. Then the full moon will be over. Within the next month you should have the remote out of the lab."

Geoffrey nodded... he damn well better be agreeing with me since I was going through all this trouble to tell him what he wanted to hear.

I was getting ready to leave, feeling I had acted decisively, impressively, even memorably when I caught sight of Carmen Rana. She always seemed gradually to appear like a hologram forming across a beam of light. Needless to say I was aroused. Sphere must be occupied. "Have you checked your system to make sure no damage has been done to the universal remote."

"Of course."

"Well, you better check it again. If Dangus is all he's said to be, he's capable of great subtlety in these matters."

"Good point," I thought he was going to keep talking, but he started fingering the remote and his essence faded into the machine. Meanwhile, Carmen emerged from the fluorescent corners of the room. With my captop camera, I recorded her image, downloaded it onto my screen through my three-D adapter, and made her dance about my monitor. She must have wondered about my stupid smile and the far away look in my eye.

"What are you doing?" she asked.

"Do you really have six children?"

"Of course."

"Unbelievable"

"Why?"

I don't know how to explain this, but I couldn't help believing the attraction and feelings I had for the image on the screen could be shared with Carmen. I took a bizarre chance at romance when I drew her left hand into mine. I know, I know... Carmen has no plastic surgery, but Christ she is the inventor of a major high-tech breakthrough and I am lusting for her cybertext, virtual gyrating image — that's got to fit into my criteria somehow. Carmen, however, was not so plugged in as I thought.

Coolly, she tried to penetrate my screen and reach my eyes: "Nothing you can put in this hand can satisfy me the way this hand is already being satisfied." I at least had the solace of interpreting her comment as referring not to her faithful custodial husband, but to her even more faithful universal remote. "I have everything. You can give me nothing."

How strange that her rejection excites me even more. What more can one ask from a woman than the fact I could give her nothing.

"That's O.K. I don't think you could match what I have up on the screen now anyway."

"Perhaps not," she smiled, I think at that moment she started to turn sweet on me. But it was a natural sweetness, not the saccharine attraction I was so yearning for.

I liked the idea that I was leaving just when I think she decided she wanted me to stay. Don't get me wrong. Carmen would not have accepted my advances, but I think she would have drawn increasing pleasure out of each successive rejection. I might have stayed anyway, if not for my appointment with little Augie. Little Augie held out a promise to me no Technoman could reject: a dead thing more fascinating than a living one.

"I will keep in touch," I promised Geoffrey and Carmen as I stepped over the boot marks... as much as I could promise touch to anyone.

· "Hey look!" yelled Sphere.

"What?"

Sphere was opening up the microwave. He reached in and pulled something out. "Owww! They're still hot." He lifted a thick oblong brown tuber. "The son-of-bitch Dangus cooked potatoes in the microwave."

Channel 15:
The Prince of Darkness

Clapping me on the back at a quarter to five in the morning, her creepy tiny hand did nothing to calm my nerves.

"Hey, it's about time. I was almost ready to ship him out." Little Augie always spoke in a sane, deep voice as she told me the most fabulous, unfathomable tales. This time, however, she said nary a word, instead walking me over to the body, pulling back the sheet.

Twisted and grizzled, the pale, hairless figure seemed to already lose all the blood from his veins. The shrunken head sucked in his nose, and coupled with his missing eyebrows and chin, he could have passed for a hideous puppet in a bad horror film. I too began to feel part of the show as I spied the feline fingernails and the serpent tattoos that would have looked absurd on anyone else's forearms but such a misshapen spectacle. The corpse should have appeared as a hodgepodge of body parts, yet the swelled belly, smoothing a small surface of the badly wrinkled carcass, the withered, but still truncheon-length penis, drooping down near his left knee, and the clumps of ochre fur, pocking the ankles and feet all fused in a repulsive unity.

"Uggghhhh," I told small Augie.

She agreed, proud that she delivered the goods to me.

"What is this demon?"

"This is no demon," little Augie, tightened her face mockingly, surprised at my innocence. "Look again."

I looked, but did not venture a second guess.

"It's Satan himself. Don't you recognize him. I thought if anyone would know him, it would be you."

"Satan?"

"The Prince of Darkness. You are only one of four I am showing this to, so appreciate it." Little Augustina spoke so confidently I struggled to question her. Instead I was wondering that if the devil were only the Prince of Darkness, then who was king? Staring at the body another few minutes — I mean now I had to look it over more carefully — I blurted out the obvious.

"Satan's immortal. He can't die."

"That was another time, Rus, old boy." Little Augie spoke to me like I was her four-year-old nephew Stevie. "He couldn't be immortal during this day and age."

"What makes you think it's him? Even dead, why would the devil have a corpse?"

"Watch this," little Augie sliced a scalpel into the top of the body's right arm. The wound smoked and popped and bubbled, then burned back shut, returning to a similar appearance of the rest of his arm, only the wrinkles a bit tighter.

Impressive, yet I began to suspect little Augie had cut open one too many dead bodies.

"But why the corpse? How did he die?"

"Toxic shock," even little Augie noted my incredulous reaction. "Look, for the past three decades what has he been doing but hanging around every waste dump, nuclear power plant, chemical factory. He thought he saw Armageddon in a test tube. He got caught up in it all. No time to transform. Hell, he's been sprawled out in a coma ever since returning to New York, triumphant after his final annual pilgrimage to Chernobyl."

"Since Chernobyl? Who the hell has been taking care of evil all this time?"

"Naive little boy. The Prince of Darkness had been a minor figure in the evil game for a long while. Technology brushed him aside like he was some auto plant worker. He had become marginalized, irrelevant. It wasn't as if we needed help drawing in drafts of evil... we have more trouble breathing."

Something about the idea of the devil dying seemed very sad, as if I were speculating on the death of a parent. I wish little Augie hadn't mentioned the notion because now I struggle to disbelieve. I couldn't listen to this crap much longer. "Goodbye little Augie. Make sure he gets a proper burial."

"Are you kidding?" she soured, looking as if she didn't know me anymore, with a disappointment intimating I may get no more tips from my little morgue friend. "He's off to the crematories."

Channel 16:
Son of Technoman

After inspecting what little Augie called the corpse of Satan, I had this strong desire to see Zach so I picked him up at the house and brought him to my new humble home.

"Let me take a picture of you Daddy."

I posed.

"Good. Now I will download you onto my screen."

I was not sure if I were entering his world or he mine. I do know both of us were now video game characters fighting against the forces of evil who fiercely opposed our leaving the countryside and letting us into the big thrilling metropolis.

We were getting nowhere until I jumped in front of Thorg, giving my life up, so Zach could hop onto the superhighway.

"Daddy, why did you do that?"

"You were not going to get there any other way."

Zach seemed moved. I was particularly fond of making noble and self-sacrificing gestures in virtual reality.

A few minutes later Zach arrived at the Metropolis sprawl and didn't notice my body floating to the heavens. I felt like a father for the first time in a long time.

Four times I asked to play soccer with Zach, but he refused... Still a sore subject. Anyway, he did not want to play with SoccerDad but with TechnoMan.

"I am Technoman," Zach reared up and pronounced, with so much gusto I couldn't figure out whether he was honoring or mocking me. Feeling more comfortable with the mockery, I played along.

"I am Thorg," and with my Intrafacer as my armor I did resemble the powerful mutant cyborg.

"Get out of my way Thorg, you deconstructional scum," such a mouth on my boy, too many satellite hook-ups and video games and readings of my column, "You outmoded, hypercrystallic, low-thyroid, under-orificed, over-acned, mother-boarding, father-fudging, run-of-the-mill Silicon Valley factory reject."

"Huh?" My young son was already too quick-witted for me, but I had an advantage, for Zach was now Technoman and if I knew the weaknesses of any man it was he.

"Factory reject? Factory reject! They wouldn't even let you into a factory... You couldn't even be the feces-like by-product of my manufacturing. You who has to go by phony names and guises because you lack an identity, a soul, an ability to — " I think I was getting off track here by Zach's puzzled look — "to compute only the most rudimentary formulas and equations. You run like a Twentieth-Century man and you will crumble like one too. I will make you mortar for shopping malls, wastrels for web sites. You will be separated from your very self."

"Oh yeah!" Zach said, running to my computer, pulling wires, taking the keyboard and the mouse, then charging at me.

Despite the sense of deja-vu, I continued to play as we smacked against each other. Zach grew fiercer and I clunked him with my hard drive, flipping the would-be superhero over. Before

I knew, he had whacked me in the elbow with the keyboard and kicked me in the head. I pretended I was hurt, which wasn't too difficult since I was hurt, and he started punching me furiously using the mouse as brass knuckles. For seemingly a half hour, I rose and fell while he continued to pummel, yelling and crying.

"I am Technoman. You cannot stop me." Whack, whack, whack.

"Technoman cannot be stopped... Cannot be stopped... Cannot be stopped."

He punctuated each "Stopped" with a full throttle into my ribs with the keyboard. Enjoying the beating, I grew convinced that Zach would be a much better Technoman than I.

About then, Alice walked in. Zach stopped hitting me, and I wiped the blood off my face and onto my sleeve.

"Jesus Christ. What are you doing?"

"Just a little rough-housing."

"I am Technoman," Zach proclaimed, a triumphant cartoon character.

"What are you?" Alice asked me in a tone that sent four different messages and served up six different questions. I had no answer. Alice, of course, had a few.

"It's one thing not be a role model as a father. But look at you." Not just my flesh but even my Intrafacer recoiled as she spoke. "You are supposed to be Technoman and you are fighting like a Caveman. You can't even be a fake of an imaginary role model. Get your stuff Zach and let's get out of here."

For the first time since I left the house, Zach hugged and kissed me without any begrudging posturing.

As he walked out the door, I snapped his picture and downloaded it.

For the rest of the day, I played with his image.

Channel 17:
Dancing Gadget to Gadget

Pines Tar: Technoman in Clubland

I confess I am a fraud as Technoman. I did not know until I made my way to *Diodes*, you know that new stainless steel warehouse-inspired, millennium-ending proportioned, state-of-the-art-deco MegaClub.

When I stepped out of the full moon and walked upstairs into the missile silo sized hall at midnight, I could have convinced myself that I had wandered into a mannequin convention. Even as the machine loop lightning and bass thunder rumbled louder, seemingly with each passing note, urging, coaxing, banging, screaming, not a soul danced. They hovered along winding peripheries of the bar, waiting, waiting, waiting for something. They waited, so I decided I should wait too. The bartender, who would almost have been pretty if she were real, shot my whisky sour out of a soda gun. Since she was my type of woman, I watched her ply her trade for a few minutes. Incredibly, she shot everything out of that soda gun: daiquiris and coladas, Harvey Wallbangers and grasshoppers, mud slides and kamikazes. In her holster was the universal remote of bartending tools. She never lifted a bottle, tossed a shaker or consulted a blender. And when I said my whisky sour is a little weak, she told me everything was premixed and she would have to·charge me more for uncalibrated whisky.

That was the most personal exchange I had for hours as I mingled about with my Intrafacer. I thank my lucky lasers I brought the whole ensemble with me or I would not have had any prayer of fitting in at the place. I felt inadequately, insufficiently artificial, such was the shiny gaggle of plastic bouncing off the walls, staring at the football field sized empty dance floor. My only solace was the pulsing of the techno that grabbed my ears and rattled my head, its beat and synthesizers hypnotizing me, its primitive chants transporting me to a place far beyond the strobe lights and the neons, that spot where sweat mingles with machine fluid. I must have been entranced for a half hour until the navigator in my Intrafacer malfunctioned and I realized I was still waiting with everyone else at the edge of the bar.

I had decided that I had never felt so lonely as in this crowd of people when old man Miller came up to me [Miller, recovering nicely from his latest chemistry class performance, thank you]. He sported a pseudo-retro illuminated leisure suit, looking geriatric and oh so cool. He seemed to be a magnet for fairly short, very made-up, and very very tight shirted women who danced about him like he was their cult leader.

"Hey," he said.

"Hey," I replied.

He was smiling and shuffling rhythmically as the ladies lifted up the backs of their bleached blonde manes, howled insincerely, and pointed at him. "Watch my dance move   I call the Paddy Dangus."

"O.K." I was becoming convinced Dangus had replaced Nicola Telsa as old man Miller's idol.

"Ready, watch... Did you see that?"

"I didn't see nothing."

"I know you didn't. That's why I call it the Paddy Dangus: You see nothing even though I did something."

"What did you do?"

"I flicked my ring and pinkie fingers."

"But those are the two digits you cut off."

"Exactly."

Surrounding Miller, I finally met a girl with artificial limbs who couldn't keep her one good eye off my Intrafacer.

"Do you want to dance?" she asked, sounding even more curious to see how I would rattle my equipment than I was about hers.

I typed in, tweaking the volume of my computer-generated voice. "I would love to."

I pointed my camera at her, called her up on my monitor, and took to the floor, with my keyboard shimmering, my hard drive waffling, and my butt contorting like I was trying to get out of a strait jacket.

During the third dance, I started to look at my date. Funny how all her prosthetics seemed so loose and free while her flesh grew stiff and hard — my type of woman.

Purely by chance, atoms crashing off each other, her resin hand touched my keyboard setting off a whole swirl of static images.

"Wow, I think I'm in love."

"With me, or what's on there," she tapped the monitor.

"Both."

"I can live with that."

"I think you can live with a lot of things." By now, almost suddenly, every human being on Long Island was moving about on the dance floor.

For the remainder of the night we were within an inch of each other, rocking and gyrating. Amazingly after the keyboard incident, we never touched again. That's the moment I, Technoman, made a genuine connection.

Channel 18:
Amputated Love

When I got down to Diodes, I hadn't planned on seducing an amputee, but the opportunity presented itself, and, after all, I'm only human. Sheila wore her limbs with pride, the whole left side of her body a prosthetic menagerie, with one of those high-tech, resin-flexing, joint twisting hands, and decent arm and leg to boot. She led with that leg, that arm, that shoulder as she came to me after I zoomed in on her one good eye.

"Wow! Let me look at that," I said of her hand the way I would if I were checking out a new ultra-elastic, dayglo spandex jumpsuit. "Does it work?"

"What do you think?" She ran those magic fingers through my hair. In a bad movie she would have clapped the claw around my pecker and sent it into orbit, but Sheila knew the soft touch. As it was, the little tousle sent me muttering "oh boy, oh boy."

Yet I was a purist and had to ask, "How did you get these?"

Would I still want her if she said birth defects?

Perhaps...

But a maiming, now that would be pure wish fulfillment.

"A tractor-trailer backed up into me."

Jesus, my fantasies and my experiences seemed to merge effortlessly. Yet, I worked harder with Sheila than at any time since I tried to get back with Alice. I poured champagne and charm into her till she must have felt like my princess. Then I carried her over the threshold of the Commack Motor Inn with the mirrors virtually papered on the ceiling and every wall: I would not miss an angle of this night.

I lay in bed as she took off her clothes and her limbs, disassembling before me... the ultimate strip tease. I wanted to beg her to keep on the prostheses, but she even popped out the glass eye before she dropped her half of body into bed. Then I wanted to ask her if she would at least leave the limbs in the jumble on the bed with us, but she had her one good hand about my pecker so fast I was in no position to think and prosecute the business of the bed. Leaning on those stumps of limbs, she nuzzled up against me, flopping about, seemingly having spasms across my torso. Needless to say, I was considerably aroused and distracted by all this movement, as she arched her back and faced me square, her one lost eye a mere sunken lid, the other fluttering, all lashes and whites, dropping her face tongue first into my mouth, the scar along her left cheekbone undulating rhythmically against my nose.

Up again she rose like a porpoise from the sea, twisting about with one good arm the way few can do with two, her single leg wrapped through and about mine, her chest seeming to swell with every heave, blood rushing to it as if responding to an emergency. She let me inside her as far as any woman had ever let me: I believe I could tickle her chin. I don't believe I've ever felt closer to another and not because of the depth of my penetration.

It was something else that I desired after she rose up about a dozen times, defying me and gravity in a single bound. Until I grew comfortable, I only touched her good side. But then I turned obsessed with pawing her scars, starting from the cheek, to the eye socket, to the arm, to the leg and the crotch. She could hardly feel my fingers, I might as well have rubbed a fingernail or a shell. Fortunately by mistake I slipped my hand just below her arm socket to a soft and lively skin. She gasped for air. I rubbed back along it and she gasped some more; caressing the patch gently I shivered as her torso vibrated against me. My other hand dropped across her and attended to just above the leg socket.

Now she was screaming and smacking against me. The cries seemed too loud and passionate to be real, but they were. Not a minute passed before she dropped in sweet ecstasy upon me, sleep appearing to overcome her. Yet as I stroked above her sockets tenderly, she soon rose up in whimpers and twists, sweating and charging until she fell upon me again. One or two more forays had me out of my mind. Christ, Sheila was practically battery-operated. She kept running and I couldn't stop her, except to punctuate with my own halloos, till I could yell no more, my throat unwilling to start what my satisfied hunger could not sustain.

When I collapsed, she could not revive me. She gamely searched my body for wounds... poor girl just didn't know I was without any. With her one good eye and hand and leg she explored me, searching, completely unsatisfied. I thought this flattering, until her hand returned to my pecker. She gave a squeeze and a stare the way one would who picks up an apple to eat disappointingly discovers what she has in her hands is a piece of wax fruit.

The silence grew too deadly for me not to speak: "Will I see you again?"

"I don't know," she said wonderingly. "I don't know," this time more convincingly. "There's something about you. There's just something missing. Something you lost that I can't put my finger on."

"What do you mean? You were howling like a banshee."

"But that's all I did was howl. You are missing something. No... I don't think I will see you anymore."

If she would have stayed, I think I could have convinced her otherwise, but she didn't remain a minute longer. She would not even take the time to reattach her limbs. She just threw on some clothes, gathered up her prosthetics and limped out.

Channel 19:
When Diodes Snap

Does the phone only ring once I finally get to sleep?

"Sorry so late lover boy," it was Angelica, "but I heard something off the police radio thirty seconds ago about a disturbance at Prometheus Laboratories. I thought you might be interested."

"Sure thanks." I hung up before I developed the urge to talk to her.

I assembled myself and made my way down in what was becoming a nightly journey. This time instead of Geoffrey at the door, it was the police.

"Russell," said Detective Peterson, "long time, no speak. I was afraid Technoman became too busy to be bothered with light industrial accidents."

"Accident?"

"Maybe, or theft and assault."

"What? Let me see."

"Now hold on, we have two injured people in there. This is a police scene. We can't let you stroll in."

"I worked with those people. I can help you. I know them and I know what they were working on there — very sensitive high tech stuff."

"Yeah?"

"If I am of no use to you, you throw me out. O.K.?"

"Don't worry, I will."

Anyway, I was in and once I saw Geoffrey and Carmen sprawled out on the floor, I started talking, all the time looking around for the universal remote. I described it to Peterson and the other officers, asking whether they had spotted it. They were pretty clear in their negatives. Somehow I think Geoffrey and Carmen would have been touched by the fact I was more concerned for the remote than I was for their persons. The EMTs were checking the two motionless bodies over, going through the procedures, treating them as classic cases of traumatic shock.

"What happened to them?"

"We don't know: we just found them knocked out cold, with no blood or apparent bruises."

"Well, then what *could have* happened to them?"

"That we won't know for a while. From what I see no one appears to have entered, although an alarm was tripped, that's how we got here in the first place."

"If no one came in, the universal remote would not have been removed from the office."

"Well, if someone did come in, he seemed to have touched nothing, not even the two victims; they don't appear to have a mark on them."

I looked out the window: the full moon was falling below the horizon. I walked over to the microwave and opened the door. More hot potatoes. Geoffrey and Carmen were being rolled out in stretchers. I asked one of the EMTs whether they would be alright.

"They are no worse than when we got here. Their vital signs are stable, but they are unconscious." He told these bits of information as if they were much more than he is authorized to offer.

Funny, as they headed off to the ambulance, I could tell something was not quite right about the room, but couldn't figure out what it was. Something about the smell perhaps, although that could be a bizarre residual of prosthetic lubrication, love juices, sweaty plastics, and a seemingly melting Intrafacer... layers of the night's movements. My senses were dulling and I grew distant from the truth of this office. Even the cops had a better sense of what had happened than I did, piecing together something that I should have been able to call up whole on my computer screen.

Why were Geoffrey and Carmen still alive? Death is so much easier to explain than this. Why let the creators live to create again? Why take the remote then?

I headed back to the potatoes searching for clues, picking up the largest one. I couldn't hold onto it though, so ridiculously hot it remained. This wasn't my type of work at all. I lived with mysteries; I didn't try to resolve them.

I couldn't tell Peterson about the vague notions I had of strange odors, nor could I tell him about the aura of electrical pulses that seemed to be shooting through the room (or was it through my head?), but I could drop a name. I might not even be able put a sentence together, but I could make Peterson understand.

"Peterson"

"Yeah."

"Paddy Dangus."

"I was afraid he would come up."

"I can't believe I'm the one who raised him."

"Do you realize blaming a crime on Paddy Dangus is just calling it an unsolved mystery?"

"Yes, but you must admit the nature of the crime scene points to him, especially with the remote dump at the landfill last week."

"Might as well point to an abyss."

"Well that's where I'm heading anyway," and I started walking out for both dramatic effect and efficient departure.

"Where are you going?"

"To follow another mystery. This one's a little too close to me right now to hang around. I'm certainly not going to get any peace here." Before I walked out the door, I remembered to swipe an old remote control that Geoffrey used to study and, on occasion, to mock. I thought he wouldn't mind my borrowing it, since my controls in the bedroom seem to have vanished into thin air. The instrument would be more comfort to me in the hours of dusk than one could imagine.

Channel 20:
A Visit To Tsarsas

With Geoffrey and Carmen lying comatose in the hospital, my thoughts returned strangely to the prone figure of Satan. I visited little Augie more than I had planned. I just had a nagging question or two. Every answer would start the same way:

"He died at peace in Tsarsas, PA. Right by the power plant. That wouldn't be reported of course, since the nuclear technocrats have enough problems without getting that PR debacle strung about their necks."

After awhile, I thought little Augie spoke to me in code, wanting to tell me to go to Tsarsas, but knowing I wouldn't listen if she asked me to go. So I went... because I had to, taking nuke gadfly Stan Peyton with me, who had been to Tsarsas, and every other nuclear power plant countless times. Tsarsas management didn't like Stan, didn't want him to be there, but Stan knew his legal rights and knew the plant, and for the price of having to listen to his bullshit, I would know too.

That he didn't shut up from the time we hit Route 80 to the moment we approached the security gate made the trip more of a painful necessity. He spoke only of the waste fuel: "You see, the bullet-sized pellets of uranium," he would keep saying, as if to brainwash me that even the shape of these things is deadly. "The bullet-sized pellets of enriched uranium are loaded into long rods. They're the fuel that turn the coolant into steam which, in turn, turns the turbines to make electricity. But every year, year-and-a-half, the fuel rods of pellets shoot their load and are spent. But that's O.K., the spent fuel will only be radioactive for at least, say 10,000 years. That seems a good exchange huh? One year's worth of fuel for 10,000 worth of waste..."

Soon Stan grew philosophic talking about how previous generations left behind centuries later art and buildings and culture while we would just leave radioactive waste. I turned the radio louder. As we drove into nowhere and I could only find country music stations transmitting, I listened for heartbroken lovers.

Satan better have died in the waste storage because that was the only place Stan showed me with any time for contemplation. The rods, the tanks, the stacks, the holding facilities... he walked by them like they were cheap furniture. The token gadfly on the nuclear regulatory commission, Stan had presidential access. The engineers and guards even gave him respectful distance. "That storage pool is 40 feet deep and at the bottom are tons of fuel assemblies holding millions of curies of iodine-131 shooting about. The deep water is supposed to cool the fuel and absorb the radioactivity. But it only does so much."

Stan kept talking but he didn't understand that I wasn't here to learn anything, only to look. The pool gave off this beautiful soft blue light — Stan said it emitted off the high-energy particles from the fuel shooting out across the water — I grew mesmerized by it.

"I want to jump in."

"You dope," said Stan. "You'd die."

"Look at it. It's a grotto of hidden life."

"Hidden death, you mean."

I was going to ask workers if they found a body around, but after seeing the pool, I didn't want to or have to. Although more than twenty feet below the surface, those shimmering blue rods seemed right in front of me, almost in my hands, each one a cell of eternal life. Now that's energy and vitality. Would you forgive me if I found radioactivity more fascinating than the Prince of Darkness?

Stan kept talking... of furies, of curies, of scandals and boondoggles, of untamed tigers, unleashed titans and cold sores. I stood soothed, lost in a fog of blue, staring at the light I imagine I might see only at death or if an alien space ship landed. With the glow in the fuel rods emanating off the clear, cool water, I hummed again and again a slow tune I had made up on Route 80. I leaned closer to the surface. It was more comforting than the flashing lights of the television on those long insomniac nights.

A pointed question from Stan awoke me from my spell. "Why aren't you writing anything down?"

"We'll have plenty of time on the way home. I just want to absorb the ambiance."

"Jesus, you better watch yourself there, buddy. You're almost over the rail."

"So I am." I looked down at the footing of the ledge. I had not been the only leaner lately. A big clump of ochre fur rested along the otherwise gleaming, sterile ramparts.

Off a cloven hoof? "Shit."

"Pull back, we're lucky a guard hasn't thrown us out already."

I was in no mood to awaken, but I snatched the fur up into my pocket and signaled Stan to go before I discovered something else.

Channel 21:
Sheep Meadow

Pines Tar: When the Grass Isn't Always Greener

"You could lie on the turf and think you were on the finest mattress money could buy," said Sheep Meadow resident Ralph Lorenzo. "Now look at it," his arms out wide, disgusted and exasperated. The full acre surrounding his huge house stands overgrown and patchy, bits of many flowers and grasses of all shapes and colors chewing away at the last remnant of suburban grandeur.

Ralph Lorenzo isn't alone. Almost every resident in Sheep Meadow seems to have the same problem of wild grasses and flowers, like a swarm of locusts, invading the plush green lawns. Once called the "Sod Garden of the World," Sheep Meadow is losing its turf and, with that turf, its identity.

"Our whole lifetimes have been spent making this community what it is, and now look at it," said 87-year-old Giles Packer, who first came to Sheep Meadow in the late 1940s. Back then Sheep Meadow had neither sheep nor meadow, just a cluster of maple trees and ponds. But when Wilbur Haddock bought its 5,000 acres he knew he could build a community for World War II veterans of which they could be proud. And so they have.

Each spring out come the spreaders and down goes the lime and the fertilizer and the supplemental grass seed and then come late June the crab grass killer is scattered about, followed in the heat of summer by the grub killer, finally topped off come harvest time by a major dose of every useful chemical known to landscapers. And through all these years, past the cold war and recessions and oil crises and even droughts that could test a water sprinkler system, the plush carpets of Sheep Meadow flourished.

But now, those lawns look like their residents have abandoned these homes, the wild flowers and weeds so pervasive that they seem to be climbing up the sides of the stately ranches and colonials. "I don't wait more than three days before I mow the lawn again," said Sara Logan, a 67-year-old widow whose impeccably tidy flower boxes belie the rest of the yard.

How could such a thing happen to what may have been Long Island's loveliest community? From resident to resident, Sheep Meadow homeowners place the blame in the same hands: "I can't prove anything, but I just know Paddy Dangus is responsible," said Sara.

Giles says he even knows when Paddy Dangus contaminated the land. "It was one evening in March about 2:30 in the a.m. when I heard a truck stopping and starting along the road. I wouldn't have even noticed if the truck didn't need a brake job. Anyway, all I saw was a shadow moving across my lawn. But you know Paddy Dangus... that's enough for him to do his damage. Next morning, my lawn was filled with claw marks.

Come spring, wildflowers sprouted where my soft thick sod used to grow. I can't tell you how devastated we are."

Despite accounts like that one from Giles, police are no closer to pinning the widespread acts of private property destruction to Paddy Dangus. "Remember we don't even possess a clear sketch of Dangus, so we are having great difficulty apprehending him. We think we have a motive, given Dangus's pattern of attacking some of the finer aspects of suburban living on Long Island, but that is not enough to track him down."

Police are asking anyone with information about Paddy Dangus or members of his organization to step forward. Meanwhile, for the residents of Sheep Meadow, relief could be on the way. Harley Blinford, chief agriculturist for the Long Island Landscaping Cooperative, is prepared to implement a solution. "I am now mixing large quantities of chemical compound that will kill everything on the ground. After we wipe everything out, the residents can add top soil and start again."

For Giles Packer that day can't come soon enough: "I can't imagine dying with my lawn looking like this."

Channel 22:
Fade and Disintegrate

Within three hours of each other Geoffrey and Carmen had awakened. And they didn't remember anything, not of that fateful night, not of the remote, not of me, not of each other, not even of their identities.

"Amnesia, oh fuck," I said out loud, more to you the audience than to myself. "What kind of melodrama serial did I walk into?" I had never met anyone who suffered more than a drunken blackout, let alone a wholesale memory loss.

When I first came in to see Geoffrey, I would have bet he was involved in a put-on. "Now who are you?" he asked, like right out of the movies.

"Do you know anything about a remote control?"

He looked at me puzzled. I picked up the remote for his hospital room TV. "The remote — This." I handed it to him.

He looked at it more courteously than carefully, then put it down, turning away from me.

"Paddy Dangus. Do you know Paddy Dangus?"

"Who is Paddy Dangus?" he asked.

"Wouldn't we all like to know," I said.

"I wouldn't," he confessed.

"Perhaps you're right. Things might have been better off that way."

"What's all that stuff on you," pointing most particularly to my flip-down monitor.

"That's my Intrafacer."

"I like it. It makes you look intelligent."

I headed into Carmen's room as Federique was corralling his pack of kids toward the elevator. From what I could gather between doctor, nurse and family talk, the problems seemed to be connected to temporal lobe seizures, but the diagnosis was accompanied by the strongest of noncommittals, an extraordinary level of hedging even in these days of shell-shocked malpractice concern. Not helping the situation was the inability to find a blow to the head that could explain the strange stew of epileptic symptoms apparently manifesting themselves from the moment of awakening. All I glommed from the discussion was a jumble of words with no meaning attached to them. I typed them into my hard drive as a keepsake, even though I had no intention of looking any of them up: tegretol, automatism, ideation, deja vecu, vertiginous, PET-scan, ictal, Grand and Petite Mal, provoking factors, etiology, Video-EEG monitoring, Acute Insults, dysphasia, Choroid plexis, audiosensory cortex, amgydala... the more they spoke of the brain, the more my head hurt. I needed someone my speed, and I walked into Carmen's room hoping she had been sufficiently damaged to disintegrate to my level.

I tried to engage Carmen in communication but she was doing a fine job of conversing without me. Her neck was flipped back and her nose bobbed up above all else the way a duck's body buoys above the water. Sniffing and squinting, she seemed very far away from me, from her bed, from the hospital, from the turn of the millennium.

"Rotten eggs," she thrashed about. "God damn."

"What?"

"I'm running out of time," she tapped on her wrist, on a watch that wasn't there. She was back sniffing, "Rotten eggs."

I don't think you'll believe me, but a strange thing was happening right then and there to your friend Technoman. I was experiencing deja vu, or deja vecu, whatever that is. I knew Carmen and I were soul mates, thinking exactly at the same level. I had entered into her memory, into her past, into her secret consciousness.

"What, is there sulfur burning?"

"Oh yeah," she smiled, "Sulfur everywhere."

You see, I told you. I could smell it myself. I *was* there. I *am* there.

"What are you running out of time for?"

"For the test."

"But this is no ordinary test is it?" I know, I am there.

"No, no ordinary test. This is the biggest test of my life."

What'd I tell you. My next question seemed. like a conversation killer, even as I was asking it, but I had to anyway; it was the dialogue that had to follow, no matter what I thought of it.

"What type of watch are you wearing?"

"A Casio C-80."

Of course, now the whole scene was clear. I was not only in her mind, but I was in there watching a TV episode in the late 1970s. Sulfur and a Casio C-80, amazing how it just took two notes for me to name that show... to name that episode. Carmen was obviously reliving the best *Bionic Woman* segment of them all. You know, I don't even have to tell you, do I? The one with Jaime running at sixty miles per hour, through a field of burning sulfur after a couple creeps raided a fertilizer factory and threw the toxic barrels in Jaime's path to prevent her from beating them to the missile silos. They were clever creeps and doubtless they would have launched the missiles and brought the world to an end if Jaime didn't have her bionic body and her Casio C-80. With her telescopic eyes she spotted the creeps running a mere 1357 meters from the silo, so Jaime plugged in her coordinates to the watch computer and calculated the distance of the throw she would have to make with her state-of-the-art grenade, allowing for the flight time of the explosive and the speed at which the creeps were moving.

"I shouldn't worry," she was talking to me. "I have the equipment, I have the technology, I can do anything."

She sure did. When that grenade hit, I remember back as a mere boy feeling, for the first time, that any vile aspect of the nuclear world could be neutralized with enough technological ingenuity and resolve, nor did it hurt that such a pretty, strong woman hurling a weapon across time and space gave me one hell of an erection.

"The world was at your fingertips, wasn't it?" I asked, knowing the answer.

"Oh yes," she said softly, now incredibly relaxed.

The return of the bumbling Frederique shut down our moment of intimacy.

"Hey," I said, trying my best to look sympathetic.

"Hey," he replied.

"I think she was having a flashback or something."

"A flashback?"

"Yeah, I think she was actually thinking about an old TV show."

"Huh."

"Well, she seemed to smell sulfur and she mentioned something about an old calculator watch and she spoke of the biggest test of her life and how she had the technology and could do anything."

Frederique flushed. "Oh, I know what she was remembering." He too looked like he was Carmen's soul mate. I didn't have the heart to tell him he was only her husband. "She's thinking about her entrance exam at MIT."

"What?" Now this was farfetched. What would the smell of sulfur, the Casio C-80, and high tech empowerment have to do with that?

"She used that calculator watch to take the exam. She'd probably kill me for telling you this, since she wasn't exactly supposed to have a calculator on the exam. Some might call it cheating, but I call it what Carmen called it: Using the tools of the age to be in a position to create tools for the next age."

Funny how I started to believe him after that last statement; it's just the type of ambitious rationalization that needs repeating until one grows comfortable with it. Frederique could not have remembered such a line if Carmen had not said it to him a few hundred times over the years. Yet I still believed my interpretation much more.

"What about the sulfur smell?"

"Oh that's the part that clinched it for me. All Carmen did for weeks is complain about the rotten egg smell of the lab room where she took the exam. She has always been convinced that those sadistic bastards at MIT included that unbearable smell as part of the test, to make sure the candidates could focus under any condition."

What else was there for me to say? Was her life like a TV show, or was the TV show like her life, or was my life like a TV show? I picked up the hospital room remote.

"Do you know what this is?"

She said nothing, but took it in her hands. She starting pressing the numbers like she was calculating some extraordinary mathematical problem. All her operations on .the remote did not add to anything, but as she tapped away, the TV screen sure did flash and crackle like a pile of photographs in a bonfire.

"You've got the whole world at your fingertips don't you?" I asked her, as I was sliding out the door.

In response, she smiled at me: I wasn't sure if it was because she agreed with my assessment or she recognized the line as one off a memorable commercial from the 1970s.

Channel 23:
Found and Lost

It took the whole ride home to figure out I should have called the nurse. Was I witnessing a seizure? If I did, it was far too intriguing to be interrupted by the medical professionals. They wouldn't have wanted to get to the bottom of the memory; they would have tried to end it, to restore her. I knew Geoffrey and

Carmen would not be in this state for long. The doctors sounded too confident in the medication and their conviction that both would soon have their memories and their old thoughts back: they would lose the bizarre haziness that I too have been infected with since that late lost full moon at Prometheus Laboratories. I liked not knowing what had happened or what is happening right now.

Could I explain that every time I thought of the universal remote, Paddy Dangus and even my life as Technoman, I grew strangely drawn to Satan? For the past three days I've left messages with Little Augie, at work and at home, but she has returned no calls. Every mystery presents itself to me mockingly, closing its zipper each time I reach inside, yet I stitch together these sealed pieces, making patterns of everything, yoking metaphors more than mixing them. I have been handed a series of mysteries with which to penetrate the randomness of my life.

I was filled with more desire than memory: I wanted to find that universal remote, I wanted to get laid, I wanted to find out if Satan really died at a nuclear power plant, I wanted to find a container of guar gum. I seemed incapable of getting anything, especially satisfaction. I guess to be Technoman is to be content with dissatisfaction. Searching for something, anything, I head to Prometheus Laboratories. It was locked. I short-circuited the alarm system with a pocket laser beam — donated by a dedicated reader — and broke in, half-hoping I would get arrested: at least I would have verification of my doing something, guided, misguided or otherwise. I could describe my impressively stealthy moves as I made my way up to Sphere's office; it will make a fine ten-minute suspense scene of the movie, when the rights to this docudrama finally get sorted out. But I should tell you about now that I found Angelica up there in the office — obviously she discovered an easier break-in route — collecting all types of electronic specimens along the way.

My first instinct was to yell at her, but then a strange feeling came over me that Angelica was the Indiana Jones of postmodern archeological digs and I would in that scenario merely serve as some minor villain to be disposed with more flair than effort. Anyway her lovely back was mighty distracting (she was wearing a tight black rayon blouse), so I was too confused to speak. After all, this back looked terribly natural... I secretly hoped for scoliosis scars, but knew I was kidding myself, so I typed in the only thing I could come up with that represented at least one of my desires.

"Have you found anything?" the computer-generated voice seemed particularly impersonal tonight.

"Yes," she said, soft and sexy, but not just role-playing, like I'm so used to; instead my distance made her that much closer to me. "But are you prepared to see what I've got."

"No," I confessed. "But I'd like to know anyway."

"How badly do you want it?"

"Bad."

"How bad?"

"What does that mean? How bad? Sometimes your movie dialogue is not too clear, or maybe the problem is the tone."

"I mean would you be willing to let me have your Intrafacer for the night."

"The Intrafacer? Are you kidding me?"

"Hey, I'm not asking for an arm and a leg."

"You have a better chance of getting them from me."

"I thought you wanted to know what I know. Or maybe you'd like to wallow in the Stone Age as far as your understanding of Paddy Dangus goes?"

"All night long?"

"What's a matter. It's like that Intrafacer alone is what makes you Technoman."

"The idea has crossed my mind."

"The Intrafacer now or you're leaving with nothing." Her tone was just totalitarian enough to make me both receptive and aroused.

Unstrapping the Intrafacer, I turned naked and cold, yet I confess I grew erect as Angelica hooked the whole apparatus up. Hardware really does make the woman. Impressively, she whipped out her own arsenal of gauges, sensors, and other electronic wizardry which I liked even more because I couldn't recognize them. I pulled close to her and started kissing her monitor gently as she typed and talked. I didn't hear anything; I nuzzled right up to her cheek and looked at her monitor.

"You must donate this to my collection when you are done with it."

"What about Dangus?" I asked, one hand of mine playing patty cake with hers on the pocket mouse, the other all over the hard drive. I refuse to keep my hands off my Intrafacer even if that means keeping my hands on the unsurgically enhanced Angelica.

"Come over here." She took me by a wall of exposed wiring. "Dangus has been fucking with the electricity."

She saw how confused I looked. She pointed a sensor at the wall and it lit up like a game show tote board.

"I think he created an electro-magnetic field."

"What? Why?"

"I was hoping you'd help me with this information."

"Well I can tell you the impact of whatever he did on Carmen and Geoffrey is enough to explain the why. I confess the what I'm not too concerned about."

"But the what may be the key to it all."

She was looking for that key to it all while I grabbed her. When I threw myself into the Intrafacer, I decided I had found myself. Angelica wanted what I wanted; I lived, she collected, now she took my livelihood — at least for the night — and I collected. She snapped a picture of me, loaded it onto the hard drive and popped it up on the screen. I did the same with her. It was her idea to put us cheek-to-cheek like Valentine's Day lovers. For hours we stared at that image. We fell in love with that picture. Time passed.

Occasionally we'd talk about Dangus's ingenious electromagnetic field and whether he, himself, actually lifted the remote and dropped the potatoes in the microwave, but we were too busy mooning over the picture to contemplate what this meant in the overall scheme of life. We theorized that if Carmen and Geoffrey got zapped with enough juice, it could have brought on the frontal lobe seizures, but the wild idea seemed more like sweet small talk than a plausible scenario. Sci Fi fantasy ruled over truth tonight and God it was wonderful.

"Why are you here anyway?"

"Where else would I be?" she answered my question with a question. "If I'm going to understand anything about what I'm looking for, it starts right here."

I looked her over: she was talking electromagnetic fields and reverse charges, and then onto concepts I really couldn't follow at all. I was too busy checking out her hardware, her equipment, her back — the pieces of her looked like they had been assembled many years ago, manufactured by a crack team... she was a veritable prototype.

"Are you the Bionic Woman?"

She smiled. Reader would you believe I was in love with Angelica? Remember we were wrapped in the same mystery. I confess, it seems a bit fast. But you should believe me. Did you know I told her about the death of Satan and asked her to come with me to visit Little Augie? She looked at me as if I were a little loopy. To her, all these upscale remotes, underground figures, overcooked potatoes, and undercooked scientists made sense, but a basic concept like Satan seemed foreign indeed. I kept pressing her to come with me to see Little Augie. I knew I was betraying the trust Little Augie had in me, but I somehow couldn't care about her faith in me right now.

"I'll show you a real relic."

"Now?" she asked, unable to pull herself away from the screen.

"Yes. Remember the Intrafacer just doesn't come with you, but is you."

"O.K. then."

Little Augie wasn't home and she couldn't be working, since it was Tuesday night. Where could she at 2:00 a.m.? Emboldened by the presence of another pattern maker, one stronger and wiser and more acquisitive than I could ever manage, I decided to break in, attempting to find clues about the Dark Angel. I sized up the door.

"Tell you what," I propositioned Angelica. "You give me the Intrafacer back if I can get into Little Augie's apartment without damaging anything."

She studied me, figuring I was one of those useless gadgets incapable of accomplishing anything practical. "O.K., but if you don't, I get to keep it for a week."

"Deal." I took out my MasterCard and started working at the soft, primitive latch. Within seconds I had the hard plastic snapping back the soft metal and I was in. Before I stepped through the doorway, I got my fix, Intrafacer back on. Angelica seemed diminished, less formidable. Without that spine of hers, she'd be nothing. Now, I was less in love. Little Augie's apartment looked like a newly cleaned hotel room; even Angelica was impressed.

"When was the last time she had been here?"

"Good question. From the looks of things," I said opening drawers, many of them empty, "days and days."

"Maybe she went on a trip."

"Maybe, but that's not like her. She lives for her job at the morgue."

"You think she's doing something with the corpse?" She asked me this question as if she started to believe in Satan's body. Perhaps the Intrafacer had an effect; with it off, I grew convinced that last week I had witnessed Satan's corpse; but with it on...

We both searched the room for relics. Out of the corner of my monitor, I thought I saw Angelica snatch something up without telling me. That was O.K. for in Little Augie's night table drawer I found this black speckled composition notebook, some pages ripped out but I noticed the word Satan occasionally scrawled within the entries. Angelica was too busy swiping some other bizarre artifact — I think it was a rusty and bulky old electric can opener — to notice my shoving the book beneath my shirt and into my underwear.

"Did you find anything?"

"No," she said. "How about you?"

"No, sorry to waste your time."

"Don't be silly. Anytime with Technoman is special time."

"Yeah, I know what you mean. I feel I have something that I haven't before."

"Louie, I feel this is the beginning of a beautiful friendship."

Hard to explain how oddly close I felt to Angelica at that moment, even as I wanted get the hell away from her and to open that journal.

Channel 24:
Satan at Branacci

From the forgotten logs of Little Augie:
I chased him, down the nights and down the days; I chased him, down the arches of the years; I chased him, down the labyrinthine ways of my own mind. And I have learned how to steal the way he has stolen and I have picked up the pins and needles that he has left in the basilicas. I even keep this little black book like he has kept his book, and I have signed it every day. I chased him under running laughter and one cold January day I found him by the fish tanks at the Cathedral of St. John the Divine. Who else would steal an African tree frog from a church but Satan? I followed him out, back to his home, I even followed him, months later, to Europe where I had figured, examining his condition, that he had flown there to die. And when he made his way to Florence, I was there. I am now convinced that he knew I was always behind him, although he never looked into my eyes. Otherwise, how would I know what he was thinking? How would I know what he had done all these years? He was communicating. I understood, even though he offered me no words. Therefore, I steal everyone else's. Why Florence? Where else? For those who have not been enlightened, allow me to explain...

Satan followed the Lord's shadow here one rainy day early in 1425, followed him into the baptistry and the churches only to see himself on the wall as a grotesque fallen angel, a hideous beast surrounded by motley demons. He even knelt with the medieval parishoners as they lifted their heads toward his image and prayed for salvation from his wrath. As for his very real and pungent presence next to them, no one noticed him as anything more than another sinner: they did not fear Satan, but his image. "Am I merely a tool of God?" he muttered, loud enough so that many in the pew nodded affirmatively.

Satan waited till mass had ended at the Santa Maria del Carmine and the parishoners had gone in peace. At a small chapel, he found a young man drawing a series of Biblical stories.

"Do you have a name?" Satan asked.

"No," replied the youth.

"Would you like one?"

"Yes." That's all Satan needed to know about the youth he now dubbed "Masaccio," so the old teacher bedded down at the Branacci Chapel for the next month, slowly breathing the breath of life into the prodigy's oils. Soon Masaccio could make Adam and Eve at their very moment of expulsion jump off the wall and could bestow upon man dimension only previously reserved for God. Other artists began to gather at the chapel and notice how mankind appeared to be reborn through Masaccio's frescoes. And when the clergy came to see the wonders, Satan joined with them, a soothing spiritual voice who helped convince them that Masaccio depicted man so monumentally solely to reflect God's glory. Only he who persuaded our greatest grandparents to eat the fruit could make man swallow such juicy lies, pits and all; of course, any such artistic achievement would marginalize, rather than glorify, God. How appropriate that Masaccio picked man's fall, the fallen angel's greatest moment in a fresco that would sear through Donatello, Ghiberti, Leonardo and Michelangelo right into the machinery of our times.

Satan rejoiced when man no longer turned to the Almighty for enlightenment. Unfortunately, Satan had not figured that with God pushed aside, man would find fewer uses for him too. Now, more than a half a millennium later, Satan had returned nostalgically for the Branacci Chapel's restoration. Was it good fortune or Satan's intervention that preserved the Chapel when a fire ripped through the church? Surely, when he saw the newly cleaned Chapel, Satan understood that men kept better care of the frescoes than they took care of him.

The final indignity was that he, like a mere tourist, was only given fifteen minutes to look at the frescoes, his powers of persuasion being no match for the ticket collector who had known more confidence men than art lovers. Even he had to conclude that his time was running out as he stepped in front of his

Expulsion of Adam and Eve, the weariness of centuries passing him by. "I should have known back then," he muttered, hardly a hiss left in his throat. As he studied Eve's shadowy, moist anguish, he now felt his own expulsion. He might as well have been bearing the burden of their heavy, bare bodies. Glancing downward, away from the fresco to himself, he stewed about how he no longer grew hair on the upper portion of his body; he looked like he had been through chemo.

He did not want to stay any longer than fifteen minutes anyway.

"How could I not have known?" he questioned himself as he shuffled through the cloisters, into the shoddy piazza, eventually trekking to the via di Santo Spirito over the Ponte alla Carraia across to the tourist-laden side of the Arno, up the via de Fossi to the Basilica di Santa Maria Novella. There he could see Masaccio's "Holy Trinity" for as many minutes as he wanted. If Satan regretted any decision in his short life, it would be over letting Masaccio live long enough to finish this fresco. Any other man who openly rebelled the way Masaccio did when he finished the top walls of the Branacci Chapel would have been dead before paint dried. But with Masaccio, Satan was... how should I say... curious about what would come next. Well, the "Holy Trinity" was. what was fucking next, and after that Masaccio would be pushing boulders up the rolling hills of Tartarus.

Not only did Satan let Masaccio get that perspective monstrosity onto the wall, but here he now stood at the absolutely darkest spot of the entire basilica with a handful of 200 lira coins to drop into the illumination machine. He spent 45 minutes and 7000 Lira in front of that painting as if he were some religious zealot who saw the light. How could this happen? The old feeling returned, the one he had never felt before the "Holy Trinity" nor anytime after he banished Masaccio to the Netherworld. It was strangely... a tremendous pity for God. The content did not stir the emotion, Satan had stood in front of powerful crucifixions for many years to come, and God's sublime solemnity only bred contempt. No, it was the painting's obliteration of the sacred space between man and God that evoked the pity. How long could man maintain interest in God after in the hand of one man eight layers of real life emerged from a flat wall? Even Satan was not prepared to accept this. The decline took longer than Satan calculated, but the end had come.

In my hotel room next to his, I listened by the wall, heard him clicking the remote across Italian stations, eventually settling in on a sex farce. I put it on too. That night I heard nothing else from him except during the moment when the priest embraced an inflatable doll. The exclamation was such that I could not tell if it were one of uproarious approval or disgust.

Channel 25:
Economy

Pines Tar: If You Think I'm Paying for This Stuff...

To be Technoman means to spend more money in a month than I have in any year of my life. To be Technoman means to be deeply, irretrievably, inconsolably, ridiculously in debt. Hey, prototypes are expensive, those experiments, those first off the line, all the creativity, all the design, all the refinement ballooning into one big price tag.

To be Technoman is to collect the first of everything before public consumption — I have no time to discover whether something works, is effective, is utilitarian... I don't care.

Desimplify, I say. Gather the gadgets while I may, I say. I myself am a prototype, I say, and that makes me damn expensive. Can I worry about paying the bills? No! My life is a bill and I cannot charge it and pay it in the same breath.

Who will pay, you say? Not Technoman, I say. But, don't fret, the bills will be paid. We are not living in the dark ages, we live in the age of desimplification. There are trusts, foundations, endowments, grants, fellowships, annuities, shelters, corporate charities, special interests, unions, political action committees, research and development collectives, etc. that will pay. How could they not, with an ambulatory product who writes his own reports, does his own PR, generates his own interest, and most importantly keeps strict and accurate records of everything he spends. And if I ever die, anyone can just retrieve the impeccable annual report off my Intrafacer hard drive under the file:

Necessary Expenses. I don't fill out forms, since I am a form. For every funding application, I write *See Attached Floppy Disk.* I know if my potential benefactors open that disk, they will pay up, for I am merely purchasing what no self-respecting Technoman could do without. Let me just show you my account of last Friday's purchases.

Expense Report

Interior Decorating

Cosmic Windows (keeps the interior spinning and the outside world out)	$42.99
TechoDisks (how could I resist?)	$35.95
Spindex (my own little world that turns)	$33.99
Lumaglass (I can now see myself fractured and reconfigured in the mirror)	$273.47
Cascading Fiber Optic Lights (an electric flower for the green thumb in me)	$249.95
Subtotal:	**$636.35**

Home Entertainment

SuperDeluxe Play Station (take my toilet before you take my video game hardware)	$427.27
Microsoft Flight Simulator (for trips at home)	$21.99
Carmegeddon (the racing game for the chemically imbalanced)	$21.99
Heavy Gear (the new breed of 3-D combat simulators)	$65.95
Dark Reign (the future of war)	$45.00
Jane's Fighter Anthology (the very best of mass destruction)	$65.95
Fallout (a post-nuclear role-playing game)	$75.00
A Supercalibrated Solar Flexor (the machine does the exercising for me) — six easy monthly payments of	$129.95
Sonic Thunder (a radio controlled car with full function transmitter)	$35.00
Subtotal:	**$888.10**

Household Necessities

Full Saturation Cellular Phone (now I can call anyone

at anytime, anywhere)	$119.95
Unlimited Monthly Calling Minutes (and call 24/7/60)	$119.95
Immortal Security System (for Technoman must be secure)	
— beyond the infrared motion and heat sensors and night vision cameras	
— seventy-two easy monthly payments of	$489.93
3-D-DDS Satellite System (Technoman must be informed and aware)	$476.95
Beyond DVD High Tech Disk System (How else can I see the world?)	$399.99
Mowbot (a fully robotic lawnmower, since I can't be outdoors too long)	$999.99
Subtotal:	**$2606.76**
Daily Total:	**$4131.21**

I picked such a day for it is close to typical of my daily expenses, although I usually average over $5,000 most days, not including my monthly expenses for car loans, rent, insurance, etc. (Hey, don't even get me started on clothing and dietary expenses). If the list looks large, imagine what it would be if I didn't receive donations from all your fine institutions, corporations and citizenry out there? I guess I could seek alternatives. I considered not buying the Mowbot for my grass and instead blanketing a plastic lining over the entire lawn putting an end to everything, but I felt not to buy the Mowbot was to betray the wiry, diode driven soul of Technoman. Hey, and all this stuff is just for me. My buddy old man Miller mentioned Christmas is coming. Now I know that is a vague statement; after all, from August on, Christmas is coming. I can't tell you what month it is, haven't looked outside for I don't know how many weeks to give me a clue. Anyway for Technoman, everyday is a pre-Christmas shopping spree, for what I buy becomes an accessory of me, and you can see I grow larger, containing multitudes. By the by, if you'd like to feed those hungry multitudes, I've instituted a 1-800 number to let all of you have the opportunity to be a part of the ever expanding me too — 1-800-101-0101. And for a limited time, stock options are available.

I just want to remind you that I have only purchased that which is necessary to my life. Who else could design my bed but NASA? I have opened myself and my wallet to the wide, endlessly productive and inventive world.

My attention span demands complications, pile up the phenomenon over my head, make it come out my ears, and let me pay through the nose. I will not live without. I ask you: Would you let me live without? Might as well make me a slave. To not pay for my liberation would be un-American. Hey, I'm at this 24/7/60/365. I don't ask you to put yourself in my electromagnetic, moonwalker shoes, but the least you could do is pay for them.

P.S.: I don't want to have to ask you again. If you respond generously, I won't have to use this column to present another pledge drive for quite some time.

Channel 26:
Post-Satanic Combat

I put Little Augie's journal down, picked up Zach, and decided to take him to the library. It was not my nature to check up on facts and seek out truth, but I had a funny feeling today. I had already been on the Internet to find out about this Masaccio character, and Little Augie's story made sense until I came across some information about "The Holy Trinity." According to this web site, Masaccio painted that fresco a year earlier than the Branacci Chapel frescoes. What was I supposed to make of that information and what was I to extrapolate from Little Augie's account now?

I tell you one thing it did: make me break one of my cardinal rules and head off to the library to, heaven forefend, open a book. Alice has always told me that most of what's on the net is inaccurate, unregulated crap, and despite everything between us, I still live under the spell that Alice is right most of the time. So I figured take Zach to the library, show him some of the real funky software on the computers and sneak off for a few minutes to find an art book. What I got instead was a lesson in fatherhood. We made our way to the computer lab to discover crowds only acceptable at a really good restaurant on a Saturday night. I kept trying to sneak Zach in to get his hands on the software, but he was so polite and considerate that he never got in front of the keyboard. Now something about his kindness was sweet, but ridiculously inappropriate for the age in which he lives. Technoman was concerned enough to plan on taking decisive action with him after I resolved my Masaccio mystery.

I dragged him over to book shelves. They were desolate: we were the only ones there, our footsteps echoing through the aisles. When I found the library's one Masaccio book, I learned that the book's author was in agreement with the web page. I did not know in whom I was more disappointed: Little Augie for her story being not fully accurate or myself for not putting my faith in technology with the same zeal my thoughts, time and money have been. However, I couldn't worry about these matters right now because Zach brought forth a more pressing concern. You see, he was actually sitting reading books off the shelf. If he stayed in the stacks much longer, who knows if there would be any way of getting him back.

Before he realized it, titles tumbled out of his hands, I had him out of the canyons, past the soothingly twisting, clicking, whirring computers and out into the Smart Car.

Within minutes we were in the huge parking lot of Laser Survival, high-impact family warfare that as the advertisements say, "Lets you save and destroy the galaxy in a single afternoon." As we headed in the door, I was handed two weapons packs. While we were locking and loading rays, beams, transmitters, wavers and lasers, some dope yelled out:

"Hey, it's Technoman!" Donning the Intrafacer for my column photo did nothing to maintain my low profile. Since I started this journey, I have been continually barraged with stupid comments like "Hey Technoman! Eat any chemicals lately?" or "Hey Technoman, you become addicted to the touch of silicon yet?" or "Hey Technoman, you look like you're wearing a big condom over your body" or "Hey Technoman, play any good sites lately"... hundreds of greetings and not one intelligent comment yet.

"Hey, Techoman, does that Smart Car of yours know how to play chess?" — the streak continues. The masses soon fondle my keyboard and look at my monitor instead of staring at me. They touch my hardware, but touch me not as I pull Zach close and turn away toward the take-off portal for Laser Survival.

Zach and I enter the dark zone of strobe lights and smoke — a disco with semi-automatics. We are partners out to destroy all other partners and to get past the all powerful Translucifer, a post-satanic meanie with good circuitry and a bad attitude. We weren't into the zone two seconds before a laser nails Zach, I think the shot came from one of my neighbors. Zach was down. I tried to get in front of my boy to protect him, but the more I shielded him, the greater the number of beams zipped through. Everything moved so quickly, before I knew it, Zach had already been killed ten times. By all rights we should have been kicked out, since that one scene had exhausted all the terminations we had coming to us.

I fired away, killing my distant and helmeted foes with more alacrity than any simulated, virtual experience I had ever had, shooting with speed, determination and ruthless efficiency. Yet the more I killed the less I seemed able to protect Zach. In fact, whether I killed or not didn't matter: I couldn't protect Zach either way. For some reason everyone wanted to beam Son of Technoman, my boy, for within five minutes he looked like a target sheet at a postmodern firing range.

As I continued to battle, hurtling over fences and under shelters to hide Zach, I decided that my boy's story could be written out in only one of two ways. Either the constant barrage would drive him loony or it would make him tough, skillful and triumphant. Yet the appearance of Translucifer soon made the fact abundantly clear that neither two possibilities would appear today. When Translucifer grinded, clicked, beeped and buzzed to spread his doom, he turned his ultra-zoom, night vision sights of course on my boy (What does Zach have a magnet in his navel? Radioactivity in his shorts?).

Translucifer singed every orifice of Zach's body. If Satan apes God, then Translucifer apes Satan. He was annihilating my boy and simultaneously mock-annihilating him, he with his #222 stamped everywhere across his soulless steel thorax, his grand social security number, or UPC code, or ISDN number, as much his identity as his cheesy compound name. He who hurled my son headlong with his jets instead of wings, his antennas instead of horns, wheels instead of cloven hoofs, smelling like motor oil instead of shit, gives my boy a lube job.

Before long, I had to confess as far as this game was concerned, my son became a ghost and with every shot he grew more comfortable with that role. He did not grow crazy, he did not grow up, he grew accustomed to the idea of dying. Across a black field the beams kept coming in pulses, a series of X-rays, of chemotherapies, of electric shocks. Except for the motor oil, the odor was sterile and the sounds were canned. The only true echo came from the thump of Zach's scrambled carcass hitting the floor. Even after a few minutes of all the unloadings, movings and shootings, it became apparent that Zach's neighbors and Translucifer had done their worst. Their worst was not good enough.

Zach would make them kill better.

Even as I so intensely grew Han Solo and paternal, a space hero for suburban shopping malls, even as I transformed myself into a full-lead jacket to block the lethal microwaves from the tender flesh of my boy, Zach manufactured new ways to be hit. No misfire would go unabsorbed; he would live no moment without dying, and did he ever die! I call them his falls, but they are no falls; they are the descents of rocket. He's the fastest victim in the west.

"Wow, cool!" I heard exclaimed more than once by a killer who saw his pray extinguish before he had the chance to put his weapon back into his holster. I even spotted Translucifer shake his mainframe minimally in mock honor. Soon the manager had to drag Zach's continually redegenerating corpse on out of the place because no respectable star fighter seemed capable of focusing on anything else but on annihilating my boy. I felt an awkward sense of pride in Zach, since he did achieve attention, and isn't that after all what we are after?

In the Smart Car, he looked so weak and vital that I pretended to shoot him with my mouse clicker, just to watch him turn strong and lifeless. Our new game reminded me of other errands. On the way back to his mother's (and my old) house, I tried to call Little Augie, but again there was no answer. I left a message, even though I figured the next one to listen to the machine would be me.

Zach headed up the sidewalk with a little spring in step, the kind of lift one gains when he realizes he is truly gifted at something.

"What did you do with him?" asked Alice.

"I gave him the chance to die for a change. See you next week Zach."

Channel 27:
The 7 Synthetic Voyages of Technoman, Voyage I

Because she truly cares about me, Angelica procured seven pills of the experimental synthetic drug Somnoid, with preintroductory hype about it "giving you the dream of your dreams." In the spirit of my Technoman manifesto, I graciously accepted her gift, and took them in the witching hours of the night. Here's the first of the seven part series:

Voyage I

I didn't float toward the clouds: I took the construction elevator. I was up on the beam Jackson during the warm October afternoon walking 945 feet above 34th and 5th, putting together the pieces of the huge erector set known as the Empire State Building. The Mohawk chief told me, "Never look down," a cliché turned meaningful as I watched him step calmly across the open, skinny links of steel like he were strolling along the sidewalk below.

Might as well have run a line of hot coals along the beams just to make the path even more ritualistically absurd. On the open end of the biggest building ever made, I am more fragile than majestic, yet more of a man than I will be when I awaken.

For the Mohawks, this vertical journey has become the great hunt, their new rites of ascension; they are the great skywalkers, always starting the next floor before I can traverse the one we had just joined.

I follow them, but I catch my foot on a rivet, losing my balance, looking down at a street closer to my guts than the rest of my body. I hug the beam with such ridiculous fearful intensity that I could not fall even if it were my greatest desire. Four stout Mohawks were required to pry my grip and to carry my paralyzed carcass onto the elevator.

I took a leak down on the ground floor, wondering why I could never get my wavering frame to indulge in the fantasy of pissing off the Empire State Building's peaks... When the Mohawk chief released his stream from the rafters, I saw the fountain of a god.

Suffering just enough shame to return to the top floor, I look in front of me and walk, the autumn wind kicking up just a bit. Rising up from the street, a babble of voices murmur and reverberate, a polyglot of languages years before it should speak. Plans are being made by the architect, by the site managers, by the chief engineers, for wiring and plumbing and carpentry and tiling. Nobody seems to understand a word the others are saying, but we keep building, and it is beautiful and stronger than the whole lot of us put together.

Further up town, the Chrysler building flashes a chrome, art-deco smile as we surge higher, erecting beam after beam. Dizzy and lightheaded, I suspect we won't stop until we reach the harvest moon now rising in the twilight sky. But I am wrong. When the architects, the site managers, the chief engineers see that the building will inevitably rise above the Chrysler Building, they hand me my lunchbucket, stuffing in my last four day's pay, and send me home.

On that final afternoon, seeds and twigs and grains pelted me as I shielded my eyes. I asked the Mohawk chief if this were manna from heaven, realizing the stupid Christianity of the question a few words too late. He said it was barley from the midwest, blowing across America, some gusting direct from the fields, others flying off the trucks, and the rest lifting out of the canal barges. Then I remember what he told me about the snow, that out here most of the flakes float up instead of down, and curse that I am being sent away months before that would happen. So at home, sleeping inside of my dream, I tried to conjure up a memory of the rising snow. It never came, for how could it? Snow would only rise many years later as I clicked the remote and slowly rewound an image on my VCR.

We finished the grand inhuman building and waited for it to come to life, waited and wondered, would they fill it up, would they ascend its heights, its interiors as we had its exteriors?

Yes we waited... we waited for King Kong to clamber up in a movie with damsel in hand, hang from its impossible antenna, and make it all real.

Channel 28:
Call Waiting

Pines Tar: Who's Behind the Cell Phone Mystery.

Although they are not announcing the news publicly, county police now believe they know who caused the great cell phone blackout last month. "Let's just say, this terrorist act of equipment damage did after all occur during a full moon," said one senior police department official, who spoke to Technoman under the condition of anonymity.

Originally, police officers did not list Paddy Dangus as one of their official suspects. Why, considering the nature of the crime, especially the deftly performed tinkering of the central site transmitter, they didn't immediately point the finger at Dangus is anybody's guess. The senior official shed a little light on the matter however. "To blame Dangus is to blame someone whose whereabouts we don't know, nor do we seem likely to ascertain. To blame a crime on someone who cannot be apprehended is a ludicrous notion. Why not just blame it on God or the Devil then?"

Perhaps the oddest aspect of the case derives from the investigators themselves who when they raise the name Dangus raise the spectre of bafflement and awe. Yet the officers, after investigating every non-Dangus lead, had to return to the obvious.

"No ordinary vandal could take communication on Long Island and bring it to its knees for almost a full day," the senior official added. "Our phone technicians say it requires tremendous skill to cross signals the way they were executed here."

An estimated 322,000 consumers, including yours truly, were affected by the large-scale, virtually complete cellular blackout. The problem started two weeks ago Friday at apparently 3:30 a.m. when cell phone calls were rerouted from their number destination to sites with coded messages. Shirley Banks of Smithtown reports a call to her insurance agent resulted in the following message: "I'm sorry. You are going to have to find another means of communication because this one is completely inappropriate."

Numerous cell phone users interviewed said they received identical or similar messages, most fast to mention that the tone of the respondent [police theorize these were taped replies] was hardly serious; many even described it as gleeful.

Others received different messages. Jessica Nussbaum in a call to her stock broker was offered only a question. "Don't you think true, sincere inconvenience is so much better than artificial conveniences?"

Nicko Inglesos, in a call to his therapist, claims he received an admonishment: "Stop reaching out and touching people. Hey, hands off... No·lo tangere...' hang up." We have yet to find another caller to corroborate such a message was put out that day. However, for many, the messages were the least of the problem.

"The bottom line is that many people were left alone and isolated by this terrible terrorist act," said Ms. Banks. "It will be a long time before people recover from this type of betrayal. Think about what it is like to take your phone out of your purse, turn it on, call a number, and not know who you will get on the other end of the line."

Fortunately, full service was restored by the next day and happily no further cell phone problems have occurred since. Yet the Long Island populace is not about to let go of this incident. Many are keeping a much closer eye on the lunar cycles than they ever have in their lives. Dave Miller, who is writing an unauthorized biography on Paddy Dangus, said that act had the exact impact the underground figure desires.

"With Dangus, it's all about disruption — disruption of technological rhythms, of suburban lifestyle, of distant communication, of deadening comforts. He wants to sensitize us and perhaps the only way to break through our barriers is to loose entropy upon the world. That sounds dramatic, but for Dangus that means to switch a few wires, break a few frequencies, shift a few signal trays and directionals. He reminds us the more complex our machines and systems are and the more we are comfortable with and dependent upon them, the easier it is to create chaos and confusion."

Miller went on to indicate that the man who has taken down complicated systems is hardly complicated. "His mystique results from the inability to find him, but believe me if we find him, I couldn't imagine most people being able to tell the difference between him and a skilled buildings and grounds worker."

One officer who has been looking for the hidden Dangus for more than four months seems confident he will ultimately get his man. "Dangus is careful and leaves little evidence, but he is just too active to remain loose for much longer," said Richard Mason, who spoke with the determination of a Captain Ahab after his White Whale. When I asked him what clues and leads he had on Dangus's whereabouts, Detective Mason laughed maniacally, one of those Hollywood sociopath laughs, and then acted like his cell phone wasn't working, making fake static sounds and all. "I'll have to call you back when I get better reception." I asked whether he thought his reception would improve before or after the next full moon. "I'd say right after — ," and then hung up. Repeated return calls to the detective resulted in the following message: "Stop reaching out and touching people. Hey, hands off... No lo tangere... hang up." For the record, the message was in Mason's voice.

Nobody seems to be able to send clear signals anymore.

THIS COLUMN HAS BEEN SPONSORED BY THE GOOD AMERICANS AT NATIONWIDE BEEPER. WHEN EVERYTHING ELSE TURNS STATIC IN THIS CRAZY

WORLD OF OURS, THE SIGNALS ON OUR BEEPERS
REMAIN CLEAR. NATIONWIDE BEEPER, SENDING
MESSAGES THROUGH AMBER WAVES OF GRAIN &
ACROSS PURPLE MOUNTAINS MAJESTY.

Channel 29:
Blowing a Fuse

I heard the word idiopathic enough at the hospital to run the term through my dictionary: it means the doctors don't know what caused the seizures — not the one at Prometheus Laboratories, not the ones at the hospital with all the finger drumming, lip smacking, arm tingling, bug-eyed hand-wringing, tongue-licking classic reactions that of course I was absent for. I am forever showing up after the action... in the mop up phase, that point where the police officer says, "Nothing to see here, move along."

Both Geoffrey and Carmen have improved with imperfect majesty, lost in expression, but restored in memory. Sphere remembered enough to scowl at me, with boss's look to an underling who hadn't been earning his salary.

"Where the hell have you been?"

I had been too many places to explain.

"Jesus, we've got so much work to do. I didn't even find out about the remote from you. The police had to tell me. You wearing clean socks?"

"Yes."

"Good. I'm going to need help remembering."

"I don't really know anything," I reminded him.

"Hey, I *can* recall that much. What I mean is I need for you to get back to the office and start piecing together all over again, and you can help me get the hell out of this hospital."

"But your seizures are happening more frequently."

"Ah, they gave me Tegretol; I should be all clear in a matter of days."

"But you're not well."

"Hey, my remote's in worse shape than I am. The world can live fine with a damaged me, but to deal with this damaged piece of equipment would leave a hole as large in the American psyche as the one in my punctured frontal lobe."

"I don't think it's safe."

"I'll tell you what's not safe. The fuse room... No, that's not safe at all. I start tingling and twitching just when I think about it. You go into that Fuse Room and check that it's not safe. You must go in there."

"If it is not safe, why would I go in there?"

"Because you must report to me what's in there if we are to start again. And we *will* start again."

"But do you think it's wise to send me in there if it's dangerous? I mean can't we send a probe or some sensors or monitors?"

"Some things, even in our field, require the human touch. I must know what you feel when you go in there."

"In the fuse room? What the hell could I feel?"

"I don't want to prejudice you."

"But you don't mind hurting me."

"Hey aren't you Technoman?"

"Full memory return, huh?"

"Yup. Now isn't it strange that Technoman would be afraid to walk into a room with a little high voltage and a few wires?"

"Alright, O.K., I'll go down there next week."

"No, not next week, by next week the moon will be full." He didn't even have to mention his name. "Go there tonight."

"Alright, tonight."

"O.K."

"O.K., how's Carmen?"

"Alright."

"Does she have all her wits about her?"

"How should I know? I'm not even sure if I have mine. Go check her for yourself."

I headed down the hall to where Carmen sat up in a small corner of her bed. Bits of gadgetry and scraps of paper littered the mattress. She had disassembled her hospital remote, but she did not stop there, also taking apart the nurse's page, the bed controls, the monitor probes and even the temperature gauges.

"What are you doing?" I asked her gently.

"Trying to teach these guys to talk to each other."

"Any luck?"

"Yeah, but they communicate in a language I can't understand."

"I know what you mean." I suddenly grew tender. Her passionate concentration, eyes down puzzling about the circuitry, reminded me of Alice, when she was still in the young, intense blush of love as she pieced together a psychological on one of her troubled young charges while rubbing my back and planning a trip to Europe with me. Little wonder I can still manage to remember Alice as the most exciting woman alive.

Behind and beneath Carmen's thin wires, tiny diodes and barely graspable screws were hospital insurance forms, Christmas cards and a food shopping list, all of which seemed almost complete. She could juggle entropies within the endless demands of suburban domesticities, and she could do so with sufficient scar tissue in her head to easily misdiagnose her malady as a tumor. Carmen returned to the remote with a matter-of-fact dutifulness of a housewife replacing shelving paper. It seemed to hardly enter her thinking that she had her brains scrambled for that little twitching inanimate device.

"How do you jump back into this cold, hard stuff after what happened to you?"

"Where else can I jump?"

I had no answer. I recorded the image of her toiling onto my hard drive, pulled it onto my monitor, and headed out.

"Hey, where are you going?"

"To jump into a fuse room."

Channel 30:
Technoman's Home Page

Technoman's Website is brought to you today by NihlSeek.
Click here to find out more.

Hit Any of These Topics
- Today's Itinerary
- Technoman's 6 Favorite Products of the Month
- How You Can Become a Technoman Supporter
- The Latest Pines Tar Columns
- How You Can Be a Technoman Sponsor
- The Latest Paddy Dangus Activities
- Excerpts from Dave Miller's Upcoming Unauthorized Paddy Dangus Biography
- How You Can Be a Technoman Benefactor
- Technoman's Top 6 Video Games.
- How You Can Own a Piece of Technoman
- Technoman's Favorite Recipes
- Technoman's Gateway to the Future: The Sphere Universal Remote
- How You Can Own Technoman Artifacts
- Technoman's Favorite Stores to Shop in
- The Technoman Product Line
- The favorite state-of-the-art toys of Zach, Technoman's son
- Technoman's 6 Favorite Pharmaceuticals
- A List of Technoman's Corporate Sponsors

• Technoman's 6 Best Techniques to Pick up a Woman on Web Chat Lines

Channel 31:
The Fallen Resurrection
from the Journal of Little Augie

They call it the oncology ward or the extended patient care wing or another name, but this is the ward where people come to die at St. Francis Hospital. It is what the nurses and the doctors dub the terminal ward, where those in the last stages of cancer, corrosive muscle disorders, slowly dying hearts gather and wait months, often years, and sometimes even decades to stop breathing and beating. And it is in this "oncology" ward that Satan came to visit one fine sunny day wearing the austere collar and black robes of a particularly saintly priest and claiming to anyone who asked him that he was Father Jeremiah.

It helps to look like you have been touched by God when you play the part of a priest; therefore, Satan appeared more like the real thing than almost any priest I had encountered in my lifetime. When he stepped into that land of death, heads weakly lifted seeking his blessing. As for me, I had difficulty not staring at the patients attempting vainly to distinguish them from those I open up at the morgue. While Father Jeremiah turned to a craggy middle-aged man with an enormous forehead, I tried to behave as if I were not trailing him. I pretended I knew the stinky old fossil three beds down.

I read off his chart that his name was Hank, I called out to him and responded dreamily like I was a long-lost, if minor, lover. The pretense was an odd one to follow while eavesdropping on Satan. Satan must know he was being followed (hey with years of following others and him being Satan and all), but I eavesdrop anyway.

"My son," began Father Jeremiah — calling him Satan seems disrespectful under the circumstances — with a timbrous voice that sounded if it had been there at the beginning and would be there at the end, "what brought you to this condition?"

As the craggy man drew a breath and prepared to tell a story he had told before, I took the opportunity to ask Hank the same question. Since I was listening to the two stories at the same time without the luxury of a tape recorder or a note pad, I will try to tell you what transpired with as few confusions and revisions as possible.

"I had just finished law school," started Bill, the craggy faced man.

"I had just finished high school," started my old man.

Bill spoke of a high-powered law firm, fast success and disenchantment, an inability to buy into corporate hypocrisy, to live with himself. Hank spoke of chemicals, a magic word for him, a formula for the future, and he wanted to be there at the beginning... and he was, especially for the early, misbegotten toxic products, the ones he demonstrated, fertilizers and cleaning fluids and even radioactive compounds that would penetrate the impenetrable.

Bill left the law firm and joined the utility company, becoming the king of the power lines, giving electricity to the poor of upstate and even on special charity missions out to Appalachia and, once, to Nicaragua. Hank rubbed his hands like· Lady Macbeth, showing me more than liver spots on his paws: looked like he had been washing his hands with battery acid. Bill brought the lights to those in darkness. Hank washed dirt quickly and wondrously from a filthy world. Bill could feel good about himself; after all he put in a day-and-a-half work each shift in good, honest contributive employment. Hank could feel better about himself, making money yeah, but making more crops grow, more clogs pass, more sticky situations unstuck.

Bill lived on the power lines. Hank lived with his chemical canisters. The transmission lines might have been high powered, but to live with them is to nuzzle up to extremely low-frequency radiation, sitting humbly at the end of the electromagnetic spectrum. The chemicals might have fortified a nation, but they dissolved an individual like he was a bad grease stain. Somebody, it could have been Bill, it could have been Hank, spoke of slow insinuations, entering cell-by-cell, creeping across lymph nodes.

"I've done my share," said Bill.

Hank overhead him, responding, "I've done my share."

With their catheters and their IVs, their spit cups and their piss bags, their monitors that had more vital signs than their carcasses — the monitors were plugged in after all — they seemed content and ready for the end.

Father Jeremiah lifted his right hand to Bill's forehead and made the sign of the cross.

"My son, will you let me heal you?"

"Yes."

I wanted to offer the same to my victim, but alas the words would not come.

Father Jeremiah stared into Bill's dying eyes and brought them back to life. Then he put his hands to Bill's cheek and the victim soon looked like he had been injected with a pint of blood. Jeremiah's hands were everywhere on Bill's body, massaging him to life, ending at that big generous, magnificent forehead. Malignant cancerous cells were transforming one-by-one. Bill looked like an electric current was running slowly, sweetly, gently through him. He got out of his bed prematurely, yet Bill could stand. He looked out beyond the door of the terminal ward, as he prepared to wander the rooms of the living.

I was too astounded to attend to Hank, but Father Jeremiah was not. The priest must have been eavesdropping on our conversation too, from his grope across the countless wrinkles of that old man. No more than a minute passed before Hank pulled off his catheter and showed a mighty erection, winking at me, like he was ready to rekindle the old romance one of us had imagined.

Both Bill and Hank seem to struggle with a question of etiquette and decorum: do they thank Father Jeremiah? How do you thank someone for such an act? Or do they just rise?

The silence in all the turbulence of these cell transformations was unbearable, like a wildly, swirling blender without the accompanying whirring sound. I could not help but speak to Bill.

"What are you going to do?"

"I'm going home to watch some TV, maybe cut my grass, wash my car."

I thought he might want to go dancing or take off on a long trip. But before I suggested as much, Hank chimed in: "That's a good idea... Do you have any idea how long I've been dreaming of starting up my lawn mower and getting out in my front yard?"

They were talking about how wonderful it would be to watch reruns of *I Love Lucy* on their own couches when I spotted Father Jeremiah sneaking out, pulling up his long robe high enough not to step on it, and high enough for a careful observer to catch the ochre tufts of his cloven hoofs. I trailed behind him like a newfound disciple.

So the terminal ward had become the court of miracles. Did he save Bill and Hank because he felt some empathy for them, he too dying from simply living in the postmodern world? Or was this not just part of the larger cover up — that when those dying on the front lines are saved, how can we worry about living in this high tension line, chemically-charged, radioactive world?

Why worry, why worry?

No one after all loves a cover-up, a scam, a myth, a legend more than Satan. I burned to ask Satan, but you know, whatever answer he'd give, it would be a lie inside of a lie inside of a lie, and whether that would then ultimately be the truth or just another lie I could not figure out.

Channel 32:
The Fuse Room

So I didn't go right to the fuse room, like I said I would. I needed to do some light reading from Little Augie's journal to calm my nerves a bit. And you know what else: I sent an e-mail to Angelica and asked her to come with me.

We made our way to the fuse room quickly, but that was the smoothest part of our journey, for from the moment we stepped in, the room contained more energy than either of us knew how to handle. The dimly lit room — I think sparks from an army of flying electrodes kept us from darkness — was all steel clamps and copper wiring resting in front of the buzzes, hums and rumbles of the juice, erecting magnetic walls inside of walls, even as those walls turned and flipped on end. To make matters more disorienting, all of Angelica's monitors went on the fritz — I thought they were supposed to measure these currents, not be conquered by them. What's worse is my Intrafacer went down. Angelica and I were shedding equipment like we were in a sinking ship on an electrical sea. We looked at each other, all our equipment off, able to make out the shadows of our figures and we felt great shame. Our eyes desperately turned away from each other, before we'd crumble under the annihilating vulnerability, and we searched for clues. Thankfully, I spotted one in less time than it took to toss off the equipment.

"Looky here," I pointed up near the top of the wall. A wicked apparatus apparently designed to send a sharp, nasty stream of electricity hovered above us, currently inanimate, but continually threatening to come to life.

"Holy shit," said Angelica. "Look at that thing. It could have been stolen off the set of a Frankenstein movie. Well, if that don't look like a Dangus creation enough, just sufficiently artificial in appearance to be real, just cheesy enough to be menacing."

Both of us wanted to make the next cliched statement — that the wild beamer must have fired off that fateful night when Geoffrey and Carmen had their brains microwaved — but we didn't want to turn this mission into a fully realized Scooby-Doo cartoon.

We kept looking up at the menacing needle waiting to get zapped, but it just stared at us stupidly as if it had never been alive. Still the longer I stayed in the fuse room, the dizzier I grew; maybe the loss of the Intrafacer disoriented me, for I turned alternately weary and goofy as my eyes rolled out beyond the monitor. I swam in a pool of rays that splashed and whooshed around me, responsive to my every movement, searching for a pore to enter.

The activity, the vibrations, stimulated me to the point of rarefied, completely uncharacteristic arousal. Here I was in a small room with Angelica, who was carefully cleaning my comatose Intrafacer like it was her father lying in a hospital bed. I imagined my body shutting down and she doing the same for me. I stepped across the electromagnetic field to her, electrons swirling about her body like the wind created for models in top-end commercials. Basking in this glow, she stepped up to me, reaching out her hand, placing her open palm within an inch of my face.

I made the same gesture, almost touching her cheek by mistake. She closed her eyes and sighed. My legs shivered and my loins shuddered. I step toward Angelica as she glides back, retreating in a slow shuffle until she was pinned against the circuit breaker. Spread wide, my arms pressed up against the panels, keeping my legs together as she opened hers — both of us managing to never touch the other. Within the gentle dreamscape of more breathing and eyes closing, electricity now seemed both in our way and a passage to the other, currents attracting and repulsing, like perpetually twisting magnets.

As time passed in this bizarre, frictive, fractious ecstasy, we had no desire either to step forward or back. "We better get out of here," I said, ready to dazzle her with my knowledge. "The extremely low frequency radiation could do us harm."

"Who could say the radiation is low in here?". Angelica mused. "I'd say I'm completely contaminated."

"Mmmm."

We were powerless in this field. Cloudy and sopped, our eyes mingled vapors until all either of us could see was the other, until neither of us could see any more. Blind, I groped my way past many a switch and on out the door. From what I could gather Angelica must have been tossing currents at me like snowballs, the pulses stinging and chilling.

"What do you think?" she asked.

"I think even without that hairy Frankenstein zapper equipment, there's enough in that fuse room to jeopardize any well-laid plans."

"I think I'll go glom that Frankenstein zapper and bring it home."

"No you won't. I've got to show Geoffrey and Carmen."

"Well, then what can I take home? I must have some keepsake, a souvenir, a memento, an artifact, if you will, for the effort."

"How about a remote."

"I have enough of them to turn on every appliance from here to China. No, I need something else."

In a gesture of almost love, I took off my calculator, stereo, cellular, thermometer watch and ceremoniously handed it to her, the measure made all the more noble by the fact that I now had on me hardly a piece left of functioning, sophisticated equipment.

"Let me guess, since you can't give me your hand, you will give me what's in it."

"No, more like, since my hand is worthless, I give you what is in it."

She said nothing, so I added: "It will last longer, it's more reliable, and more accurate. Besides, it's the only thing that remained unaffected by the electromagnetic field."

"Who would want such a thing then?"

As she walked away with the watch cavalierly in hand, she indicated that she was throwing it away, but I saw her irresistibly and slyly pocketing it.

I felt a burden off me getting rid of the thing and then considered which corporate sponsor to hit up in order to procure a new one.

Channel 33:
Lost Remote

Pines Tar: Why This Column is so short

It was gone. Not under the couch or cushions, or in the kitchen, or by the stereo. The remote just vanished. What's worse my Intrafacer had gone down, and wouldn't be fixed until morning. Some sick trick by the gods. I redoubled my efforts for the remote. Not even in the fridge. After I had to endure one TV show for 10 minutes straight, St. Anthony must have taken pity on me for I discovered the instrument on the window sill. When I had captured it, a strange possibility overtook me. What if I refused to use the remote for the night? With a twinge of betrayal to my manifesto, I stored it in the freezer and prosecuted the night's business.

So what did I manage to accomplish in one entire night of refusing to use the remote while watching television: read a novel, sanded down an old lacquer table, ate a half gallon of ice cream, wrote this column; sliced a wart from my thumb, cleaned ears, cut toenails, flushed belly-button, rated the attractiveness of the women on the shows I watched, showered twice, blew-dry my hair for the first time since I was seventeen, and ended up drawing a still-life of the television screen filled with erasure marks and images scattered atop each other like some orgiers who can't seem to get to a prospective partner. With that I turn off the T.V., take my twice-showered body to the office, column and still life in hand, sit in my cubicle, waiting for the quick shifts that make life bearable.

Funding for this column was provided by the fine people at J.C. Brand Foundation, dedicated to making the future the present and the present the past and the past much less the past than the present will be past. The J.C. Brand Foundation, supporters of the advancement of technology across the globe.

Channel 34:
The Sounds and the Fury

For the first time in months, I saw Zach and Alice without the Intrafacer. I brought over a ManuBot, one of those robots that converts with a few choice pulls of torso and limbs from a mechanical man to a truck, to a tank, to a supersonic jet, to a rocket launcher. Zach was happy to get it, much happier than I was when I saw him line it up next to three other Manubots: I took some solace in the fact that mine was the newest, shiniest and most flexible — the others brandished only a wimpy rocket launcher, while this one could start World War III.

Alice had Zach attentive on the couch, reading *Where the Wild Things Are* to her.

"He's finally getting better with his reading," she reported, talking to me for the first time in a long time like we were still married — I think it was the absence of the Intrafacer. "He's been so delayed for so long that I was starting to worry."

"That's great," I said sincerely. She usually drove me crazy because she cared so much about everything, but for the moment I was touched by how much she cared.

Zach read the part where the boy sailed off to the island, and he generated a mechanical roar that sounded so much like a Sport 42 powerboat that Alice and I laughed.

"He does that pretty good, doesn't he?" she said.

"Yeah."

"Zach, do the Ford Windstar," and out of his mouth came the very sound of the ignition cranking and the minivan starting, a noise I had heard every morning for three years of my life, so I could judge its accuracy. Zach even had the toot of the horn down cold. Alice and I chuckled proudly. Encouraged, Zach vibrated out our dehumidifier, warbled out the white noise of our air conditioner, beeped and whirled our microwave, and even reverberated the hum of my laptop.

"That's amazing," I said.

"Isn't it now."

Alice tried to get·back to the story, but I kept asking for more imitations and Zach just got better and more sophisticated with his noises, the report of a 357 magnum, with and without silencer, the launch of the shuttle Discovery 13, the static of an off-line, scrambled cable channel. If Zach were born even 50 years earlier, this gift he had would not manifest itself. But he was born at the right time. In a tour-de-force, he simulated the audio that accompanied the various transformations of the Manubot, even delivering the fusing and welding hisses and crackles required for the transitional phases.

Alice, more patient with Zach than with his father, returned him to the text.

"How can you focus on the story when you hear this miracle, this gift, this genius before your ears?" I questioned her.

"What does it do for him?"

"Are you kidding. He can do sound for every commercial and every movie out there. His voice is as much a gift as Pavarotti's or Sinatra's."

"C'mon, anything he can do can be glommed off a synthesizer or some other machine. The most he can do with all those sounds is appear in a *Police Academy* sequel."

"He is a sonic phenomenon." She just didn't understand.

"What are you talking about? Last check you were a columnist, and before you became Technoman, that would almost make you a writer of sorts. How could you be a writer and do nothing to teach your son how to read?"

The question was too good for a response. I wanted to say what good did writing ever do for me, but I was afraid her reply would even leave me in a greater quandary for a follow-up answer. She did shut me up, which I guess was the purpose.

She drew Zach back into the book, but now neither of them were too quiet, for their reading had become cinematic and multisensory. Literature did not come to life here; instead it came to virtual life. Alice with her structure and Zach with his multimedia contributions made *Where the Wild Things Are* a Las Vegas extravaganza — replete with flashing lights, sophisticated audio, and the visuals of Alice's and Zach's occasional descent into mime, charades, puppetry and grotesque gesticulation.

"Can I help?" I offered, more left out than usual.

"Daddy, you can be a monster like you used to be."

The like you used to be was a quiet disapproval from Zach of my Intrafacer self. With the Intrafacer I was liberated; I no longer needed to play the monster, no longer trapped in my identity, but without the Intrafacer I guess I could play the monster one more time.

I spoke not a word as the monster, just growling and glowering, until I started staring deeply at Alice, devouring her with my eyes. Moving fiercer and closer, the intensity absurdly tight, I wish I could record the moments and play it back onto my monitor. I had an erection that almost popped its way through the book, an accumulation of a decade and a half of love and misery welling up inside — a longing for forgiveness and reconciliation.

Naked and stark, I touched Alice's face with fingers coarse, callused, and a little desensitized from excessive keyboard work. Behind her sweaty, dark hair and the glassy moisture in her amber eyes rose a pity that passed by my mistakes, my childishness, and my no longer appealing inability to adapt.

"Don't worry," Alice said gently, "I still love you."

With that, I knew she was signaling me to leave. If I stayed any longer, I would have put Zach to bed and made love to Alice on the kitchen table. Neither of us could bear another of those nights.

So instead of the monster, I switched roles, becoming the boy who sailed off and awoke from his dream.

Channel 35:
The 7 Synthetic Voyages of Technoman,
Voyage II — Eating Crow

Zach carries bulky, ratty cushions out on Route 22 and stumbles to the shoulder where he finds the white truck of Paddy Dangus. It is empty, so he puts the cushions atop the driver's seat, climbs up, starts the ignition. A horribly coughing awakening spits out of the ancient engine, and he takes to the upstate roads, driving out across the depression era '30s. Finding a box of old prunes on the front seat, he begins eating one, probing about with his teeth for a pit, but the prune has been pitted. Nevertheless, he pretends to be choking on the absent seed, shuddering and shaking behind the wheel, the truck's movements following his herky-jerky gyrations.

Gradually looking up, he spots in front of him Angelica, thumb out, calmly hitchhiking. He pulls up too quickly and she has to walk backward seventy years to get to the truck. Hopping out, Zach yanks the latch of the flatbed, opens up a big battered trunk that could carry the possessions of an entire Tuckahoe family, and gestures sweetly to her. Angelica climbs into the trunk and Zach continues up the road a spell.

On the radio is Robert Johnson's "Crossroad Blues" as Zach keeps time and eats prunes. The front seat smells like stale camphor oil and he looks in the glove compartment for cigarettes, but all he finds is an old red hunting cap. Laughing, he throws the cap on backwards and looks out the rear view. No one is coming, he thinks, but he can't tell for sure because a shotgun, handsomely mounted to the top of the flatbed, obstructs his view.

He drives a few miles until songs change. It's another Robert Johnson tune, "Me and the Devil Blues", and Zach announces to himself, "It must be two for Tuesday." Eventually, he comes to a corn field infested with thousands of crows. Stopping the truck, he climbs up into the flatbed, pulls down the shotgun, and stands erect, aiming the gun at the crows. All of a sudden he draws his finger away from the trigger, pretends to squeeze it, and sounds off a wonderfully realistic imitation of an exploding cartridge. Never mind that he *pretends* to shoot, about two dozen crows fall to the earth.

Out of the fields rise the gaunt, unshaven men. They move to the crows and gather them. Scared, Zach drops just like another dead bird. One man, I think it is the balding knife sharpener Platt, takes the shotgun, aims at the gaggle of black fowl feasting on the corn, and fires. Nothing happens. All the peddlers try the gun: Hayes the rag man, Cohen the fish man, Gallagher the coal man, Baker the milk man, Schmidt the egg man, Foster the bread man and even Procino the fruit man. Since the shotgun would not work, they return their attention to the crows, starting a campfire in the fields, plucking the fowl, and cooking them just long enough to smell like chicken.

Not much to a crow though, especially when you haven't eaten well since 1930, so they are not pleased with Zach playing dead. The peddlers start kicking the life back into him. Genuinely surprised that they are happy to see him now looking so healthy, Zach has no other choice but to oblige when Hayes shoves a shotgun back into his hands and says, "Bring us some more manna from the heavens, boy." Zach pretends to trip the trigger, the crows fall.

As the gaunt men gather, Zach runs back to Dangus's truck, opens the beat-up trunk, and asks Angelica, "What should I do? They want me to keep shooting and they don't like when I die either."

"What did you expect when you decided to drive *his* truck?"

"Not this."

Angelica breathed deeply for a moment and then rose from the trunk. "O.K., give me the gun and the keys."

Relieved, Zach chucked both at her, Angelica catching the gun, the keys clanging on the flatbed. The men were stoking the fire and plucking feathers, but Hayes looked out from the fields to the road, scanning for Zach.

"If you don't want to help them, you better run."

"Where?"

"Follow the crows."

"Can't I just die here?"

"No, who would let *you* die with so many others in so much worse shape? The way I see it, you got 70 years of running to do. Then, just maybe, you'll find a nice place to die."

Zach began to protest, then decided to put his energies into following the crows that had taken off, flying south, down the Hudson, crows that no doubt wouldn't stop flying until they reached the salt marshes of Long Island. Tracking the flight patterns, Zach points and aims with his finger, but can't kill a single bird. Even as he continues to chase, he regrets giving up the instrument. I follow Zach into the corn fields, but the stalks grow too high and soon I can't see my boy anymore, only those black crows he chases. I chase them too, all the way south, until those winged devils fly right out of my dream.

Channel 36:
Retrofitting

Geoffrey and Carmen were checked out of the hospital that afternoon and that evening I was meeting them at Prometheus Laboratories.

"Have a flashlight," Geoffrey offered, he and Carmen already brandishing them.

"Why?"

"Because tonight I think we are going to need them."

I had told them everything about the fuse room, except for Angelica's participation in the investigation — I saw nothing to gain from the revelation, except a new suspect for the remote control thefts of the office. They were dying to see the high powered beam for themselves.

"Holy Shit!" said Geoffrey. "And I never noticed this?"

I could have said something, but what was there after all to say? The pulsing currents had no less effect on Geoffrey and Carmen than it had on me, for they looked like astronauts whose capsule had dropped into rough coastal waters after a long mission in space. We might as well have been fondling electric sockets.

"That must be ripped from the wall," Geoffrey pronounced. I started to move toward the beam and Geoffrey grabbed my arm. "No, I must do it."

"But you are just out of the hospital, you look like someone just knocked you over the head with a shovel, you better let me handle this."

"No, I must do this myself if I'm ever going to get back on my feet and put this remote back together."

"Hey, it hasn't even been a month. Don't rush. Have patience."

"Don't rush? Don't rush? Absurd. What do you think we are doing here? No patience is involved in this creation. There is no time. Get out of my way."

His talk just seemed too melodramatic to be denied, so I stepped out of the way and he scaled up to the great beam.

"Shit," he muttered. "Shit."

"What?" I asked.

"Fucking Dangus wrapped every electrical wire in the room around his laser beam. If I rip out his beam, I take down all the electrical in the entire place with me."

"Fucking Dangus," I repeated offering support.

"Then cut the wiring away," said Carmen, speaking for the first time.

"But we would cut off our electricity."

"Do you feel right with that thing in the fuse room? Will we get anywhere with it still around?"

"No," answered Geoffrey.

"Then cut all the wires and get it out of here," she said. "We'll spend all night splicing them back together again and get on with our lives and our remote."

"Alright then. Turn on your flashlights and Carmen shut down every circuit in the room. Don't miss one since I think I've had my fill of juice and currents today." He smiled, either at his little pun or in his wisdom of having Carmen turn off the switches instead of me. At this point I could have really used my Intrafacer, for I came off now as no more than a beam of light.

That light was reserved for Geoffrey as I passed him the wire cutters and Carmen switched us out into a black silent hole, the last of the fans and gears stopped by stale air and metal teeth.

Spending the better part of an hour clipping and disentangling, Geoffrey cursed with admiration the carefully compulsive entwining Dangus achieved. "The guy's a fuckin' technician at heart. All complicated patterns and orderings, like he had followed a set of instructions. No random willy-nilliness here."

As he continued to free the campy, rusty electric beam, I thought of the thousand action toys I had liberated from the shackles of their boxes in packaging made to hold through a plane crash. A half dozen times Geoffrey claimed he had the laser out of this web before he actually did.

"Shit, it is heavy. Carmen, it didn't even have to fire at us to hurt us. If it would have fallen, we would have been both dead."

Under the dual spots of Carmen's and my flashlights, Geoffrey dragged down his huge cumbersome trophy like he were Beowulf displaying Grendel's great head. In his triumphant descent, he staggered a bit but would not let me take his hand. Seemingly unconscious of our presence, Geoffrey strutted and stuttered awkwardly out of the fuse room, the great metal beamer aloft, his own Stanley Cup. We followed out into the darkness of the central remote room. He clicked his flashlight, pointing it towards us, acting as if we were a couple of muggers or something.

"You did it!" I said.

"Yeah!" added Carmen.

We were going to add more, but rays from Geoffrey's flashlight started whizzing across the room the way one only sees during a security crisis. He was spinning around with his laser beamer and his flashlight like he belonged atop an emergency vehicle. The next thing we knew, he dropped to the floor, light and laser pointing to the ceiling, casting shadows about our faces. Running over to him, we flashed our lights on a grey pained face, convulsed with just enough foam frothing from the mouth for even a dope like me to figure out what was happening. Stiff and jerking, Geoffrey held light and laser tight in his outstretched hands. He might as well have been shot through with a thunderbolt.

Carmen had a dazed look that was a little too clinical for my liking, especially since such an image has deja vu or deja vecu written all over it. "An overstimulated insular cortex," she mused.

"Call 911," I said, getting her the fuck away, as I, even as I revealed an ictal fear — boy could I have used the Intrafacer about now — that neither of my remote friends manifested. Out of Geoffrey came a stink that was pretty close to vomit, but I moved past all that in the wild febrility of the moment. Hell with all the vibrating pulses and the surrealistic movements of the flashlight, I could well have been guest DJing at Diodes.

"They'll be right here," said Carmen. "In the end, they'll say etiology unknown."

"Help me get the laser and the flashlight from him."

"Don't touch him," she warned.

"What are you talking about?" I said, realizing Carmen for once knew nothing, and I had to know everything. I grabbed hold of his forearms, but God he was strong. I thought I was wrestling Popeye. I had a better chance ripping the head off a marble statue than I did getting anything away from him. Instead I just tried to hold him down.

"Don't do that," Carmen warned.

I pressed him down more forcefully and noticed his eyes lost out well beyond the fuse room into a space no walls could hold. To make matters worse his tongue gyrated and undulated in paroxysms that were the stuff of bad horror films. This was not right at all. I pulled from my pocket a pencil — hey without the Intrafacer I had to record my information some way, so I went native — and shoved it in his mouth.

"Don't do that," Carmen warned.

He snapped the pencil in two, as he did the next three. I ran out of pencils. His mouth was indestructible. With those electrical explosions firing off in his brain, Geoffrey seemed every bit as powerful as the grotesque instrument he held in his head.

About that time the EMTs arrived. The lead technician was the same guy as last time. I wanted to ask him whether he worked twenty-four hours a day, but that seemed inappropriate given the situation. By the time they arrived, Geoffrey had shot most of his fireworks; they prepped him for the stretcher.

"Did you hold him down?" he asked.

"Yes."

He shook his head and grimaced worse than Geoffrey did. "You shouldn't have."

"What's all these broken pencils here."

"I didn't want him to bite his tongue."

"You shouldn't have." The head EMT looked at me fatherly. "For next time, because I have a strange feeling I'll see you again, don't restrain him, don't put anything in his mouth, keep things out his way so he can't be hurt by them, and if you feel you have to touch him, just loosen his clothing so he can't hurt himself with them."

I wanted to ask him how he could hurt himself with his own clothing, but he was busy with Geoffrey and I was feeling a little less confident than usual.

Soon Geoffrey and the EMTs were gone, the lights flashing in our window like so many had previously that evening. I was left alone with Carmen in darkness. I figured she would have followed Geoffrey to the hospital, but she had other matters on her mind. She took my hand and guided me into the fuse room.

"Point the flashlight at me," she said and I did. "Good, now get closer and follow as I head toward the wiring, take my flashlight too... Now, go get me some electrical tape."

All night I had the flashlights pointed at Carmen as she untangled wire after wire and started the slow, arduous process of splicing them back together. When she had finished, the morning light streamed through the eastern window.

"Hit the circuit breakers," she commanded and I obeyed. The office again was illuminated and the appliances hummed. In the fuse room electricity bounced across the walls, and Carmen smiled dreamily.

"We're back in business," she said.

Channel 37:
Waiting for the Moon

Pines Tar: I See A Full Moon Rising

I turn my camera to the sky and watch it through my monitor. As I pan up and out, I don't see the sky, but hundreds of heads turned to the sky, up and out into the clouds, waiting, waiting...

Waiting for the bright moon to find a way through the vapors, searching a way through the emissions of the chemical stacks, discovering a means past the crazy light pollution of Yuletide shopping.

They wait for the moon and they wait for Paddy Dangus. It is almost full and he is almost here. A few blasphemers have even compared the vigil to those following a certain star some 2000 years ago.

"I've been swamped with calls," said old Dave Miller, who is writing an unauthorized biography of Paddy Dangus. "They want to know what he is going to do next. They might as well ask me for a winning lottery number. All I know is if you expect something big, you probably won't be disappointed, but if that big thing affects you personally, then you will be really disappointed."

Dangus seems to be developing quite a cult following among youths and anti-establishment types. "We don't know what he stands for, which is kind of appealing," said Steve Bradley, president of L.I.E. [Long Island Environmentalism]. "We do know that he doesn't like fertilizers and high tech gadgetry, so he can't be all bad. I must say we are very curious, even excited, about what he will do next."

Representatives of the Walt Whitman Industrial Park [W.I.P.], Long Island's own little Silicon Valley, look forward to Dangus's next move for different reasons. "Dangus has a better chance of getting into Fort Knox than vandalizing our facilities," said W.I.P. spokesman Clyde Cunningham. "Our state-of-the-art security system will pick him off faster than he can take a potato out of his pants."

When I respectfully asked Mr. Cunningham if he thought it wise to taunt Dangus in such a brazen manner, he questioned my patriotism, my manhood, and my identity as Technoman. "People have not taken Dangus seriously enough. That's why he has succeeded. He is just an annoying gnat and it is time to swat him down."

Last night for the first time during the holiday season, the moon broke through every barrier of the polluted, moist suburban evening — it was almost full. And from the e-mails I received, I guess people noticed. Loyal reader Rafter Simpkins said, "It's like I could feel his presence in the air, like I could smell his tuberous odors wafting through the back roads. He's coming alright and I wait for him like I've never waited for anyone in my life."

For Simpkins, for Cunningham, for Bradley, for Miller, for all of you, for even Technoman, the wait is over. I type in the forecast: After a cloudy early evening, tonight the moon will fully open its bleary eye.

THIS COLUMN HAS BEEN BROUGHT TO YOU BY HOME OBSERVATORY TELESCOPE. MOST PRODUCTS PROMISE YOU THE UNIVERSE, WE DELIVER IT. HOME OBSERVATORY TELESCOPE: FOR EVERY STAR IN THE SKY AND FOR EVERY PHASE OF THE MOON.

Channel 38:
Adolf Khan's Leap of Faith

from the lost journal of Little Augie

I had to pay $150 to a scalper outside of Madison Square Garden in order to follow Satan into the Adolf Khan concert. I would have felt more comfortable shelling out the money if I knew who Adolf Khan was. I got to meet his audience, but not the star — no one was over twenty-four years old except the dark angel and myself. At first I thought I didn't fit in — hey even Satan did not look nearly sinister enough to belong — but many of those with the warpaint, the tattoos, and the hair of wildly varying dayglo, oils, lengths, twists and directions accepted me into their culture.

"Nice old lady mask," the very skinny girl with the three nose rings, five lip rings and seven eyebrow rings complimented me. "Cool."

"Thanks," I replied in the most youthful voice I could muster.

"You going moshing?" she asked, eyeing the big open space where people gathered as the lights started dimming.

I spotted Satan heading into the shadows of that pit, so I followed. After a great deal of noise, smoke, multi-colored beams of light, explosions and images of snakes, bats, fires, cauldrons and screaming visages, Adolf Khan slithered onto the stage amid crimson explosions. His long black mane fell just above his skinny buttocks and his imitation cadaverous face (not the type I see at the morgue, but the type you see at the funeral parlor) was distinguished only by a series of horror flick inspired scars and a Hitler mustache.

One look at the pale androgynous performer gave me a hint of why I was here. Satan's expression of restrained repulsion provided more clues. In the mosh pit I drew closer to Satan than I had previously dared. I somehow felt safer bumping up against him than the rest of the crowd. He communicated to me with his eyes. Strangely, I think he was almost as relieved as I was that neither of us stood alone in this place.

The sound from the thick 15-foot-high speakers swelled so fully and tumultuously that I could hardly hear anything at all; except for Satan and me, the audience uniformly caught a rhythm, jerking and gyrating, now forward, then backward. The din grew to bedlam proportions every time Mr. Khan wagged, curled or projected his tongue, which he was inclined to do often.

The ruckus and spectacle making me lightheaded, I turned to Satan, almost giggling. "Is his last name Khan or Con?" I asked him in innocent tones. He smiled a smile only he could give, with all the knowingness of the ages, of confidence games that relied more on faith than on pyrotechnics.

Some low-budget ghoul pretended to play guitar next to Khan, while all the music blasted from a wondrous synthesizer in the back of the stage. As the words echoed to the rafters, *"Come to me Lucifer's children,"* Khan often looked like he was actually singing the words rather than lip-synching them. Satan almost smiled at the display, especially when Khan rubbed goat's blood all over his body, yet I noticed that as the concert dragged on, and boy did it ever drag on, the old man grew increasingly disturbed. I can't say for sure, but I don't think he drew any pleasure from watching Khan bite off the wings of a live dove, leaving the maimed animal on the stage bleeding, dying. And his wrath grew as Khan chanted an invocation to the devil — some gibberish that concluded with "*vene, bene, Mephistopholenny, any menny, Mephistopholenny*," replete with conflagrations and miserably acrid sulfur fumes.

The longer I stared at Satan the more attractive he appeared. It wasn't a change in my attitude, but in   his physical transformation. As he continued to watch this devil-worshipping act, Satan turned virtually incorporeal, almost bodiless and weightless. If he weren't holding my hand, I felt Satan would float to ceiling. No gravity could affect him; he was an astral body; he was an —

Angel.. A brilliant light exuded from him, a number of gawkers taking their eyes off Adolf Khan for a few precious moments must have thought a misguided laser locked in on my companion. This was not merely Satan, but the Lucifer God knew well at the beginning, the most luminous of the angels. If the archangel Michael was he "who is like unto God," then what was Satan? If Adolf Kahn is matter, then Satan is antimatter.   Like the angel he once was, he has metamorphosed, broken down and diffused like a radio signal. Was it seeing Khan as a mockery of him, as a mockery of a mockery of a mockery that turned him ethereal?

Soon, even the hardcore fans were getting distracted by Satan's glow, reaching out to touch and lick its flames; in response, the dark angel extinguished his internal lights, and they all turned back to the stage, to a neglected, yet still tongue-wagging Adolf Khan. Maybe it was the sensory overload they were experiencing or the contact high they absorbed from the hash floating about the room, but once the glow dimmed in Satan the fans failed to notice the power plant level of energy generating out of his body. The kinetic waves and vibrations became so great that I grew numb to the other phenomena around me. Satan muttered incantations invoking himself: "Lalle, Bachera, Magotte, Baphia, Dajam, Vagoth Henche Ammi Nagaz..." A gust of wind swept through the arena and the sparks flew from the synthesizer. Everyone else thought the effects were part of the show, but I knew better.

The intensity of his words growing, Satan simmered and stewed in a fury: "Adomator Raphael Immanuel Christu, Tetragrammaton Agra Jod Loi. Konig! Konig!" The crowd grew frenzied, chanting and yelling, banging into each other with their make-up and their masks and their malevolence. They were one angry mob. Nothing annoys Satan more than a manufactured, nutrasweet-maddened crowd. Adolf Khan bore down on his closing song like he was giving the greatest concert in world history and for the megafinale he clambered up on one of those massive 15-foot speakers and screamed out what, from the response, must have been his biggest hit. He might as well have ripped out his vocal chords and chucked them into the crowd.

Meanwhile, Satan incantated *sotto voce*: "Anion, Lalle, Sabolos, Dado, Pata, Aziel Adonai Sado..." And then in a hissing whisper to the shouting Adolf Kahn: "Vagoth Agra, Jod, Baphra! Komm! Komm!"

Cleanly, quickly, economically, fiber optic size rays of electricity left Satan's fingertips toward the speaker. Khan cried out like he was suddenly being dropped from the top of the world down into a canyon. Crazy went the crowd, even one inured to theatrical highjinks and multimedia hyperspace couldn't have expected such emotional intensity. Khan staggered like he had been buffeted and battered by a tidal wave; then he squinted out past a veil of glare to the audience and prepared for what the moshers called *The Leap of Faith*. Off the speakers Khan would jump to a waiting, semi-adoring audience who would catch him.

Well Khan's was more a Fall of Faith than a leap, as he dropped down, barely clearing the speakers. After they caught him, the moshers found out what Satan and I already knew. That Adolf Khan, the devil's son, was dead before he landed. Everyone around those few moshers thought that the falling, dying Adolf was part of the act, one that even those catching moshers were in on, but most people know a corpse when they feel one. Half the audience got word before the synthesizer stopped playing and cheers exploded.

Even with the body of Adolf Khan sprawled out in the mosh pit and the house lights turned up, the audience members flicked lighters and kept their vigil for an encore. Knowing there would be none — although we grimly noted few would miss Khan's presence in the encore if the synthesizer, smoke and lights were operating efficiently — Satan and I left the Garden.

In the papers and in media the next couple of days, both pundits and public theorized that Khan's death was some form of divine justice. Even my buddy Russell Pines in his column quoted a concert-goer named Rafter Simpkins, suggesting an angel might have been in the audience. "Something crazy was out there man," is what I recall him saying.

The next time I saw Satan was at Kahn's funeral. Giving the eulogy, Mick Jagger pronounced through his crimson protruding lips, "Dying the way he did, Adolf Khan will live on forever." Satan cackled high and guffawed low, the hearty belly laughs of the living. At another funeral, the audience would have thought him rude, but here for the first time in a very long time, he was considered the coolest guy in the room.

Channel 39:
How Many Shopping Days Until Christmas?

Pines Tars: Dangus Brings the Year Without Santa

A couple of e-mails from sources said I might want to go to the mall on the first night of the full moon. So I was eating at Biosphere III, you know that new theme restaurant with all the ecosystems and endangered species, and I'm feeling very uncomfortable: you see here I was with a brand new Intrafacer (off the lot this week) sitting with all my Technoman accouterments, trying to find some processed food on the organic menu, vines hanging down all around, birds chirping everywhere, waterfalls splashing about my table... I was in a suburban jungle.

As I called the safari guide (a.k.a. waiter) over to order off the survival pack section, featuring a savory blend of chemicals and preservatives, the lights went out all over the restaurant. Not only the lights shut down, but the birds choked off, the rivers stopped flowing, not a peep from frog nor cricket was heard in the jungle. The packed house murmured and grumbled.

I felt much more comfortable now, knowing the nothing at Biosphere III was living, at least whatever lived was brought to animation by electricity. (Initially, I thought the crocodile was real, then knew it was not, since it had moved around so much). Even the waves of ocean that serve as the romantic backdrop stopped breaking and the winds of the lobby desert ceased blowing. Though I now wanted to remain in the restaurant for hours, the reporter in me signaled that I should get out into the rest of the mall and look around. If the diners at Biosphere III were turning increasingly hostile, imagine what the ire of holiday shoppers must be should the rest of the mall suffer a similar fate.

One step out into the Roosevelt Field Mall's great boulevard told me this crisis could only be the work of Paddy Dangus, for the entire facility, bigger than most Long Island towns, was subjected to the blackout. For miles in any direction only the battery-operated emergency exit lights could be seen. The moon rises early in the dark sky this time of year, so Dangus was given plenty of time to wreak havoc for the mall's Midnight Madness sales.

· Shoppers were shuffling quickly, close to frantically, from store to store, looking for one with an operating register. No matter how dark the store seemed, desperate shoppers entered asking if they could buy merchandise now. Some even went to the extreme of offering cold cash for their goods, as if they were living in black market Russia or something.

As I made my way into Macy's, I encountered dozens of shoppers patiently queuing up at each register line of the many departments waiting for the electricity to return. Many already dragged five or six shopping bags of goodies in tow, overburdening their arms with more. Everyone seemed afraid to get off the line; nothing could be worse than losing your place in this time of need.

The buying public behaved in a much less civilized manner at Transistor Metropolis, where the Midnight Madness sale on all CDs, TVs, VCRs, cellulars, digitals, and monitors started at 8:00.

CDs, TVs, VCRs, cellulars, digitals, and monitors started at 8:00. The once-in-a-lifetime prices would never be offered again (I guess that's where the once-in-a-lifetime component comes in), and electrical appliance shoppers were laden with these huge, heavily packaged boxes containing very small equipment. Credit cards were out, but no scanners worked, and with each passing moment of darkness it became increasingly apparent — despite claims by sales staff to the contrary — that the once-in-lifetime sale would pass them by.

What is it about electronic appliance stores that bring out the rioter in all of us? I confess even I was tempted to chuck my Intrafacer through the gargantuan glass window and drag out everything I could carry, perhaps even ram my Smart Car through and load up the trunk. Growing violent, the shoppers kicked empty boxes, screamed at each other for being so annoying, and threw an occasional elbow. The manager tried to assuage the customers by releasing to them some special inside information that next week Transistor Metropolis would have a once-in-a-millennium sale, which was even bigger and better than the once-in-a-lifetime sale. Unfortunately, this revelation did little to soothe and cool the crowd's passions. In fact, the unruliness grew, the Nassau police came in, and I decided to head on to other stores.

As I moved about, I was continually hounded by the public, first because they were bored and recognized me (nobody else at the mall seemed to have any claim-to-fame whatsoever), second because they wanted me to purchase discount merchandise for them off my Intrafacer. Even though I could have made tremendous money off the endeavor, I have too much integrity as Technoman to stoop to such activities.

Instead, I typed in their comments, most too horrible and shrill to relay. Let's just say Elizabeth Freeman of Commack spoke for many: "I thought I'd never see such a thing, but it has happened. It's the year without Christmas."

Even without any hard evidence against him, most customers were inclined to blame Paddy Dangus for the blackout. Arnold Pedersen, Nassau County police captain in charge of the investigation, said, "We certainly cannot rule Dangus out, given the apparent pattern of his activity and the nature of the crime."

I stepped outside of the mall and walked toward its electrical plant facilities. I couldn't drive my Smart Car to it because the parking lot was a gridlock nightmare. Fire trucks blocked even my pedestrian access as puffs of smoke coughed out of the facility. Clearly, if the firefighters didn't take care of the problem soon, the mall would have to be evacuated. Retail managers had to get the county supervisor involved already to prevent the fire chiefs from taking such precautions. Meanwhile, huge generators were being transported into the mall to restore power.

All around me out in the vast asphalt lots people gathered, hugging each other and sobbing, as if they had witnessed a plane wreck, the victims their loved ones. Fortunately, the generators soon got the parking lot lights restored, so I could record the spectacle onto my Intrafacer. Would you believe some even sang Christmas carols in their sadness? No? That's why I recorded it, knowing I was capturing an important piece of history.

As a group of melancholy teenage girls serenaded the other mourners with "Silent Night," even Technoman's eyes grew moist. I, like other shoppers, wandered toward my car so empty of hand and heart, cursed the moon, and waited in my car either for the traffic to clear up or for the lights to return at the mall.

Neither happened, so I spent the rest of the evening replaying on my Intrafacer the night of the mourners and singers, the night of the shopper's vigil, the darkest night of Christmas.

THIS COLUMN HAS BEEN BROUGHT TO YOU BY THE FINE PEOPLE AT ENDLESSCHARGE BATTERIES, THE POWER THAT'S THERE WHEN YOU NEED IT, THE POWER NOBODY CAN EVER TAKE AWAY FROM YOU.

Channel 40:
False Advertising

All my best friends have had plastic surgery. The last time I have been out in the fresh air was in the previous millennium, and I don't put anything in my mouth unless its been wrapped in plastic and UPC-stickered first. I am Techoman and I come to you through a fiber optic line and fly across your terminals screens, your television sets, your computer-generated comic books. I am here to once and for all raise the base of this country, its mud dwellers, its Appalachian poor, its migrant workers, its sad sacks on the old warped docks, and its blemished diseased faces of the past.

I am not who you think I am. I am not some Prozac pushing superhero, some killer, some conqueror, some robot who can convert himself into a truck or a battleship or a jet fighter; no, I am not some Fascist zealot of the New Age. I am Technoman. That means I am the first man who fully and truly embraces the technological world. You see, the techno world is not some means to the end, something to exploit to make a bundle of money and to indulge in lives of sweet convenience and diversion. It is man's vision uncontaminated by nature. And as its purest vessel, I spend my days on the sidewalks and the road shoulders, never touching the dirt or, heaven forbid, the grass.

So my first question at the nightclub is? "Have your breasts been enhanced?"

The rare one who thinks my remark flattering will reply, "No, they are not."

"Too bad," I tell her, scanning my eyes across the horizon forever searching for the woman whom I can comfortably rub up against.

Last night, I sought out a woman who felt perfectly comfortable with the unnaturalness of her entire self, a woman who could take me by the hand and show me how to embrace heightened flesh, a woman whose love would be as indestructible and resilient as the implants and the enhancements that elevated her very being.

So I returned to Diodes in search of that woman, in search of a meaningful relationship in a place where everyone pretends to be shallow. Four processed martinis later— yes Virginia, there is imitation alcohol out there, not twelve-year-old scotch, but gin that would last into another geological age — she came into the bar with a set of zeppelins that defied gravity. She was the one. We spoke of romance and silicon. She called herself Dolly — Christ even her name was perfectly artificial — and seemed to pick me before I picked her.

"Come take a walk with me, Techno... man." Our conversations were embarrassingly bad, which made them all the more of a sparkling fantasy. What a turn-on! I could marry this woman. Better yet she took me to what seemed like an all-formica hotel, bouncing me about the room. I could have been her big old inflatable toy. The energy that ricocheted across the vinyl space, boy, Jesus, I felt like an atom split in two. But I talk too much. I don't want to talk about it. We made love for what I thought was hours, but I now believe it wasn't even minutes, only seconds. In the end, she smothered me in those huge, bouncy breasts of hers, and I dropped down, spasmodically, legs giving way to relief and satisfaction, eyes drooping, arms flopped out across the bed. Now, finally could I lay me down to sleep. Straddling me, she lifted a limp limb to her breasts. "You thought these were silicon. Think again." They were warm and blood surged through them; I had been too excited to notice their unsurgical sag and the absence of inhuman roundness. How in God's name could Dolly be real? What was the world coming to? Who could you trust anymore?

"Oh Fuck." It would be another sleepless night.

Channel 41:
Curing the Sick Patient

Until you have looked at an abandoned Intrafacer, one that you have known intimately for months, you cannot understand the guilt I feel. Yes, this Intrafacer hasn't been working since the first time I visited the fuse room. Yes, the Intrafacer 3000 is faster with more memory, more applications and more possibilities than the older model, but you try spending a few minutes staring at the old boy's dim pulsing lights, every transistor in its body weeping, and you tell me you could walk away.

The Intrafacer wasn't fried; it was salvageable, but I guess I had been willing to mask a coldheartedness behind the manifestoes of Technoman: I was ready to dispose of it quickly and ruthlessly. In this life, I found myself continually confronted with two choices: either live with the equipment for years and deal with the constant misery of endless maintenance and repair, or

"Poor baby, you'll be O.K.," she caressed my hand, running her soft skinny fingers through mine. "Just get some rest."

For the first since I became Technoman, I really did rest, completely shutting down all my functions, sprawled out on the bed like I never had to worry about doing another thing again.

On the next day, I didn't wake until 7:20 p.m. I thought it was morning, until I turned on the Intrafacer and it started synthesizing a complete report of the evening news and the day's events. I was still groggy; in contrast, my Intrafacer seemed completely recovered, its lighting as sharp as the day I got it, the functions and applications sliding effortlessly from one environment to another. Life had begun again. I felt celebratory, so I wanted to get outside with the Intrafacer and to thank my family for all they have done. Figured I take everybody out for ice cream or something.

When I came downstairs, all wired up again, I found Alice stretched out on the couch and Zach curled up on the loveseat. As I touched their heads, I knew they caught my fever. So I grabbed the pharmaceuticals on my end table and started administering them. I tell you if I was half as sick as them, then I was in really bad shape yesterday, because the two of them should have been hospitalized. Yet to hospitalize them seemed like a betrayal of what had happened during the past 24 hours. I rode the fevers out, pouring and wiping and caressing the night away. The four of us had been in the house for two days, trapped by illness, quarantined by our commitments.

By 6:00 in the morning, the fevers had been broken, Zach's by 4:00.

"Thank God," I said, for I had to be in Manhattan by 7:30 that morning to meet with corporate executives before I received a substantial donation to the Technoman Benefactor Fund. After washing myself and my Intrafacer, I kissed Alice and Zach goodbye, promising to return later that morning. Both looked at me skeptically, as if the temporary illness infused and awakened within me a few moments of latent humanity that would be snuffed out the minute I walked out the door.

In a rare act of recognition and lucidity, I knew what I must do. Carefully and ceremoniously, I detached the Intrafacer from my body, and left it resting on the floor between the two of them. In my absence, the Intrafacer would be my surrogate. The least I could do was walk out the door naked... They were my family, after all.

Channel 42:
The Book of Joe

from Little Augie's Journal

Today, it finally happened: Satan called me over as I was scrawling down notes in front of Joe Crayola's house.

"Are you a Dante or a Milton?" he inquired.

"Huh?"

"Are you portraying me as cold, dumb and trapped or fiery, cunning and fluid?"

"Neither. I am a woman of science."

"Oh, so that means I'm guaranteed you'll fudge the results. Well come on in anyway. I need you to play God for me. Since you've been acting as my chronicler, I figure you've had good practice."

He spoke commonly, but just condescending enough to remind me of the chasm he had to cross to communicate with me.

"What are we doing here?"

"Conducting a little experiment with Joey Crayola. You, being a woman of science and all, should appreciate it."

"What's your attraction to him?"

"Look in the window. He's got a beautiful high tech Smart House. Everything is computerized, climate controlled, secured, insulated. He made his fortune peddling microchips and now he sits there all day, playing with his TV, his stereo, his computer, his monitoring systems, his video cameras, and his audio-digital communication systems."

"So what do you plan to do to him?"

"Make all of his high tech equipment slowly and methodically become inoperative."

"And what will that do?"

"Well, after a few days, I'd say it would turn him into a savage, a complete ape. He will revert to his primitive instincts."

"That's the stupidest thing I've heard in a long time."

"Hast not thou made an electronic hedge about him and about his house and about all that he hath on every side?"

"You quote scripture to mock scripture."

"No, I quote scripture to quote scripture. Thou hast blessed the instruments in his hands, and his substance beams in and out across the land."

"That substance is too much a part of his very essence to lose."

"Well, let's see, shall we?"

First went the portable phone/answering machine which had the courtesy to tell Joey, "The phone does not work and you cannot receive messages. Call the 1-800-237-3232 for assistance."

"How can I call if I can't use the phone?"

Joey pushed the "Help" button three more times and received the same message until the notification died too. As he attended to the phone, his computer beeped. A coffin rose from the bottom of the screen, with little disk doctors and security icons serving as pall bearers. "Your computer has lost its drive, try www.liferaft.com for assistance."

"How can I log on if my computer doesn't work?"

I could go through every piece of equipment, every appliance, every electronic, but it is too long and too terribly graphic to bother relating. Just know that within a few hours, Joey was left without anything working in his existence… left in abject, unrelenting darkness.

In the ensuing moments following the all-encompassing loss, Joey did not cry, he did not sob, he did not shout. He moved from machine to machine touching their buttons, tapping, massaging, pounding, caressing those buttons like he was trying to revive loved ones. Hours passed and Joey continued to push those lifeless buttons. As the moon climbed into the sky, three of Joey's friends came visiting because they wondered what was wrong since their complex and intimate communications network had been cut, and even attempts to contact him on the phone were fruitless. The first words out of their mouths were that they feared him dead.

Joey said nothing. He just clicked and punched the buttons showing them how the lights, the waves, the signals had left his world. The three friends prepared to lament and to contemplate his loss. At least they had intended to discuss everything, but without a computer, TV, phone, fax, or beeper, they had nothing to interact with, so they had no means of discourse. Each silently drank one of Joey's beers, bad and warm — the fridge had gone out too — and then left.

Satan smiled a smile only Satan can smile as Joey left the house, turning the ignition on his luxury car that would not start, and then closed the door and took to walking.

"Look, he's going native."

We followed, very carefully, for Joey grew increasingly paranoid, oddly thinking someone was out to get him. We were not hurting him, after all, just his machines. He arrived at Diode City, a computer and electronics megastore and started gathering replacements for everything malfunctioning in the house. I guess he figured he would just dispose of the failed equipment, but when he tried to pay with his debit card, Joey soon discovered a return to his life would not be so easy, for that card and every other in his wallet had been demagnetized. He could not pay for the new equipment.

He walked back home angered and frustrated, picked up the phone and dialed, "Mom! Mom!" He was calling out, but he had no signal. "Damn!" he smashed down the phone. And then, he smashed it again.

"Just like an ape," said Satan triumphantly.

And he smashed it again, breaking its guts open, springs, buttons and wires exposed. As he charged over to his computer, ready to attack it with his phone like a caveman would turn toward a lamb with his club, he suddenly stopped and stared at the innards of his phone receiver, then poking his finger around in them like he had with the button. Soon, he takes out a screwdriver and pliers and fiddles around with the wiring, realigning it in endless configurations.

Satan anticipated his every effort to revive the phone, smiling as Joey failed again and again. He waited for Joey to curse the phone.

"He will curse it and every piece of equipment in the entire house before he is done, and he will smash them to bits."

That night Joey fell asleep with the phone in hand. He worked on it for much of the next morning and early afternoon, failing repeatedly, endlessly, interminably, until he finally decided to move onto the fax machine. By the following day, Joey was failing to fix the computer. Weeks passed, and Joey seemed inexhaustible in the things he couldn't fix. He knew the machines had worked and could work, even if he could not make them work.

For Satan, the test had ended. He laughed and seemed happy, even though I wondered why since he was proven wrong again.

"Go on in and tell Joey that he has proven his worth. All his equipment shall work again and none of his equipment shall ever need repair or fail until each has reached its planned obsolescence." He chuckled a bit and added, "Tell him his ancestors too shall be so blessed. Go now."

I told Joey as a tidal wave of energy surged through the house and the entire neighborhood seemed to go on line. The pulses from the various monitors and the blinking from reactivated electronic clocks gave Joey an aura about him.

Funny with all the interactive material now available — Joey's three friends soon returned, yakking and typing up a storm — Satan said not a word. That is when things started to turn phantasmagoric and surreal.

Out of his pocket Satan drew forth a small trident, and toyed with the three prongs like they belonged to a particularly tacky piece of costume jewelry. Impersonating a magician, he reshaped the prongs to that of an electrical plug, the staff melting to a snake-like wire. It hissed and struck right toward my vagina. Fortunately, I had my hand at my crotch at the time and could bar the way. It smote my palm hot and sharp and then dropped harmlessly to the ground like an unplugged cord.

Now imitating a rejected lover, Satan slunk away, his clumsy attempt to make a connection only preserved by the three marks on my palm that looked terribly like a TB test. That night I thought better than to follow him. Anyway, he was off to the dwarf pine barrens out near the Hamptons in what I figured would be his own failed attempt to go native. After these past two weeks, I've had my fill of chronicling failures, and even if it were that of the devil himself, I had no stomach for another one.

Channel 43:
Get the Picture?

The Carmen at Prometheus Laboratories today was not a Carmen I met before. She propped herself in front of the terminal laughing and cursing. She winked at me, conversing as if I understood. "What else?" she wondered, smiling and raking her fingers through her kinky hair, "What else could fucking .go wrong?"

"I don't know, what else could go wrong?"

"Hey Technoman, maybe *you* know, maybe you can help me. All my universal remote files refuse to come up from this disk. You're Technoman. Technoman, save me, save me," she said this in tones more worshipping than mocking. I wanted to ask: "What, are you drunk?" but she was too busy chanting, "Save me, save me Technoman. If you save·my disk, you save me. You'll be my hero."

I wanted to explain to her that I am "Technoman" not "Technician Man", but I saw nothing gained by it. Instead I listened to her as she loopily explained her efforts, her hours of frustrations and futile attempts, and ultimately how she came to this daffy and spent state. Asking her the obvious questions, about key commands, disk doctors, translators and retrieval programs, I concluded she supplied all the right answers, had followed all the proper procedures.

Then I said, "Let me look." I switched off the frozen computer and rebooted it, then shoved in her disk, finally double-clicking her universal remote file. Everything was going smoothly until I clicked that file: then I heard all types of whirrings and grindings, slowly pumping up the file, the screen blinking and waving, getting ready to throw up the image, and then, and then, and then I wait. Silence. Nothing moves. I tap the mouse and tickle the keyboards, but no response, no pulse. The machine is frozen.

"Well it's nice to see it isn't just me," said Carmen, chuckling softly. "That is pretty much what happened the last twenty-seven times I called up the file."

I kept tapping, tickling, poking and prodding out of compulsion: in my life, I've never turned off a frozen computer until a good twenty minutes of futile revival procedures. "Fucking Dangus," I said, giving up.

"Fucking Dangus right," she supported. "Now you want to see something really sick? Watch this."

She prepared to turn off the computer from the back, and asked, "Are you watching this?"

"Yeah."

"Are you sure?"

"Yeah."

As she shut down, the screen flashed and what appeared for a split second but a blueprint of the universal remote.

"Woah!" I said.

"Shit yeah woah," she agreed.

"It's still there. The file's still there."

"Yeah, it's there, but not really, just a ghost in the machine. I took out my digital camera to at least get a copy of the screen, but the image moves too fast for me to capture. I can see it, but I can't record it."

"How about back-up disks?"

"There are none." She saw my expression. "Don't look at me like that. There was no time for back-ups. We were inspired. We had to keep pressing ahead. We were making too good of progress for backups."

"How about printouts, hard copy?"

"No time for that either. It seemed like a wasted step. We could see it all on the screen. It was right there before us, as hard and clear as anything on a piece of paper. Who knew this would happen to us? How could it be expected?"

I acted more sympathetically than I felt at that point as I watched her boot the machine for the 29th time. This time she spotted another file called "Aldo." Since Aldo was the name of one of her many sons, I figured naively that it must be a sensitive portion of the remote blueprint, especially given the nervous and frantic way she pointed and clicked the mouse at it.

Her efforts gathered the same results as the universal remote file. She slammed down the mouse and tears started to well in her face. I switched off the machine, and what flashed before my eyes were Carmen and a bunch of kids in party hats. This was no ordinary business file.

She started sobbing uncontrollably and called up the file again, this time taking out the digital camera and shooting the split-second image of the party scene. Rebooting, she loaded the picture onto the hard drive and called it up. What came onto the monitor was the perfectly clear image of a blank, frozen computer screen. She hurled the camera across the room, "Piece of shit."

"What was it a picture of?"

"Aldo's fifth birthday party. I remember it as one of the happiest days of my life. Not one of my children cried that day; everyone giggled and hugged and had ice cream cake. I remember how content I was that day. We had almost completed getting the kinks out of the remote. I remember thinking I could become a better mother and spend more time with the kids real soon. That was a week before all this shit started happening... It was one of the better moments of my life and now it's lost."

"But you still have the memories."

"Yeah, but the pictures would be better."

I found myself developing this miserable tendency of staying around people who are distraught, comforting them. I lost my skill of the graceful exit. Carmen grew even more weepy and more sentimental, spending the ensuing hours telling me of Easter egg hunts and Halloween tricks and Christmas caroling. Somehow she connected with me the way only a truly fine TV commercial — one with all the trappings of suburbia — could. The more she spoke the more she waxed poetic, until she told me the story of her friend Georgia, a librarian who refused to have a picture taken of herself her entire life. Carmen spoke of Georgia with all the grace an angel blesses upon a lost soul.

"She took no pictures and now she is dead and so she will be forgotten."

"But *you* remember."

"For now, for now. Oh hear me Technoman and record for I soon will forget her, even though she supplied me with more books and data at MIT than I will ever know again. Oh hear me Technoman." She was dramatic and affected enough for me to play along. So I typed as she spoke, she all the time staring at the blank screen as is she deciphered a secret code that bubbled up beneath its dark surface.

"Behind the Infotrack, behind the stacks, behind the years of kindness, giving out information for free, Georgia emerged, a walking, waltzing reference book I could take out of the library... Behind her 38 years, unmarried, parents dead from the cancer, behind years of humble answers, the right answers, behind accommodation after accommodation, behind a freight train of electronic information clacking along rusty tracks, behind the wheel of her stalled vehicle, behind her 250 pounds, behind her mild complaints of discomfort, and behind her ensuing doctor's appointments...There..."

I thought I was witnessing another seizure here, with another convulsing body and a visit from my dour EMT. Instead she was groping for words.

"...There lay her childless womb. The doctors told Georgia she would need a hysterectomy on Saturday. Behind the incision, the uterus, the ovaries, bred the cancer the doctors found that morning, a cancer so deep and profound all the doctors could do was sew her back up."

"That night she fell into a coma and died."

"Behind 38 years of kindness was a student complaining that the library was closed today in remembrance."

"I doubt he would have been able to get the information he needed anyway..."

Suddenly Carmen rose from the screen. Georgia was forgotten. She retrieved the digital camera from the corner of the room, shaking and staring through the viewfinder.

"It still works. I'll see you later."

"Where are you going?"

"To get some party hats and recreate Aldo's birthday party."

She was so hopeful and happy. I couldn't resist trying the file one more time. The computer froze again. Don't feel sorry for me though; I drew comfort by the inability to access the image.

Channel 44:
Computer Sex

Pines Tar: The Love Line

I am no longer a technological virgin. I met her in a dingy web chat room and we had a keyboard fling. Who was the lucky maiden, you ask? To protect her identity, let's call her Angelica. Some of the language (very little) has been expurgated by my good friend Rachel, editor and censor extraordinaire, to protect the innocent.

"Hey where has your desktop been all my life?"

"I've been saving my screen for you."

"Have you ever? Ever? Ever!"

"Never? Never? Never!"

"Neither have I. Could Ya? Would Ya?"

"I could, I would, I haven't."

"Why not?"

"I haven't found someone to push the right buttons."

"I have magic fingers."

"Where have I heard that before?"

"From clumsy oafs who confuse plunking hard on a keyboard for passion. I caress before I press."

"I believe you do."

"Best to know my home keys."

"I believe I will."

"Touch"

"Me"

"Touch"

"Me"

"K, K, K, K, K, K"

"I, I, I, I, I, I, I"

"S, S, S, S, S, S, S, S, S"

"S, S, S, S, S, S, S, S, S, S... This is embarrassing."

"No, it's alright."

"It's tacky."

"It's L'Amour."

"It's…"

"It's…"

"Stop pressing the CONTROL key."

"How about the OPTION key?"

"I didn't take you for the adventurous type."

"I'm any type, any font, you want me to be."

"You are, you are."

"☞"

"Ohh!"

"☞"

"$f1$"

"Wow"

"$f2$"

"$f6$"

"I think I love you"

"$f7$"

"I can't…"

"$f8$"

"$f3$"

"$f9$"

"$f4…f5$"

"Mmmmmmm…Multiples!?!"

"$f10$"

"Wooo! Ahhhhhh…"

"That was fast."

"What'd you expect with twin modem lines linked to the power surge. These babies are built for speed."

"Hey, your keys are sticky."

"Shut up… Well are you staying?"

"Well, I have to write a column."

"And I was going to make you breakfast."

"That's sounds lovely. I'm sorry."

"That's O.K. Just roll over, put on your screen saver, and get out of here."

"You were the best I ever had."

"Please, this is awkward enough; the whole thing is so awkward."

"Too bad the desire wasn't so great."

"Yeah."

I type in many more words, a great number of them I am thankful not to repeat here, before I realized she logged off and I was speaking only to my machine.

This column was brought to you by the good people at Hormodem.

For greater sensitivity, stimulation, and pleasure, use Hormodem every time you surf the love lines.

Channel 45:
Technoman's Daily Schedule

Technoman's Planned Itinerary for January 3

12:00-12:47	Go to 24-hour market and purchase the finest in diet goods
12:24-1:14	Guest D.J. at Diodes
1:15-1:37	Pick up surgically enhanced woman
1:38-2:02	Find romance in Smart Car with surgically enhanced woman
2:03-2:08	Hold surgically enhanced woman and exchange farewells
2:09-2:25	Drive home
2:26-2:45	Give equipment and person a chemical wash
2:46-3:18	Have insomnia
3:19-6:23	Activate screen saver of Intrafacer, get R.E.M. sleep
6:24-6:57	Chemical scrub and dress
6:58-7:33	Ingest many pills, power bars, protein diet shakes and egg beaters
7:34-7:37	Consider how I can be a better Technoman today
7:38-11:29	Saturate my hard drive with as much new information from my three perpetually channel shifting, digital satellite TVs, my Intrafacer net

surf, plus my mega-accelerated web cruiser, with special accentuation on commercials

11:30-12:30	Make appearance at Crazy Woody's Gadget Shack
12:31-12:49	Visit *Herald* office electronically, pick up paycheck
12:50-12:59	Try out necessary inventions and state-of-the-art equipment
1:00-2:30	Make appearance at the Bill Gates Memorial Video Arcade
2:31-3:30	Attend luncheon in my honor at the Silicon Club
3:31-5:30	Make appearance and do my wardrobe, accessory, apparel and equipment purchases at ResinWorld, your one-stop shop for the Postmodern universe.
5:31-7:27	Attend Sci-Fi convention and make speech
7:27-9:17	Network, interface and dialog with Technoman sponsors and potential ones
9:18-9:46	Cultivate Technoman cultural activities
9:47-10:36	Family time: take Zach to Warner Von Braun Galactica where I make guest appearance
10:37-11:21	Do necessary reporting and write Technoman column
11:22-11:41	Read E-mail and exchange correspondence while eating a microwave dinner
11:42-11:46	Use bathroom facilities and cogitate about increased efficiency in daily activities
11:47-11:59	Write itinerary for January 4.

Channel 46:
Getting Relief

I estimate it has been three days since I used the bathroom... Perhaps I took too literally my offhand comment: "Technoman is so hyperextended that he doesn't even have time to piss."

All I know I found myself having to go again and again over those days and repeatedly curbing the urge. So, I decide right then I better relieve myself quick before the urine starts spouting out of my ears. Unfortunately, like always, somebody wanted me just as I unzipped my fly. This time, old man Miller came by looking as if he was on the dole, as if he needed something. I had to make a promotional appearance in a few minutes, so I told him:

"I can't talk to you now because I have to piss."

"Can't it wait for a minute."

"No, I really have to go."

"Can't I talk to you as you go?"

"Alright."

Old man Miller followed me into the bathroom, and he was yapping before I got my pecker out. I don't know if it was his talking or just all the restraints and delay, but I took a full minute before the floodgates lifted and the stream began. Meanwhile, Miller made this convoluted, windy request to download all the material I have written, collected and interpreted on my Intrafacer since I became Technoman.

"I will be your archivist."

"Download everything?"

"Yup."

"But if I give you everything, what will I have?

"What do you mean?"

"I mean if you have all my Intrafacer files, what do I have? I might as well give up my self, my identity."

"On the contrary, if you don't give your files to me, you will have given up your identity. Rus, I've know you long enough to figure out you are not going to archive this material. It's not your nature. You're a great one for gathering phenomena, but not one to spend the time necessary to turn them into permanent records, into history."

All the time he spoke I was still pissing a steady stream, my penis held up by the pressure. My bladder seemed larger than a swimming pool, and the draining took on an overnight, overflowing inevitability.

"If I don't bother archiving my own life, why should you?"

"Because I figure I might find a nugget or two for the Dangus bio, and after that I'm going to need another project. My lawyer confirmed just yesterday that I won't be going back into the classroom, that I'd have to accept the district's generous buyout package."

"I'm sorry to hear that. You'll be missed in the chemistry labs."

He nodded in acknowledgment while I continued pissing, pissing through business and sympathy. The odor turning overpowering, I flushed some of it away even as I manufactured more. Alternately scared and impressed, I was the great fount — with enough urine to scent every fire hydrant on the island as my territory. Who more deserving of being recorded for posterity? Old man Miller certainly thought so. He called me the human microchip, digitizing my soul through every wire of the networked world. He said more too, comparing me to microprocessors, transistor circuits, Pentium chips and pretzel logics until my head washed hazy and I became another one of his lost, inattentive students. Did I happen to mention I've been pissing during the entire discourse?

"When would you plan on downloading this information?"

"Right away, if possible."

"It'll take hours and I simply don't have the time."

"You don't have to have the time."

"I'm not giving up the Intrafacer to do this, if that's what you're implying, not even for a couple of hours. I almost went nuts when I left it with Alice and Zach for a morning."

"You don't have to give it up. Let me follow you around for a couple of hours with this transfer box, and I'll just be periodically inserting disks."

"But how will we record what's happening today, right now?" keeping in mind that this five-minute (and still going) leak merits notation.

"Those will become the soon-to-be-famous 'Lost Hours of Technoman.' Everyone needs a little mystery. I'll insert something cryptic and conspiratorial for the missing time."

My great archivist didn't even notice how long I was pissing, the oblivious, monomaniacal bastard. And yet just as I wondered whether all the fluids in my body would eventually spill out if I stood here long enough, old man Miller clamped an eye on my penis.

"You ever consider a catheter? It would save you time and sure add mobility, besides a few extra tubes wouldn't hurt your look."

We continued talking, working out the details of the archiving as I watched the last trickles drop into the toilet, stopped for now, but threatening for more. After I zipped up my fly, gave a surgical scrub to my hands, and shook his big meaty paw to seal the deal, the both of us looked very relieved. He shifted to what I thought would be idle chit-chat.

"I'm sure glad we could come to an arrangement. I never told you this before, but I think I grew fascinated with Paddy Dangus because I knew his father. He was a shell-shocked sergeant half out-of-his-gourd when I knew him. He was brought to Mason General Hospital where I was stationed after the second world war to take care of loonies, you know with the sedatives, the electroshock, the whole magilla."

"I've heard of Mason General."

"That's right, sounds familiar doesn't it?"

"Yeah."

"If you are wondering whether your father was there with me, yes he was. As a matter of fact he was my boss and buddy; I'd believe he'd tell you that too if he were around to say. So there we were, me, your dad and old man Dangus in a post-war insane asylum."

"Huh," I responded, having nothing else to say.

"I guess by recording the legacies of the sons I record a bit of my own."

"Why don't you record Angelica's too then?"

"She doesn't have a legacy: she's too busy collecting other pasts, histories and artifacts to generate her own one."

"Like father, like daughter."

What I might have meant as an insult he took proudly as a compliment, smiling and waving goodbye, promising a return in a few minutes, once he assembled the proper materials.

So my old man knew Dangus's old man, probably even stopped him from flying out a window once or twice. Shit. My innards tightened up. Miller pulled out of the driveway.

I returned to the toilet, finding that I, once again, had to relieve myself.

Channel 47:
The 7 Synthetic Voyages of Technoman, Voyage 3

Fighting the War on the 7th Floor

Old man Miller is a very young man and he already has Jimmy Dangus in the tub ten hours by the time my father, an 18-year-old sergeant, walks in. For Dangus's particularly violent form of mental anguish drawn from the war, hydrotherapy often seems the best way to go. For days, Dangus sits in those hot tubs, the canvas on top strapping in the heat and the patient. The whole time, Private Miller, a 16-year-old who used his brother's identification to get drafted in the first place, stays by his side like his best buddy. Even in his thermal stupor, Dangus is more alive than most men and that's what Miller feeds on.

Dad stops in because it's finally time to get Dangus out... with Dangus, the hospital staff never has fewer than five people surrounding him during any of those ever treacherous transitions from one ward to the next. One time we staff members let down our guard after Dangus, with that fast right hand, had already beaten the crap out of everyone on the ward and finally seemed mollified by the very knowledge that without weapons he could do no worse damage than already achieved to the members on the floor. Of course that was the night he raised his pudding spoon and starting hacking at any white coat in sight. By the second victim, the staff knew he must have been filing the spoon feverishly, scraping away very late during many consecutive nights, for it was sharper than most Swiss Army Knives. What a bloody mess he made! It took five guys wielding mattresses to corner him, pounce upon him with the padding, and after almost suffocating him with the cushions, subdue him.

So now through the soupy mist of the hydrotherapy room, Dad, Miller and we three others surround him. After he gets out of the tub and puts on his maroon patient's outfit we escort him back to the seventh floor ward, the top floor, where all the extreme and dangerous crazies are assigned. Maybe it is the long hot bath that sets Dangus today on his best behavior. He goes right to the game area and gets the five of us to play Monopoly and piece together a puzzle of the Empire State Building. If it weren't for our white uniforms, Dad, Miller and the rest of us could have passed for patients, and Dangus could be the ringleader.   In between the puzzle pieces and Chance cards, Dangus tells us five medical technicians about the war, about his time in Patton's Third and four separate shells that almost got him in France. "I should be dead by now boys. Shit those explosions wiped out everyone around me, but here I am." For six nights a week working the overnight 7-7 shift, we listen with wonder to his stories, since we were all drafted too late for combat, the Nagasaki drop not even a month earlier. No one listens with more awe and admiration than Miller. He just loves Dangus, like the veteran's a big brother you know.

Next shift, Miller is all nervous. Dangus is going in for his sixth and final treatment of electroshock therapy. Miller hates the procedure. "Why don't you just shoot him in the head. You're killing the poor bastard."

Although the doctors gently explain that electroshock is the best thing that can be done for Dangus now, Miller is more disturbed and adamant than Dangus is, as he and Dad wheel the victim in on a gurney. As he straps Dangus's legs down, Miller starts to cry. Dad has to take care of the arms and torso. Miller steps back as a nurse tapes the electrodes to Dangus's temples and shoves a cotton cloth in his mouth to keep him from chewing up his tongue. Everyone now backs away from the patient the way we still do with X-Rays today. Dangus is alone as the nurse steps up to the little black box and the doctors quietly administer the procedures.

Seconds after the nurse twists the knob on the black box Dangus begins to shudder and Miller turns white. Soon the convulsions kick in: Dangus thrashes and flops, alternately fighting and embracing his restraints. Miller fares worse. "No!!!!!!!" he screams, like he cries out against bloody murder. Dangus drops unconscious, his now puffy face slumped into his clavicle. Just as he had witnessed the other five times. Miller knows what will follow for Dangus: the short-term memory loss, the stiffness, the disintegration of personal identity.

As Dad and the rest of us unstrap Dangus's limp body and slide him onto a rollaway, Miller charges over to the nurse, pushes her aside and grabs the black box. "This piece of shit! I can't stand this piece of shit!" He smashes the box down. The nurse and the doctor step back and Dad grabs Miller tight from behind. "Easy now, easy," Dad says calmly, the way he always speaks to Dangus. Miller responds like Dad is going to throw him in electroshock too, jerking and wrestling all about, punching and lashing out at anyone who stands in front of him.

With his forearm across Miller's windpipe, Dad has to make a decision and fast. His commanding officer always warned him if he ever used a choke hold to subdue any army personnel, no matter how crazed, he could face a court martial. Yet there Dad remains, a sharp muscular arm across the throat, waiting for the last weak struggle of his friend before he passes out cold.

That next day, Dad doesn't get a court martial. Instead, he finds himself walking over to the tub with a new patient. When Miller takes off his new maroon uniform and starts his hydrotherapy, he is calm and content. He dips into the tub easily, willingly. In fact, when he lies back beneath the canvas, he sighs and smiles like he is taking a good piss for himself. Dad sits tubside wishing he were as comfortable and wonders what kind of games Miller will play when he gets upstairs to the seventh floor now that he is in charge of the board.

Channel 48:
Virtual Child Care

Today, I planned to take my boy off to the Animatronics Zoo. I figured Angelica could accompany us, a good way to introduce him to her. But my strategy was thwarted. Zach came over and almost immediately said he had to go.

"Where?" I asked.

He stared lost at me, his head swimming, then stammered a little, "Oh, just out."

He circled behind me, cryptically and trickily. Being one of those "cool" fathers, I didn't press the interrogation. I mean how much trouble could a seven-year-old get into?

"I'll be back in a few hours."

"O.K."

"Can you do me a favor?"

"What?" I figured I was already doing him a favor.

"Can you take care of these?" He spread before me five big plastic digital necklaces.

"GigaPets," Angelica smiled and beamed. "Sure we'll take great care of them." Zach acted as receptive toward her as she was to the GigaPets. She leaned over his shoulder, "Have they been fed lately?"

"Just before I got here."

"How about walked?"

"They'll need a walk about an hour from now."

"How about the bathroom?"

"Real soon."

I interrupted, "When you get back, we can play with the new remote control cars I bought. I'll put them together while you're out."

"Cool."

Zach was wise to bring up the GigaPets — he knew I was vulnerable over the subject. During his first visitation last year, I almost killed the whole brood when during a wonderful father-son bonding hike around Lake Ronkonkoma I neglected them, a relationship dampener, I'll tell you. So with a quick wave, Zach left us with his gaggle of GigaPets, which Angelica immediately smothered with the greatest attention and affection.

Seconds within her inspection, she bursts out: "Great Googly Moogly! Holy Moly! How old is this one?"

"Oh, Fido," I said, recognizing the ancient, fuzzy image emanating from that dinosaur of all GigaPets, "he's probably over five years. I think Zach got him from a neighbor for his second birthday, like he'd be capable of operating the thing at that age or something. I don't know what she was thinking."

"Are you sure it's five years old?"

"Sure, I'm sure."

"Then, it's just what I thought. Your Fido is an original GigaPet. You know how much its worth?"

"$500?" I bid ridiculously high as I'm want to do whenever I get such a loaded question, especially for a $15 toy.

"More," she topped me. "It's invaluable."

That afternoon was a strange one even by my Technoman standards. You see, the more I observed Angelica caring for the GigaPets the more suspicious I grew. She tended to Lady, Tuffy, Sam and Inky with top-of-the-line care, from feeding to walking to washing to weeing. But for Fido her behavior was... how shall I describe it... erratic? When Fido beeped and barked, Angelica turned to him immediately, but never tended to his needs, always intimating to the poor dog that she would take care of him, but never quite fulfilling those promises.

What was she trying to do to poor Fido? Look how she caresses him, as if the plastic, staticky screen were charged fur. She clearly wanted Fido to herself, not to sell him mind you — Angelica is not that way. She wanted Fido for her collection, for what is a technology museum without an original GigaPet? So I watched her every move as she slowly neglected the life out of Fido. That Fido was alive today was a miracle, outlasting many of his younger counterparts; he was created before the GigaPet's obsolescence was perfected. Yet now he wheezed, his beeps becoming increasingly shallow and wispy.

To confuse matters, the remote control cars once hooked up seemed to stir and steer on their own about the room, waking and sleeping in a random manner. Every time they appeared to settle down for a few minutes, that grinding spinning started in the motors, as if tooling about in restless dreams. As I drew closer to these sleepwheelers, I received a clue to help explain the agitated movements. Sparks slid across the carpet from my fingertips to the steel hubcaps. Perhaps so many currents shot across the room that they set off the engines. Between the idlings and shudderings of the cars and the ever-present pulsing yappings of the GigaPets, I had trouble knowing for sure just which services were being provided by Angelica.

However, I conveniently managed to crash the two cars into the radiator just before Angelica began hovering at the bedside of the fast fading Fido. I had accidentally killed enough GigaPets in my day to know that one deft button-push by wicked nurse Angelica would bring Fido to the big sleep. I wanted to yell out, "Don't pull the plug," but I couldn't speak. Oh stars, is Angelica a murderer? Who was this woman I was half in love with anyway? What kind of person would kill a little boy's pet? An electric fence rose between Angelica and me. I turned away repulsed as she tapped her fingers nervously, I fathomed that edgy action was a guilt-ridden manifestation of her desire to finish him off. After what seemed like four or five minutes holding Fido in her palm without movement, she finally pressed the button...

But to my surprise, the yelp of Fido grew a little stronger, like it rose out of an aluminum canyon, an anomalous tinny resonance. She had fed him. The remote cars stirred and ground out as if awakened by this cry of life. Angelica smiled and scratched Fido's plastic coat affectionately. For the next hour and a half, she only had eyes for Fido, tending to his every need. Not having the heart to kill, she pampered him instead, as if trying to preserve him beyond realistic expectations — to increase his life expectancy to Tibetan levels. Each moment alive was to be cherished. I confess my confusion with Angelica, who struggled between keeping Fido terminally on a shelf or lovingly in her hand. Meanwhile, time kept passing and Zach hadn't returned home.

Here I am concerned about the welfare of this molded, faded GigaPet while my 7-year-old wanders the streets. I threw on my jacket and pointed to the GigaPets.

"You mind baby-sitting?

"No."

"Good. Take care of these: I'm going to find my son."

Channel 49:
Dangus Alert

A Public Service Announcement
Sponsored by the AntiEntropy Society

Attention All Citizens

During this lunar period when the full moon hangs in the sky, we advise you to exercise extreme caution in your activities. To limit your chances of being affected by the ignominious vandal known as Paddy Dangus, we are suggesting all citizenry take the following measures:

- Please engage all appliances to an absolute minimum
- Do not operate a cell phone
- Avoid all desolate, poorly lit areas
- Do not approach any white truck or other large white vehicles
- Keep remote controls in the confines of private residences
- Do not fertilize lawn
- Do not overuse credit cards
- Keep a safe distance from chemical or microchip factories
- Do not visit web sites on the Milky Way Sprawl

Be warned that while Dangus has not attacked single individuals as of yet, he has attacked and damaged many pieces of equipment that injure the collective consciousness and efficiency of society.

Channel 50:
SuperHole

Pines Tar: Dangus 28 - Network 0

They propped themselves in front of the television with their buffalo wings, their nachos, their fried mozzarella sticks, their pigs in a blanket, their pork rinds, their six types of premium beer, their NFL-authorized jerseys, their authentically autographed footballs, their gambling pool sheets, their arsenal of picture-in-picture remotes. They gathered with family and friends as they had in years past, only each year the tradition grew with more munchies, more possibilities, larger bets, bigger screens.

And when everything was in place and the preview show on NBC shifted into the pregame program and all spectators had found their chairs, their seats on the couch, their ottomans, their spots on the squad-like football bench next to the Gatorade cooler, the TV abruptly broke off from the sharp, crisp image to absolute snow.

"At first we thought it was part of a commercial," said Shane Worthington, an avid Packer fan from Lindenhurst. "You know, we figured it was a way to get our attention, make us perk up thinking there was a problem with our TV or something on the most important day for the TV to be working. Then we thought it was a promotion by NBC for its midyear sitcom schedule. But then, nothing changed, the snow continued. I switched the channel, but the reception was out everywhere. I ran next door, and Nicky Case had the same problem. I called Jason Schmidt over in Levittown and he had the same problem too. Even at the bars, nothing would come in. It was ridiculous."

Citizens from all over Long Island suffered the same fate as cable centers from Montauk to Brooklyn were cut, stripped and smashed. CableLink executive Chuck Roland said service was interrupted for more than four million customers. "This act of vandalism has taken us days to repair and has broken a valuable connection we have with our customers, one of visual trust, at a time when they rely on us most. All we can say is we are as sorry as they are and that these are times we must join together to fight such senseless and terrible acts of violence."

Long Islanders seemed to agree with Roland as the pitch of hostility aimed at Paddy Dangus — do I even have to mention him as the top suspect in this case? — has reached levels not verbalized before. "Destroying equipment, lawns, services, factories is one thing," said Congressman Robert Hockney, a well-known voice of moderation and calm in the community. "But now Dangus has gone too far. Before this incident, most of us thought he was an amusing quack, but I've come to realize he is a subversive anarchist of the worst kind."

When I asked Congressman Hockney just what was the worst kind of subversive anarchist, he replied, "One who knows his way in and out of complicated wiring and gadgetry, one who can sort through hair-thin fiber optic lines like they were strands of spaghetti or something."

While many citizens and officials see this act as a shift in Paddy Dangus's tactics and activities, Dave Miller, author of an unauthorized biography of Dangus (to be published this summer by Random House), finds the gesture in perfect keeping with a pattern developed. "Dangus is predictably unpredictable to the point that he is getting predictable in his actions," Miller said. "I had a feeling he would do something with the Superbowl, but in the past all my feelings and predictions had been incorrect, so I didn't reveal this one."

"It is important to remember that Paddy Dangus cares not one hoot about public opinion. He acts because he must. He wanted to get our attention and he certainly got it."

No one more than Fred Peterwood, vice president at NBC who is in charge of all Superbowl programming. Looking for a silver lining, Peterwood reasoned, "At least we were able to get in the Superbowl preview show which ran before the pregame program."

Peterwood explained that the early ratings for New York, the country's largest market, were outstanding and he predicted that this year's Superbowl would have been a revenue breaker. He cites the large viewing audience as the reason for the unparalleled public outcry from the disruption in services. Yet the public's most common request was not expected by the NBC executive.

"We have been getting swamped with complaints from people saying that they can always catch a report on the football game, but what they can't get are all the wonderful, first run, exclusive, big-budget commercials for which the Superbowl has become renown."

NBC officials have come up with an alternative that should satisfy the public. "We have decided to present a program of all the commercials. They will be run once before the incredible half-time spectacular and then again afterwards," said Peterwood.

He added that if the pilot program gets good ratings in the New York metro area, the network may make it an annual event nationwide.

"Dangus, or whoever the perpetrator is, may have thought he was damaging the Superbowl with this inexcusable, despicable act," said Peterwood in his conclusive spin on the events, "but he has only made it bigger and better, as if he dismantled an old stadium just for us to erect a new state-of-the-art luxury facility. He has unwittingly made the Superbowl into something greater. I wouldn't be surprised if next year we call it the Mega-Superbowl."

Nevertheless, the citizenry and fans all over Long Island were tremendously affected by the experience. "Our parents asked each other where were you when Kennedy was shot, our grandparents ask where were you when the Japanese bombed Pearl Harbor," said Worthington. "We will be asking each other, for years to come, where were you when Superbowl Sunday cut to black."

This Column Has Been Brought To You By The Responsible Drinkers at Toddler Beer, For a Lager That's Just Got Legs and Learned How To Walk. Watch The Repeat Of Our Superbowl Premiere Commercial On *The Tonight Show With Jay Leno* At 11:53 P.M.

Channel 51:
Defoe on Grub Street

from the Journals of Little Augie

After that experience with Satan, I no longer sought him out. Nevertheless, he came to me one night at the morgue, first perusing the corpses, then perusing me.

"You could follow me to London and think you understand, or you could just listen to me here."

"I don't read you."

"Like with Florence and Masaccio," he paused for me to process. "You should hear about Defoe if you care about putting any of the pieces of the puzzle together."

"Together?"

"Let's get a few things straight. At first, I was kind of disinterested in your following me and taking your notes. But as time goes along, I've come around to thinking that since I now live in this age of excessive recording and scholarship, you might as well transcribe in detail and if you get Defoe wrong, you will get it all wrong."

I grabbed my journal. "O.K., I've got my pen and I'm listening." It didn't seem to matter what I had in my hand, for he compelled me to write, and never did the words hit the page so quickly and accurately, like I had downloaded them off another file.

"Defoe, Defoe," he began, "who else could appeal to me but a Dissenter. He first came to my attention back in the 1690s when he was using these wild hugger-mugger ways in business transactions, so much so that his opponents gave him the nickname 'Devil'.

"My type of boy, I figured as I watched him through the next years wander in and out of trouble, on the 1 a.m. after the Duke of Monmouth's doomed rebellion, even on the pillory for a particularly pointed satire. Yet it was when he started writing *The Review* and became a mouthpiece for Robert Harley, that's when I knew I must step into Daniel Defoe's world.

"Down on Grub Street I met him, all hair and motion, couldn't get him to stop writing for a minute, meeting Harley in back doors under the cloak of darkness, mucking about those awful wet, puddling, disease-infested roads with his rough, ugly coat and boots. I was impressed how many lies he shot out to me in a few minutes visit. All he spoke of was Harley this, Harley that... if Defoe were going to fulfill his destiny, Harely would have to go. So Harley was soon gone."

I almost asked him about what he did to Harley, but I figured that was another story.

"Cut loose, Defoe fragmented into so many identities he was almost a god. He was not just the journalist, but secret service man Claude Guilot, and the author of secret histories, pamphlets and papers in which he adopted endlessly alternative viewpoints, often writing three arguments in the same night, each countering and opposing the others. He was filled with conviction and intensity, believing in everything with wondrous hypocritical absolutism. And as he described the manifest world in all its multitudes, the secret, internal world of Daniel Defoe grew to proportions few men had known. He was beyond Whig and Tory, beyond Townsend, Sunderland, the Queen and even Walpole."

That I knew little of these figures seemed not to matter to Satan, only that I continued to transcribe his words.

"Defoe was the man of secrets, he was the template for what modern man would become. His was the world hidden in his memory, his duplicities and even his subconscious. And even then, you know what it took me to get him to write about secret worlds in a full-length form. When he wrote what would become the first English novel with *Robinson Crusoe*, Defoe would insist to me on masking the whole thing in a religious conversion. What the fuck was that? Good thing Defoe had just enough brilliant evil within him to let the vicious, self-deifying mercenary in Crusoe emerge a bit. Well when the response came in (of course his identity as an author was a secret), I no longer needed to encourage him, his secret worlds of rogue narratives that followed turned criminal, murderous, and even, heaven forfend, incestual."

"By the time a heroine gave a complicit nod to the murder of her own child just to maintain a secret, Defoe had felt he had gone too far. He started to write novels at 59 and by 66 he shot his load, couldn't even finish his last novel, so repulsed was he

Defoe acted God without God, just as I am like a God. He was eating a bigger fruit, with his newspapers, his novels, his political, sociological, and economic tracts. Who needs God when you have cheap paper and an efficient press? Defoe produced, yet did not die like Masaccio. He lived and lived. Even in those final five fading years, fighting for redemption, writing treatises designed to stop the very rogue characters he implicitly glorified in his novels, Defoe couldn't help but make himself Godlike."

"Who needs God when man can reason out his own social, economic and political reforms? One night I came to him and quoted Milton quoting me (I thought that had just enough hidden narrative layers and internal subtexts to perk his ears): 'The mind is its own place, and in itself/ Can make a Heaven of Hell, a Hell of Heaven.' Old Defoe responded by pumping out *The Political History of the Devil*, whether he intended the work to be an attack on me mattered less than how he described me. Now I did Defoe the honor of quoting his depiction of me: 'being confined to stratagem, and soft still methods, such as persuasion, allurement, feeding the appetite, prompting, and then gratifying corrupt desires, and the like, he finds it for his purpose not to appear in person, except very rarely, and then in disguise... in the dark... making use of methods and persons concealed.'"

"I put my arm to his shoulder as Defoe all the while compulsively worked at his writing desk. 'Let me ask you, does that description sound more like you or me?' He didn't answer, but kept trying to write his way far distant from me. But we both knew the more he wrote, the closer he came to me. If all of humanity could see man as a god when Masaccio painted, then when Defoe wrote in his plunky, simple prose, each man now knew he too could be a god. It would not even take a pen, merely a private life."

Satan now rose and came to me, softly caressing my chin, "And who comes knocking more in a woman's private life than I?" He tried to kiss me and I turned away like a 14-year-old school girl from a dirty old man.

"Why does everything have to be personal with you?"

"Because everything is personal... Don't you see that's what Defoe signaled. That the masses would now turn very personal. Everyone would have an identity."

"But be a servant of yours?"

"The minute a man becomes truly himself, truly independent, he must come to me."

I considered whether I was independent and started growing a bit weak in the knees. I turned away from him very consciously and methodically and looked to the corpses. I tried to complete my lab reports, but I could not. His hair flowing softly over his face, Satan kept reaching out to me. I refused to grab his hand, yet I could not help but continue to write his story.

Satan lifted his fist in triumph. Evil had conquered good and the energy Satan gave off in the room made the fluorescent lights pulse and beat a jaundiced aura throughout the morgue. I grew terribly woozy, even cracking some smelling salt to revive my senses, but to no avail. As he touched my cheek in an effort to restore me — the way he must have touched Defoe's cheek centuries earlier - I swooned onto the chilly cement floor.

Channel 52:
Paddy ~~Dangus~~ Dingus

Pines Tar: The Wannabes OutPaddy Dangus

What is the most popular car on Long Island?

The Camry? The Sable? The Beemer? One of the endless minivans? The off-road vehicle? The Taurus?

"Two years ago, they'd all be in the running," said Rick Barnes at Pynchon Chevrolet. "Now I'd trade each and every one of them to get a few more white Searcher pick-up trucks in here, preferably used instead of new."

Just how tremendous is the Paddy Dangus phenomenon? Big enough for car dealers all down auto-strip row to spray every vehicle with a mangy flatbed the creamy dirty off-white that has captured the modern imagination the way the Lone Ranger's mask did generations earlier.

Down at Pynchon Chevrolet the activity is monomaniacally absurd as if the dealers have no other cars on the lot except for the white pick-ups. "Until the full moon, we don't even talk about other cars," said Barnes. "We have to wait for the fever, the frenzy pitch to ebb. You sit here and tell me if this copycat obsession hasn't gotten out of control."

Call them what you will, copycats, imitators, wannabes, apprentices, protégés, Piddy Dinguses; they are out there in force and have perhaps become a more frightening spectre than Paddy Dangus himself. *The Herald* has increased its coverage of Dangus activity dramatically in the last four months to deal as much with the copycat shenanigans as with Dangus's own heightened activity. To hear Suffolk County Sheriff Ernie Cooley distinguish between the two is to note the difference between amateurs and professionals.

"When Dangus goes in there and destroys somebody's lawn, dumps some high tech equipment, or delivers toxic waste to the doorstep of a chemical mogul, the only thing we hear of is the white truck. Everything else is ghostly — like a supernatural occurrence. Nobody's ever seen the guy. It's like he's magical and protected, plus he knows what he's doing.

"Now when one of those Dinguses is out there, you only know them by the white truck; otherwise, you'd just think you came across a bunch of bumbling fools. They might as well defecate at the scene of the crime for all the clues they leave. We have a better chance of catching a Piddy Dingus than we do of a guy robbing a bank with six security cameras glaring down at him."

Cooley said even the best, most thoughtful imitators always manage to give themselves away. "The Piddy Dingus who blew up all the barbecue gas grills, now he was pretty sharp. We still haven't caught up to him. But he left enough clues at the crime scenes for us to track him down, not to mention the fact he created a situation where one poor homeowner got his arm blown off, and that is not Paddy Dangus's way at all."

My tendency is to like Paddy Dangus. Hell, you can tell that Cooley likes him, and even as Dangus and I are going in opposite directions, I can't help but admire him. But he's got more imitators than I got polyplasticine piercings on my porous body.

He must be wondering who the enemy are: those he terrorizes or those who terrorize his terrorism.

And now with a new full moon rising, *The Herald* and the rest of Long Island braces for the next surge of activity, from Dangus, from the copycats, and from a whole new host of weekend warriors in white pick-ups.

For better or worse, the least likely to show up is Dangus himself.

THIS COLUMN HAS BEEN BROUGHT TO YOU BY FARQUARD AND WHEN YOU SAY FARQUARD NOTHING ELSE NEED BE ADDED.

Channel 53:
Why Haven't We Visited Earlier?

The Paddy Dangus Shrine
You are number [612,723] to hit this site.

Welcome to the biggest, most comprehensive, most authoritative source for information on Paddy Dangus on the entire web. Check out our entirely new photo gallery (sorry still no pictures of the man, but we have a pretty good shot of what we believe is his truck) and our media commentators quotables about Dangus.

Hit any of the Headings
• Top ten theories and legends of Paddy Dangus
• Listing and map of Dangus sightings (*updated 2/14*)
• The photo gallery (*new!*)
• The Miller biography in Hypertext
• Woman who would like to have Dangus's baby
• Talking heads talk Dangus

- Related Links and Sites (not directly focused on Paddy Dangus, but mention him)
- Elton John's tribute song to Paddy Dangus
- An article on Dangus in the French Scholarly Journal Le Cirque
- Membership information for the Paddy Dangus Fan Club
- Lunar cycles for the next five years
- The most hostile comments made by public officials about Dangus
- Dangus t-shirts, accessories and apparel
- Security systems installed at malls, factories and corporate centers to thwart Dangus
- Drawings of Dangus as imagined by six prize-winning illustrators
- Car dealerships with beat-up 1979 white Ford Bronco trucks
- The joint denouncement of Dangus by Charles Manson and Theodore Kaczinski (*full transcript*)
- The latest information on Dangus (*updated every 22 minutes*)

Channel 54:
You've Gotta Believe

Top ten theories and legends of Paddy Dangus
Click on the number to get the full story
1. Dangus lives in an old fallout shelter on canned foods first stored on the shelves in the 1950s. Dangus developed immunities to whatever poisons those old foods have.
2. Dangus is an Irish Republican Army terrorist whose father was killed by a Long Islander and now he takes out his vengeance on the entire community.
3. Dangus is a government experiment run amuck. Embedded with millions of ultrasensitive transistors in incredibly complex microchips, he has superhuman intelligence and skills. The training and brainwashing by the CIA is a classic case of the creators being unable to control their awesome creation.
4. Dangus is the last of a long line of Knight Templars, preserving a code of beliefs and honors this epoch knows little of. He is the accumulation of 800 years of knowledge as he brings to

conclusion the Final Crusade, the culmination of the Holy Land Crusades as predicted by St. John in the Revelations.

5. Dangus is an intellectual wanderer who has taken hundreds of courses at the major technical universities in the nation. He has **four** doctorates: one in nuclear physics from M.I.T., another in aeronautical engineering from Cornell, another in computer design from Berkeley, and a final one in electrical engineering from Stanford.

6. Dangus is a corporate hit man hired by SONY to undermine its competitors. Why else would so few of the products assaulted be manufactured by the electronics giant?

7. Dangus is Technoman. How else would Technoman know so much about Dangus, and who else has enough equipment to commit so many terrorist activities?

8. Dangus is not a person, but a large, well-organized underground movement. A whole fleet of white trucks move along the landscape; that is why Dangus can seem ubiquitous at times, appearing during a full moon in many places simultaneously.

9. Dangus is a stunt launched by gubernatorial candidate and millionaire Donald P. Heywood. Dangus is just the presence a law-and-order guy like Heywood needs to kick off his campaign.

10. Paddy Dangus has revived the Luddites, the anti-technological group responsible for destroying massive factory· equipment during England's Industrial Revolution.

Channel 55:
A Microchip off the Old Hard Drive

I couldn't find Zach that day. He returned to my house and Angelica convinced him that she could tend better after Fido than he. So he headed home with only four GigaPets, which must have made Alice happy, she hated those little beeping buggers.

When he came over today with a similar request to slip out, I let him go, but this time I slyly followed him.

The son-of-a-gun made his way down the block to Crazy Woody's Gadget Shack. I figured he's there to pick up some funky video games, but Zach has something else on his mind. He goes right up to Crazy Woody himself and starts talking to him.

What's even more bizarre is the way Woody treats him, like a favorite nephew or something, laughing and poking him. Zach's doing some sort of elaborate imitation that sends Woody into big hearty chuckles. Soon a few customers gather around Zach and are laughing too, loud enough for more to follow. I turn my zoom lens to the mirror and catch an inverted image of my son performing.

Even without Zach drawing a crowd, the Gadget Shack constantly clanged and clamored its way into carnival state, all the twirling neons and twisting graphics perpetually upheaving whatever appeared comfortable and conventional a moment earlier. Whenever I did a promotional appearance there, I felt I was walking through cyberspace. But my boy wasn't touring cyberspace, he was the star of it. He imitated computer graphic images as if he were beamed through a picture tube.

Moving with the slight stuttering, stilted ambulations of video characters, Zach performed the ancient classical figure of Pac-Man with a singular attentiveness. He ate the air like he could discern the separate molecules, swallowing his way through a maze only he could see. While the crowd was already won over, clapping with the gusto of a television talk show audience, what really warmed them up was Zach's impression of the thickly moustached Mario brother, filled with the kind of jagged gesticulations that I had believed only animated computer graphics were capable. I thought I caught a bit of Chaplin and even Hitler in his forward march, although how could he imitate what he didn't know? Nonetheless, his was mockery with authority. Who knew that my son, heretofore an introvert with an intravenous hook-up to the TV, was a prodigy?

He called out to the audience, a 7-year-old playing a 7-year-old's game with an increasingly large crowd, "What am I?"

Then he jerked his body about in sharp perpendicular bends and drops.

"I'm a joystick." The crowd ooooh'd in recognition.

From then on, understanding the game, they yelled out guesses continually as he whirled and buzzed and stammered, collapsed and flopped and quivered. Many minutes passed and Zach seemed inexhaustible while they barked out the answers.

"A microwave!"

"An unreadable disk!"

"A fax machine!"

"A cell phone!"

"A photocopy machine!"

"A system error!"

And when all the functions and machinery were correctly identified, he told the crowd members to their great chagrin, "Last one now."

For that imitation, his body seemed to be pressed at different spots as he shot all his intensity and essence toward one of Crazy Woody's screens. He was too good at this one for even a dolt like me to miss. I yelled out the answer alright, but thank goodness it seemed the entire place caught on at the same time.

"A remote control!" They all cheered more satisfied with themselves for figuring out the correct response than with the quality of the imitation, and afterward turned back to their gadgetry purchases, happier and wiser customers. Zach struggled to regain himself after incorporating so much wiring, transistors and electricity into the very fabric of his consciousness.

Was he aping humans or computers or some fusion of the two? Christ, he can make his human features robotic better than a robot can make its features human. As Zach headed out the door, Crazy Woody pronounced, "Give a last round of applause to the Son-of-Technoman." With that type of triumphant exit, *you* try keeping *your* son back at the house playing with GigaPets.

After Zach left, I went up to Crazy Woody, who seemed surprised to see me. I had a long conversation with him. But to boil it down to its thick soup, I'll tell you Woody was under the impression that I knew about the appearance (I was careful not to alter that impression), for which Zach received the tidy sum of $50, plus a complimentary copy of the Total Annihilation Intergalactic Warfare game (an additional $50 value). In fact, Woody thought the performance was my idea, especially since I couldn't make that last appearance when I was sick.

Woody even indicated that Zach could be the new star of a popular video game. "I tell you the way your son moves, he may well be the missing link between humans and computer-generated images." My whole conversation with Woody seemed filtered through Somnoid. Absurdly proud and hostile, I wanted to first pat Zach on the rump exaltedly and then beat him on the ass. How did I lose control of him so quickly?

When I returned to the apartment, I didn't confront Zach about what he did. I figured I'd sort it all out in my mind first. I don't know which of us Alice would strangle first if she found out. Certainly, if the secret came out, I'd have a hell of a time maintaining visitation rights.

Channel 56:
E-Mail from Prometheus Labs

Just when I connected with Carmen on human terms, I lost contact with her and Geoffrey. I could have passed along the e-mails to you as I received them, but I think you'll get a fuller picture from my cutting and pasting them together in one file. On the up side, the e-mails have been a refreshing substitute for wandering over to Prometheus Laboratories every other day.

February 13

Hey Rus, what's up? Geoffrey returned to the office yesterday with his head on straight and what seems to be the right type and dosage of seizure medication. Anyway, he walked in with what he tells me is a new brilliant idea for the Universal Remote. He warned me that we'll be working round-the-clock for the next few months to get the product ready for release and he told me to inform you that you don't have to stop by for at least a month since your services won't be needed for a while. We'll be e-mailing you with updates. As we get closer to the release date, you'll be sure to be working your ass off. He promises an e-mail soon. I have made pretty good progress puzzling together the pieces of the prototype. I'd say I've got about a good three-eighths of the work restored. By the way, I was able to recreate Aldo's birthday party pretty well. The hats were different and the laughter seemed a little forced, but I've had worse moments. Maybe if I try it a couple of times more, add some balloons perhaps, I'll get it perfect.

Carmen

February 16

Technoman. I'm back and better than ever. You know what? The best thing that happened to us was losing the prototype remote. That would have been an embarrassment. But now, now, I've got it. This new prototype will be bigger and better than ever. I'd love to talk about it but I'm too busy designing. Hang in there. Get psyched, because you're going to be promoting the greatest domestic advancement since the microwave oven.

Geoffrey

February 20

Techno. I don't sleep anymore, and I've got to talk to somebody, so here I am. I don't want to bitch about Carmen, given what she's been doing with the prototype, but I think she's losing her grip. Do you realize what she did today? She stopped her work right in the middle of rewiring to walk her son Aldo's GigaPet. A fuckin GigaPet! And when I laughed at her, she started to cry. I felt like shit so I asked her if I could get her a cup of tea or something. She said, no. Then two minutes later she turns to me and says, "Where's my tea?" with an attitude I might add. I said "What tea?" And she said, "The tea you were getting for me." And I said, "You said you didn't want any tea?" And she said, "Of course I wanted tea, otherwise why would I ask you where my tea is." Needless to say, I got her tea. She didn't drink the tea. Worse, she didn't finish her rewiring. Still I'm confident we'll be done in about nine weeks. Will let you know when you're needed. Take it slow.

Geoffrey

February 25

Today one of my hairs fell into the remote. I ended up thinking it was a wire and tried to connect some diodes with it. I would have never made such a bonehead move if the hair wasn't gray. I didn't know I had any of those in my head, but I guess I should just be grateful it fell out before I spotted it in the mirror. If I'm getting old working on this prototype, I have Geoffrey to thank. Do you know he pays a guy to wait at the door to receive any deliveries from the manufacturers just to rush them into my hands, like the prototype couldn't wait an hour. Every twenty minutes he cleans off my tools and sprays down my work area with chemicals. No dust has settled, I've generated no debris, yet he's there with his chemicals, hovering, waiting, like he's timing contractions or something. And to make matters worse, he keeps redesigning the remote; every few days, he drafts plans with adjustments, tinkerings, additions. He crams more and·more into this remote. By the time he's done, it should be able to do everything, maybe give a virtual blowjob, that is if anyone can figure out how to operate the equipment. "Simplify, simplify," he says, and he piles on more. I'm just warning you, because I have a feeling he's going to ask you to write the directions to this sucker. Don't be surprised if a few gray hairs come dropping down on your keyboard in a few months time. Rest up my friend.

Carmen

February 28

February is the shortest month. I bet you're feeling neglected about now. Don't worry I haven't forgotten you. If I wanted you before with the old crappy prototype, I certainly want you with this masterpiece in process. Hey, especially now that you are Technoman and have become such a celebrity and all. You could be instant credibility for our product, just be careful not to overendorse yourself in the next month or so. Simplify. I'll be needing you.

Geoff

Channel 57:
Angelica's Place in the 30s

Even though I wanted to record everything there, I took my Intrafacer off the moment I stepped into Angelica's apartment. I could say the cliché that walking into her apartment was like stepping into another decade, but I'd be more accurate to claim that I became another era, transforming with the time. Down to every decoration, appliance and label, Angelica's place inhabited the 1930s, even a dope like me had seen enough depression-era movies to figure out that much.

When I walked in she was talking on a telephone, not just any phone mind you, but the Bell 300, the black ergonomic masterpiece where the receiver sits like big old dog ears above the rotary (look Ma no touch-tone), you know the one of a thousand screwball comedies and newspaper farces, the one with the message in its rotary bullseye "Please wait for the dial tone," the one that could be slammed down conclusively in a time when people still believed conversations could end, when telephone wires would actually stop sending messages after someone hung up. As if to prove my point, Angelica delivers a firm final offer. "I'll give you $1,300 for the 79 SONY walkman. Take it or leave it. You have until high noon tomorrow. Got it ·chief?" Then "Slam!" to appropriately punctuate her ultimatum.

I, neither being an artifact nor having an historical, cultural or ergonomic value, was attended to with less of her determined acquisitiveness. "Hey," she looked me over, I wasn't sure if she was staring at my apparatus-free person or at the marks left on my torso by the Intrafacer. "I haven't seen you this naked since the fuse room."

"I'm just trying to fit in with the rest of your decor." The apartment could easily be a period room in the Smithsonian, except for the fact that it remained a working, functional living space.

Sizing up her soft, elegant floral print suit capped off with a gently rimmed hat, I wanted to give Angelica my attentions, but the objects of the room grabbed them instead. As I gawked at the fabulous art deco radio, all wood with a twisted sunburst exploding open in front of the speaker, she seemed more flattered than offended, as if I were admiring her luxurious hair or something. "I see you like my Pye radio." She twisted an octagonal knob, turning on an oldies station, just in time for a wild jazzy drum solo. "That's Gene Krupa," she said, like a honey-throated announcer, "playing with Benny Goodman, the King of Swing, doing 'Sing Sing Sing'." I don't know why but I found myself afraid to laugh at all this. I always have trouble laughing when the absurd turns real on me.

She led me into the kitchen past a black Aga stove where iron skillets and steel pots bubbled on the boiling plates, the burners flickering gas, emitting odors stronger than the vegetables cooking above them. I followed her to the Coldspot Super Six, a sleek white refrigerator that boasted the pressed-steel styling of a top-of-the-line Chevy.

"What, no ice box?"

"I used to have one until I picked up this baby."

"Another garage sale?"

"No, even I couldn't find something like this at a garage sale. It took a very well-cultivated relationship with a geriatric friend to get my paws on this," she waved her hands in front of it like a game show model. "Do you believe he was able to buy this for $169.99, and they let him pay for it in easy monthly installments. Even then, they knew how to suck people into bigger, better and newer appliances."

I couldn't get her to shut up about all her thirties still-operating artifacts. I'll spare you the description of the Kenmore Toperator, a primitive washing machine that looked like a huge crock pot on wheels. Nor will I have you live through our romantic moments in front of the Toast-O-Lator; a wondrous gadget that allowed us to feed bread in one side and to view it through a peep hole as it toasts along a conveyor belt, coming out golden crispy on the other end.

I confess I found the demonstrations increasingly amusing after enjoying a king-sized, bizarrely concocted Old Fashioned for which she managed to employ a juicer, a billy-club muddler, and a silver cocktail shaker shaped like a penguin — perhaps being true to the recipe was less important than finding uses for her bar accessories. No matter, my spirits soon became so elevated that I crashed to the floor where I rolled about a heavy, die-cast metal Dinky toy car, much the way Zach used to play with Manubots.

As I collapsed on a wonderfully uncomfortable couch, I asked Angelica: "This is nice and all, but why did you pick the thirties, especially since I pegged you as a girl who would find say, the 50s or the 70s much more appealing."

She thought for a moment and smiled wistfully, "I don't know, I just always had a soft spot for this decade, maybe because it was the last period in this century when the American masses felt deprivation, when the bounty wasn't endless."

The concept seemed too foreign to even contemplate, so I scoped out the room again in search of the exotic, only to lock in on an object oddly familiar.

"You like this?" she said pointing to the faceless dark head of plastic, with a speaker where its countenance belonged.

"No." The hideous, awkwardly shiny mold (even after all these years its tacky slickness undisturbed) sat terribly out of place compared to the other artifacts.

"It's called the Radio Nurse, created in '37 after the Lindbergh kidnapping. In the baby's room would be a microphone and this receiver would be with the parents. I couldn't believe I was so lucky to find it at a garage sale for $10."

"Unbelievable."

"Of course, for that price, they couldn't have the microphone."

"Of course."

"But what would I need with the microphone, since I don't have a baby or anything."

Somehow at this point neither of us had a word to say. She stared at the object, or shall I call her the nurse, and was back yakking again.

"Even though I like the look of it, so ultramodern and ahead of its time and all, the real attraction to it is that it's made out of Bakelite."

"It looks like plastic to me."

She hardly tried to hide her amusement. "Bakelite is a plastic, really the first used widely." From there she kept going, talking away my embarrassments.

"That's why the thirties are so cool. They had the materials of the new era embedded in them, even as the depression dragged on. Plastics changed everything. They made artifacts cheap and therefore disposable."

I chuckled at her endless analysis of her objects, of her trophies. "Do you live in theory or do you live?"

"I live with *things* baby, which is a helluva lot better than living with nothing, see," spreading her arms out wide, and then turning on me, "What do you live with? That fog of a machine, that filthy screen, the moments that fade with every run-down of the battery or intensify with every power surge?"

Changing the subject, I asked her, "Why don't you have the old-time product advertisements, the packing and posters that I always see around? You know, memorabilia?"

"Hey this is not a theme restaurant; this is where and how I live."

"Sorry, you're absolutely right. I guess I'm a bit disoriented that's all."

In no mood to chastise me further, she took my hand and led me off the couch. "You must be hungry, let's eat."

She had cooked chicken in a pot, some canned green beans, split pea soup, and roasted potatoes. Everything was terribly hot and overcooked. On that cold February evening close to Valentine's Day, Angelica and I turned to childhood memories, swapping stories about how we accumulated the scars on our bodies, how I chipped my tooth smacking into a pole during a January sleigh ride, how she earned nine stitches in the eyebrow following a whack with a tennis racket, how my finger gnarled up after I caught a screaming line drive with my bare hand, and how her shoulder skin turned into a freckled mass of melanomas following a summer at Fire Island with no suntan lotion.

Nostalgically, we wondered where have all the wounds gone. What scars do we have from the last couple of decades? Searching and probing our bodies, we could neither see nor touch them. Then we held hands, thinking but never speaking of ways we might be able to open up fresh wounds.

She served me coffee from a double decker Wear-Ever aluminum pot. The coffee tasted old but good. We played Monopoly, but ever-so delicately and daintily, figuring the ancient fake bills were worth more than the currency denominations printed on them. By the time she built hotels on all her properties and largely depleted my money through rental payments, I grew enraptured by her pale powdered, rougeless face, the thin, arched eyebrows, her moist black eyelashes, the intensely languid pupils, the impossibly red lips, the naked ears, the mystery that emerges out of good old bald openness.

"Do you have a camera?" I asked.

"Sure. Try my Beau Brownie," she said, passing me this bizarre box. After a ten-minute explanation from her, I snapped Angelica's portrait. She promised to give me a print, this in lieu of unbridled intimacy, since we were, after all, in a thirties movie — a black and white print, of course.

After I had taken my shot, we both knew the night was over, so I gave her a goodnight kiss that belonged to those 30s movies and stepped out into the end of the century.

Channel 58:
The 7 Synthetic Voyages of Technoman, Voyage IV

My mother shook the dying peach tree, setting free the last two small shriveled pieces of fruit. She was ten now, but she could remember when she was younger the huge bounty of those trees, such that her brother Tony would pelt her with perfectly delicious cherries and pears no one would bother to eat for everyone had his fill. But each year, one or two of those trees grew diseased and rotten, bearing nothing but mangy branches. The peach was the last... it would bear no more. The only thing that seemed to grow any more was the family size — now up to nine. There had been seven in 1937, and nine in '39.

The basement had been transformed into a kitchen, the only place to handle the big stove and the long institutional table, where six nights a week they ate pasta fagoli, fortified by an occasional scrawny chicken that had obliviously stutter-stepped and clucked about the yard.

Outside, mom goofed around with her toy sock, pretending it a snake as she chased the runt pig Ralphie. Soon that mean bitch of a goose Suzie was chasing her. Dropping its long, undulating neck down, Suzie lifted her bill and charged, webbed feet and clipped wings bent on taking mom's kneecap off.

As she dove behind the shed, my father for some reason met her there. He should have been off in Westchester and older than the seven years he appears here. But, nonetheless, mom took dad by the hand and showed him around. Scurrying intensely past them as only a goose can, Suzie now focused on chasing down brother Tony's ass.

Together, my parents looked up at the front of the house. To see it, they had to stand across the road, not because the house was so huge mind you — to fit all those kids in there was a logistical miracle — but because the house was on top of the road, an old servant's quarters for an already run-down small estate (its decay ahead of its time). Standing in the middle of the road, they had no fear of being run over, the only car to ever go by was Grandpa's old flatbed to and from the shop. As they looked at the ugly house longer than any of us would now be capable of concentrating on a stationery object, the spell was only interrupted by mom grabbing her gut, trying to ride out the flips and flops of menstrual cramps. Growing into womanhood far too early, she staggered and stumbled with the pangs of an adolescence that ripped by much faster than the rest of her life.

Trying to support her, dad guided her to the well where they pumped water, smudged charcoal on their teeth and brushed them clean with their fingers, splashing water into their mouths and across their cheeks. Nauseous and fatigued by the drinking and brushing, mom could barely speak when she spotted Millie the chicken clucking by. Doubling over, searching for air, she lifted her head and pointed at Millie, "Get her." So dad was off chasing Millie in a broken field run, in and out of barely standing sheds, wood with rusty nails leaning against their sides waiting for the repairs, across little grass tufts and patches of dusty dirt, following the zigging and zagging chicken. His hunger making him fast and flexible, dad tracked Millie mercilessly. Twice he dove for her snaring only a falling feather, mom's voice strengthening, "Get her." Up again, dust covering his pants like he slid into second base, dad grew angry and supple. He stretched out and snatched Millie's left claw, pulling her in. She pecked him on the hand. "Shit," he said, a rare curse, but then again how often had he been pecked by a chicken? Hands around Millie's neck, he passed mom the prize, struggling past the frantic clucking, flapping, and clawing of the prisoner.

Mom looked at dad oddly, wondering what he was doing, for when she got her hands about Millie's neck, mom snapped it deftly. For a second, dad looked a bit horrified at the suddenly silent and stifled chicken before he came to his manly senses. Mom had seen enough though to take matters into her own hands.

"You wait out here while I clean the chicken."

A little hurt, dad asked, "Can I watch?"

"No. Did you ever smell the inside of a chicken? It stinks."

When mom returned from the shed nearly an hour later, with the plucked and gutted bird, dad was petting Nana, a big old black goat with white speckles and huge full teats almost dragging along the dirt.

"You sure look beat," she said, eyeing dad with the goat. "How 'bout a Nana ice."

"What's Nana ice?"

Without a word, she headed inside, the chicken her ticket to admittance. Dad knew he shouldn't follow for he would not be let in: he could not know the inside of that house. He just stood there trying to figure where each of the family members slept, calculating the doubling and tripling in various beds. About a half hour later, mom returned with two small jars all frozen on the bottom: they had obviously been sitting on a block of ice. Dad wondered which brother did mom have to beat down in order to get that prized jar for him. These meager jars, after all, were the last of Nana's load from yesterday, a miracle that they saw daylight past those dry, thin throats.

Dad drank the frosty goat's milk, thinner and flatter than cow's milk. Somehow it tasted warmer than it should be, like it could never rid itself of the heat in Nana's teat. Thirsty, he tried to savor its tangy sourness, but the jar finished so sharp that he found himself wagging his tongue. "A bit fungusy," he said, trying to comment without complaining about it, "It's like Nana stuck her hoof in it or something." Chuckling, he stuck his tongue in the jar, lapping out the last melting puddles. He made the jar just clean enough so that it served as atonement to mom for the comments about the milk's flavor.

Mom ate her Nana ice more slowly, yet still when she was done, she rubbed her tummy in pangs, the cramps returning. Picking up the jars, she told dad, "wash them," and he went to the well, rinsing them clear. By then, mom carried a bent tin bucket in hand and walked over to Nana. Dad followed.

"Take this rag and put some water on it." Dad obliged and found mom sitting on a stool by Nana. Struggling for breath and looking mighty pale (despite her dark olive skin), she washed the teats with the rag and stepped off the stool.

"Sit down," she told dad. He sat.

"Yank her utters a bit, stretch them out." Dad handled them sheepishly, like they were hanging turds or something.

"Don't be afraid. She needs them tugged." Slowly, he warmed up to the task until mom told him, "Now that's enough."

"Where's the milk?" dad asked.

She giggled, even when another cramp came, she giggled more.

"You grab the teat at the top, like this, and pinch it off with these two fingers, see?" Dad nodded. "Now you make sure you've got a nice sack of milk in there. Then close your hand and squeeze." She aimed the teat at dad's head. "Like this." A sharp stream of hot milk shot against dad's cheek, like thick white piss.

"Augghhhh!" Dad wiped his face. Teasingly, Mom laughed, all the time holding her gut, growing increasingly wan.

"Now you try."

Dad grabbed the teat aggressively, no more squeamishness here, aimed the teat at mom and squeezed. Nothing came out. Falling to the dirt in hilarity, mom rolled about the ground for a few choice seconds before she rose up to go through the milking steps again. This time dad seemed to understand fully, enough so that she warned him, "Now don't try to shoot me because we don't have enough milk as it is." The sobriety of her tone checked any of my father's mischievousness. Too many of her hungry brothers lurked around the ramshackle sheds for him to let a drop miss the bucket.

Assured, he pinched and squeezed as milk splashed into the tin. He pumped and pumped, his wrists weakening and his hands stiffening, but he kept contracting his fists filling that bucket. Soon his right arm grew so engorged with blood it no longer seemed to belong to the rest of dad's body. Though he expected the whole limb to fall off any moment, he would be a man around mom, even if it meant to be a one-armed man at that. So he proudly turned to her after he milked Nana dry. Mom tried to smile approvingly, but her eyes were rolling back up into her forehead and she fell face-first to the earth.

Dad turned her anemic body over, wiping the tiny twigs and muck from her face. She was lost, unconscious. He dipped his fingers into the bucket and slid them gently across her closed lips.

Channel 59:
Making A NewMan

Old man Miller kept his lab coat, but instead of hydrochloric acid and a test tube in his pocket, he carried some Phalo Blue and a one-point, chisel edge paint brush. Each day he made his pilgrimage to the third floor of the Long Island Museum of Modern Art, breezing by "Winter Rhythm," waving to a flushed Marilyn Monroe, straight to Barnett Newman and his painting "One." In earlier days when he had more digits than he knew what to do with, Miller would shove his snout right up to the canvas.

"It's only a line," he'd mutter, hoping someone would hear him, even a guard would do. A field of blue, with one red line, roughly five-sixteenths across the canvas. From his personal measurement, a full cubit from elbow to forefinger of the edge. About once a month Miller wondered when Barnett would get around to finishing up the painting.

Now that he had more time on his hands, Miller decided he'd might as well finish it himself. For weeks he'd been home practicing, lining his pockets so he could get a neat little dab of paint on the brush, dropping a little blue at the top of the line to at least cover a few millimeters. He would hit the top and bottom at first, make it look like Barnett meant for the line to be enveloped by the field of blue. If he did it carefully enough, it would take him only about seven weeks to make that line all Phalo, just a tiny chromatic shadow line on the field, hardly discernible unless a snout was snuffling right up to the canvas. He practiced tirelessly for his brush to become seamlessly an extension of his middle finger, to be whipped out and returned to its holster with the speed of a gunfighter.

The first couple of swipes were hugely successful, along the tops and bottoms he could stipple in almost a whole centimeter, so lax was the security around the Newman, even though the lights would flash just before the brush hit the canvas. As the sensor detectors piled up activity, guards creeped over with greater regularity and Miller had to wait for the changing guard periods to bring the Newman painting any closer to completion.

Whether it was sloppiness or just the law of averages is unclear, but on the eighteenth day, a dignified, and let's just admit it, on-the-beam-Jackson guard actually caught Miller in the act.

"What are you doing?" he asked, a smooth voice and smooth mustache, a veritable keeper of the shrine.

"I just wanted to see how far the line went," answered Miller, beginning a grin in goofy anticipation of being hauled off to jail, mulling over just how he was going to explain this crime to his fellow prisoners.

"What's that in your hand? What were you doing to that painting?"

"Nothing," implying the answer would suit both questions. Miller held out his open hand to the guard. The guard somehow didn't see the brush hooked to the middle finger... any television or surveillance camera would have spotted it, but all the guard saw was what wasn't there — those two missing fingers, he couldn't take his eyes off the mutilated stumps. All that occurred to the guard was the idea that hedge clippers were at the root of the problem here. Miller would not let the sympathy end there. "I'm sorry, when a painting like this one is reduced to the terror of the unknowable I just had to touch it to get a better sense of it."

Miller had his hand back in his pocket quickly; the guard, embarrassed, figured his freak-show staring at the mutilated paw was the cause.

After that moment of crisis, Miller steadily and lovingly completed the painting. Ultimately, Miller had crafted a beautiful blue field, one he could walk into, that every visitor could enter without fighting past the vertical hold Newman offered, his test signal on a cheap TV screen.

Now the painting is nothing at all, and it's a much better work of art for it.

Upon completion, Miller looked again and discovered it wasn't all blue after all, for Barnett Newman's signature broke in at the bottom right of the surface.

"This is no longer a Barnett Newman," he chuckled to himself. Even Barnett Newman would not recognize it as his own. It took Miller three days to blue over the signature. It took him two more days to replace it with an artist more worthy.

He signed it: *Paddy Dangus.*

Channel 60:
Father-Son Talk

Alice brought Zach in with an all-pervasive Americana sweetness that only a father who had grown recently paranoid would suspect. Not that I could find any fault with Alice. She was teaching him state capitals as they headed into the hallway. Yet I noticed something about Zach: his response to every suggestion from Alice was the beautiful, perfectly appropriate response, "Great."

"Make sure you put on chapstick before you head outside because you know that your lips will start bleeding if you're not careful."

"Yeah, great." This "great" was no sardonic response or even perfunctory: you would think Alice just gave him concert tickets.

"If you go to the arcade, try the Manic Geography Trivia Game."

"Great."

"I'll pick you up at seven on Sunday."

"Great."

So when Alice left, and I suggested we spend the day around the house and he said, "Funky," I wasn't as sanguine about his enthusiasm as I normally am. I have always loved when Zach said, "Funky" to me: it meant that he thought whatever I said was really cool. Instead, I was beginning to discover that "Funky" meant that I thought he thought whatever I said was really cool.

"Do you like my new shirt?"

"Funky."

I asked him that question because the one thing I know is that my shirt is not funky; it is repulsive. Even *I* knew that, after all. I got it as a birthday present from senile Aunt Connie who dragged it off a discount rack that seems to specialize in unfunky clothes.

And worse just to throw him off, I give him an Alice request. "Now, in case I forget later, make sure you wear your hat when we go out to dinner tonight because it's a little chillier than it appears."

"Great," he says. That's right, he gave me a "great" instead of a "funky," the reflexive little bastard. Could I find any comfort in the knowledge that he tuned me out with care and alacrity equal to that with which he offered Alice?

To seal matters, Zach put his headphones on and started listening to his tapes. The more I spoke the more convinced I grew that he only heard the walkman. His deliberate withdrawal was less of a surprise than a deflation. Obviously, I am not the first father to find himself completely excluded the moment his child enters into a world with machinery. And yet one of my more erosive fatherhood revelations derives from knowing that I live a series of clichés.

So my kid bobbed and nodded with those headphones on, in his own little world like one of those child actors in so many sitcoms. I grew tempted to make a mocking comment just to test whether I would hear the raucous chuckles from a laugh track.

But I could only pose as the hapless father for so long. After all, ladies and gentlemen, I am Technoman. I tune out the world, the world does not tune me out, and that includes my son. So within a half hour I had bypassed his tape player and his video-game cartridge. Boldly infiltrating his world, I sent a message through his headphones and across his screen with surgical precision.

"Hey there funky son," I said over the airwaves, in a computer generated voice, just to assure I would get his attention. "I've been watching you. I know where you've been going. I know all about your appearance at Crazy Woody's Gadget Shack." Across his monitor I sent a series of explosions and crashes just to assure him of the gravity of this discovery. "You have been lying to you Mom and Dad and that, my boy, is completely unacceptable and inexcusable." Here I made the monitor look like it was short-circuited. "I have trusted you and you have betrayed my trust. You will not be permitted to leave my sight again. Do you understand?"

The whole time the message is transmitting, Zach does not look up once. Now I waited for his reply. For better or worse, he decided to type his message on a monitor with his primitive hunt-n'-peck writing and zip it over to my Intrafacer.

"Im sory."

His type was huge as if to match the magnitude of the crime.

"Yu must
no I didant
meen two
doo dis."

The words came out slow like he was crying while he was communicating.

"I sory.
I jus
wantd two
bee lik yu."

I burned to go over and hug him right then, but I knew I had better give him his space. He didn't even look up once, and I

stopped looking over as to not make him feel uncomfortable.
Fiddling around on the keyboard and scrolling about with his
mouse, Zach struggled with how to explain himself. I calmly and
patiently waited for him to get it all out.

"To begin
with you
must first
understand
this game
is not
for everyone"

I feverishly scrolled down on my monitor hanging on each
word, not sure what he was talking about.

"The best
way to
do this
is to
just plunge
right in."

Here it comes.

"Just plug in
and start
playing
Total
Annihilation
Intergalactic Warfare"

Total Annihilation Intergalactic Warfare? The game? Slowly, I registered that Zach was no longer talking to me. That certainly explains the improved spelling. He must have downloaded the opening blurb of the Intergalactic Warfare game -- of course to pile insult atop insult, it was the game Crazy Woody gave him for the appearance. I lifted my head to glare at Zach, but he was no longer there. The message was just long enough of a distraction to allow him to slip out. What balls this kid has!

Here I was concerned that Zach would be too frightened by my sending the stern message through the headphones, but I was the one frightened now.

Channel 61:
The 7 Synthetic Voyages of Technoman Part V
Dritz, the Junkman

"I cash clothes!" Hayes the ragman sang out, looking to buy the duds dad's thin eleven-year-old frame had grown out of. The parade of peddlers made their way past dad's home, marching across the depression years with their sacks and barrels and bags. There was Platt the knife sharpener and Cohen the fish man and Gallagher the coal man, Baker the milk man, Schmidt the egg man, Procino the fruit and vegetable dealer, and there was Foster the Duggan Bread man who dropped off from an electric car in the winter and from a horse drawn come summer time. They all came to you because they couldn't count on dad and his family making it to them.

But they weren't the only ones to offer services. Increasingly each month more sad sorts, down and outs, came by the house looking to exchange a day's work for a meal. Today one showed up right after Hayes, after dad had collected two bits for a bag of his wool trousers and knit shirts. Out by the well, dad washed his hands with Kirkwood brown soap; the lye ate away at his palms so he dropped them back in the bucket's cool water. With his pa out of town, dad had grown accustomed to handling the day laborers. Somehow they managed to be lost, miserable and hungry without becoming thieves, molesters or murderers. All that was left to do at the house was clip the barberry hedges, a job dad easily could have performed, but he learned early how his own shiftlessness could put food in another's mouth. Handing the nameless man the clippers, dad heads out along the Mount Vernon streets where everyone is selling something but hardly anyone is buying.

The entire town seems to be crying out, to sell becomes breathing, becomes survival... mere survival that is for all but one.

Although no one knew it until long after his death, Dritz owned a house that a good eight or nine of the Mount Vernon three-story stone and stuccoes could fit into. Yet what was Dritz but a junk man, albeit a magnificent junk man, a junk man nonetheless. The WASP housewives out sweeping the walk murmur, "Look at the shabby, ragged old Jew." Always dressed in the destitute clothes of the lowliest of beggars, Dritz in his scraggly miserable beard and his stooped frame made the down-and-out seem comparably upright and respectable. Little wonder not a soul knew of his wealth — nothing is more repulsive to a consumer than a fat, well-dressed peddler. Later in life, dad always puzzled over whether Dritz turned rich by gathering junk, then selling it, or if he procured his money from other means.

Wandering to the western edge of town, dad eventually reached Dritz's huge plot of land where he collected all his junk.

In an old deserted armory, Dritz's twice-chewed empire operated behind great stone walls. Tugging at the thick ivy vines, dad dragged his ass up and over, on into the forbidden world of rejected machinery. Essentially, what Dritz ran was a parts place, for hardly any whole set of equipment worked, but most of the pieces did. Piled up more like in a landfill than a pawn shop, the scattered, broken and mangled equipment collectively created a non-functional universe.

To even get to Dritz, dad shifted a heap of mutilated umbrellas, tilted an old gas tank, and clambered over a discarded washing machine. Notorious for taking anything and everything from the neighbor's garbage, Dritz found his way into the Pines' pails before dad could retrieve a smudged and tattered pad even his rat-packing mother could not help but relinquish.

Stern and wild like an old prophet, Dritz cast a very warm eye at dad until dad opened the palm with the two bits in it. "Can I see what you collected today?"

"I guess."

Unsorted, the booty consisted of mainly bent cans and dirty, rusty tools: nothing had been wiped off and it all stunk to high heaven. Dad searched this crap for a good hour, his hands all cut and sticky. "Didn't you grab a pad?"

Looking lost for minute, Dritz pulled it out of pocket: "You mean this?"

"Yeah," dad noticed how badly Dritz mangled and generally shitted it up in his short term of ownership. The old junk man started inventory lists with a crumby charcoal pencil on the back of the pages and had dog-eared the corners by stuffing it in his stinky ancient peacoat.

"How much you want for it?" Dad asks. The pad was worth a nickel new.

Dritz had seen dad's palm and recognized many decades before his time how age can increase the value of such items.

"Two bits," Dritz spit it out with enough gall that dad didn't even bargain, he just handed over the money. The pad for a short lifetime's worth of clothes.

By the time he returned home, the man had finished the barberry hedges and was collecting money from ma... changing his mind the day laborer asked for cash instead of a big lunch. Dad had just enough time to study the laborer's profile and begin to draw. Some people had a guest sign-in book; dad compiled a visual history.

When I was eleven, dad showed me that pad. He basically drew the same man eighty-three times, the last being in '41, believe or not, when I later was taught the depression had long ended, just four months before Pearl Harbor. When I thumbed through the drawings, I remember trying to act more excited by the father-son sharing than I was. Sadly, dad drew like an eleven-year-old.

I never saw the pad again. Yet whenever I awaken from a Somnoid dream, I behold that damn pad, each picture flicking by like a card in an animated deck. I sit up with that pad stifling my thoughts, unable to progress, my mind a disk laboring to be called up on the hard drive, somehow lost between positions, a clock icon telling me to wait, never quite engaged nor ejected, just trapped with the only means to escape being to reboot the machine.

And there's the pad, too clear are the amateurish drawings for foggy visions. Never milky, I see his collection of one-faced ne'er-do-wells through a weak, calm glance, a mental state not quite up to speling correctly.

In those lost hours of the night, I retrieve the way my father retrieved who in all my years I never saw throw away a thing. The remnants of my broken, mushy cooked carrots and my mashed potatoes, gravy grossly coagulating, always ended in his plate, down his gullet. How else could I explain why he never threw me away?

And tonight, as many, too many nights have gone, I hurl myself over the stone wall with two bits in my hand talking to Dritz.

Channel 62:
Not *My* Secret World

from the Journal of Little Augie
When I regained consciousness, Satan was talking, talking as he has continuously since Adam and Eve wandered into the land of Nod. Even in a morgue, his odor predominated, one of breathing excrement.

"But the world was already running through my fingers even as I grasped it fully for the first time. Things seemed promising, not only with Defoe and the other scribblers, but with the large-scale emergence of the Freemasons, a secret society of devil worshipers if I ever met one. I'm still grappling with what happened next. For me, it was one of those endless falls, such a fall that an optimist could describe it as a resurrection."

Satan had been talking to himself for quite some time, but now he was talking to me, or at least he was talking on the record for publication.

"Even as Defoe was working for me, Antoni van Leeuwenhoek was working against me. I would have known how to handle him if he were acting for the glory of God, but he was out there grinding the lens of his microscope and looking at semen, of all things, finding the spermatozoa, finding creation. What a blow to the Lord of Life! I was a little slow in realizing what a blow to me."

Satan removed his overcoat. At his sides rested his intricately folded wings. I had not seen them previously and he caught me gawking at them before I could turn away, so he spread the soft, sable appendages out majestically. He could still grab one's attention.

"With his microscope, Leeuwenhoek tapped into a secret world that had nothing to do with me — a world pricks like Leonardo and Newton seemed to find without instrumentation, but now Leeuwenhoek provided for the common schmuck a powerful magnifying glass to that hidden world. Nor did it help that Vitus Bering was navigating and charting hidden openings in the manifest world. How could man focus on just my secret world when I could have no monopoly?"

Restlessly, Satan began flapping his wings and before I knew he flew about the low-ceilinged morgue, a ghostly raven who glided about the dead. He landed behind a curtain sheltering new bodies and spoke to me through the veil like I was his confessor.

"I thought things would get better after Newton's death: they only got worse. Shit, Linnaeus was classifying plants, Bonnot was spouting empiricism, Black was finding hidden heat during the melting phase, Cavendish was discovering "inflammable air," Priestley was composing an electrical history, Holbach was philosophizing a godless, mechanistic interpretation of the universe. It was insane, the advancements piled atop each other: Black and Cavendish were pulling gases out of thin air, and Priestley added more, while Lavoisier reduced water to hydrogen and oxygen. Everybody was jumping aboard: Rutherford, Scheele, along with Priestley and Cavendish all discovered nitrogen independently. If I stopped one guy, another would jump in. There were just too many. To make matters worse, Herschel built a telescope that could look into an angel's asshole if so required."

Beyond the sight of him, where he was merely an echo and beating wings, I grew suspicious. His presentation had been designed and marketed for my consumption. How could a woman of science resist such a litany of names, such a flattering compliment from the dark angel to my sensibilities? He sounded too much like the victim and even as I reconsidered, he redirected, for he followed:

"Not that I didn't try to stop the madness. Mere scientific knowledge could not harm me without physical applications, and who could have predicted I would have had my greatest problems controlling the spread of invention. When Kay invented the flying shuttle and cut the mill operatives' labor in half, I screwed him. I sent the message that inventors would gain nothing from their efforts, that technological advancement would only mean personal pain. But not even I could undermine the financial boons that result from time and labor-saving advancements."

Satan pulled the curtain away and looked hypnotically into my eyes. He was transforming again, as the wings drew inward. He was no angel or demon, but now just a frail little man, all vulnerability and openness — an accessible, approachable vessel that belied his language.

"I grew increasingly desperate, even taking the godlike measure of the terrible Lisbon earthquake. But the fuckers, instead of shutting down for a while, they started studying the causes of the land shaking and rattling. They did not want to create the world, they wanted to solve it."

Now he appeared to me as nothing less than a Man of Sorrows. Even though he cast the shadow of a fallen angel, I thought I saw Adam and Christ wandering around his eyes. If I hadn't prudently glanced down at his hairy ankles and hooves, I would have most naturally held him in the bosom of compassion and consolation.

"I don't think I felt closer to God since my rebellion than when all those secret worlds rose beyond me, transcended me. Sure I knew of them, but who figured they would fascinate man?... it all seemed like intolerably dull textbook fodder. What were these physical secrets, hidden molecules and currents? Where was the temptation, the allure, the physical beauty, the attraction? Much later on Freud was some help, but even with his dreams, his id, his subconscious, he could keep hope alive short-term. Incredibly my incorrigible magnetism and Freud's demons of the mind disintegrated once the pharmaceuticals were passed around at the psychiatric clinics."

As Satan spoke, he grew increasingly turbulent, shuddering and shaking like an angry old man who had been cheated out of his social security. Seeing him simultaneously intense and beaten down, I waited for a blood vessel to pop, some aneurysm perhaps like my Clarence had a few months before a massive stroke killed him. But Satan kept talking, ignoring every graceful and mannered social signal I offered to quiet him down.

"What the hell? Even I tried some of these," pulling a rainbow of pills from his pocket, "... not half bad..." I waited for him to press ahead.

"Shoveling shit against the tide, I say," breathing heavy, winded, struggling. "Fighting," more gasps, "the good fight."

I tried to interrupt, to lift him, to soothe him, to ease his pain, but he waved me off, gathering his energies for some final words. "The fire down below has been extinguished."

With that he collapsed on one of my morgue stretchers, sprawling out stiff, pretending to be a corpse, mocking the dead even as he seemed nearer to joining them.

"Put me in cold storage; it'll make me feel like one of those vampires. At the very least, I could get a role playing Dracula."

I obliged his wish. As I shut the stainless steel drawer, I heard him whistling an old folk song... I think it was "O John Henry."

Channel 63:
Get the Message?

February — Pines Tar: Was That Rush Hour?

Following the first night of the full moon, my morning commute started like the opening scene of a horror flick. Along with so many a commuter that morning, the first electronic highway message sign that greeted me read:

"THIS RIDE WILL NOT BE A SMOOTH ONE."

I should have been philosophical about the warning ... What trip on Long Island roadways is a smooth one? But I, like everyone else knew, Paddy Dangus was the one putting his stamp on the rush hour by controlling the signs — that's got to be a sunrise coffee stain on a driver's trousers. As if heeding the message, the cars in front of me started to slow cautiously, the way commuters do when they spy an accident or emergency vehicles in the offing.

I clicked on the radio to get a traffic update, slogging through a series of commercials, only to receive the following comment from the newsradio anchorman: "As for traffic today, we seem to be experiencing some technical difficulties at Transit Central. According to our Nexar SuperDopplerRadar map we have gridlock everywhere across the highways, which we know cannot be accurate. Furthermore, the only data we are receiving on our screens is the superfluous question. HAVE YOU DEVOTED THIS TIME TO DRIVING IN YOUR CAR? We will provide a traffic update the minute our systems are up and running again."

As if everyone on the highway heard the same report or a similar one (a friend tells me on the other stations they provided a briefer, less detailed explanation of technical difficulties), we collectively tapped the breaks and then inched forward, waiting for the impending jam up. We puttered along for the next few miles until we rode up to the next sign.

"THERE IS TRAFFIC ON ALL MAJOR ROADWAYS, THERE ARE BACK-UPS, ACCIDENTS AND CONSTRUCTION DELAYS."

The message was just vague and innocuous enough to give hope that Department of Transportation officials had regained control of the electronic boards -- even though they obviously as of yet could not organize traffic data. Most assuring was the veracity of the statement, since we figured Dangus had no interest in providing accurate information, no matter how useless it is. We figured wrong, as we soon discovered upon crawling up to the next message board.

"DO YOU EVER PASS A SIGN WITHOUT READING IT?"

Feeling increasingly helpless, I clicked on the NorthCom state-of-the-art-traffic analyzer in my Smart Car. Damn, what else would scroll across the screen but "DO YOU EVER PASS A SIGN WITHOUT READING IT?" A week after Valentine's Day, Dangus was sending no love letters. Traffic stumbled and tumbled to a halt as each commuter independently responded to the messages at a different pace and rhythm, so much so that a few bumpers were kissed or rapped. Fortunately, or I *guess* fortunately, I sat stuck right in front of the message board, like it was my own personal drive-in movie. After about five minutes, a new message flashed.

"YOU ARE READING A MESSAGE BOARD. THAT IS WHAT YOU ARE DOING."

For the ensuing five minutes, I continued to read the sign, trying to interpret it. The maroon Lexus in front of me with the vanity plate "HOOPSHAPPY" lurched five feet forward, but I wasn't moving since I'd lose view of the sign, and after all, considering the speed at which we were going, what was the difference anyway? Unfortunately the green Tercel with the "THINK GLOBALLY, ACT LOCALLY" bumper sticker disagreed and was bomping at my Smart Car vehemently, an occasional fist shaking out the window on this cold winter's morning. Maybe it was all the distractions that made me struggle in my understanding of the sign. But no matter, another five minutes later a new message flashed on.

"THIS MESSAGE BOARD IS FULLY OPERATIONAL AND IS FUNCTIONING JUST FINE, THANK YOU."

Again hope swelled in the bosom of every commuter that perhaps the Department of Transportation had regained control of the electronic message board, if not the traffic itself. Like those times over the radio when we hear of a huge accident finally cleared from the roadway, we waited for relief just around the next turn. But relief did not come in the next five minutes; instead a new message was delivered.

"TRAFFIC WILL BE LOVELY AT 2:00 A.M. ON NIGHTS WHEN THE MOON IS FULL."

I bet it will. The rush hour hell seemed endless. I concluded Dangus would hold on all day. I revised that conclusion when the next message came up ten minutes later, one that gave all of us more than hope.

"NORMAL TRAFFIC CONDITIONS AHEAD."

Now that was a message we were familiar with. Normal traffic conditions are acceptable. That means the Department of Transportation has a handle on the situation, and we'll all be getting to work soon. And as if someone opened a magic gate somewhere in the distance, the traffic started to roll forward again, at first punctuated by short taps of the accelerator and the brake, but soon eased to a steady five miles per hour, then ten, then fifteen, and finally up to twenty. Normal traffic conditions indeed! We gladly took twenty the rest of the way in. The signs kept reading the same message, and we kept going at the same pace with nary a pause.

When I walked into the *Herald* newsroom, I caught an earful from every commuter in the office (which meant every employee and customer) about how Dangus ruined the morning. Then I made some calls to the State Highway Police. Captain Richard Striker said he couldn't even tell me how bad conditions were since his patrol cars could not get from one sector to another, their vehicles trapped in the same hideous gridlock as the rest of us.

. Detective Richard Mason, who has been tracking Dangus for the past six months, was already armed with data by the time I contacted his office at noon. "Six accidents and two fatalities, all because of Dangus's prank. People don't seem to realize how serious this situation has become. Like most terrorists, Dangus is pure and simply a murderer."

The victims were Alice Flick of Huntington, who had dedicated most of her life to charity work, and Peter Karp, a real estate broker for Century 21. Dave Miller, whose unauthorized biography of Dangus comes out in a few months, argued that Dangus cannot be held responsible for these deaths.

"Tell me the last day no one died in an accident on Long Island roads and then you can start criticizing Dangus," said Miller. "He didn't knock out the traffic lights or reverse one-way signs or erect dangerous roadblocks or something like that. He just communicated with us over the electronic message board. I think it was one of his kinder, gentler moments."

Nonetheless, others are not as willing to read good intentions from Dangus's latest highjinks. As Dangus returns monthly with his disruptive visitations, more citizens seem to be questioning his intention and purpose. What is his point after all? "After a while, you have got to ask yourself why doesn't Dangus just leave us alone?" asked moderate Congressman Robert Hockney, long a voice of the people. "What have we ever done to him that he would do this to us?"

This column has been brought to you by the fine people at Fort Knox Computer Systems who produce the world's most secure data resources. With specialized three-dimensional encryption codes, Fort Knox provides its customers with the type of tightly sealed network that even Paddy Dangus can't penetrate.

For more information, call 1-800-CLOSE-ME.

Channel 64:
Polishing Jeremiah

Angelica sprayed Fido the GigaPet with a blast of Fantastik.
"What are you doing?" I looked at her with horror.
"Giving the pooch a bath."
"Won't that hurt him?"
"You? You're concerned about my use of cleaning fluids on Fido? You? The talking toxic waste site?"
When she was done with Fido, Angelica eyed up the rest of the place. "How could you treat your things this way? Every piece of equipment you have here in your house needs either to be serviced, cleaned or repaired. Don't you care about your stuff at all?"
"Sure I do," feeling a bit embarrassed, remembering my early maintenance vigilance as Technoman.
"Well, start acting like it."
I now understand that Angelica truly loves me, just by the way she treats all my possessions. Yesterday, she took my

SmartCar to Jiffy Lube and then to the CarWash. I ask you
reader could such care be anything less than love?

Lying on the bed watching her cleanse and purify my space, I
clicked the remote, scrolling from channel to channel long enough
to catch an image and a phrase: "the final umbrella, national
security, *hair-care product*, premature ejaculations,
top-twenty countdown, you wascally wabbit, *lift those thighs,*
I can't go on like this, hits the three-pointer, call now, *you can't
go Lucy*, have you used the move?, I'm falling and I
can't get up, oh sugar that's right, life begins anew for the
salmon, that's not a sabersaw Al, *Hitler's propaganda
campaign*, Cindy Crawford's new movie— "

"Hey!" I protested as Angelica grabbed the remote from me.
"I was watching that."

"Watching what?" she examined the buttons. "Yuch, how can
you hold this thing? It's disgusting."

"Yeah, but it's the only one I got."

"It's filthy," furiously shooting the Fantastik at it, attempting
to wipe away years of dust, gunk and germs.

As she cleaned across the buttons, more images and phrases
fly across the screen. "*Somebody stop me*, I'm sick of you
Clarisse, *You're supposed to be my best friend and then
you make love to my husband?*, the Lord said unto David,
the Universe is linked by strings, Nostradamus predicted all
these things, *now we'll never get off this island*, Father
Jeremiah saved me, the Klingons will join the alliance, *you go
girl*, Princess Di marched through the land mines, are you really
the invisible man?, Gainey breaks up the blue line pass, Sir you
haven't been listening, what a pair of knockers on her, *sangue
qua sangue*, only forty-nine hats left— "

Slow registering, I finally halted the cleansing process.
"Father Jeremiah?"

I clicked back to the "Father Jeremiah" comment trying to
remember where I heard that name before, originally thinking it
part of a hit song currently being overplayed on the F.M. stations.
I had to hear one older fellow repeat the name again, then I finally
associated the figure with Little Augie's Journals. Two men were
interviewed by Wilfredo Holmes, who if you haven't seen him is

one of the better talk show hosts out there. With talk shows now overparodied, Wilfredo decided to make his show a parody of a parody so that the interview became nothing less than very serious business, even Wilfredo's tone indicates that the last thing he'd ever take serious was serious business.

I tried to listen over Angelica's frantic spraying, as every gadget in her sight caught a dose of her ionic love. While she washed away a layer of film from my life, two figures I eventually understood to be Hank and Bill spoke of the man they called their savior. With his huge craggy forehead filling much of the screen, Bill did much of the talking.

"From the minute he came over to my bed, Father Jeremiah had a light around him that I can only describe as angelic."

"Pretty weird, Bill."

"Yeah, tell me about it. I thought he was there to take me to heaven. Who knew he would instead save me for earth?" Obviously, I must have missed the whole stories of Bill and Hank's illnesses, which was O.K. since Little Augie gave a pretty good idea of how far gone they were. Their mere appearance on television was sufficient to now make me a believer of everything Little Augie wrote in her journal.

"So are you saying he's an angel?"

"No, I'm not saying anything. I'm just saying I was at death's door and he brought me back to life. Now I can mow my lawn and I can watch TV on my couch." The audience spontaneously applauded at this revelation.

"That's very heart wrenching, that's very beautiful," said Wilfredo in a tone indicating the saving of Bill's life could well have been neither.

As Hank described his magical healing process and how Father Jeremiah touched him all over, Angelica cleaned my Intrafacer. Folks, she cleaned it while I still wore the thing, delicate fingers running gracefully across my keypad, fondling my mouse, breathing her steamy breath onto my monitor and wiping it away. She took her time and was still going at it when a doctor from St. Francis came on verifying the gravity of their illnesses and the incredible recovery of the patients. "I am a doctor and men of science usually don't say such things, but what happened to these two men was a... Miracle." The television audience was wildly pleased.

Using a soft cloth, Angelica slowly and softly rubbed my wires, right down to the scuzzy port. She was cleansing me, baptizing me, and I became a new man. Sweetly she whispered to me cheap movie dialogue, "Is that a hard drive in your pocket or are you just happy to see me?" I laughed deeply the laugh of grand dreamy contentment. Can I tell you I haven't had such an erotic and arousing experience in a long time.

Two other guests came on, claiming they were also saved by Father Jeremiah. As I mentioned before, I didn't hear Bill and Hank's full stories, but I can't imagine they were as sketchy as these two, as the physical description of Father Jeremiah progressed no further than a bearded man, monk-like in a long, hooded robe. Wilfredo, too cognizant that these two may well be sham artists, cut them off quickly and returned to Hank and Bill.

"You know the strangest thing is," said Hank, "I never saw Father Jeremiah before he healed me and I haven't seen him since. In fact, I have found no one at the hospital who has seen him except on that one magnificent day."

The show was coming to its end and as if to keep everything neat, Angelica was finishing her thorough job on my Intrafacer. Bill ended the discussion with a plea: "Father Jeremiah, if you are out there, thank you man. I love you. Remember that others need saving too, others need your gift."

Because of either the subject matter or the cleansing, I kept the Wilfredo Holmes show on the entire twenty minutes, the longest distance I have gone with unpaid programming since 1993. Completely relaxed, feeling shiny and new, I fell asleep in Angelica's arms like a newborn. With her one free hand, she returned to cleaning the remote.

Channel 65:
Remote Language

Until I pulled up to Geoffrey Sphere's mansion on a spit of land between the ocean and Mecox Bay out in Bridgehampton, I had no idea of the old inventor's wealth. Little wonder

Prometheus Laboratories had been able to fight off two hostile takeovers, even during those days when Sphere's frontal lobe was exploding.

After the old guy who played the role of the butler took my coat, I relieved myself in an outrageous fuscia marble bathroom that ascended twenty feet to a porcelain campanile. My piddling echoed and whooshed into a rushing waterfall. I won't even describe the flush.

In a ridiculously sharp white suit — especially since it is March and all — Sphere greeted me looking every bit the Jay Gatsby or the Tom Wolfe or whoever currently evokes the past and embodies the fantasy of Long Island's affluent mystery. He held court with an intimate cadre of guests: Linda, the Dean of Mount Holyoke; Charles, the grand bourbon distributor from Alabama, and JoJo, the self-made carpet mogul who rolled his Brooklyn burbers and shags out to the swanker shopping malls of the Gold Coast. I, playing the role of Technoman, completed the carefully orchestrated quartet. Two drinks behind, I caught up quickly as Sphere demonstrated his latest advancement with the Universal Remote — voice-activated capability.

"What is the biggest hassle with the remote?" he hardly waited for anyone to answer — "The buttons. First finding the right one, then pushing it, although the present company knows well how to push buttons." The quartet smiled and chuckled, appreciating the admittance inside the compliment.

"Especially with a Universal Remote, where the buttons mean different things for different appliances. Very confusing for the masses." And yes he said "masses" with sufficient contempt to exclude the quartet.

"Now with this new voice activation remote, I just have to say –'Turn on the C.D. and' — " Miles Davis's cool opening signature from Kind of Blue wafted through the speakers, "Wallah."

We appreciated the showmanship, an audience to a most urbane and elite infomercial. Over the boisterous conversation of four dominant types enjoying the fine cocktails, Sphere, the powerful sorcerer, continued making demands of his machine, turning on microwaves, ranges, blenders, cuisinarts, toaster ovens, espresso makers.

The intimacy of the evening made me eventually flip up my monitor and swap stories and jokes with the other guests. Steadily and skillfully, Sphere tugged away each of the other guests to be alone with his remote. I eavesdropped on his request of JoJo as I told the others of my bizarre rock-star style appearance at a computer convention.

"I'm trying a little experiment: I've been tinkering with the voice activator and I want to see if it responds to a particular modulation." Sphere pulled JoJo close, giving him the old *sotto voce.* "Just ask it to put on the cuisinart."

JoJo couldn't have been more open and willing, speaking to the remote like he was talking to one of his carpet installers: "Hey, tewn ahn da keysanart."

The cuisinart gives the silent treatment.

"Good," Sphere said reassuringly, "you've been very helpful."

JoJo seemed pleased too. "Pieca shit," he mumbled. A few polite minutes later Linda was lured to the remote. Sphere, more *sotto voce,* gently urged Linda to ask it to get his Lexus going.

"Remote Control, unlack tha ca. Staat tha ca."

Out the window she looked to see if the Lexus lights up, flashes and purrs. Sphere didn't even bother to check; he knew his luxury vehicle would be dumb to such a request.

Charles was next. "How about you get the remote to fire up the toaster oven?"

"Cluehk ahwn dat toedsta uvin, wouldya?"

Given the experiment, I wondered what Sphere scratched about for when he called me over. He started with the same request he gave JoJo. A bit mischievous, I passed along my best Brooklyn accent to the grand unresponsiveness of the remote. It just blinked, subtly signaling me that I must be inadequately communicating. I gave the next request straight in my most mechanical voice and the cuisinart whirred instantaneously. I followed with a call to the Lexus in haughty Boston nasality, but Sphere's machine didn't know from New England clam chowder, so then I spoke in the slow impersonal language of the remote and

jump-started the engine. Naturally, I gave the toaster oven a
Southern dialect, subsequently followed by a cold, clear monotone
and soon the mozzarella sticks were warming.

Completing my work here, I wanted to say "Hey, you think
Zach is the only Pines clan member who can do voices," but I
figured since I had been lucid with the machine, why should I
confuse everyone else in the room?

Little time passed before Sphere cornered me and proposed
that I create a tape instructing consumers how to speak properly
to the remote control. I asked the obvious, "Why don't you just
give the voice activation system learning capabilities so it can
pick up regional dialects?"

Amused by my comment, perhaps he thought it was naive,
Sphere shook his head: "Do you realize how many staff members
I had to employ just to get it to this point? I even stole away Tony
Phillips," he said the name like I should recognize it. Then he
continued, gawking at me like he was talking to a moron or
something, "The best voice activation man in the business?" I
tried to pretend I understood. "Anyway, Tony said we would be at
least eighteen months away from any such design. With the
current prototype, we could introduce this sucker a month from
now."

Now it was my turn to look incredulous. And yet allowing for
Sphere's standard hyperbole, I grew impressed that with all the
setbacks, he'd still have his remote, new and improved mind you,
out in... perhaps... ten weeks time.

"No, I can't put the extra investment in right now. I've got to
get this out before SONY puts out its model and before Digital
Associates returns for another bid on the company. The tape will
be just the thing we need."

"Then why don't you get an anchorman to do this?"

"I thought about that, to be honest with you. But I think you
just might be the right man at the right time. Hey you're hot right
now, and those goofy accents of yours might just make the tape
damn entertaining. Anyway, do you realize what I am offering
you? Your voice will define the way we talk to our machines for
years to come. I even have the name for it: RemoteSpeak. Eh?
You like? I thought of Remote Language, but RemoteSpeak is

faster, like the instrument itself. Think about it. Your voice will come off a machine, the consumer will imitate your voice; it will be picked up anywhere in the house, bounced into the sensors to the remote, the remote will respond and bounce its signal back off the sensors and the command will shoot off to the appliance. Yours will be the voice of a god."

I laughed at the absurdity of the statement, even as I pulsed with charges of electricity surging through me.

Shit, I *am* Technoman.

RemoteSpeak. Wait until Dangus gets wind of this — and Dangus will get wind, since he is even more wired and connected than Technoman.

"How are you feeling? Any more seizures?"

"No, I've never felt better. Why do you ask?"

"No reason."

Even if I professed a reason, Geoffrey would not have been interested, since he was too busy talking about the script and booking a recording studio and about his increasingly large staff and his careful expansion of responsibilities for Carmen and about his plans to introduce the prototype at one of the huge high-tech conventions in Manhattan either next month or the following month. In other words, Sphere no longer acted as the engaging host, and the quartet soon took the hint and took our collective leave.

Outside in front of the driftwood shingles, JoJo spoke to his cell phone, telling a stout-armed, big-bellied minion in Flatbush to get some indigo double-density, scotch-guarded shag into his Econoline and over to Bridgehampton in a hurry because we have a carpeting emergency out here. Linda dragged a videocamera from her Beemer and recorded the image of the prototype remote. Exalting the model's sleek ergonomic design, Linda communicated with the camera beautifully, her words completing the image, even at times fully seizing the visual space. Meanwhile, Charles plugged in his portable fax machine, zapping out an order for a case of 18-year-old Jack Daniels to show up at Sphere's doorstep within the hour.

In wee tickings of the night, Sphere sprawled out on the floor across his new shag, a glass of the finest JD in his hand, watching a videotape of Linda's paean to his prototype remote. In fact he turned the TV and tape on with the very instrument.

Even though I appeared to have left with the others, I actually hung around, since I felt the need to bond with that remote, if it was going to be my partner in the upcoming weeks. I reactivated my Intrafacer and pumping up the sound, made it talk back to me in a variety of computer-generated voices. When I noted how well the prototype responded to my Intrafacer, that's when I knew we would all get along together just fine, thank you.

.Channel 66:
A Rival Paper's Take on Technoman

It's Official: Technoman's a Fad

One definition of a fad is something that catches on which had no right whatsoever to succeed in the world. Mindful of that definition, Technoman must now be considered a fad, as bars are filled with patrons in Technoman costumes while media coverage of his columns and activities has reached absurd proportions. So when TV tabloid magazines follow Technoman [a.k.a. Russell Pines] around the supermarket, even *The Daily News* has to take note.

Ironically, Technoman has gained fame most prominently not for his own exploits, but for his coverage of the anti-technology underground figure Paddy Dangus. As Dangus has inveigled his way increasingly into our consciousness, so, like the ramora to the shark, has Technoman. *The Daily News* even contacted through secret and carefully cultivated sources the almost impossibly reclusive Dangus. And for the first time in the history of the media, Paddy Dangus has spoken — a *Daily News* exclusive, not even Technoman can make such a boast.

"I can't comment on Technoman," said Dangus, filtered through a number of intermediaries, "but he does merit comment if I did that type of thing, which I don't."

One of Technoman's journalistic subjects and a self-proclaimed friend, Dave Miller, supported Pines' column work. "He's the only one out there telling the truth. He uncovers what is beneath all the complicated networks, smoke screens and jargons in the world today. He's the only one telling the truth, except of course for that fine, young reporter Rafter Simpkins, whose been blowing the lid off that conspiracy about aliens landing in the New Mexico desert."

Good journalist or not, Technoman has received the kind of fan adulation usually reserved for cult science fiction actors. One rumor reports that he gets paid at least $100,000 just to put in an appearance at a high tech convention. Furthermore, a call-in on-line chat with Technoman garnered the greatest number of hits at any time since the introductory offer for time-release Demerol.

"What Technoman provides is common sense talk and examples in a time that has no common sense at all," said sociologist Harold A. Kennedy. "Here is a man fearlessly walking through the furious hail of phenomena that is neo-postmodern life. What could be more heroic?"

Not everyone buys into Pines' identity as Technoman however. His ex-wife, Alice Pines, explains, "I love Russell and all, but Technoman? We are talking about a man who can't figure out how to put batteries into a flashlight."

Whether Technoman is a mere charlatan or the Pied Piper to a new age is only one of the debates surrounding a cultural icon whose face seems perpetually blocked by a screen. Doctors have been considering the possible health effects of Pines' new lifestyle. Some even predict that he will be dead before his yearlong experiment comes to an end.

"Obviously, this mode of living cannot be good for Mr. Pines," said Dr. Patrick Salatto. "Most living organisms can only take in so many toxic substances before their metabolic functions just give up. He's essentially making himself an environmental Superfund waste site. Even if he gets through the year, with all the chemicals he's pumping into himself, Mr. Pines cannot be long for this world."

Some scientists who spoke on condition of anonymity said they look forward to the day they can cut him open and take a look inside. "It's bad enough that I think when he takes off the Intrafacer he'll have that pasty, half-cooked look that Darth Vader revealed when he finally pulled off his helmet. But imagine the fluids in that body of his and what they must be doing to his organs."

Other representatives of the medical field are much more optimistic that Pines will be around long after the Technoman fad has faded. "What doesn't kill you makes you stronger," said Dr. Matthew Walker. "We should note that Pines is not dead and by all conventional wisdom should be. Think about the antibodies, immunities, individual adaptability and personal resiliency he has developed. He may be equipping himself better than most for the future. Anyway, given his diet, the man's a walking preservative. He may be around decades beyond the rest of us."

Channel 67:
Satan the Giftgiver

from the Journals of Little Augie

He stepped out of cold storage with a beautiful locked case in his long fingernails. Like an innocent suitor, he passed me the case and handed me the key. Awkwardly, I blushed.

"What's this?"

"For you."

"Should I open it?"

"I'd like you to but you don't have to."

"You'd like me to."

"Yes, you've got the key if you want to use it."

All in-laid silver with enough details to pass for a Roman sarcophagus, the case belonged in a museum. I wanted to open it, but how can I open such a present from such a giver? Beware of Satan bearing gifts. A new age Pandora's box. What? What?

He said nothing. Instead he lit a cigarette. I hadn't noticed before that he smoked. He looked a little like Joe Camel when he puffed. Hardly did he seem to care whether I put the case up on the shelf next to my specimen jars or cracked it open.

After more anxiety than deliberation, I turned the key and opened the box... I must say I was most surprised by his conventionality. He gave me a silver necklace, a simple elegant cut that glowed and sparkled even in the dim morgue lighting.

"You shouldn't have," I said, draping the jewels across my neck.

"You're right, but I couldn't help myself, my little Gretchen." Gretchen? I let it go, figuring it was a term of endearment.

"Would you help me put it on."

"I'd love to."

I looked in the mirror and Satan came up behind me — should I have been able to see him, I would have caught a most sinister smile.

"You look like a million dollars. How do you feel?"

"Wonderful."

"That's because you are dying."

I paused for a minute, not sure whether to take him seriously. He didn't wait for me to figure out what he was trying to say.

"Do you feel a tingling sensation?"

"Yes..." I said hesitantly, as much a question as an answer.

"That's because you are wearing radioactive plutonium. You wear it well." Then he added gleefully, "Look, you are positively glowing."

Oddly, in this devastating moment, I took the high road, more concerned for his immortal soul than for my terminal carcass. "What have you disintegrated to? A petty villain in a James Bond film."

"You cannot shame me into getting your life back. Your cells are being riddled with malignancy as we speak, multiplying, spreading."

"You've contaminated everyone."

"It's a morgue, my little Augie. Everyone is dead."

"Oh. Still..."

"Everyone is dead that is but you and I, my little Gretchen."

I tugged desperately at the necklace, fumbling with my fingers, trying to snap open the latch. I was wasting my time. I might as well try breaking adamantine chains.

"How long do I have?"

"I'd say 72 hours at most."

"Don't you want me alive? How can I be your chronicler if you don't let me survive?"

"Why do you want to live?"

"Because I don't feel like dying."

"I do."

"Is that why you've been on this endless journey of yours sniffing around every toxic site you could get near?"

"You know about Chernobyl?"

"Of course I do. There is not much you can hide from me, you dark angel you." I wasn't finished with my interrogation though. "How did you get the plutonium anyway?"

He said nothing, but stepped back, appearing absurdly ashamed. He gave himself away.

"Look at you. You can't stay away from it, can you?"

He pretended he didn't know what I was talking about.

"You're a nuclear junkie. That's all you are. Pathetic. Just pathetic. My, the mighty hath fallen." I do not know if it is the radioactivity or what, but I grow strong and cruel.

"I will save your life, if you would like."

"I would like."

"Then I will."

"Why did you decide to kill me in the first place?"

"I figured I owed it to you."

"How will you save me?"

"By sucking the poison from you."

"But won't you be contamin... hey, I see, you are just using me to kill yourself."

"Why didn't I just put on the necklace in the first place then."

"Would you do anything that directly?"

"Absurd, but I do believe you care about me; I haven't come across anyone who's been so interested in me since that doctoral candidate from Texas in the early 90s."

"Well, I can tell you this: I care much more about my life than I care about yours, so let's get back to that part of the discussion."

"I will heal you, if you do one thing for me."

"What?" I had a bit of hostility in my voice, since his one thing usually has a way of multiplying.

"Promise to burn my corpse when I die."

"Aren't you immortal?"

"That makes matters more difficult... Just promise true that you will cremate my last remains."

"But you would be the corpse of the millennium. Science and research — "

"Fuck science and research. Don't let them carve me up like a Christmas turkey."

"I promise."

"O.K., sign here then."   ·

No contract in my life did I peruse so obsessively as the lovely document he rolled out in front of me. It looked like the Declaration of Independence. After assuring myself that the word "soul" was not mentioned once in the agreement — I would lose merely my life if I reneged — I signed with a flourish.

With that, Satan donned the black collar and transformed himself into Father Jeremiah. He gently touched my forehead and drew his palm slowly down my body. Cells were correcting their irregularity and my body healed as easily as it was contaminated. The good father's own person took the cure hard though, even as he let loose a hollow, morose laugh that echoed through his dry lungs.

"A couple more of these and I should be dead within a week."

Straightening his collar, he headed out of the morgue with a visionary look in his eyes that intimated he would be embarking on another long journey. Feeling rejuvenated, I followed him. As I opened the morgue door, the necklace fell off me. Hearing the jangling, he stopped, straightening his neck, waiting for me to put the jewelry on him.

As we wandered out into the sweet clean light of day, he displayed it to me proudly, like one does a retirement watch.

Channel 68:
Heather Marks, or Sex at a Senior Citizen Discount

If you haven't figured it out by now, I've avoided the *Herald* newsroom as much as possible since I became Technoman. My absence explains how so many months could pass without me ever catching a glimpse of the new Managing Editor. She was striking. The scuttlebutt in the office was that she was sixty-four, but I would not have guessed her being a day over fifty-nine. Nothing about her appeared real, what with her bleached hair, her snare-drum skin, her tummy-tucked sweet little waist, her high-beam breasts. God! My kinda woman! What have I been missing by not coming into the newsroom?

She shook my hand firmly, said she was "delighted and excited" to meet me and told me her name was Heather Marks. Imagine that, a sixty-four-year-old woman named Heather. I think I'm in love.

"I'm delighted and excited to meet you too." I gave her the look: the one that said I'm not interested in your age, your management position, your flattery, your small-talk... I want you.

Go ahead, keep talking, feel me out. Yes, I really mean it. Are you afraid? You've seen enough prime time soap operas to know what's happening here.

"Let me show you some files on Paddy Dangus in my office."

I followed and what an office she had. You could bowl on her conference table. I stood too close to her. She closed the blinds under pretense she had obtained top-secret information she could only share with me.

I spoke of *Dynasty*, *Dallas* and *Melrose Place*, and she understood. If we did not have this common ground, I don't think such an arrangement could ever have transpired. Had we met any other year of our lives, if I had not become Technoman, neither of us would have been aroused by the other. For Heather, I was the newfangled, trendy gadget she must possess, especially if she could procure me on layaway. And I, even confessing a smidgen of repulsion in my sentiments for Heather, knew if I were going to know intimately the time I live in, I better know this woman. She was the forbidden waxed fruit and I melted her like a candle.

With a woman like Heather, I highly recommend tossing the mouse chord about her waist like a lasso. Instead of my pulling her in the way a cowboy would a young calf, she snatched the wire and reeled me in like some debris-laden fish. Somehow, the tugging and rustling transformed into foreplay as my monitor flipped up and my lips landed on her stem-taut neck, her skin pulled and tucked so intensely that her nape responded with grand sensitivity, with the febrility of finger tips. Absolutely writhing, she pressed her breasts into my face. Now it was my turn to wriggle. These, my friends, were the real things. Not saline folks. Heather must have gotten her implants before silicon became illegal for they rolled and wrestled like they had a life of their own. They sure as hell don't make breasts like they used to. I am confident they will endure long after I depart.

Needless to say, my pants were soon around my ankles. Christ I even took the Intrafacer off as Heather dropped me onto her king-sized conference table and I was fucking the three layers of make-up right off her. Thank goodness for the six or seven thick coats of polyurethane that protected the conference table's particle board; otherwise, boy the splinters I would have endured... Splinters anywhere and everywhere for Heather couldn't stand me in one position. We shifted like volleyball players. After what seemed like an hour of this rotation, I began to hope someone would knock on the door or something because I was in no condition to continue. I flip-flopped between her presence and pictures of magazine covers unable to commit myself to any one particular vision. Obviously, Heather was one of these workout queens with a personal trainer because she was thinking orgasm while I was thinking heart-attack. Thankfully, each of us got what we expected and caught our connubial breaths as our skin stuck to the gunky table surface.

I could have used some somnoïd about then. Instead, she scooted over to her desk drawer and passed me a shoe shine brush. Apparently, I was supposed to clean myself up with this.

"What do you want me to do, polish my dick?" She laughed but offered me nothing else as she took care of herself with something from her purse. Under the conditions, I did the best I could.

Heather had known too many men to say too much after whatever that was.

"So if you have any difficulties or need any more material, don't hesitate to drop by."

"Thanks," I said, truly appreciative.

The experience was so thoroughly artificial and thrilling, I thought I just might need a bit more material.

Channel 69:
Riders to the Curb

Pines Tar: The Tragic Past of Paddy Dangus — March 17

I confess my resistance to writing this column, but the demand from you for more Paddy Dangus stories has reached Elvis/Princess Di proportions. So reluctantly I give you an Internet account from Rafter Simpkins about the miserable legacy of the Dangus family. Simpkins explains he was told by some guy he met at an Irish Pub named Sing, who claimed to be Paddy's oldest .and dearest friend. Even though we have been unable to locate Sing, old Dave Miller respects the story sufficiently to throw it into his upcoming biography. I admit more revision to the tale than Simpkins would have liked, but then again, it's my column. Gather round the campfire and listen up because I can't see another Dangus story out there for publication until at least April.

The Simpkins Account

When the U.S. Motors Guardian flipped over the Meadowbrook guardrail and sent family patriarch James Dangus to his death, the Dangus clan figured it was just crazy pa's time. And when his son Seamus Dangus took the Guardian out, crashed into a Buick and lay in a coma for three weeks, the family merely chalked it up to hard luck. So when Moira Dangus drove her Guardian off the Robert Moses Causeway, they were a little surprised to see a pattern developing.

Yet it couldn't be the Guardian. After all, the car was called the Guardian for a reason. The advertisements explained it was "the safest of all vehicles, especially designed for the new rules of the road." Those new rules emerged after the energy crisis in '74 with the gas lines, skyrocketing prices and an unaccustomed outlook of limitation along the limitless conveyor belt that is America. With its small, light frame and its incredible, downright Japanese, gas mileage per gallon, the Guardian would drive the country out to the horizon again. The Danguses were a four-Guardian family — they even appeared in a local commercial representing a new breed of Americans up to the challenge of the new breed of car. And every time a Dangus corpse was removed from a crumpled car, insurance would supply another Guardian for the totaled one. With three dead, the Danguses still had four Guardians among the five remaining family members.

The matriarch Patricia Dangus asked her boys not to take the car out anymore. But where can one go and what can one do without a car on Long Island? On the Tuesday after Thanksgiving, the last day of November, mother begged her eldest Mickey not to go off to Fortunoff to buy an engagement ring for his pale red-headed love Maude. Mickey bought the ring, but never made it home. The calls were becoming familiar: "Mrs. Dangus, your son has been in an accident."

"Oh, my Mickey! Not my Mickey," she keened, staggered and then tried to steady herself for the next question, "Is he dead?"

"We don't know of his condition. All we know he's in an accident. You'll have to come down to North Shore University General to find out more." She hung up.

"Oh, he's dead! My Mickey's dead!"

Though she didn't even bother going to the hospital to confirm, no one would deny she was right, especially at Mickey's funeral. "Those cars are cursed. We can't drive them anymore."

"That's stupid," said Sean. "We have these perfectly good vehicles, the finest America can offer and no one is going to stop me from riding them."

And the very next morning as Sean prepared to get down to the construction site, Mrs. Dangus cried, "Oh, Sean my darling, if you care at all for your mother, you will not go today in that death car."

"Oh mother, I'm fine. I can't stop living my life," and off he went in his grey Guardian with his lunchbox and his hardhat. When the police found his car smacked into a telephone pole after fishtailing down a hill in the early December snow, even the Thermos inside of the lunchbox was crushed.

"Why do my sons ignore me?" she asked her remaining two boys Eamon and Paddy.

"Let me just take this Guardian to the dealer and see if we can trade it in," volunteered Eamon.

"O.K.," mother said reluctantly, "but be careful."

Eamon was gone an hour when the snow started falling heavy to the point where you could hardly see in front of your eyes, and everybody knows drivers on Long Island have not a clue of how to handle even the lightest of flurries. Eamon didn't return and the police didn't call. Paddy watched his mother pace for two hours while cooking a roast.

"Why haven't we heard?" she asked, expecting the death call, even more shaken by the absence of its certainty. As about four inches of snow blanketed the roadways, she put on a pair of Paddy's galoshes, the teenager and his mother having about the same foot size. She took off in her Guardian in search of her lost son.

If she found him, it was in purgatory because she never made it to the used car lot. Paddy could hear her keen in death with the passion and lamentations she cursed her life. Oddly the police called about a half hour earlier to report mom's accident than Eamon's. They were buried, however, at the same time.

Paddy didn't even bother contacting the insurance adjusters. He just called a U.S. Motors car dealer and offered him the two remaining Guardians in exchange for an old beat up Searcher pick-up truck. The dealer agreed readily, even to Paddy's one condition: that the dealer drop off the white Searcher and drive the Guardians away for him. The Searcher was one of those bizarre cult vehicles (more so now, naturally, than before), ugly as sin, but ran forever. When Dangus got his Searcher, it already looked ancient, even though it was merely a couple years old. Fourteen years ago U.S. Motors plunged under, yet today Dangus's Searcher rides on.

PostScript: And what did the dead Danguses leave for Paddy besides the Guardians? Well... not much... except... something mighty bizarre. They left him lifetime service contracts from the major manufacturers of all the appliances in the Dangus home. In theory, Dangus could hold onto his oven, refrigerator, washer-dryer, TV, etc., until the day he died. The manufacturers never counted on having a true lifetime customer like Dangus. They had figured even the most frugal and diehard would only hold onto an appliance at most fifteen years. But Paddy Dangus would cling to an appliance like it was his very own spleen. No, considering the way I heard Dangus drinks, much better than his spleen, even if the appliance had to be replaced piece by piece.

Dangus continually, doggedly corresponded with GE, Kenmore and SONY to get repairs and replacement parts for his equipment. Eventually, all the manufacturers gave in and offered Paddy new appliances rather than attempt to track down obsolete materials. In fact, he procured twenty new appliances in the two years before he started his terrorist activities.

Store clerks at A.C. Antenna's, Circuit Town, and Sears give varying descriptions of Dangus: blonde crewcut, long black mane, bearded, clean-shaven, short, tall, clear-eyed, bespeckled, boisterous, quiet — either he sent different representatives or is quite the master of disguise. I figure we must see Dangus surface within the next few years because most his appliances are bound to give out soon. Meanwhile, Dangus sold the home on Newbridge Street almost two years ago. Where he carted off his new appliances in his Searcher remains a mystery.

Channel 70:
Appearance at Mediocrities

With my growing popularity and my endless parade of appearances, I felt compelled to mock myself before someone else got the idea. So I accepted the lucrative invitation to make a promotional stop at Mediocrities, a place well designed to tear away my last shreds of dignity and decorum. The establishment promises dissatisfaction and no one is ever disappointed. Don't believe me? Have the coffee sometime, which is older than most software programs, that is if the waitress makes her way to your table. If you don't desire the coffee or you are not hungry, just scan the menu: everything is overpriced and freezer-burn to boot. As far as entertainment, Mediocrities has as much quantity as it has little quality. The musicians can't play and they can't sing, but perform each task with a convincing attempt at apathy. Watch them wince when they mistakenly hit the correct key or strike the right chord.

Of course, I fit in quite well at the place. "Senora, may I have a large cappuccino?"

"No, we don't have large."

"It says on the menu right here: large cappuccino for $11.95."

"We don't have a large cappuccino."

"But — "

"We do have a small cappuccino for $12.95."

"Alright then, I'll have that."

"Anything else?"

"Yes, I'll have a— "

Too late, she was gone, talking to another customer, not about his order mind you, but asking him why he would wear a tie in a place like this.

I made the rounds, shaking hands, talking to the men about my sexual exploits as Technoman, to the ladies about my increased sensitivity to their plight in my own captivity, to the children how if they eat their junk foods they can grow up just like me. Twenty minutes later, my cappuccino had not found it's way to me, but I noticed the presence of something more disturbing. Zach, whom I hadn't seen in weeks, was also making the rounds, squawking out bad imitations, gamely partaking in the spirit of the place. Apparently, he was booked for an appearance too.

I met him over by the arcade pressing convulsively on the flippers of a cheesy looking pinball machine. It was truly the worst of pinball machines, for no ball, no matter how skilled the operator, remained in play for longer than ten seconds. Zach kept plunking in quarters seeing if he could break his record low score. Even more awkward than usual, I became charged with an inability to play both Technoman and father in public; so I tried to act nicely to Zach, although I confess baleful undercurrents. A large group of customers were watching as we played "Pong" — an ancient video game, impossible to lose, a patty cake exercise. The longer we tapped the virtual ball back from one paddle to the other, the more the crowd dispersed. I pulled the monitor away from my eyes and looked penetratingly straight at Zach. He pretended not to notice my hurt and disappointment, continuing to play on.

After a while, he attempted to thaw me. "Oh dad, I was just playing with you the last time we met. Don't be mad. Won't you fight me in Intergalactic warfare, dad? Why don't you annihilate me a few times. It'll make you feel better and you won't be so angry with me."

Collectively, we destroyed the world more than a dozen times, but I still didn't feel any better. What made it worse was how perfectly charming and attractive Zach behaved. No father wants to be so disillusioned by his son so early; the smooth liar seemed destined for corporate law. As he moved beyond intergalactic warfare and beyond me, I couldn't help but notice his hyperactivity, hopping from customer to customer. If he weren't supposed to be making an appearance here, he'd be quite annoying.

My cappuccino finally arrived when Alice walked in to pick up Zach. She looked even more beaten than I did. Still I could not refrain from asking her, "Why do you let Zach make these appearances?"

"I can't help it. The only time he seems happy is when he's making a public appearance."

"He's gotten that bad?"

She looks at me for every ounce of the detached and deluded father I am. "Four months ago I was actually hopeful; he seemed to be turning a corner, he was just about up to grade level and he was even socializing with other children at school. Now, I don't know what to think? Can you believe he has snuck out of school a half dozen times to go to computer bars." She turned away from me visibly shaken and headed out the door. I grabbed my check — it was wrong, but I paid the $19.37, plus tip, anyway — and followed her. I know I should have stayed with Zach, kept an eye on him, but I figured he could get no worse at Mediocrities. Alice sobbed in her car and I got in the passenger side.

"I don't know what to do with him. He sneaks down in the middle of the night and watches every violent show along the channels, he turns on sex cartoons and scrolls across the satellite stations. When·he's not doing that, he takes overstimulated over-intense virtual trips, virtual roller-coasters, white water rafting..."

"Holy shit."

"Don't you see it? He's living the hyperreal life of his old man. Christ, he even drinks Jolt Cola. The kid lives his life wired."

"What are you going to do?"

"I'm going to disconnect him."

"What do you mean, *disconnect him*?"

"I'm throwing out the TV and the computer and going from there."

"That's a great idea."

"Yeah, sure it is. Now why don't you help out a bit and start acting like a father."

"How?"

"Well, if you'd get rid of that Technoman act, you'd sure make a huge difference in his life."

"Get rid of Technoman, what are you kidding me?"

"Is that such a big deal?"

"A big deal? It's my whole life. I can't get rid of Technoman."

"Are you telling me that being Technoman is more important than saving your son?"

"Aren't you the overdramatic one. Don't be ridiculous. Zach's behavior has nothing to do with Technoman. You act like he never had problems before Technoman."

"And you act as if his problems were half as severe before you became this absurd piece of cheap hardware."

"Are you blaming what's happened to Zach on me?"

"No, I'm not. I'm just asking for your support. Zach gets about four hours of sleep a night. Does that sound familiar?"

"A bit."

"Well, are you going to do anything about it?"

I paused, confused, even a little anguished. "I can't stop being Technoman, at least not yet."

"Why not?"

"I can't explain it to you. But if I give up Technoman right now, I give up myself." I followed fast upon that statement before she could question me more. "I can spend more time with him, even take off the Intrafacer on occasion, try to break him away from the wired world a little bit. Maybe if he sees his old man finding other things in life, he'll follow."

Alice drew me close. I looked gently into her eyes and whispered to her, "You're not alone in this." She grew misty and kissed me, but a soft tap on the foggy windshield awakened us from the spell. It was Zach. He gnarled up his hands to create mouse prints on the window. God they were good. Like we were viewing a scary drive-in movie, we looked out at Zach with amusement and horror.

Channel 71:
Seven Somnoid Voyages of Technoman —
Part VI, Grandpa's Cane

By the time he limped and hobbled about his twelve children, Grandpa Guido brandished a cane that had taken on mythic qualities. While the 20/20 eyes missed much, the cane caught all. And no one knew this better than Louie, who found a deft turn about the house's sharp corners provided no escape. When Guido wanted to get you, that fucking cane was a virtual boomerang that found your ankles with the deadly efficiency of a rattlesnake.

Forever in trouble for pulling one's hair or squeezing another's ass, Louie tested the cane from every angle. One day instead of running, he stood straight in front of his old man, hypothesizing that Guido's cane possessed too much natural movement to hit him dead on. When the bottom kicked up and thudded square on the bridge of his nose, Louie decided from here on in he would forever sprint from that cane. And every time he ran the cane tracked him down. That is until the last time when he had spent the money he was supposed to pitch in for coal on some Polish chippie.

He had escaped that great cane attack because he wisely did not even answer Guido's inquiry about his weekly contribution; instead he just ran. Caught off guard, Guido delayed a few seconds before he cranked up the mighty staff. When the spinning brown hook clattered two feet short of him, Louie stumbled by reflex. He didn't fall though. Returning to the house the next morning — he had a date with that Polish chippie the night before — Louie dragged his ass in like a condemned man and waited patiently for his beating.

Instead, Guido handed him a draft notice: how's that for a caning?

For perhaps the first time in his life, Louie now looked behind and beyond his old man's cane. He clamped an eye on that stubby twisted shortened leg lost in Guido's baggy pants. In 1915, Guido got off the boat from Naples onto Ellis Island and then found himself cutting thick Sicilian heads in Little Italy. Within two years, he was on a boat again, this time to France to fight the Krauts through mustard gas and barbed wire. In the trenches, he burned leeches off his belly with matches and monthly tossed his wet clothes into the bonfire. Not two months passes down in the bowels along the Somme before a shell made his thigh look like a domino, dark, smoky and speckled.

Dragging his leg with honors back to his humble Long Island home, he would shuffle about the barber shop with a ridiculous number of aches and discomforts. At night, he pulled off his pants and tenderly fingered his wounds, amazed how close the shrapnel came to his groin without piercing it. So he turned to Mary, flopped his bad leg over her and made himself whole again.

Louie would now go off to a war where the shells were bigger and better than in the previous one — the Krauts had made refinements. If their shells had one shred of the sense of direction that his old man's cane possessed, Louie would find soft and narrow accommodations on his way home. Following Frankie off to the front, Louie gave his family something even his father could not provide — the first telephone in the home. The U.S. government kindly offered installation for any family with two GIs or more.

The first call my mom ever made went to sturdy, gentle Bill, who she hoped one day would take her out of the range of the cane. Mom too knew the cane: one time after little provocation she found it thumping into her forehead. In fact, in her childhood, she feared no object more: it stood for the fierce, absurd authority of family. And when did she stop fearing the cane? Well, her young strong husband made her overcome this weakness. Not by his life though, but his death. You see, when the man you love climbs up on a telephone pole only to tumble down with ten thousand volts sent through him, a cane suddenly becomes a quaint and affectionate image of a simpler time.

When Mom greeted Louie off the boat two years after she lost her future, neither thought they could move around without their own walking sticks, even though nothing was physically wrong with either of them. How could they not look for support when they witnessed the rapidity with which their wired world could send messages, alternately convenient and deadly? Little surprise that the two headed together to Wallachs and picked out sturdy mahogany canes.

That night they drank burgundy and lifted the staffs above their heads, imitating the old man's technique. "It was the twist of the hip, even with the bum leg, that made all the difference," mom explained. "Always from the side he tossed it."

"Shit," said Louie, "That cane was like his pet Doberman or something."

"If that's so, then even though some times that beast thought we were raw meat, more of the time it must have figured us for a couple of fire hydrants."

Louie laughed. "Yeah, yellow and stubby." They chuckled a little more before mom started to cry and Louie soon followed, their canes rattling as they weakly embraced. From that day onward, Louie and mom clung onto their canes. Despite their expertise and the family tradition, neither of them ever let it fly out of their hands.

Channel 72:
Dangus Takes a Holiday

Pines Tar: The Full Moon Without A Dangus

Most people will admit it was the most anticipated evening in recent Long Island history. Hell, it was Friday the 13th on the night of a full moon.

"All my friends stayed up waiting for Dangus," said Joe Crayola. "And what does he do? Stands us up. It's enough to make us not believe he exists at all."

Crayola and his buddies weren't the only ones waiting. I heard rumors from at least a dozen sources that Dangus would shut down the airports in the New York-metropolitan area and render the space over the island an aerial desert. So I made a few trips to the FAA's radar central in Garden City only to find the controllers had heard the rumors too. The director boasted of all the additional generators fired up to guarantee continued air control service. Everybody knew if Dangus were going to wreak havoc with air traffic it would have to be here at TRACON where all the flights are monitored, tracked and guided in and out.

. I don't care how many generators the director lined up, I smelled the fear and anxiety when I walked into the guts of the place — TRACON's control central. In that black pit, I felt right at home with my Intrafacer. Almost all the lighting of the windowless computer arena came off the little yellow blips on the monitors. One screen pulsed into the next as starlights popped above and across others. Each of the controllers had their own little air space, one clustered, another zoned up, another zoomed in. "Look at this screen," senior manager Arnold Cancelliere told me. "It's just a swatch of space in the atmosphere. You don't think that Dangus, with all he's taken, couldn't grab that with a click of the button?"

I reminded Cancelliere of federal encryption and security coding. He glanced back at me like I was a child and took me to where the national screen displayed every plane flying in the United States at that moment and time. "That's 5046 planes. It's a little slow right now. All Dangus needs to do is shake us up a little." I asked whether the FAA had emergency back-up plans. "Of course, but they do mean long delays and lots of problems. When a nut like Dangus comes along, he reminds us how fragile the whole system is."

Or does he? Cancelliere had worried unnecessarily for Dangus never stepped into his night sky. In fact, for this full moon Dangus was completely out of the picture. While Cancelliere blew a sigh of relief, he asked the question on everybody's minds: "Not that I'm complaining, but what the hell happened to Dangus? Where'd he go?"

I confess my own personal disappointment over Dangus's absence. At TRACON central waiting for the impending doom, I felt like I belonged in a James Bond movie. When Dangus didn't show, I grew more intensely aware I dwelled in a suburban world than at anytime since being trapped in Home Depot last month. A number of people have theorized that Dangus is running scared.

During the previous weeks, detective Richard Mason had leaked to the media that he knew exactly what Dangus would be doing in this lunar cycle and that the underground figure would be in police custody any day now. "The fact that he didn't do anything shows you how fearful he is to even make a move," said Mason. "He well knows his shenanigans are coming to an end and he is just prolonging the inevitable." Mason stuck to his prediction that he would harpoon Dangus soon. "Unless somebody has misinformed me, we get a full moon every month, and I don't think Dangus can control himself, even though he knows he will be caught."

Perhaps more damaging to Dangus's reputation is the theory that the terrorist refrained from acting due, not to fear of being caught, but to the absence of a good idea. "I hate to admit it, but I can't help but believe Dangus has hit a creative wall," said a weary sounding Dave Miller, his unauthorized biographer. "Jeez, consider the absurd pressure of Friday the 13th piled atop the increasing frenzy swirling about his subversive activities. Anything less than detonating a nuclear warhead on the Island would have been considered a disappointment." While Miller speculates that Dangus has lost some of his luster, the biographer admits his decision to not act had more integrity than acting halfheartedly.

"Thank goodness the vandalism of the Woody Hollow Golf Course proved to be the work of Dangus copycats," Miller added. Of course Miller is referring to the rototilling of thirteen of the course's greens Friday night. Police have now arrested Aaron Tully, Sam Steigerwald and Anthony Abogato in connection to the incident. Police also compounded their U.S. Motors Searcher, which had recently been painted white over its original turquoise coat. While pleased about the arrest, course manager George Buchanan could not resist implicating Dangus in the vandalism. "I don't care if he doesn't even know these boys, it's Dangus's influence that made them do it. No one would even think of committing such a senselessly ugly and destructive crime until Dangus started his mission to destroy everything that is wonderful about life here on the island." As Buchanan looked out on the 13th hole, naturally the one with the most severe and brutal damage, tears welled up in his eyes. "Satan himself would not do something so cruel and gratuitous. That S.O.B. needs to fry."

Even before those boys were arrested, you heard first in this column on Sunday that Dangus could not have been responsible for such an act, for no other reason than the fact that the vandalism was too close in style to his Sheep Meadow triumph, and Dangus stands against nothing if not against repeating himself. A true Dangus groupie, Rafter Simpkins actually believes Dangus did the best possible thing in his decision to not act at all.

"Think about how on edge all of Long Island was, just waiting for Dangus to strike," he said. "If he wants to mock suburbia, what would be more mocking than making the dumb bastards in their bedroom communities wait for nothing? Dangus is all about the unexpected. The masses were expecting Dangus so Dangus decided this would not do at all."

Well, one thing is for sure, if Dangus is retiring, some of us are going to have to get a new hobby.

THIS COLUMN HAS BEEN BROUGHT TO YOU BY FRIDAY THE 13TH, PART XIII, NOW APPEARING AT

YOUR LOCAL MOVIE THEATRE. IF THE OTHER TWELVE
BLOCKBUSTERS SCARED YOU SENSELESS, IMAGINE
WHAT WILL HAPPEN TO YOU IN THE 13TH & FINAL
CHAPTER. GET TO THE THEATRE, BEFORE IT GETS TO
YOU!

Channel 73:
All for the Machine

I could not believe how hard Geoffrey Sphere was working
me. Between the voice activation instructional tape and the
endless series of press releases, manufacturer inquiries and sundry
correspondences, I hardly had time to be Technoman anymore.
When I lodged such a complaint, Sphere groused: "What are you
talking about? For the first time you are truly Technoman, giving
your all for the machine, rather than the costume role you've been
playing for the last ten months."

The way he worked, Sphere left me little to gripe about. I
don't think the crazy bastard slept. And Carmen, I'd be surprised
if she even knew her children's names anymore. But don't just
believe me, listen to their barroom talk one late night when I
invited them out to Tara's. Hell, I figured it was the only way I
was going to see old man Miller and Angelica, my time otherwise
so monopolized of late. When I arrived with my two remote
buddies, Angelica had already wiped away the spittle and the
ashes from the back edge of the bar and her father was telling the
bartender old missing finger jokes accompanied by goofy squints
and gesticulations with the digits in and the tongue out.

Carmen didn't even get a chance to order a drink before some
toothless old salt made his best offer to pick her up. Yet the
wrinkled advances had the effect of a first margherita, and by the
second sip of her initial drink she giggled and snorted
contagiously. Geoffrey, meanwhile, had stored up three months of
pent-up bitching that was given tongue by a gin martini.

"This sucks. Every time I fix one thing another problem
arises."

Old man Miller, who learned long ago how to agree, chimed
in, "Ain't it the truth."

"You know the worst thing?"

"What?"

"That sometimes there is no answer. Even when there is an answer. The thing just won't work. And you know what I do?"

"You walk away," said Miller.

"You bet your ass I walk away. Wouldn't you?"

"Of course I would."

"But you know what else?"

"You always come back."

"You bet your ass I do."

"I shall return."

"That's right. I shall return. You think a fucking remote is going to beat me?"

"How could it beat you? You, I can tell just by looking at you, are a man. The remote is a machine. A machine cannot beat a man."

"Not a real man."

"No, not a real man. And you my friend," Miller lifted his bottom-of-the-keg tap beer, "are a real man."

"Damn right I am. Do you know I haven't slept more than three hours in six weeks."

"That so."

"Yeah."

"That so."

"And I've got a pain in my head that any normal person would be hospitalized for."

"Really?"

"Sure would. But I can't let go. About a month and a half ago I thought I had it. I thought the remote was done. All the insights had come to me, as if God had handed down the blueprints himself. But who knew what it would entail fine tuning the thing."

"Who knew?"

"Who knew? It's not like I've been looking for overnight success here. I've been working on this machine for a little over six fucking years. I was forty-three when I started and now menopause is kicking in. Do you know how many prototypes I've plowed through."

"No, how many?"

"I'd say seventeen or eighteen."

Lifting her antenna, Angelica inquired, "Where are those prototypes now?"

"Oh, they're long gone. Pieces of shit. How could I bear to look at them once I knew I could create something better. And now with this model, and I can honestly tell you, this will be the last one, once a week something goes terribly wrong. The machine explodes in my hand."

Geoffrey squeezed tight his empty glass — no olives, no ice, no nothing — and I ordered another round. Carmen and Angelica were talking, finding each other more attractive than I deserved. I grew distracted by everything around me, particularly by the way a biker lifted and twisted the pinball machine and by a potential fight brewing over the pool table. Geoffrey kept talking through a haze of smoke, for I introduced my friends to a synthetic brand of cigarette — those tobacco companies, what will they think of next — and every one joined in the spirit of lighting up. In such a lurid atmosphere, Sphere seemed to be an underworld informant clueing us in on the organized crimes of humanity.

"Nothing is more temperamental than a universal product. I have spent these past three weeks expunging the last remnants of my personality from the machine. I believe finally the remote is a pure vessel."

"Are you sure?"

"Do you think I would be drinking with you undesirables if I were not?"

"Perhaps you are deluding yourself," shot back Carmen, who as his office wife knows damn straight how to strike a nerve.

Geoffrey only shivered a little before he sipped his martini and agreed, "Perhaps."

Much talk continued late into the night. I heard less than I usually do, my hand on Angelica's thigh, as I grew disturbed by my negligence toward that section and the remainder of the limb in the preceding weeks. Most of the bar was singing a revised tune from the seventies whose chorus for the rest of America went:

"Oh, Super Spaceman, put a helmet on our face
Oh, Super Spaceman, come take us to this place"

But at Tara's the only lyrics to the chorus were:
"Oh, Paddy Dangus, come wipe away our face.
Oh, Paddy Dangus, please come destroy this place."
The references to Dangus relegated Geoffrey and Carmen to clutching their skulls. I tried to soothe the tense moment with shop talk.

"What did the SONY representatives want today?"

"Oh, they just want to buy the new prototype."

"Well, what do you think about their proposal?"

"At the money they are offering, I'm listening. They're a little late in the game though. Hey, they are my sixth suitor. But we are talking deep pockets here."

"How do you feel about giving up your prototype though?"

"Yeah, that's the problem. I'm not naive enough to ignore the possibility that they want to buy me out just so they can kill the prototype and maintain their current stranglehold on the remote market."

I nodded, Miller nodded, we all nodded.

"Hey, it's strange. I thought I was in it for the money. But now the prototype is ready, and I want to see it come to the market, even though I now know that will probably take another year... Yet, though I won't get into specific figures, SONY gave me some offer." He smiled, but not for long, the chorus had come around again, and seemingly everyone at Tara's but the five of us was shouting:

"Oh, Paddy Dangus, come wipe away our face.
Oh, Paddy Dangus, please come destroy this place."

Geoffrey tried to continue, but as he heard the chorus repeated, this time more boisterously, he grabbed the smallest of male serenaders by the rugby shirt and started smacking him. Needless to say, this is Tara's after all, the beatings began, so I got my Intrafacer out of there. Old man Miller giggled in the corner. As I headed toward the door, I nostalgically eyed up the bar remote, wanting this time to offer it with great gentility to the fair Lady Angelica. Geoffrey was finding out personally what it felt like to be tinkered with a bit until I regained a conscience and dragged him out of the bar.

Outside, in the warm April night, an early heat wave mind you, I tenderly used my shirt sleeve to wipe the blood from Geoffrey's lip. Old man Miller played with Geoffrey's head, asking how many fingers he had up, no amputee got more mileage out of what's missing than old man Miller. Geoffrey was weak, but garrulous.

"Get me back to Prometheus Laboratories, I've got an idea."

"You are in no condition to work," I reminded him.

"I am in no condition for anything else... I have an idea."

I drove him alright. He talked Carmen into returning to work too. I don't know how it happened, but instead of spraying Pledge on Angelica's thighs, I felt the obligation to return to write the next correspondence with SONY in preparation for ensuing negotiations.

When we got inside the office, Geoffrey, Carmen and I gathered about the remote and mockingly genuflected to the idol, and then we hunkered down to business.

Channel 74:
Carmen's Checklist for Today

☐ Make Lunches
☐ Fill Out Insurance Forms
☐ Call Voice Activation Designers
☐ File Nails
☐ Use K-Pro Scalp Remoisturizer, Split End Repairer
☐ Go 2 Dry Cleaners
☐ Clean Linen Closet
☐ Repair Diode Connections
☐ Meet W/ Jim Ruppert, SONY Marketing Director
☐ Go 2 Jiffy Lube 4 Oil Change
☐ Get 2 Merlot, 1 Pinot Grigio
☐ Clean Oil Burner
☐ Get Migraine Medication Prescription Filled
☐ Drop Off Pant Suit at Dry Cleaners
☐ Pick Up Repaired Cell Phone
☐ Call In 2 Up Reuben's Ritalin Dosage
☐ Reprogram Microwave Codes

- ❑ Solder Wiring 4 Connectors Again
- ❑ ✓ Prototype 4 T Remote Cover W/ Stereoligthographer
- ❑ Update Encryption Codes
- ❑ Buy Briefs 4 Frederique & 6 Pair of Panty Hose
- ❑ Install New Version of Windows
- ❑ Run Norton Disk Doctor Program
- ❑ Get Film Developed & Transfer 8 MM Videotape 2 VHS format
- ❑ Get RoseEllen's, Brendan's & Anthony's Birthday Presents At ToysRUs
- ❑ Make Copy of Promotional Materials 4 JTD Marketing
- ❑ Go 2 Car Wash
- ❑ Replace Toner Cartridge 4 Laser Printer
- ❑ Call Louise About Chemo Treatments
- ❑ Call Michael About Missing Gerbil
- ❑ Get Seat Designation 4 Las Vegas Flight
- ❑ Meet Pfister at TGI Fridays at 3
- ❑ Talk 2 Geoffrey About Payroll Deduction
- ❑ Bedsheets
- ❑ Drink 64 Oz of H20
- ❑ Eat Banana
- ❑ Change Kitchen Bulb
- ❑ Get New Batteries 4 Remote
- ❑ Program VCR 2 Tape at 9:30 4 Innovations
- ❑ Floss
- ❑ Take Advils
- ❑ Get Cup of Coffee
- ❑ Quit Smoking
- ❑ Fill Out Patent Application 4 Diode Centrifuge
- ❑ Apply Eye Liner
- ❑ Thank Lawrence 4 Flowers
- ❑ Do Back Exercises
- ❑ Ignore Calls From RCA
- ❑ Get Rus 2 Make Manual Revisions
- ❑ Pluck Eyebrows
- ❑ Get Fax Machine Serviced
- ❑ Revise Supply Data Base
- ❑ Clean Up Hard Drive

☐ Spray & Squeegee Off Monitor
☐ ✓ On Sanyo Stock

Channel 75:
Sister Livia

The last entry in Little Augie's journal was one lousy line:
"Tomorrow I must see Sister Livia."
I didn't know Little Augie had a sister. When I told Angelica about this wild goose chase, she looked at me with exasperation: "Where the hell have you been? Don't you know who Sister Livia is? Get your head out of the microwave and live in the real world."

Angelica explained to me how Sister Livia had come out to the East End to take care of the sick after the Vullem Scandal. I had written about the Vullem Scandal, but heard nothing about Sister Livia. Vullem was supposed to be the greatest product since Teflon. It was supposed to provide a protective coat over 3 1/2 inch disks to make them virtually indestructible. That is until the workers applying the Vullem started getting this hideous skin disease, and then the community of Green Island suddenly started looking like a Leper Colony.

Angelica tells me Sister Livia has been out there tending them ever since. "Be nice to her," Angelica warned. "A good number of people think she is a Saint."

If she weren't a Saint, she certainly looked the part, with her premature wrinkles (Angelica told me she was only 35), her frail fasting body, her thick skin, and her warm eyes. She would not stop her work to speak with me, so I had to pretend I wasn't horrified and transfixed by the crawling, stinking, pukey pink skin that ran from a worker's wrist to his elbow as she softly padded the wound with a cloth soaked in green solution.

"More chemicals to heal the chemicals." She ignored me; obviously she was not the idle chit-chat type. I would get to the point.

"Would you do the same for Satan?"

She looked into my eyes, with more pity than she administered to the mangled man, "I would do the same for you."

"Hey, what are you trying to say?"

"I don't *try* to say anything. I *try* to help people."

"Have you ever seen Satan?"

She shot a look straight into my eyes. "I have seen his face many times."

"I mean have you met him? Do you know him?"

"Why do you ask such questions? I can't arrange a meeting between the two of you. I believe you can do that yourself, if you haven't made arrangements already."

Easier to get a straight answer from a politician or a lawyer than from a saint.

"Did Little Augie come to see you?"

"Little Augie?"

"A short old woman. She works in the morgue, handles dead bodies all the time, probably spoke to you about them."

"Do you know how many people speak to me about the dead and dying? I'm sure I spoke to her."

"What did she say to you?"

"*That* I don't remember just as when someone asks me tomorrow if I spoke with you. I will tell him, yes I have spoken with you, but I don't remember what transpired in the conversation."

"And if someone asks me if I have seen you, I will say no, but I will remember what you have said to me."

"May you find peace," she said to me and I believe she meant it. She placed her hands on my left cheek, gently and caressed a bad rash below my jaw and neck — I got it from wearing a funky, polystyrene collar beneath my Intrafacer.

"My son, you are pained, let me heal it." Tenderly she spoke and dropped her cloth in the green solution.

I too almost fell under her spell, but the green goop whisked near my face awakened me. I turned away.

"No thank you, I don't want to be healed. I am different from the others."

"No, you are the same as all the rest. Nobody wants to be healed anymore. It takes a strong man to want to be healed."

"Have you healed Satan? Is Satan a strong man?"

"I have renounced Satan, his works, his empty promises, but I would heal him. Yet Satan will not be healed. He is the example which all of you follow. He has been carrying around his wounds longer than Adam. He will not be healed just as you will not be healed. You hold your wounds like a badge, let them fester, and spread the disease, the plague of our age."

Not fond of sermons, I respectfully said farewell.

"Goodbye my son, bless you, may you find your peace as I believe your friend Little Augie has found hers at the eastern tip of Fire Island."

She told me this information as she turned away toward a patient whose entire carcass seemed to be rotted away, one whom she figured I would not have the courage to pursue; instead to let my wound take precedence. She was right. I took my cue as I took my blessing, with uncomfortable gratitude and with suspicion — suspicion that I was being sent to the end of Fire Island to be converted at some cultist retreat and that Little Augie had never mentioned : to Sister Livia about going there. Yet I grew increasingly attracted to the idea of showing up there and finding no sight of Little Augie, but a sanctuary for myself.

What does it mean when I have trouble trusting a saint?

Channel 76:
Technoman on Damage Control

I lasted nine months as Technoman before I discovered technology can only have so much appeal to the public without sex. I hesitate to discuss the most unfortunate moment during my tenure as a mechanical icon, but so much has been written about the incident I feel compelled to at least defend myself.

I wrestled a female robot not because I wanted to or because I am a perverse human being... I was just so used to agreeing to engage myself in all technological possibilities that I could not say no.

Let me explain:

As I physically broke down, my TV appearances increased dramatically. Who cares that my head continually spun about like it sat on the carousel of a microwave and my sinuses grew more congested than the Long Island Expressway, we are talking air time here and I figured air time must mean dollars and more dollars to fill up that pit of debt I excavated.

I proudly profess that I became an even more popular talking head than Henry Kissinger. I emerged as the all-purpose futurist, invention commentator, computer hack analyst. No product was legitimate high-tech until I deigned to regale it with a review. I wandered from studio to studio offering my insights in thirty-second sound bites. If we were in a movie, Angelica would have played my femme fatale, my leggy seductress, in booking these segments, but she never actually sought my corruption out. Instead, she came because I needed an assistant, an exclusive entourage, plus she didn't mind glomming an occasional specimen for the Tesla Institute.

So I punctuated each appearance with a cliché: "This machine points us away from the stark inconveniences that characterize postmodern life and propels us toward a world of smooth clear paths."

Or: "Finally, a product is on the market that takes the hassle and the boredom out of getting from Point A to Point B."

Or: "The newest in this audio-visual technology will change the way we see and hear the world around us."

Or: "The last time we had an invention as monumental as this one was the Gutenberg printing press."

Or: "The amount of leisure time gained through using this equipment will make it seem that we hardly have to work at all anymore."

Or… Or… Or. After a few weeks of clichés, I couldn't endure watching myself on television anymore. Yet cheap thrills compounded. On the cable network Speedvision, I rode the brand new minivan motorcycle which gave me a suburban erection you would not believe.

When I spoke of low-life women with high-tech bodies on the *Jerry Springer Show*, I thought I could not stoop to greater depths, but I knew myself less than I could have fathomed. Dean Fudera came to me looking less sleazy than he had any right to be, with his Armani suit and his nicely quaffed balding skull. With the utmost dignity, Dean told me of the Venus 2000, a robot so far advanced that it would engage and interact with humanity the way none had in the past. Dean was right. Essentially a full-sized Barbie-doll, Regina moved in limited directions and motions, but those were nonetheless substantive activity.

"Wrestle with Regina and you'll lose pounds and have fun at the same time," professed the ads. As I mentioned before, I had no qualms mocking myself, but I could not have known just how humiliating wrestling Regina would be. I figured wrestling Regina would be similar in workout and stimulation to jacking up a car.

Admittedly, Angelica warned me. "Look at those heavy resin breasts and the way the nipples poke through her body suit. You're telling me you don't find that a little stimulating."

"What are you kidding me? We're talking a doll here. I might well as get aroused by my keyboard or a trash pail."

"O.K., but I think you are fooling yourself."

If I had a dress rehearsal like Angelica suggested, I might have drawn the same conclusion. But I could not make the free time, so we filmed live. Yes, Regina could only push into me — her lateral movements were minimal, but when we stepped into the ring I had not counted on two other determining factors. When I pulled her neck toward me, I immediately knew though.

Her stiff right arm tugged down on my head and sent my face into those hard strong breasts. I wanted to pull back but when my cheeks slid across her electrified nipples I lost one will and gained another. Dean, the little fuck, didn't tell me that her whole body surged and vibrated, didn't tell me how strong she was and that every time I hit an erogenous zone, Regina would undulate and convulse. If you look at the tape, you will see I honestly tried to extricate myself from her grasp, but when her right leg hooked itself behind mine, I grew involved in something from which I could no longer disengage myself. When I fell onto my back, I had no alternative but to arch and press into Regina until I could twist her over.

I know the picture that has appeared in the tabloids, the one I fought so vigorously to suppress, the one I thought I paid a sufficient price to squelch. But can you destroy my persona from one picture of me atop a full-sized doll? All I can say is thank

God I committed no crime because my image would have been obliterated rather than merely tarnished.

Is this an apology? I don't know. Yes, I'm embarrassed. But perhaps that is because I've been asked to explain myself more with the Regina incident than collectively everything else I have done as Technoman. How is it that I have become more popular and more of a joke at the same time?

And how do I explain that ever since I wrestled Regina I grew obsessed with the idea of making love to Angelica. Yet she, like the rest of the admiring public, takes me less seriously than at any time previously.

Channel 77:
Alice's Letter

The following handwritten letter was left at my doorstep in pretty Laura Ashley stationery.

Dear Rus,

I was cleaning out our closet the other day and found the first thing you composed on the typewriter I bought you. Maybe it was how the sweetness of the love poem you wrote makes me so many years later return the favor. I hope you remember. I remember everything, especially the night before I gave you that typewriter.

Do you remember when we were out picking blackberries and you got your leg caught in the stickers? When we got back home, I washed your scrapes and doused them with mercurochrome. At the Artie's party everyone laughed at you like a little kid, drank daiquiris and danced wryly to disco music. You slicked back your hair and made fun of John Travolta and I early on played the trashy slut and then after the sweet ingenue.

And late that night I took you to the wilderness for the first time. We sat on long grass, only shortened by the summer sun, and tasted the friction in the night air. The grass had bugs . . . bugs of the night, millions and millions of bugs that didn't fly high, just to the level of my crotch. And I smelt insecticide — the chemicals that cause mutation in their offspring. If the bugs weren't dying, who was?   Oh what fields those were for bugs of the crotch!

The ground was still damp from the rain. I was itchy. From forearm, to shin, to tricep, to legpit, I scratched. My scalp itched — I raked it from top to forehead. You grabbed my butt and pulled me close and I squeezed your arms and legs. We seemed to stare through the darkness at each other for hours. You smelt of Ivory soap and sweat. It seemed like we made love for years that night, made love almost up to this very day. The friction was gentle, as gentle as we could generate it; as a matter of fact, we barely touched at all.

Somehow I can't stop thinking about that night. Amazing how I can remember something when my mind was hardly working. So I write you out of a memory and to let you know the typewriter is still here if you want it.

> With Love,
> Alice

Channel 78:
The Ashbag School

I confess remiss in my efforts to wear completely artificial and unnatural clothing. I have been true to my manifesto, but rayons and polyesters do not constitute a new wardrobe. Plastics have helped, yet not until the Trash Bag Clothes Company (TBCC) sent me about forty promotional e-mails did I embrace the Technoman ensemble entirely.

Yes, not until I put on the trash bags did I feel truly disposable, at one with styrofoam cups, CD wrappers and baby diapers. And when I donned TBCC's special red bag waste, my body responded with an instinctive detachment. The message I send with my new clothing is that I am something worth containing, packaging, ticketing. I am merchandise, a commodity, even if discarded merchandise at that.

In my new outfit I came over to the house to do some manly chores for Alice and to try again to patch things up with Zach. With typical acerbity, Alice greeted my new TBCC yellow jump suit: "What is that you're wearing? A big condom?" She chuckled, I wasn't sure if it was over my outfit or over what she had in store for me. "Look at these babies Rus." Piled to the ceiling were three mighty boxes containing the Millennium 3000, the most up-to-date computer system on the market. "Good luck putting that sucker together. If assembling the gas grill took you five hours, I can't imagine how many months you'll spend on this.

I made up a bed for you to sleep in. I figure you'll need at least the weekend."

I don't know if the boxes or Alice's lack of confidence intimidated me more, but I admit some regrets in buying the monstrosity already. Alice and I agreed that the Millennium 3000 might be the one way to keep Zach from running off somewhere — what more could he desire? But as with every purchase, I rarely consider what is required to start up and maintain the thing.

All it takes is a simple motion like picking your nose to get a sweat going in my TBCC so you could imagine the juices flowing as I opened the boxes. Styrofoam wedged inside each box, beyond the styrofoam rested bubble wrap, then heavy plastic and thin plastic and tape and labels and warning messages and registration information. Beneath this pile lay pieces of the machine. A soup simmered in my plastic clothes as I lifted the equipment monumentally from the boxes like I raised some hidden golden calf to its rightful position as deity.

"Look at you Rus, with that suit you could be a brilliant technician from a sci-fi movie," said Alice. "I think I'm getting turned on." First time today Alice might not have been completely sardonic. Indeed, the assurance and machismo I brandished upon handling the equipment invigorated me. I knew the parts as well as a soldier knows those of his rifle. Plugging in wires into all types of ports, sockets and surge protectors, I drew the breath of life into the nostrils of the machine. Talking the whole time about what this computer might do for Zach, Alice kept calling me *Rus*, but now I felt fully that I was *Technoman*.

Never mind that the iconography and the diagrams were shockingly direct and simple and that the machine essentially told me how to put itself together, I didn't pass this information to Alice. I enjoyed the novelty of her thinking I was brilliant, even if soon she would revert to believing otherwise. "My, how you are growing Rus. There's hope for you yet." Within an hour, I had the machine up and was registering everything from the system to the printer to CD-ROMs to my pecker. Within two hours Alice played Risk against the machine and was winning. Now *I* got turned on.

The whole time I had not heard a peep from Zach. "He's in the bedroom talking to his GigaPets and getting his daily nourishment of cartoons." Emboldened by my success on the Millennium 3000, I snapped my hands to my hips and stiffened my jaw, looking every mega-ounce the superhero. Then I stepped into Zach's animated space, hoisted him onto my shoulders, and headed out the door.

He giggled like I was a caped crusader, and followed, only tugging me briefly upon spotting the new computer — "Hey, what's that?" "Not now my boy" — and then looked straight ahead. "Let's give you a test flight on the lunar cycle." Today, he was ready to believe it was a rocket ship; all other days Zach would have said, "that's a bike, just a bike, even though I wish it was more than a bike."

For a while we had been teaching Zach how to ride the lunar cycle — Alice did most of the teaching. He'd been slow in learning, struggling to push the petals — never being able to keep his balance. For a boy turning eight not to be able to ride a bike is to consign him to a level of outcast even Zach had not heretofore experienced. So today I determined I would finally set him free. We must have looked incongruously radioactive with my yellow plastic suit, he with his virtual reality gear beneath his bicycle helmet. I held onto the edge of the bike seat steadying him as he gained momentum, my back sore and my body dripping from the awkward motion inside the suit — not that any movement in the suit would avoid perspiration.

"Son, I at 1300 hours, 6 minutes and 40 seconds, will release you."

"How long is that from now?"

"2 minutes and 10 seconds."

"Alright," he said tentatively, skeptically. All the while I had been loosening my grip and my control of the seat, as much because my back couldn't take the pressure as from his increasing steadiness. Even before the release time, I let go. As he moved away from me, neighbors stepped out of their houses and watched one of the grand clichés of the Long Island streets. An old man with one working arm hollered, "Atta' way, my boy."

A woman holding a newborn chimed in, "Look at him go."

Even Alice contributed to the growing chorus, "Oh, Zach that's wonderful." I expected to hear exultant music play. I imagine if he were alone on the street, Zach might have actually felt liberated by the experience, but how could he now? Not only did Alice take out the camera to record the event for posterity, a neighbor absurdly whipped out his video camera and began shooting.

"How hokey is this dad?"

"Pretty hokey," I confessed.

Not a fan of what was transpiring and unable to resist a media opportunity, Zach promptly spun out of control on the bike and aimed straight for the mailbox. He hit his target with enough velocity to knock the pole out of the ground.

"Wow," said the filming neighbor.

Zach tumbled dramatically and staggered back up with bloody raspberries on the knees and elbows. "Get that?" he asked the neighbor.

"Yeah."

"Send it in to *Video Bloopers*."

I carried Zach and the mangled lunar cycle back into the garage: "Good shot huh, worth twenty points, wouldn't you say dad?"

"I'm not sure if it's worth anything son."

"Sure it is. At least it should be worth a ride on the Millennium 3000."

"Alright."

Not even giving me time to bandage his scrapes, Zach jumped right onto the machine, dropped in the *Cyclokiller* CD and raced about in the deadly bicycle challenge. Zach tinkled on the mouse and the keyboard like a virtuoso, a prodigy, perhaps a young Mozart. No chance of Zach falling here, even as he cut and slashed his way through the most treacherous turns and obstacles. "Now, *this* is how to ride a bike dad."

"That's not how to ride a bike," said Alice. "You were just riding a bike. Now you are wasting your time." I knew enough to shut my mouth here.

"Mom, this computer makes you feel right in the action."

"It should, since with all the time you spend on computers, you'll never be in the action, so you might as well feel like you're in the action. Look at the your father; he's the most inactive active man I know."

Given how I had comported myself today, the cheap shot stung particularly hard, having a broad numbing effect on me. In contrast, Zach heard not a word. He survived while six murderous cyclists fell off cliffs or smashed into walls.

Alice must have noticed the hurt in my eyes, for she consoled, "I'm sorry Rus. I just get so frustrated. Look at him."

We both stared at Zach as he stared at the machine, his mouse dancing magically.

"How can he have any prayer with you as a father?"

"I'm trying."

"I know. That's the saddest part. You are a good guy. I love you. But you are Technoman and that is not good for Zach."

"Perhaps you're right."

"I wish I weren't."

"I'm only Technoman for a couple more months."

"Thank God. Then maybe we can fix everything."

"I hope so," and I embraced her, the plastic crinkling coldly against her warm body.

"I feel like I'm hugging my kitchen trash."

"You are, but I thought you would have figured that out in all the years we were married."

"Strange how I still think of you as my husband, even though you don't live here anymore."

"That's nothing, you still think of Zach as your son." Zach rode out there on the blue on a smile and a shoeshine, sending bikers off cliffs, a thousand miles away from either of us. I tried so hard not to be cruel, but I couldn't help it. Alice had marginalized me, and despite my better intentions, I had to diminish her too. Tears welled in her eyes quicker than I've been used to lately.   "I'm sorry."

"You are a shithead. You are trash."

"I'm sorry. I love you."

She didn't bother answering me and opened the front door. Alice showed me to the curb

Channel 79:
Hedonism in the Rubble

When Dolly called me on-line out of the blue, I blossomed more vulnerable to her charms than I would have been at anytime since becoming Technoman. I confess it was not her bleach-blonde hair nor the neon trinkets in her ears, but the farm-fed midwestern breasts that I thought might nurse me back to health.

I don't think my accumulated months as Technoman brought me to my present state of infirmary, but the incessant schedule, with its sharp cutbacks, shifts and adaptations doomed me. My bones are no longer supple; they're brittle. I own rashes that any Vullem worker would be proud to bare, my belly rumbles with a golf course worth of ulcers, and sciatica shoots down my left side. My heart rate pumps either too fast or too slow, but that's O.K. because it matches my breathing. At my advancing age, I have finally discovered the beauties of the three "A's" — acne, asthma and allergies. I move from one itinerary spot to another itching, wheezing and sneezing, and to soothe my ills, I take pharmaceuticals, chemicals and specially manufactured elixirs.

So when Dolly clanged on my Intrafacer with an anodyne for my digitally remastered sufferings, I flipped up my monitor and listened carefully.

"After I tried this new synthetic drug, all I could think of is you, for no one deserves to be turned on to this more than Technoman."

"Another synthetic drug?"

"I know, they come out with a new flavor every week, but Hedonism is different. It's the real thing. It'll cure your ills."

I didn't get into this mess without believing in people, and I believe in Dolly. "So when do you want to meet?"

"How about now?"

"Now? My schedule..."

"You always have a schedule. If you look at your schedule, you'll never know Hedonism."

"Let me ask you something: you're not trying to pass along any of those natural, herbal homeopathic medications on me are you? I mean I have not forgotten your bosom deception."

Dolly giggled. "Of course not. I swear upon these real breas
of mine, there is not one speck of reality in Hedonism."

Wearing enough makeup to create a mannequin's mask, s
came over in supersonic time and she dropped a pill on my tong
as she kissed me.

"I like what you've done with the place," Dolly said, forev
the one to use lines from cheesy sitcoms. In what might I
considered as Disney's version of an inventor's laboratory, n
apartment housed a gadget junkyard, toxic and glowing — wh
an undiscerning woman might consider exotic and arousing.

We talked and tongued and I tried to inveigle out of Dolly ju
what I had taken, the first product I had interacted with in to
months without a user's manual. As the minutes passed, she to
me with a nasal stuffiness of either plastic surgery or cocai
usage, "You'll find out soon enough."

"But what is it like?"

She eyed me with vague deceptiveness "It's... *hard*
describe."

"Is it like I'm sleeping when I'm awake?"

"Sort of," unconvincingly.

"Have you taken any?"

"Of course I have," falling into my waist.

"Ow!" she bit me on the gut. Correction, she took a chunk
me. Normally, I would recoil, but now I bit back, first on tl
thigh, then on the rump. We were chewing on each other for
good two or three minutes — given my respiratory rate I had
come up for air pretty quickly — before I knew Hedonism kick
in.

We spoke no more.

On the kitchen table, against the cabinet, across tl
countertop, along the ironing board, we tousled and snapped ar
snatched and wriggled. I found myself in orifices, but never f
long. One of us always grew restless. We could never sustain, ju
shoving and thrusting and shifting and mawing and mauling. W
groped inside of each other and then dived out, in a bloomir
rash, all prickly heat and kinetic energy. Flipping about tl
other's limbs like acrobats, we rubbed and kindled, compoundir

riction and fluids. The next thing I know her bicuspids ground
nto my thigh.

Obviously, if this kept up, we would have chewed up each
other's limbs. I found myself crashing against the kitchen tile just
o save the shards of our broken intimacies. We tried to kiss, but
ve head butted, my searching fingers dislodging blonde curls and
black roots. We tried to be animals, but were objects. Despite our
ntanglements, somehow together we were aroused and alone; we
plit off, breathing heavily, missing each other when we attempted
o reunite.

Then it happened.

Dolly, coming at me again, cracked into a state-of-the-art
adar detector — even effective from a mile distance. Turning
.way from me, Dolly raised her arms mightily, like an Amazon
varrior, and smashed down onto the radar detector, crushing it
eroically.

"Ourrgh," she growled triumphantly.

That bitch wrecked my Funkpig MegaBeam Radar Detector!
3oy, that gave me a fury and an erection I couldn't believe. That
er breasts suddenly appeared to have been pumped with an extra
int of blood didn't help matters. I entered into a perverse porno
artoon, as if a porno cartoon could be anything but perverse. I
vrestled with her: I'm not sure, but I believe Dolly is not a robot.
he discovered the huge new microwave GE sent me that could
oast a 25-pound turkey and she jumped up and down on it, until I
nocked her out of the way. Too late. That bitch broke my
;argantuan Laser Baster!

Tackling Dolly, I took her tumbling into a whole stockpile of
adgetry that she rolled about erotically. Her heavy make-up,
specially the thick rouge and mascara, melted and dripped until
er face became the mask of an exotic warrior. As if the hardware
ave her superhuman strength — like they were cans of spinach
r something — she emerged wildly powerful and charged. The
ombination pocket calculator/Nintendo game? Rubble. The
lender/ice cream maker? Shattered. The remote suburban
ninivan car set? Wrecked. The new human gigapets? D.O.A. The
irtual reality soldiers? M.I.A.

Somehow in the effort to stop her, I grew less aggres
toward Dolly and more toward my equipment. My stockpi
essentially distributed chronologically and as Dolly made her
to the bottom, she unearthed my first gifts as Technoman —
soup to nuts food processor with its bread machine, pasta ma
and coffee urn; the cell phone with the microprocessor
recorder and baby laser beam; the dayglo blue electric suit
2,727 small bulbs; the combination electric shaver, walkman
smoke alarm. When Dolly pounced on those sentimental objec
savagely tossed her aside and found myself sending a forearm
the food processor.

"Shit!" That hurt. Goddamn heavy resin doesn't even
while my arm bounced, burned and trembled. No match one
one with the machine, I picked up the broken steel arm of an
muscle-group aerobic powerciser and whacked down brut;
taking out the pasta-making component in one fell swoop. F
there, I refused to desist as not even the accessories escaped
wrath. Awed and excited, Dolly joined in and we hacked a
through this jungle of technology for at least three or four s
minutes, huffing and wheezing.

We continued to destroy until we grew soft and tire
touched her cheek, part of it came off in my hand, and the
caressed her. We lay down to sleep, pawing scraps of
wreckage and pulling it over us as a jagged fragmented quilt.

Channel 80:
Remote Realizations

After that night of debauchery, I slept more than I ha
months, so I awoke desolate, groping and starving. Thoug
craved breakfast, I ran out of the house for a meeting
Geoffrey and Carmen, clamping my Intrafacer on the
Fortunately, a SonicMart sat on the right side of the road nex
Prometheus Laboratories. There I filled up a 64-ounce S
Thirst Annihilator, snatched a three pack of yodels, a two-pac
Suzie-Q's, a tube of Pringles, a six-pack of Slim Jims, a baby
of Fluffer-Nutter, a microwaveable melting breakfast sn
Pseudo-Nachos topped with Imitation Cheez Whiz... $4'

ater, I carried two grocery bags into the meeting. Talk about the
ostpartum Hedonism munchies. Geoffrey had his own
reoccupations, however.

"I've done it, Russell," he pronounced. "Correction," with a
od to Carmen, "We've done it."

"The remote is completed?"

"All the bugs are out and we are fully operational."

"Weren't you supposed to be done a few weeks from now?"

"Next month. We're ahead of schedule. Do you believe it?"

"Wow," I tried to seem excited, but I confess, I had to stuff a
Suzy-Q in my mouth before I could hear any more. In two bites, I
ook care of that, skimming my fingers across the cardboard
upport and the plastic packaging for the remnants stuck there.
Damn, nothing better than a Suzy-Q, chocolate tempered by
reservatives, something unearthly in its sponginess, and then the
cream filling, a subtle hydration and whipping of coagulated non-
lairy coffee toppings.

"That's the good news, but now we have problems."

"Problems?"

"Now that it's done, how do we protect it?"

"You have a patent right?"

"Sure, but what about imitators?"

"Well, then, you protect it by putting it out to the public.
Why don't you release it?"

"Mass manufacture is months away. But imitators are the
least of it."

"Then what is it?"

"Dangus."

"Dangus?"

"Dangus."

"Shit."

"Shit-yeah."

I ripped open the Devil Dog two-pack and shoved them in.
Good. But what the hell, could they be any drier? I might as well
have been eating sand the way I choked and coughed, gagging and
banging the chest, tossing a convenience store smorgasbord onto
the table before I unearthed the 64-ounce Sleet Thirst Annihilator,
stabbing a ruler-long straw into it, and sucking away. It cured me

of the parches, but I had to contend with the huge cup already deconstructing under the strong compound bubbling and kicking inside.

"Dangus?"

"Shit-yeah."

"How do you know? How could it be? Everybody thinks Dangus is done. Since his no-show in April, the media doesn't even pay attention to him. I think Dangus has shot his load."

"Don't kid yourself. Dangus has a few more bullets in the holster."

"How do you know?"

"Come with me." Geoffrey led me into fuse room. "Look here." He pointed down to the three dirty left bootprints that appeared in a line toward the wiring.

"Yeah?"

"That's his boot."

After studying the prints carefully and noshing on Slim Jims the way Bugs Bunny eats carrots, I asked, "Where's his right boot?"

"Who cares? We've got one boot, a Dangus boot, who the hell else would go into the fuse room? What do we need with another foot?"

"It'd be nice that's all. What does he hop?"

"Shit."

"Could he be a pegleg?"

"What's the difference? He's after me."

"What would he want with you? He's already zapped you. He doesn't tend to repeat himself."

"The remote's complete."

"How does he know?"

"He knows. He always knows."

Carmen, who shadowed us, definitively added, "He knows." I tried to digest this paranoia as I took bites out of my two Twinkies simultaneously, their yellow sponge collapsing, the indestructible processed albino filling shooting across my molars like toothpaste. Only the difficulty of tearing open all the air-tight thick plastic packaging slowed my feeding frenzy.

"I don't think Dangus is too happy about us finishing," Carmen explained.

Geoffrey signaled me over to him, "Come with me," he whispered. With my arms around my remaining grocery bag, Geoffrey led me to a storage closet as Carmen followed. "This is the only place I can guarantee Dangus is not listening," he explained, *sotto voce.*

"What?"

"I turned around the microcamera and sent muzak into the bugs."

"Are you kidding me?"

"No, why should I kid you?"

"I don't know." I confess I couldn't believe a word he was saying. Microcameras and bugs! Bullshit! Anyway with his whispering and my crunching PseudoNachos and Pringles slathered in imitation Cheez Whiz, I could hardly hear him.

I caught no verbs, only nouns, and most of them proper ones: "Dangus... SONY... hostile takeover... MRIs... NASA... JFK... Suzy-Q's... microwaves... potatoes... Carmen... Slomin's Security... Bill Gates... Carpal Tunnel Syndrome... Lithium... Javit's Center... your home."

"My home?"

With every chip gone, I could hear a little better as I popped open the Fluffer-Nutter and scooped two fingers into the little jar. "I want to wire your home for the remote."

While my lips smacked shut to hold in the marshmallow-peanut spackling and my sticky fingers dived back into the jar, I swallowed three times to free my tongue for speech, "Why in God's name?"

"Insurance. If Dangus gets us, then the remote lives on."

"And what if Dangus decides to come after me?"

"He wouldn't dare come after Technoman."

"On the contrary, I think he wouldn't dare *not* go after Technoman."

"What are you afraid of? You don't even think he is after us. How could you be concerned about him coming after you?"

I don't know if it were the food or what, but I became awfully queasy. "Uhh, my house is a little messed up right now."

"All the more reason you need the remote. It'll bring order into your life."

When Geoffrey made that stupid of a statement, I had nothing left to say, except, of course, to agree to his request. "Whatever. I don't care. Hook me up. Wire me so that when I fart the fan comes on for all I care. Just let me go now."

"Go? Why?"

I didn't answer. I couldn't: my gluey tongue cleaved to the roof of my mouth. I flipped my Intrafacer monitor up and down for a formal farewell and slipped quickly into the elevator then out onto the street, first shuffling, then jogging, then sprinting, my hardware jangling, toward SonicMart, still holding the collapsing 64-ounce Sleet Thirst Annihilator cup in hand. I tried to refill, but the bottom fell out. I had to get a brand new cup, and I dispensed the sloppy fluid with one hand and stretched for a fruit rolled crack jack with the other. I made an evening of it, eating an aisle at a time, occasionally dropping a buck at the virtual reality games to allow for proper digestion. When I finally walked out into the late evening sky, a three-quarter moon guiding my way, I strangely found myself still hungry and wide awake.

Channel 81:
Fire Island

What a surprise, I couldn't sleep. Since I was going off to Fire Island anyway, I figured I might as well get there for sunrise, so I rode east with streaks of light kicking up in the dim gray milky sky, till I turned south to the ocean and crossed the causeway, the late March winds still breaking green waves cold and choppy. Unfortunately, the island did not end where the road did. Robert Moses must not have had a chance to finish paving. Instead, I wandered through a few miles of sand dunes and scrub oaks, staring right at the bleary eye of the sun that splattered crimson and turquoise dapplings about the cottony clouds. Admittedly, I felt so ridiculous with my Intrafacer on that I unstrapped the whole apparatus carrying it like it was my occupational burden.

At the end of Fire Island lies a storybook cottage. As I grew closer to it, I spotted a single scrawny figure on the beach running, hands in her hair. Rarely do I search for something and it actually appears. But wouldn't you know that little Augie emerged, this mirage on a spit of land at the very edge of America. And to make matters more surreal, she was yelling and crying hysterically. When I caught up with her, little Augie threw her arms around me, not even bothering to say hello. So I didn't ask her where she'd run off to all this time.

"What's a matter?"

"Oh, it's terrible."

"It's alright now," I assured, caressing her tenderly. "I understand. I have read your journal."

She looked sad and surprised. "You invaded my most sacred space?" Little Augie collapsed into me. "I appreciate the effort."

We seemed reconciled and connected, so I pressed on.

"Now, what's terrible?"

"Him! Him!"

"Who him? Satan?"

"Who else?"

"But he's dead."

"Yeah, that's the problem."

"What?"

"Look over there," she pointed to the breakfront at the beach. A body could be discerned even from this distance. "No, don't look over there. It's too horrible."

"Satan killed a man?"

"No, you idiot. That's Satan."

"But he died months ago. You showed me the body."

"Yeah and there he is washed up on the beach, dead again."

"I don't get it. How can he die again?"

"I don't know. I guess the same way he dies every day since I've been here."

"Every day?" This awkward questioning continued until she explained that each morning Satan's body washed ashore, "sometimes, even dressed like Father Jeremiah."

"Are you sure it's not the same corpse?"

"Impossible. Every evening I burn the body."

"Oh yeah," I should have remembered that.

"It's getting pretty bad ... I'm running out of wood."

"You've got to get back to the morgue."

"I can't. A promise is a promise. I must get to the corpse before anyone else."

"Yeah, now you can, through the dead of winter, but summer's coming and there'll be boats on the shore, walkers, swimmers, jet-skiers, power-sailors, dune-buggies, road-rangers, dirt-bikers, all-terrain vehicles, horseback riders ..."

"O.K. I get the idea, but what am I supposed to do?"

"Don't you realize the only reason the bodies show up on the shore is because you're here to burn them. He wouldn't dare die if you take off."

"You think?"

"I think."

"Yeah?"

"Yeah. Look, gather your things, burn today and tomorrow, then meet me on Friday at the morgue."

She agreed resignedly. "In my next life, I'm coming back as an atheist."

I helped her collect the wood and then we walked to the shore to drag the waterlogged corpse. Like a beached seal, Satan's body flopped and sprawled; hair salty and tangled, he presented a perfectly ordinary corpse, repulsive and ripe for decay; he could have been a homeless man, a drug dealer, or both. That he might not have even been Satan didn't seem to matter to me. I had read enough to be a believer.

Later on as night fell and the almost-spring sky became virtually overloaded and overdetermined with so many stars that blackness served merely as a backdrop, we lit the fire that would be the hot bed for Satan's body. Out here where it is so irrevocably land's end that it could be considered the offing, where even the light pollution could not find its way, the flames dived and weaved through the wood, cracking and dancing till they found their eternal partner who (incredibly) stunk even worse in death than in life, as if the skin held in a sack of sulfur. Thankfully he burned hot and fast. We watched carefully, half expecting, even hoping, to witness a spirit rise up out of the smoke and float out over the waves.

As the flames grew higher and the wood popped and he sizzled, I yearned to sing campfire songs or roast marshmallows or something. I put my arm around little Augie like she was my mother and, as Satan's body cooked to ash, she spoke of my days as a cub reporter and all the bodies she'd shown me over the years.

Channel 82:
Just When You Thought It Was Safe to Use Your Computer

Pines Tar: Dangus Shuts Down the Web

After disappearing last month, Paddy Dangus has returned with perhaps his most dramatic and damaging act yet. Yes, I say Paddy Dangus did it, even while the Police will not, even as the *Herald's* libel lawyer urged against reporting the news, for I know Dangus shut down the Internet throughout Long Island as well as I know the monitor in front of my face.

No matter what they say publicly, sources in the police department and the district attorney's office have privately confirmed that they are almost certain that Dangus committed the act. For the record, however, law enforcement officials are providing only the basic facts.

"The alleged perpetrator or perpetrators — and in this case we definitely think it was multiple perps — caused service on the Web to shutdown from midnight on May 5 until providers could repair links late in the evening the next night," said Arnold Pedersen, Nassau County police captain coordinating the investigation.

Nassau and Suffolk county detectives are not the only ones involved in the case. The FBI has now indicated that its number one priority in the region is the capture of Dangus. "These acts have affected commerce and the infrastructure, affected the very fabric of American life in this area," said Rupert Darr, regional FBI spokesman. "We are prepared to take aggressive and decisive action."

Too aggressive and too decisive, according to Richard Mason, former Suffolk County detective, who has been carefully tracking Dangus activities for the past six months. Mason has been highly critical of the FBI's effort, criticism that apparently led to his suspension from the force. "I had Dangus right where I wanted him and then those buffoons from the feds got their big suits in the way and loused everything up."

All signs indicate that huge forces within the criminal justice systems have hunkered down to an old-fashioned manhunt, replete with search warrants being handed out like parking tickets, special access permits, bulked-up street patrols, furious D.A. evidence gathering, and a barrage of full-moon all-night stakeouts. An officer friend of mine said he can never remember the overtime being so good.

However, police are tight-lipped about how Dangus shut down the Web in the first place. "That information cannot be released to the public for its confidentiality is vital to the investigation," said Pedersen.

One thing for sure is the way officers bristle and scoff when I suggest that perhaps Dangus sent a 24-hour virus through the system. "Don't be ridiculous," said Darr. "This is not a science fiction movie you know. Dangus does not have the capability to do that. I can tell you one thing: Dangus may have caused the problem, but he certainly didn't correct it. The Internet providers did a heroic job of getting the Island back on line. That's a fact."

Neither would police comment on whether Dangus merely cut the central lines that sprawl out throughout Long Island to service the communities.

"Nobody's talking because there is nothing to say," said Dave Miller, whose unauthorized biography on Paddy Dangus, *Suburban Menace*, was to appear in book stores next week, but will be delayed another week as a final chapter on the Web triumph is rushed to the printer. "Systems that are supposed to be impenetrable, ways of life that are supposed to be permanent, are sent spiraling off into chaos, entropy you might say, all by one man."

Of course, many tragedies have occurred because of the incident (See the *Herald's* special wraparound section, "The Web Massacre," for more). Trevor Hoffman of Upper Brookville claims he lost $1.3 million because of the inability to shift stocks; the Sloans of Farmingdale said they lost an entire family vacation to Las Vegas because of reservations that lapsed that day from their inability to get on the Internet ("Oh, what might have been," lamented matriarch Emma Sloan. "I think we as a family will always look wistfully back on this missed opportunity"); Mary Paggione of Holtsville suffered from a terrible angina attack because her prescription was never filled when the Web shut down; aspiring actress Lisa Bialek of Dix Hills missed the final casting auditions for all Dorothies for Broadway's new version of the *Wizard of Oz*, a role for which her mother explains she was lock; and have I mentioned the thousands who got sick because they couldn't get the updated weather report off the Web, a report which warned of plummeting, unseasonable temperatures and cold rain that day. Add to these woes, the obvious: the missed flights, misbegotten traffic accidents, misplaced orders, and miscommunications.

However, perhaps the biggest gripe Long Islanders had with the Internet shutdown was boredom. "Thank goodness it was a weekday," said Wayne Mills, a bartender at Tara's. "People would have known what do to with themselves if the Web broke up on their free time." As it was, none of the employees could get their banking done or their bills paid. LILCO reports more delinquent checks for utility payments this month than in any other in recent history. "Dangus lost us thousands of dollars on interest alone," said LILCO spokesman Nora Meyland.

How big was the Internet disaster and how big has Dangus gotten? Big enough for the President of the United States to respond to a question about him. "This type of behavior cannot and will not be tolerated," said President Curmen. "You can be assured that my staff is keeping me fully informed of the subversive activities of one Paddy Dangus and we will take appropriate action."

Channel 83:
Preserving the Wreckage

As Angelica entered my apartment, I decided not even to try to explain what had happened. She turned to my broken pile of gadgets like she walked into a war zone, immediately tending to the casualties.

"Rus, what is all this?" Answering the question was more awkward than I expected since I had sort of indicated to Angelica months ago that I would donate all my gadgetry to her institute after my year came to an end.

"I'm sorry. Things got out of hand."

Her eyes were welling up and her voice breaking, "What got out of hand Rus? What got out of hand?" She crumbled next to the pile like she too was a broken piece of fine equipment.

I didn't think I needed to explain my actions to her any more than I need to explain them to you, and yet she was sobbing and fumbling gently with the pasta maker to see if it could be reattached to the rest of the food processor. And she carefully gathered the bits of plastic on the floor like they were pieces of an ancient puzzle. For Angelica, these were her ruins of Pompeii, her Dead Sea Scrolls. From the pile, she kept looking up at me, so I too would catalog the enormity of devastation. Even as I cowered behind the monitor of my Intrafacer, I began to believe that not since Caesar burned the great library at Alexandria had such a barbaric act been committed.

My first instinct was to blame Dolly, my second was to blame Hedonism, my third was to displace: "You were planning on using these objects for a display on the year of Technoman, isn't that right?"

"Yes."

"So there you are."

I wasn't trying to be mean; in fact, I think I was trying to be kind. Nevertheless, Angelica keened and wept. She caressed the wires of the MegaBeam Radar Detector like they were hairs attached to a little bleeding boy. "The waste, the senseless destruction."

Every time I stiffened my resolve to explain, I choked and clammed up, nervously tapping my keypad. Somehow I think Angelica knew what had happened. All I could do was try to save what was left.

"I know I said you might be able to have all this stuff one day. Why don't you take it today?"

"But you are not finished being Technoman."

"I only have a little while left and I want to transfer all these things before anything else happens to them."

Angelica recoiled from the suggestion that more damage could occur. "All right then."

The agreement lifted a bit of the accumulated tension in the room. Angelica stopped lamenting and started planning. "You have any plastic bags?"

"Are you kidding? I am still Technoman you know."

"How many bags do you have?"

I opened my cabinets revealing hundreds of bags: sandwich baggies, little freezer bags, food storage bags, small pail trash bags, tall kitchen garbage bags, hefty, heavy duty synch sacks, and finally huge all-purpose leaf bags.

"Good," she said, sizing up the formidable task in front of her. "We are going to need every last one of them. And I'll need masking tape too."

Hours passed as every bag was carefully labeled and the pieces set down gingerly like they were car accident victims or something. Every time I tried to shove equipment in quickly, Angelica's patience and solemnity eased my exertions. Painstakingly, we excavated this archeological dig, extracting the artifacts from the resin and silicon layers that emerged from months of intense activity. Soon her dad appeared at my front door, with an extended length van in the driveway, and helped us carry everything out.

As they drove off, I started to ruminate that I had given the best part of myself away. But these contemplations were cut short because when I returned to the kitchen, *she* was waiting for me.

"Jesus, I thought they'd never leave."

"Dolly, what— "

"I need money."

"For what?"

"You know what," today's makeup was particularly heavy and her attitude particularly confrontational.

I attempted to respond, but had no idea what to say. The whole scene felt like some anti-drug video that I had been hooked into performing.

"Be serious."

"I'm not kidding. I need the money and that's not all."

"What else?" the question coming out less incredulous and more compliant than I wanted it to.

"I want you to pick it up with me."

Suddenly, I understood and became firm. "No, you got me all wrong. You offered it to me. We tried it. It was interesting, but that's all."

"You mean you didn't like it." She rubbed up against me, remarkably sexy in a terribly, aggressively grotesque way.

"Well…" I couldn't help smiling at Dolly fondly.

"So, let's do it again."

I confess arousal, yet I remained immovable, the body bags Angelica carted off still fresh in my mind. "No, I'm done. That's it. I'm just a dabbler and I dabbled and now I'm done."

"You can't just dabble in Hedonism. You are in now for the long haul."

"I am not."

"You are too."

"Oh yeah."

"Yeah." Looking around, Dolly seized upon the thick metal accessory tube of my Hoover Vortex 3000 Vacuum and then brandished it at me threateningly.

"Don't even think about it." However wild and strong Dolly turned in her frenzy, I figured with a good eighty pounds over her, I could restrain her.

"I'm going to get exactly what I want."

"And how are you going to do that?" I readied myself for a good fight.

"I'm going to bash in your Intrafacer until you come with me."

"My... Intrafacer." That caught me off guard.

"That's right," and she smacked down straight toward my monitor.

"No!" I screamed, blocking the blow with my forearms and backing away as I absorbed the bruising thud and moved the Intrafacer to a temporarily safe distance.

"Hey, what's the matter?!? Don't want to lose your Intrafacer?" I quickly understood that I could protect my person much better than I could my Intrafacer. I was much more vulnerable to this little woman than I had initially figured. She lifted the vacuum pipe again. I cringed and covered. This time she pulled back. "I didn't think so."

I stepped even further away from her, thinking of even making a run for it. Then she asked gently and meekly, "Won't you come with me? I need you."

I nodded compliantly and Dolly hugged me with warmth and affection. Looking into my Intrafacer monitor, seeing the reflection of my gray eyes, she offered sweetly, "Everything's going to be fine. Go get some money now dear." She spoke to me like we were an old married couple.

As I grabbed the cash from my bedroom, I thought about taking off my Intrafacer and putting it safely away in a huge, heavy-duty trash bag, giving it over to Angelica so it could be protected forever. But instead I kept it on as I headed out with Dolly. I knew without it, I would not be myself.

Channel 84:
Zach's Birthday Party

Alice gave me one job for Zach's party, so I stand at the express supermarket counter line with birthday candles in my hand, waiting for an incorrect price to be re-entered into the computer, you know with the manager's keys and the rest, then waiting for an outmoded grocery card to be updated, then waiting for coupons to be validated, then waiting for new codes to be inserted for the fresh vegetables. Four times I consider hopping off this line for a regular line, but I am next, forever next, so I stay and finally the check-out boy scans the candles, but the scanner doesn't beep no matter how many ways he points and clicks.

"Something must be wrong with the UPC code. Hold on I'll get a manager and I'm going to need keys too."

I say nothing to all this, only flashing my debit card to express my full willingness to pay. As I wait and wait, I try not to completely waste my time, so I tickle some keys on the Intrafacer only to discover that the computer froze up. No matter, I dial Alice on my cell phone, but the call does not go through. Fortunately, by this time the manager comes and guesses that the candles are $1.19 — quite a bargain. I slide my debit card through the register and it beeps at me confusedly. Three more times I slide the card, but it fails to respond. The check-out boy tries the card another half dozen times to no avail. The line grows longer. "It must have gotten demagnetized."

I have no cash in my pockets. As I leave, the check-out boy is calling once again for the manager, with his magical overring slips and keys.

The birthday parties at Anima World are only forty-five minutes long, and I've already missed the first five minutes, plus I had no candles either. Alice will love this, boy oh boy. As I step into the party room, each of Zach's friends sits at a separate study carrel in front of a computer and sends out typical eight-year-old birthday greetings to Zach. Instead of a shot-in-arm for each year of the birthday boy's life, these kids send computed-generated assassins across the network to kill the cartoon image of Zach on his machine. For every time Zach is machine-gunned, macheted, knifed, ninja'd, poisoned, or exploded, the boy squeals with glee.

Never more animated than when he is being killed, Zach uses the computer table as a platform to perform all types of wacky cartoon and video game voices, each one concludes in a choke, a cough, then a dying fall.

"Hey buddy," I say, "Why don't you try this on for size now that you're a mature 8-year-old."

I hand him my Intrafacer and he straps it on. Immediately, he becomes the coolest kid in the room, like he were driving around in a Porsche or something. "Woah!" says one friend. "Psych!" says another. "Rom!" says still another. Who knew my boy had so many friends?

While Zach dies two dozen times and then performs as a space-age alien in my Intrafacer, I try to keep up with a party moving at warp speed. Alice helps the 12-year-old who is running the festivities for Anima World take out the robotized cryogenic pets for the boys to play with. First comes the animatronics baby goats that each boy gets to feed a bottle. "The goat's cool," says Clifton Alberti, "but the bottle stuff is gay." Clifton grows happier when the barely artificial alligator waddles out and opens his mouth so the boys can feed it toy turtles, the big reptile's teeth even crunching up the plastic shells. Then wanders out the grand buffalo who ceremoniously drops chips out of his butt that the boys indelicately toss about like frisbees. To Alice's great satisfaction — especially following the months of *sturm und drang* that had gone into the planning and decisions (not to mention the $790 price tag) — all the boys agree that this party is the greatest they've ever been to. The animatronic rattler moves like only a fake snake can, with a marvelously clunky recoil and the boys stick a glass with a rubber top in front of its menacing fangs to extract its venom. Yes these are thrills and chills that any red-blooded American kid would desire, but they are nothing compared to the Shark Attack finale. Instead of the shark twisting about in some tank, the creators of Anima World brilliantly load him up on the computer screens, hand each of the boys 3-D glasses, splash out the most realistic, state-of-the-art nautical graphics and let the boys go. Each one gets a chance to feed Jaws either an arm or a leg, and when the shark clamps down, blood spurts out and dozens of other sharks come rushing in to join in the feeding frenzy.

The party rushes forward as the sharks swim away and the words "Happy Birthday" appear on the screens and a computer-generated voice drones out: "Everybody pick a voice to sing Happy Birthday to Zach."

After each of the boys clicks on a different voice, the computers start serenading Zach. There are laughers and gassers, opera singers and hum-dingers, football tacklers and count draculas, Germans and vermins, all regaling Zach as a Buzz Lightyear theme cake rolls out. The cake tastes so good it could almost be fake and Zach opens the presents quickly for another group of kids are already lined up for the next party. Wads of cake stuck in his cheeks, Zach entertains his guests with imitations appropriate to each gift he receives. This achievement is all the more impressive given the move to retro-computer goods currently dominating the kid toy scene. Zach gets scads of comparatively old-fashioned computer games, nostalgic Pac-Mans and Space Invaders, pre-64-bit Mario Brothers, not too mention, wacky, primitive Gameboys. Some of the gifts are bizarre amalgamations of present technologies and past trends like the GigaPet Rocks and Plants and the lava-lamp/kaleidoscope screensavers. One wise-ass kid has the nerve to present Zach with a baseball glove. Zach rips wrappers and whips out imitations with increasing urgency.

As the 12-year-old host leads us out and ushers the next party in, Zach is still talking, still performing, even as his friends hop into their off-road vehicles for their on-road departures. During the entire party, Zach has not spoken once using his real voice. With his friends gone, even he realizes that he is still talking in the voice of "Fred," a computer-generated character best known and loved for his dopey drawl.

"I gosh I gut to tuk en my reo voice nowwww." Zach touches his lips as he sits in Alice's car with the two of us. "WOAHOH, I carnt doodoo it." I figure Zach's joking, a final encore from the prankster, but then he acts more and more disturbed.

"Hayja! HAAAYJA! I carnt stup my fuk voice!" Zach grows frustrated and teary. "Ware's my reo voice! Ware— " he struggles to recapture his own modulations and frequencies, "Ware? Wa? Waa? Waaaaaaaa!" Now he's crying and mumbling, listening to hear himself and only hearing Fred.

Even if he regained his voice in the murmurs, neither I nor Alice could know since he cries louder and angrier with each passing failure. Soon, he stamps and whacks his hands against the dashboard. Zach's crying and tantrums build till he produces an entire series of staggered, convulsive ticks, most particularly a few fast breaths followed by a blinding twist of the head. Once he could be reached, Alice gathers him in, gently holding and rocking Zach, even as his tick hurtles him temporarily from her arms. Lovingly, Alice sings to Zach an old Ramones song, "Nothing to do, nowhere to go, I want to be sedated," not at the Ramones' break-neck pace mind you, but quarter-speed, sweetly, gingerly, whispering the lyrics like they were "Hush, little baby." She sings that song six times: first two through crying and ticks, the second two through just crying, the final two in relative silence. When it ends, Zach asks, "Why did you stop Mom? Sing again." Zach's words are finally clear.

"Mom?" Zach asked, "whose voice am I using now?"

"Yours," she told him with relief. He smiles. Even though he is unable to recognize his own voice, he is satisfied that at least his mother can identify it.

Channel 85:
Geoffrey Builds a Smart House

Wiring my house, Geoffrey might as well have wired himsel[f] yapping and controlling, all fears and triumphs rolling forwar[d] like old tires through potholes. I thought too much to talk. Tha[t] was O.K. because Geoffrey opened no spaces in the ears fo[r] response. Not even old Dave Miller could slip in a joke an[d] Angelica managed to sign a contract without ever uttering a word[.]

"So with the Tesla Institute contribution you'll be permitte[d] to rip the house out of its foundation the minute Rus is done wit[h] it and drag the whole fucking thing out east to that potato farm o[f] yours." Geoff didn't even wait for the nod. "Now, let me sho[w] you a few other things Rus. To turn on the fireplace, you hit this.[.]" Flames shot up. "Pretty warm and cozy, huh. And if you want t[o] water the plants, hit this." The edges of the house rained. "And i[f] you want to dim the lights, you hit this." The volume of Mile[s] Davis's *Kind of Blue* dropped a few notches. "No, I mean you hi[t] this." The ceiling fans jumped on like helicopters readying fo[r] takeoff. "No, no, this." The room grew soft into shadows. "Yes[,] watch that again. Hit this for light up and down." The nigh[t] followed the day. "Now watch this," pointing the apparatus to the bathroom. A thundering came from the toilet.

"And that's where I'm heading." He dropped in a chair like a fallen king, his remote his sceptre. "The greatest invention since the computer and I am to be brought down by a Mick in a flatbed. Did I tell you about the potatoes left in my fireplace? I did? Oh yeah. But anyway. You know what that buffoon Mason said, 'Dangus just shut down the Web. Why would he deal with small potatoes like you?' You know what I said to that dumb bastard, 'Small potatoes. You talk to SONY and tell me I'm small potatoes.' He didn't even believe Dangus zapped Carmen and me in the first place. The authorities can't be bothered with me. And the very night after the police came calling, Dangus came calling." We all looked at him. "No, I didn't see him, but the next morning at the lab the lights were all fucked up and my transistors were tampered with. He's juicing up my lab to fry me again.

Jesus, I look at the night sky and I see him. He's the fucking man in the moon. It's like I'm being stalked in a low-budget horror film. Every unrecognizable noise and I scream like a little girl. I'm a total wreck. You know what else, I've got diarrhea."

We winced in repulsion. I had half a mind to turn him on to a dose of Hedonism. "And you know what's worse, when Mason came back the next day, you know what he asked me: 'Are you sure *you* are not Dangus?' " That made us listen up. "Yeah, he said it just like that: 'Are you sure *you* are not Dangus?' So I said, 'Are *you*?' That bastard, Mason, smiled. 'You certainly have the technical skills to be Dangus.' So I spent the next hour defending myself to Mason instead of trying to convince him to put his goons at my lab waiting to nab Dangus."

I told Geoff not be so offended, since Mason asked me the same thing. "Technoman as Dangus!" Sphere laughed gleefully. "That's great. Hey, I could see why he'd ask that... You aren't Dangus, are you?" I didn't respond, just looked at him blankly. "No, you're right. You're not smart enough to be Dangus."

Then old man Miller confessed that Mason had too questioned him. "Of course," said Geoff, "who else could be Dangus but his biographer. That would explain how much you know about him and all that inside information you seem to magically gather." Miller chuckled comfortably. "I could see you: the mad scientist doing all types of wacky rewiring with your three fingers tickling about the diodes... I guess I better shut up. There's no reason to piss you off, just in case you are Dangus.

"Mmmmmm. They didn't ask Angelica if she was Dangus. You know what that means. She must be Dangus then. Ha, Ha. I'm sure you'll have his white truck before it's all over, you acquisitive temptress you."

Geoff turned his attention away from us and onto the two boxes still unopened in the middle of my living room, remaining even though the wiring of my Smart House was completed. Past the styrofoam, bubble-wrap, plastic and tape, Geoffrey pulled out what seemed to be an Intrafacer. "This is the finest in wearable computers." He started strapping it on. "Look at this 233 Megahertz Pentium processor with 48 megs of RAM, and a 689-meg hard drive running Windows 01. And forget about the shoulder and cap deal. Instead the touch-screen display fits in the belt holster and look at this nice flat panel." He's started ripping open the other box. "The best thing about it is that it works with this virtual view golf cap. Feel that baby. It's as light as a toupee. See this eyepiece, that's 960-by-720 pixel computer display, and the headphone sound is CD quality. Better yet, it's got this noise-canceling microphone for issuing voice-recognition commands to wearable computing devices. If I live through this next month. I could see me transforming myself into one big remote control. How fucking cool would that be! Look at this thing, would you. Rus, it relegates your Intrafacer to a piece of shit. Isn't that sad, the technological world is already passing Technoman by.

"Angelica, Annnnnngelica, I see the way you're looking at me," insinuating, "I see, I see the lust in your eyes. Don't worry, when I'm through with this stuff, you can have it, every scrap and tittle. I see why you and Rus run together. Well, you'll have a third in your party soon because I can't see how our friend Mr. Dangus could ignore a place like this. Anyway, Rus remember, when Dangus gets me, you become the keeper of the flame, the one who has the true fully operational universal remote, of course until he gets you. Then perhaps Dangus will be the keeper of the flame."

He laughed and then turned on his body-mounted computer. For a few minutes, Geoff withdrew from us and turned in to the machine. For the last time, he looked directly at me, matching up my hardware to his. "I want to know what it's like to be you, Technoman, especially since the job I did on your house assures me that you are going to know what it's like to be me."

Channel 86:
A Trinity at the Morgue

Visiting her on the solitary midnight shift, I greeted Little Augie at the morgue. I don't think her return home agreed with her. Since I saw her last, she grew quite a substantial mustache and a few whiskers twirled about her chin.

Embracing me, she whispered, "Rus, Rus, come quickly, for you must see these before I burn them." She led me into the back room, the room which everyone knew was Little Augie's very own, hers in which to examine and to sleep –– hey, if you worked at the morgue as long as Little Augie the least you could get is your own private space.

Three shrouds rested across three rolling tables.

"The Easter Bunny left me a basket," she said, dramatically pulling away the sheets. I examined the bodies as carefully as the wicked sulfurous fumes would permit me.

"Let's see here. Well this one looks like Satan, and this one... looks like... Satan, and this one looks... like... Satan." Over the past year, I confess I have grown comfortable, even at peace, with not understanding things, yet the sight of three devils all in a row even caused me to ruminate and puzzle.

Little Augie explained, "He's multiplying. Isn't that sweet of him."

"How can he multiply if he's dead?"

"I don't know. Why don't you ask him?"

"Which one?"

"Look at them, look at their hands."

I half expected their paws to be at their crotches, but that wasn't the case at all, for their gestures were solemn and full of prayer. The middle one had his right hand to his forehead, the one to his right had a hand on the heart, and the one on his left spread his arm across his chest. "What is this? They look like they belong on a totem pole."

"Not quite." Then she genuflected and moved from one gesture to the other to the other. "Father, Son, and Holy Ghost. Don't you see he gave me a mock Trinity in death, just as the Trident has always been his mock Trinity in life."

"Why? Why would he bother with you?"

"Why would he put this on my arm?" She flashed a big, purplish pussy blotch across my eyes. I recoiled. Overall, this was turning out to be one of the more disgusting evenings of my repulsive little life. "And why this?" She yanked up a pantleg and showed me a tuft of fur on her ankle. "Why? I can't tell you. But I can guarantee this is all happening. Perhaps it is because I believe."

"Keep the faith sister."

Neither of us knew what to say after I made that stupid comment. So as always in such situations I found words.

"What are you going to do with them now?"

"Burn them."

"Shouldn't you show them to somebody, some of the other M.E.s, even a technician."

"I've shown them to you."

"If you haven't figured it out, I'm not enough."

"I don't want to share these bodies with the world. I want them to be my own little secret."

"If you don't show them, you may never get rid of them. Satan returned day after day at Fire Island. What makes you think he's going to leave you alone here?"

"Nothing. But I won't expose him like some societal freak show, even if he is trying to get me to succumb to his temptation, with all these outrageous dyings. Martin Luther dealt with Satan throwing nuts on his roof and with Satan's demons stalking him; Saint Theresa dealt with him striking her with invisible blows. I can certainly deal with this nonsense. To reveal him to science would destroy the mystery."

"Don't you understand, nobody's interested in him anymore. If you don't reveal his body to science, you are making him even more dead than he already is."

"At least he won't be bobbing in formaldehyde in some specimen jar. Once he is put in cold storage, that's it. He can never come out again. When I burn him, his spirit is released, his ashes return to the earth. Even the devil needs to be reborn every once in a while."

"And this is a good thing? You realize you have started your own conservation program for Satan."

"He's on the endangered species list after all."

"So are God and the angels."

"They're making a comeback, especially the angels; they're treated like the buffalo, given all types of space and protection. Satan is like the wolf. We have a real hard time protecting the wolf."

I had been in some absurd conversations before, especially in the past year, but this one strained my incredulity. I haven't fully

described Little Augie. Besides all the hair and the blotches, she has deteriorated to such an extent that she could very well portray the grim reaper — bony, gray and sunken. She can babble all she wants about her mission, but Little Augie has died a bit with every one of Satan's deaths, and as she noted, those deaths are multiplying. I had half a mind to drag her off to a nursing home. She must have been partially reading my thoughts because she shifted her line of reasoning.

"I'm not saying this dead bastard isn't testing me. Look at the three of them, alternately campy and sinister. What will he deform himself next into, three dead stooges? He's done a pretty good job of making me feel even more marginalized than he does. That's why I can't expose him to the world. If I do, he wins. Then he has taken my soul."

I didn't understand what she was talking about, but I didn't question or argue. Instead, I lingered around for the incineration. I desired to see Satan the way Tundale saw him a millennium ago, over hot coals sucking all the lost souls into his maw when he inhaled. One after the other the three headed into the incinerator. I confess I remained because I half expected to hear one of them cry out in the night as the flesh met the eternal flames. I heard nothing, yet I saw something much more frightening than anything imagined.

As we called back the rack following the final burning, I stared at the wall and noticed my impressive shadow. Though she stood right next to me, Little Augie cast no shadow.

"Look," I said to her, pointing to the wall.

She gasped, genuflected and fainted. Since she was hardly more than a robe and a bag of bones, I easily lifted her up and put her on a table reserved for the dead, giving her one of the crinkly plastic shrouds for a blanket. I left her sleeping comfortably and peacefully on the autopsy table.

Channel 87:
The Other Dangus Manhunt

Pines Tar: A Fuller Picture of Paddy Dangus

In addition to the one run by the authorities f
Technoterrorist Paddy Dangus, an entirely other type of manhu
is coursing through the major arteries of Long Island as reporte
are searching every trash can, web shrine, and white truck for tl
mystery man of the hour.

The Nielsen Ratings report that news programs leading wi
Paddy Dangus have cleaned up during sweeps week and the NB
newsmagazine special, "Paddy Dangus: A Dragon in Our Mids
topped the ratings. One message has come through loud and cle.
to the media:

Paddy Dangus = Profits^2

In fact, Dave Miller has been given a $100,000 bonus f
rushing the final pages of his much-anticipated unauthoriz
biography of Dangus to Random House. Meanwhil
Glamour/Cosmopolitan Books, Inc. has offered Dangus $
million for his story. "The only problem is we can't find him
offer the contract," said publisher Paulina Baldwin. "A number
agents said they represent him, even claimed power of attorne
but no one has produced an authoritative document yet, not th
we'd know what his signature looks like."

Well, after this edition of *Pines Tar*, I guess the public w
have a better idea. I didn't want to publish the picture to the upp
left of this story, a *Herald* and Technoman exclusive, by the wa
I had been holding onto it for five months. But I heard a Frenc
journal got their hands on it and figured I was about to g
scooped, so I better let it out, although I confess a few misgiving
about Dangus's privacy. But then I figured Dangus knows wh
he is doing anyway and if you look at the picture, he is only a bc
of 15. If he hasn't changed from 37 years of aging and tl
compulsory disguises required of a private man like Dangus, the
I would feel a greater twinge of regret.

Well, anyway, there it is, Dangus's senior yearbook pictu
from Oyster Bay High School, the genius was even in a rush bac

n. Despite the fact he had barely reached puberty, note all the ial hair.

If you are studying that picture carefully right now, you are alone. Dangus is clearly the man of the hour. Hollywood has ne calling for his story. How do I know? Walt Disney ductions asked me to be a consultant, along with Miller: they uldn't tell me whether they would do a live action or animated sion, frankly I don't think they know themselves. Rumor has it t Warner Brothers, HBO and Fox are considering their own sions of the Dangus tale.

In addition to the film plans, Oprah, Jerry, Rosy, Geraldo and rest are in a bidding war among the talk shows for an lusive appearance. They are even willing to meet him in a ation of his choice, put him behind a dark screen, and distort voice so the authorities won't catch up with him.

"O.J.? Princess Diana? They're nothing compared to what ngus can be," said Wilfredo Holmes, talk-show host raordinaire. "Remember he has had no direct exposure. The nera hasn't even seen his face. When that face finally appears, en that voice speaks, who's not going to watch and listen. We talking Superbowl ratings." When I mentioned to Holmes that shouldn't refer to the Superbowl when courting Dangus, he n't seem to understand.

Longtime Dangus watcher Rafter Simpkins does not think ngus will be drawn in to any of this stuff, not for all the money fame in the world.

"I thought about Dangus selling out, just so he could make a ckery of selling out, but I can't help but think that the only y you'll ever see him is in handcuffs," Simpkins said. "Look, I s calling up my Paddy Dangus Shrine right at the time he shut wn the Net. That crazy bugger even knocked out his own web ge. He's self-destructive. How could you not like a guy like t?"

Channel 88:
The Chevy Master Deluxe

Still playing off my guilt for destroying much of r
accumulated gadgetry, Angelica asked me to drive her
Farmingville in the very heart of Long Island to pick up a class
car for the Tesla Institute. I could tell just by the way she ask
me that this field trip would have multiple purposes. Recent
closing on 100 acres of potato fields out east to store t
institute's acquisitions, Angelica behaved like a woman in
titanic battle with time itself.

Except for an occasional 7-Eleven, video store, a
McDonalds, Farmingville contained almost exclusively business
associated with the automobile. It had collision shops and o
change pit stops, 18-wheelers and car dealers, transmission ca
and muffler repair, specialty diesel gas and bright-star auto glas
it had buyers, sellers, leasers, traders, renters, borrowers, stealer
crushers, wreckers, towers, reupholsterers, detailers, pin-striper
customizers, restorers, inspectors, waxers, engine rebuilders, de
removers, rustproofers, undercoaters, tinters, polishers,   whee
aligners,   and transporters; in Farmingville, you could fir
security alarms, radiators, car sound systems and car phone
tires, tools, and trim, sunroofs, seat covers, springs, storage, ar
shock absorbers, air conditioners, floor coverings, heaters, hu
caps, jacks, bumpers, and accessories, accessories, accessorie
and you could get brake jobs, tune-ups,   diagnostics, brushle
car washes, electricals,   consultants, brokers, drive awa
companies, and, with these, the options of all-foreign, all-truc
all-van, all-sport, all-guaranteed.

Yet these businesses are dwarfed by the proliferation
discount auto parts stores that somehow managed to stay aflo
despite   the   one-store-to-every-hundred-citizen   ratio
Farmingville — you know stores named Roadside and Barn ar
Parts and Parts Plus and AID and Castle and U.S.-1 and A(
Delco and... Clearly, the fine citizens of Farmingville take bett
care of their cars than they do themselves.

In this engine revving carnival, how could I resist a trip
Spiffy Lube for a servicing.

"You're late," said the lube man.

"Late? Late for what?"

"Servicing. You're a thousand miles late. Otherwise you
uld have qualified for a five dollar discount."

"How many miles do you recommend before I return?"

"2000 miles."

"I'm sorry."

"Hey, it's your car man. You can abuse it if you want, but
day, man, you are going to wake-up with more problems with
ur car than you could handle and you'll have no one to blame
yourself."

I turned to my control panel. "I'm sorry."

"You want the Smart Oil?"

"Smart Oil?"

"Smart Cars need Smart Oil. It's only $9.99 more."

Angelica chimed in: "Get the Smart Oil cheapo. Take care of
ur vehicle, will you."

"O.K.," I agreed sheepishly. "I'll take the Smart Oil."

"Excellent choice sir. You won't regret it."

He ushered us inside and offered a cup of instant coffee, with
t non-dairy creamer no-less, right up my alley. After two
nutes, he was back.

"Done already, wow you guys are fast."

"Not quite done. When's the last time you've had the
ferential fluid change?"

"Do I have differential fluid?"

"Yes, but barely. It's a good thing you got to Spiffy Lube
en you did because this could lead to an engine breakdown."

"Well, it's a good thing."

"For $45.99, I'll take care of this for you."

"Do that." Now I could describe the next fifteen minutes, but
ffice it to say, but by the time my serviceman was through
ing care of me, he had kindly advised me I needed new
insmission and brake and antifreeze fluids, an air filter, an air
shener and new rugmats. For every month as Technoman I
came a softer and softer touch. Yes, by the time I finished my
wdered coffee I added a $397.49 Spiffy Lube bill to my charge

card. I drove away out into the town with a car comple
attended to and cared for: I felt like a Farmingville native.

In the center of Farmingville, as if he were the mayor and
house city hall, stood Ralphie Cancia in front of an appropria
oil-stained abode, wedged symbolically between two disco
auto parts stores. His home was almost all garage (three-
mind you) and no house (one-bedroom). When we stepped
Ralphie scarcely veiled a frown of disgust upon seeing the Sn
Car. The frail old boy scrubbed away at the hood of his
Chevy, the soap bubbles flying around the once thick crop
black-and-gray hair that was now falling out in clumps. Ange
warned me that Ralphie just completed six weeks of chemo. '
nearer I approached Ralphie the worse the smell grew; he had
stinkiest body and the cleanest car of any man I'd ever known.

He barely acknowledged my presence, looking through me
my Smart Car. "Today's cars," groused Ralphie, "look under
hood, there's no room. It's all metal, plastic, and rubber hea
on top of each other. You can't even fit your pecker in there,
alone your hands."

Angelica spoke to me many times of this 1940 si
Chevrolet Master Deluxe four-door sedan with an excitemen
her voice normally reserved only for fairy tales and h
corporate mergers. When she was just a girl and Ralph
neighbor, Angelica would hang around his garage and be
assistant, grabbing tools and oil cans. Whenever Ralphie clain
the job would take a half an hour, it lasted always at least th
hours. "The size is just a little off," he would say, "but tha
O.K., we'll make it fit."

Ralphie introduced me to his '40 Chevy with almost religio
solemnity. "You probably don't know '40 was a special year
the Chevy. In '36, GM put in the hydraulic brake system, Kn
Action ride and an all-steel body. In '37, they threw in a n
216.5 cubic inch, 85 horsepower, six cylinder engine, plus t
introduced the hypoid axle that lowered the floor a couple
inches. Look at the room in here," he waved his hand through
interior like St. Peter among the clouds. "In '39, they add
turning signals. But '40, that's when it all came together, wI
the factory lines were really cooking and they were cranking

about a million cars a year. I paid top dollar for this baby too, $934; the cheapest Chevy that year was $659, but that's O.K., I was making a long-term investment here and I knew it, even then. I bought this car on January 11, 1940 at 11 a.m.. Does that date mean anything to you?"

"No," I confessed.

He looked disappointed even though I'm sure he anticipated my ignorance. "I didn't think so. At that very moment GM produced its twenty-five-millioneth car, a silver Chevy just like this baby. Now talk about a manufacturing giant. Look carefully at this baby. You are looking at history here. This is our Gutenberg Printing Press."

"Yeah, but the engine," I said, "you've got to have a new engine in here."

"I bought all the replacement parts for the car when I was just a young man. I knew I would have this car for the rest of my life and I didn't want to get caught short. Listen to that engine — it's like a squadron of lawnmovers. Beautiful."

Angelica served me a nod of reverence toward Ralphie most people only summon for movie stars. "Look at his fingers. Look at the tips."

Ralphie opened his rugged, horny, octogenarian hands to me. They were black and lineless. "You don't have any fingerprints."

"Too much battery acid over a long life," he said proudly.

"And if you die, how would they identify you?" He flashed his upper arm which sported a tattoo. In the very shoulder spot where other generations have inoculations, that tattoo preserved the Vehicle Identification Number of his '40 Chevy. This discussion got Ralphie started on a rundown of injuries incurred during his years of preserving the auto. He showed belly burns from when as a young, impatient man he popped an overheated radiator cap, antifreeze bubbling all over him; he displayed a left knee mangled from a jack accident, not to mention a series of nicks, scars and bumps from too many years of tinkering while the engine was running.

"I could not give more to anything in the world than I have given to my Chevy Master Deluxe. I have given my life to this car, six decades."

"Any regrets?" I asked.

"Are you kidding me? Look at this baby. Jeez. My Chevy i
the one thing that never let me down. How often can a dying ma
say something like that?"

As Ralphie talked, Angelica gently ascertained the title, th
collector's certificate and even the keys. She has this gift for no
dragging out transactions any longer than absolutely necessary
She turned the ignition and I headed toward my ignominious
almost obsolete Smart Car.

"Now make sure you take care of the car will you," Ralphie
instructed. "You hear me, Angelica, treat that like it's your ow
baby. Take care of the car. Don't let me down. I'll be watching
you from heaven. Take care of the car. And take care of yoursel
too."

Angelica drove the ancient Chevy like she was taking the ol
boy off to a nursing home, and Ralphie lay down on his broke
old dolly, though he no longer had anything to slide himself under

Channel 89:
Hedonism Arcade

Dolly came knocking on my door again. I had already grow
so accustomed to negotiating with her dealers that I could chise
down prices. I also had grown accustomed to her Intraface
demolition threats. She stepped into me all depleted, drained
totally self-consciousness, forever heeding sans Hedonism, fixing
her hair and her breasts, making sure everything pointed in the
proper direction, watching for my approval, measuring her word
... a real control freak. Even without her holding my Intraface
hostage, I probably would have succumbed to her commands
merely to avoid having to listen to her unstimulated talk.

So we took off, down to a back room of Diodes where the
music dropped just enough decibels so we could hear the
cacophony of video-game audio. In the arcade room, we scoped
out Joystick, who held the keys to two kingdoms — that of both
Hedonism and Virtual Reality games. On the big screen ran
continuous drug flicks, this way Joystick could perform whateve
role he wanted, with his bandana, scraggly beard, skinny ass, and

atto tan. But the dialogue wouldn't kick in until the
iminaries were completed. Dolly and I joined Joystick in a
es of arcade battles. We looked on in awe as Joystick killed
ıy two-dimensional images ... the underlying threat being that
:ould do the same to me.

"What the fuck you think of that, Techoman?"

"Let me try." I soared above the planet Zoton in a distant
ıxy, blowing asteroids and aliens out of the sky. On the big
:en played *SegaDreams*, a very popular flick that premiered
 year precisely upon the opening of Diodes. The entire movie
: shot at the club, and for the picture they brought in the
hty ancient pinball machine Noah, an electronic, flashing
ɔsaur that had formerly commanded the plains of the Walt
itman Mall since the 1960s. It had no right to inhabit the
rkling, swank new Diodes arcade, yet Noah gave the place a
se of history and it ended up stealing the movie. In the film and
his very day in the club, its antediluvian flippers and springs
ame the training ground for the intergalactic gladiators of
se 5-D games that ran for $20 a pop. I too had learned from
ıh.

Over the past eleven months, my finger speed increased
onentially; I had gone digital. Joystick discovered I am not so
 at zapping cartoon characters. I am a *man*. Meanwhile with
 head just charged with a freshly scored double dose of
lonism, what the hell was Dolly? She challenged the both of us
Mall Ninja, only the coolest game in the whole goddamn
ade. We would fight each other in death matches set during a
zy white sale at a major department store. Before combat, the
ıera took a full body shot of each of us, exaggerating our most
jected features. I won't describe Joystick and myself, but
dless to say, the cartoon image of Dolly was front and rear
npers.

First Joystick took on Dolly, and I could describe the entire
ıfessional wrestling/high karate steel cage battle that went on
$18 worth of tokens, but ultimately Joystick's figure ended on
 canvas, the image breaking up in front of a triumphant Dolly.
:n $24 later she had me down for the count too. Needless to

say I hadn't been this excited since I saw an episode of *Baywatch* or was it *Charlie's Angels?*

Next the time came for dealing. *SegaDreams* was not realistic enough for a synthetic drug deal, so Joystick put on *Boyz in the Hood*. We were already vibrating from the courtesy samples of Hedonism, so the pumping soundtrack of the movie sent us into all types of hand twists and head turns like we were in the Crenshaw section of South Central L.A. God it was awful.

Joystick kept one hand on the remote, fastforwarding his way in and out of lines in the movie, and another on a supercharged light gun that he menacingly brandished and occasionally shot at me.

"Got some blow?" she asked on the big screen. "Got some rock? I'll suck your dick."

Like the drug deals of the movies, we were mainly about flashing our fake guns, talking tough, dropping our lips like we carried pacifiers in our mouths, like we were boyz. Looking up at the screen, we understood that hope was already lost by the time the football star was caught in the crossfire. With all the trigger play and the fuck-yous shared by the real dealers and us two actors, nobody in the place even noticed the exchange of living pills and dead presidents.

"Damn nigga, what's wrong with you?" said the screen.

"Nuthin," Joystick replied.

And then the screen: "I'm tired of this shit, this fucking shit."

"So the fuck am I," said Dolly. Joystick and I were mimicking the screen handshakes when Dolly turns an open palm toward Noah and drops her hand down on it. She smashed away at the old pinball machine while Joystick scrolled the video.

"That's what happens when the blood separates from the plasma."

"Why is the blood turning yellow?" Until now I didn't realize that Joystick was playing *Boyz in the Hood* backward. I wanted to stay and see how the movie would begin, but Dolly increased her blows to the machine.

"What the fuck are you doing?" asked Joystick, even though the line might not be in the movie, he was too disturbed by the senseless act of violence.

Dolly attacked Noah like a cable serviceman on a pirated box,
backing the thick faded plastic top with her elbows. I pulled her
way and those elbows flew up, cracking into the hard drive of
my Intrafacer. Dolly smiled at me, invigorated, and grabbed my
hand. Thankfully, so many gamers were so engrossed in their
individualized arcade challenges ("hey, this time it's personal")
that it took a few minutes for them to awaken from their spells
and figure out that their beloved godhead was being defiled. They
were rushing toward us as I dragged Dolly out to the car. I took a
last glance at the grandfatherly pinball machine. Fortunately,
Noah had been smashed and tilted so many times over the years
that even Dolly's vicious, wanton attack would not stop its
bumpers from flashing and clanging.

Rushing into the Smart Car, I discovered that my Intrafacer
was not so lucky: it had now known Hedonism too. The Intrafacer
responded sporadically and selectively to my key commands, only
obeying when it seemed to want to do the same thing anyway. I
was able to call up my applications but not access my files. The
Intrafacer appeared to have a mind of its own.

"What's a matter with your wittle Intrafacer?" Dolly asked in
sweet mockery. "I didn't hurt it, did I?"

"It's not working right."

"Let me see."

I was afraid to pass it to her, yet I didn't want to be a wimp,
I let her have it. She was gentle.

"Oh, oh I see. No problem. This works fine."

I leaned against her cheek and looked at the monitor. It was
hazy and foggy.

"You see," said Dolly. "You see how beautiful it works."

Channel 90:
Remote Dangus

Coming down from my Hedonism high, I arrive at
Prometheus Laboratories a little later than I expected. The police
were already there. They seemed to be waiting for me. They read
me my rights and then a detective told me his name (which I
immediately forgot) and said:

"Tell me about Dangus."

"Huh?"

"Dangus. You know what I am talking about."

"Where's Sphere and Carmen?"

"Don't worry about them. Tell me about Dangus."

"Are they hurt?"

"They're down. Now about Dangus."

"Zapped again?"

"Maybe."

"EMTs here?"

"Not yet."

I caught a glimpse of a prone Geoffrey aided by an officer taking out what seems to be a Bic pen and sticking it into his teeth. I moved gingerly toward Sphere.

"Don't do that," I told the officer with more than usual authority. The detective was too curious about my behavior to interrupt.

"Huh?"

"I have experience in these matters. I was here for the last one."

"What am I doing wrong?" He looked sincere, which was very helpful.

I called up the information off my Intrafacer, who was fortuitously cooperative. "Don't restrain him, don't put anything in his mouth, keep things out of his way, so he can't be hurt by them, and if you feel you have to touch him, just loosen his clothing so he can't hurt himself with anything on his person."

And the officer listened. Within two minutes the EMTs arrived. The head EMT, who had come to know me, said, "Uh oh, not you again. What'd you do this time, shove a bunch of Number 2s down his throat?"

I only responded with a confident wave toward the patient.

"Not bad," he said. "A couple more seizures and you'll be ready to take the first aid test."

The detective tugged me away and tried to ask me questions about Dangus, but I think I looked too believably lost for him to align me with the suburban terrorist. It didn't hurt the way Geoffrey, regaining consciousness, spoke to me.

"He got it. The bastard got me and it."

"Just rest, relax."

"I am resting and I am relaxing. You know why? Because I don't have it anymore. You have it. It's your burden now."

I tried to comfort Geoffrey, but we both soon understood that he should be the one comforting me. Carmen fumbled about on the floor while the EMTs tried to guide her onto a stretcher. She kept searching for something, but I don't believe it was there, at least not in front of her or around her.

"The Universal Remote is in your hands now," Geoffrey said, sliding onto the stretcher. As they started carrying him away, he raised his voice, "You hear me. It's all yours. The Universal Remote is yours. Take good care of it."

Thanks alot, Geoffrey. Now the police will really be all over me.

I turned to the detective, "Didn't you guys figure that Dangus might strike Prometheus Laboratories again?"

"Of course we did. That's why we had the place staked out."

"If you had it staked out, why didn't you protect Geoffrey and Carmen?"

"The perpetrator moved too fast. Anyway we needed to catch him in the act."

"Did you?"

"Yeah."

"Well, where is he?"

"We are on the tail of his white truck right now."

Oh great. This will be all over the news and I'm already behind the curve of the story.

"You mean they haven't caught him yet."

"We are in pursuit. Don't worry. We'll get him."

Geoffrey rocked about furiously, he didn't enjoy being trapped down. He was still talking, talking to me, although I confess I was more interested in hearing about Dangus right now.

"What'd Dangus get them with?"

"We think electric current."

"Same as last time."

"But we're not sure how he did it. I'm sure we will find out soon, once we nab his ass."

The police radios were kicking information out like crazy. Back-up units were piling into the Brentwood area. The officers at Prometheus Laboratories followed the chase like one for a fugitive on *America's Most Wanted* or something.

"Could he be that dumb? Hayes says they found Dangus's house."

"How?"

"Seems he drove his old white truck home, even though he knew we were following."

"UnFuckingReal."

"He's right off the Long Island Expressway too. Who would have figured that Dangus would live right under our noses."

"Where?"

"In some rundown shack and pond right by the old closed psychiatric institution where they used to house the nutty veterans. Hayes says there's duck shit everywhere and a load of farm animals all around the place."

"Did they get Dangus?"

"Not yet, but they've virtually got him already."

With the victims being carted off, the officers were leaving, which disturbed me, since I was following along on their police monitors — my Intrafacer behaving badly once again, complete lack of cooperation from him. The last word I heard was not from the police and not about Dangus. When I asked the officer about whether the police are now tracking Dangus on foot or what, he suddenly grew cryptic. In contrast, Geoffrey spoke clearly and directly, even as he was being dragged out the door:

"You!" he pointed at me. "You're more likely to see Dangus than the police. You have the Universal Remote now, and he'll be after you."

I giggled like a cartoon character and pushed a few buttons on my Intrafacer. I started tracking Dangus from my temperamental monitor and wondered if he had a monitor on me too.

Channel 91:
Accumulated Wisdom through Clicking the Remote

What I heard on television from 12:30-1:50 a.m.

- "Becket was stabbed by a beggar. When Becket asked the man in prison why he did it, the man replied that he had no idea."
- "When the aliens appeared in Chimora in 1964, even the sheriff had to admit their presence."
- "Wilma's right Fred, what's the worst thing that can happen, you'll be a flop?"
- "We have been fighting now for 40 years without any rest. We have been fighting so long that we won't give up our arms. The Burmese are stronger than us, but..." ·
- "The fatal school shootings at schools in recent months are apparently part of an increased wave of violence committed by juveniles."
- "But the years of excess — the cars, the girls and especially the drugs — had left Andy broke."
- "It's all right boys, I'm going to settle down. I'm through with the newspaper business."
  "Too bad. You'll miss a nice hanging Hildy."
- "In volatile markets, it makes sense to own *some* stocks that have *some* income."
- "Tell children a story that the first human beings are thrown out of their house because of one mistake and that feeds into their worst fears about family life."
- "It's true you took me in, but it's also true that when I found you, you were huddled in the corner with a pair of tweezers eating gray spaghetti."
- "And the ice cream truck is definitely under arrest."
- "You know what still bugs me? This nagging feeling that my time has passed."
- "Job's Spike Fertilizer. It's what trees want."
- "What's great about the Total Gym is that you can fluctuate your workout. There are two basic exercises that work over eighty-percent of the body."

- "This is great! Talking to you for so long for so little."
- "If it weren't for the Bronx, this rap probably would not be going on."
- "Part of it is about art, but part of it is also about campaigning."
- "I was thinking maybe we could get a minivan... If the word *minivan* scares you, think Odyssey."
- "Some people sleep well; some people don't. You're one who doesn't. ... Fortunately, across America now you have sleep disorder centers. You might even be able to get off your sleeping pills."
- "Delicate rock formations can collapse."
- "Often guns were passed down two or three generations, from their grandpa or grandma, or even their great-grandparents."
- "I will kill your wife; you will kill my momma. That's fair."
- "Tell them there are gay animals here who need a home."
- "Look for cloudy skies but not nearly as chilly as it has been."
- "I've been doing 200 dates a year for fifteen years."
- "Do you think the president is being picked on?"

Channel 92:
Plastic Traditions

I left the nightmare of the Dangus search and sought out the bosom of my dysfunctional family. Of course, they were sleeping, but I still had a key and made my way to the couch in hopes of blissful slumber. About 4:30 in the morning, I dropped off, but I was periodically awakened by the remote control car revving up involuntarily, a twitch of the engine and a shimmy of the tires, just enough to turn rest to restlessness. And then at 6:00 a.m. with the ridiculous late May sunrises, I caught an earful of an infant's musical ball that came to life without encouragement of touch, movement, wind or telepathy.

All across America, tinny electronic tunes sing out involuntarily in the background of suburban lives. We hear them, buzzing and plinking, but we don't know how to turn them off. On that couch at Alice's, at my old home, I tried again to nod the morning to sleep, but Zach's old toys — the ones he had at four, you know with the heavy duty batteries — were still awake, out of the factory endlessly rocking, playing the anti-lullaby, the song of postmodernism, discordant, mocking itself of course, but mocking you so much more. "De-Dee, De-Dee, Dee-Dee, Dee-Dee, De-De."

And if I *could* drop back off, it didn't matter anymore for Zach and Alice were up and talking and they had their hands on the remote, twisting channels furiously. All three of us were with it, alive and responsive. We took to the T.V. at our most intelligent, following every 2-second visit to a channel with a comment. I think the "Family Anti-Matters" rerun got us going, you know the one where the father says, "I don't have to worry about my daughter becoming pregnant. I taught her early on how to be a Lesbian."

So when we shifted to the History Channel and the station ran a special on the rise of the Third Reich, I was ready to be provocative. "If the Nazis never came into power, would there even be history in the Twentieth Century? Well there's always the bomb... Thank goodness for that."

From there we switched on the Lifetime Channel and we watched two minutes and forty-five seconds of a movie about a nutritional health counselor who becomes a bulimic herself. When she vomited in the bathroom, Zach asked, "Why do they call it a toilet anyway? There are no toys in the toilet."

And when we clicked to an infomercial on Viagra, Alice had her own contributions to our own little family meeting: "We have too many erections already in this world without Viagra. What we need is a way to alleviate the erections we have. Make no more of them. The more erections we have in this world, the more problems we have."

The morning continued this way until we shifted to a retro Nickelodeon show only to discover a retro commercial for whiffle balls. The commercial was so kitschy and therefore so effective that Zach asked, "What the hell is a whiffle ball?" Feeling whimsical and perhaps even nostalgic, Nickelodeon does that to even the best of us, I dragged Zach off to 7-Eleven, the corporate world's version of a mom and pop store, and picked up a whiffle ball and bat for the outrageous price of $2.49. Who knew that would be the best investment I made in eleven months? Only minutes passed before I had Zach throwing a curve ball. Who knew the whiffle ball would be my redemption? Need I remind you that we were playing with real honest-to-goodness plastic here, not imitation plastic, not virtual plastic.

In the backyard, I made a mound from a couple of frisbees and showed my boy how to push off the hill. "That's right, kick the toe up and follow through strong with the legs. If you use too much arm with a whiffle ball, you'll find your limb falling off." He watched me carefully, although I'm sure he was also recalling the way cyborg hurler Dirk Beanball delivered in Armageddon National Pastime. And when he figured out how to send the ball dropping right out of the strike zone, I put him in front of the plate.

"Choke up there. Choke up more. The bat's light, but you need to control the stick better. Now remember, just by the way you threw, you know that whiffle ball's all about the movement of the sphere. You have to wait on the curve ball. Keep your hips back and don't bail out, even if the ball's coming right at you. Most of the time it will curve across the plate and you have to prepare yourself for the break. And if it doesn't curve, remember it's a whiffle ball. You're not going to get a concussion or anything from it."

Zach stepped up to the plate and told the crowd, "And now, Number 000, the one and only, Ben Jiffy Jr." Ben was the first baseball player robot in Armageddon National Pastime to enter the league when cyborgs took over the majors in the year 2050. When I pitched in to Zach or to Ben, I pitched into the future, a high rising fastball that took the air the way only whiffle balls can. Zach took a swing over his head, missing beautifully. On the next pitch, a low sinker, he sent a twisted, spinning grounder back at me.

I put on my camera and tried to use my mouse and monitor as a radar gun, but I soon discovered that my Intrafacer didn't appreciate my involvement in a father-son whiffle ball game.

Since it refused to cooperate during the game, I removed my Intrafacer, although I confess I must have looked a bit raw and uncooked.

Was I teaching my kid skills that were already obsolete like lessons in Latin or in 8-Track Cassette cleaning or in Beta VCR repair? Yes slowly I am coming to the realization that all I can teach Zach are about things either obsolete or soon-to-be obsolete. But I must say I felt like a real Dad. As I pitched in, the accumulated burden of Technoman began to lift.

I discovered I could teach my son something. I had found a relationship with my son and its name was Whiffle Ball. Somehow I had forgotten that I once had a greatness within me and its name was also Whiffle Ball. It had been a Pines' family tradition — my dad had taught me.

Magically, all the neighborhood kids came out to play as if compelled by stage directions. I played with them too and I was a buddy, a companion, a teacher, an uncle and even a dad. The ball bounced off trees and fences and bushes and curbs. It bounded off the back stop and kids rushed to curb, blocking the storm drains, to get it back to me as fast as possible.

Alice brought out sandwiches and Kool Aid, and I half expected the Ice Cream truck to come jingle jangling down the street. Yet instead all I heard were sirens wailing, and I knew they were for Paddy Dangus as police continued to search him out. And I knew I would have to put my ball away soon and write a column, a column of a man running away from suburbia at the very moment I grew comfortable with bedding down in it.

Channel 93:
Dangus Escapes the Authorities

Pines Tar: He's Bloody and Free

The police seemed so confident. One detective even told me: "I'll bet my wife and kids that we have Dangus in custody by nightfall." Well, the moon came up and not only was Dangus still on the loose, but police, despite their best efforts to spin the story otherwise, apparently have little idea of his whereabouts.

"We've got his truck," Detective Mason proclaimed in the early morning, intimating that apprehension of that White Searcher was the beginning of the end. Furthermore, Mason dragged all types of material out of Dangus's home, obviously a treasure chest of clues and evidence, although police would tell us little more than the material was "aggressive and sordid," whatever that is supposed to mean.

By 4:30 a.m., police had surrounded the six-acre property, combing the area carefully; it was inevitable that Dangus had to turn up somewhere, and he did at approximately 7:43 a.m. As Mason describes the incident, "the perpetrator sprinted across a small, marshy meadow to the duck pond." From my visit to the Dangus property, I can tell you that pond is a murky, stagnant pool of duck doo. "Police called for him to halt, yet he ignored those calls, so we opened fire. At about five feet in front of the pond, a bullet hit its mark. The perpetrator clutched his shoulder and then staggered into the pond as police continued to fire." Police pursued, but Dangus disappeared.

What police did not realize until much later was that Dangus had headed into an underground tunnel. To the police's defense, officers did scour the pond and the tunnel's entryway looks like nothing more than a gopher hole. Yet the elusive Dangus, who appears to be taking on a Houdini-like aura, wriggled his way into the fissure and out of the clutches of police. Got away not just from officers mind you, but from every resource, material and device the authorities could bring to bear. There were bloodhounds and copters, cameras and monitors, sonars and radars, yet, when the guano settled, there was a wounded man who refused to be caught.

How did he escape? No officer will go on record for this part of the story, but a few on deep background and with assurances of anonymity corroborated the most likely scenario. Apparently, Dangus's tunnel stretched under the Long Island Expressway and emptied in a water recharge basin (a sump) on the other side. From what officers could make of the scattered footprints up and out of the sump, Dangus seemed to be headed for the African-American community of Wyandanch. When asked if he is certain that Dangus escaped out of this sump, an officer responded, "Who else would go into a sump? Those things are like quicksand."

Off the record, police confess that Dangus could not have picked a better spot than Wyandanch to hide in. "We haven't exactly made a load of friends down there, if you know what I mean," said an officer whose Second Precinct beat covers the area. Furthermore, two different officers explained that if Dangus had a previous connection to the African-American community, the police were not knowledgeable of the link prior to the escape.

So, to sum up, Dangus managed to get by an army of police, only to hide out in a sympathetic community, while police start from scratch in their search for a man they have been pursuing for many months, having just blown their best chance for apprehension.

Dave Miller, whose revised edition of *Suburban Terrorist: The Paddy Dangus Story* will come out next week and whose current edition is in bookstores everywhere, distilled the situation into its purest form. "Dangus is Speedy Gonzales and the authorities are just some well-intentioned cartoon characters who haven't seen this breed before. But they better familiarize themselves because Dangus may be the first, but I can't imagine he'll be the last."

With no better place to explore, police are scouring Dangus's house and grounds for clues. From what authorities allowed me to see of the house, Dangus lives in primitive conditions. The yard is what attracts the untrained eye, with its tortoises, snakes and endless ducks. Dangus has so many eggs and chicks in incubators, the town had to send in a team of experts to take care of the homestead; otherwise massive animal deaths would have occurred.

"It's funny, how much it looks like what I imagine would be a humble American farm in a previous century," said Professor of Sociology Martin Maresca. "The place is positively pastoral. A little rundown and swampy, but aren't most American Edens?"

Longtime Dangus observer Rafter Simpkins believes we are now entering a new phase in the suburban terrorist's existence. "He can't go home again. The Man has taken that away. He's wounded· and holed up in Wyandanch. His crisis situation just might send him spiraling into a rampage of subversive actions we cannot even fathom. People keep saying, 'Let's see what happens during the next full moon.' I keep reminding them, hey, this moon hasn't even run its course yet. I know I won't be sleeping well this week until that moon fades into the sky."

Channel 94:
Satan's Disciples

"Psssst. Rus is that you?"

"Yeah."

"Good. Get in here and shut the door. And don't turn on the lights."

"What's all this about?"

"Look around you and you'll see."

"Hey Augie, it's pretty dark in here. What am I supposed to be looking at?"

"What else but the usual."

"Shit. Look at all these bodies. Let's see here... That's one Satan... and there's another Satan... and — "

"Don't bother checking and counting. Just believe me there's twelve Satans."

"What do you think? He's doing the disciples then?"

"What else could he be doing?"

"He's multiplying again then."

"Multiplying? My God, he's mass manufacturing."

"Soooooooo, what do you make of this?"

"I don't know, but I think he may be cloning himself. But when you clone a dying thing, how long is the clone expected to live? How many clones could Satan have left in him?"

"Shit if I know, but if he's cloning, Satan may have just found immortality again."

"Now that's reassuring. But what do *I* do in the meantime?"

"What do you mean?"

"I mean I've almost been caught with corpses seven times within the past two weeks. Even with my exclusive, cloistered sanctuary of operation area, I'm having more and more problems keeping these bodies a secret. More people are creeping around. On Wednesday, Hammon walks in as I'm incinerating a body. I had to tell him I was just burning my trash. Good thing he thinks I'm eccentric."

"Good thing you've fooled him so well."

"Hey, I have to. No one must see my secret Satan."

"I should feel honored then that you have permitted me to view Satan."

"You... you, I don't concern myself with. You might as well be that air conditioner in the corner there."

"That's very sweet of you to say. I wouldn't worry if I were you. You get rid of all these bodies every time they turn up,. so what's the problem?"

"I think people are coming into my rooms when I'm not here, not just the janitors either. You know how careful I am. I'm exhausted. Now look at this mess. How the hell can I clean up this pile of devils?"

"There are quite a few to handle aren't there. My God, you can hardly move in here."

"And I don't have the strength to take care of them anymore."

"You sound like you're crying out for help here, so why don't you step back and let me start rolling bodies into the incinerator."

"Be me guest, but I'm warning you, Satan's gotten a lot heavier since you last moved him. He's not clay; he's plutonium."

"You're right. I feel like I'm dragging around a pile of dog shit, like I'm — "

"Shhhh."

"What?"

"Quiet, someone's coming. Hide, get under the sheet."

"With Satan?"

"Shhhh. You don't have any other choice, do you? Quick."

"Hey, Augie. You in there? ... Augie? ... Augie? ... I guess she's left. Jesus, it stinks in there. I can't go in there right now. I'll go in later with a gas mask."

"   ...   "

"   ...   "

"   ...   "

"   ...   "

"Rus?"

"Yeah?"

"You can get up now. The coast is clear."

"Jesus Augie. I think I'm gonna puke."

"Thanks, I know it takes a real man to lie down with the Devil, but there was no other way. We had to keep the secret. I've held on too long to give it up now."

"I smell like I've went in my pants. I'll have to wash my Intrafacer for a week to get rid of his odor. I've got a couple of his hairs in my keyboard."

"So what do you think now?"

"I think you better leave the morgue for good."

"I'm glad you're starting to see things my way. All it took is for you to appreciate what an undercover life I've been living."

"Well, let's put it this way: if you want to stay, that's your business, but I'm never returning to this place again. There are just too many bodies here. I'm overwhelmed."

"So am I."

"Tell you what, I'll get rid of them with you now, but after that we're done, O.K.?"

"You know that means He's chased us away."

"*He* hasn't. *They* have. Remember *He's* become a *They*. He's become *Them*. What's the world coming to when you can't even trust Satan?"

"He seems more tricky and sneaky dead than alive. Anyway, whether a He or They, pop star or corporate conglomerate, Satan has chased us away."

"Yeah, I know, but is that bad?"

"Probably not? Away seems to be one of the best ways to remember what it's like to be alive."

"Do you remember what it's like? I mean to be alive?

"No."

"Me neither. Good, we won't have anything to forget that may get in the way of our recollections."

"And what if we forget what it's like to not be alive?"

"No chance, I've got all that loaded on my hard drive."

"And what if your hard drive crashes?"

"Then I guess we will lose it all."

"Then we better take something from Satan so we won't forget."

"From which Satan?"

"It doesn't matter. They're all the same."

"Then how about a finger?"

"Perfect. Get that hairy one with the plutonium ring on it and the cubic zirconium marquis inset. Use that knife over there. Be careful not to lose that gorgeous long nail... That's it. Don't mind the puss. Hey, hey, don't give it to me. You take it."

"What should I do with it?"

"Where do you keep your mouse?"

"In my pocket."

"Then put the finger next to it."

"Don't I carry enough around my person already?"

"You can never carry enough with you. You see this, look what I carry with me."

"Yuck, what is that. It looks like an aborted hologram."

"A nice hunk of my skin from the late 70s. I had it laminated. Look, it doesn't even have any wrinkles."

"And you been carrying it around all this time?"

"I'd like to believe it's been carrying me around instead."

"Ridiculous."

"Oh yeah. Which way is that finger you're holding pointing?"

"Out the door?"

"Out to Fire Island and that's where I'm heading."

Channel 95:
Passing Time

If I have learned anything this year, it is I have only two ways to live: 1) to search. 2) to comfort. Never mind that I am more interested in comforting myself than others, today I would comfort Carmen. In the latest visit from Dangus, Carmen lost what she describes as "everything." Worse yet, Dangus left her with her wits, so she could understand the enormity of the loss.

I found her at her home at eight in the morning clicking the remote, skipping channels like they were rocks across a pond. "She's been at this all night," said Frederique, two kids in front of him, their eyes blinking to the flicking of the television stations. "She said she can't sleep without her clock radio."

"Why the hell not?"

"She says she knows without it, she won't wake up."

Turning away from the set toward me, Carmen gazed wearily at my monitor: "He took away my time. I have no more time."

"What was the name of your time?"

"It's Sanyo and it's 20 years old. And you can't get it anymore. It's irreplaceable."

"What if I said I may be able to give time back to you."

"Don't talk time to me. You are a little too hazy and symbolic. Let's talk specifics here. I need a Sanyo, Model No. RM 5100 from 1978. Can you deliver this kind of brand-name, historically situated time?"

I backpedaled a bit. She scared me with details, and yet I told Carmen: "I think I can. Take a ride with me."

Within minutes, Carmen stepped into my Smart Car and we drove out east to the new home of the Tesla Institute, where I knew Angelica would be none too sanguine to meet someone who was an acquirer, not a donor.

On the drive, across the scrub pines and onto the North Fork of Long Island, Carmen acted like her old self. I made her feel needed by asking her advice about Zach. "I just can't seem to get him under control."

She scoffed and chuckled. "Your problem is you let him run the place. *You're* the parent here and you are bigger and have a stronger will than he has. If you remember that, you will always have control."

That conversation ended, since she obviously didn't know what she was talking about. When we drove up to the Tesla Institute, Angelica was out arranging the history of food processors in her new home; 100 acres in wine country she had to fight the vintners off for. "Can you believe that? Those wine makers want to destroy every piece of pristine land on Long Island. The Suffolk Parks Commissioner said the county earmarked the land for preservation, and I said, 'What am I doing if not conservation here?' Needless to say, he soon understood."

Angelica gave us a tour of this work in progress. The place was magnificent, as if Walt Disney designed Home Depot, tools and equipment, colorful, shiny and abundant.

"Now this is a place I could find missing pieces of my past," mused Carmen.

"What do you think? I'm not sure if we should make this a museum or a theme park."

"Make it a museum. This is stuff that should not be cheapened."

She warmed us up with a tour of the great microwaves throughout time. "Look at the tacky wood-line paper on this one and the size? Isn't it wonderful," Angelica gushed. "This model is from the late 70s when microwaves were new to the American consumer. This period is popularly known as the Grey Age of microwave cooking for nobody could believe how fast the microwave heated up food. Therefore, everything was overcooked. And that, my friends, marked the beginning of an unfair trend in carousel cuisine, where the chef blamed the microwave, and not the practitioner, for the bad hot food that came out of its cool, smoky doors, a bum rap we unfairly perpetuate today. I will predict the conventional oven will soon be considered as useful as the icebox when open-minded gourmets finally grant the microwave the respect it so clearly deserves."

If Angelica waxed enthusiastic in the convection warming wing, how do I describe her radiance in the "Evolution to Microchip" Pavilion? As we headed down the row of vacuum tubes, Angelica was like a paleontologist displaying "in tact" dinosaur skeletons. The vacuum tubes were huge and majestic, soaring off the floor into the sky. "Look at those beasts. They chew up energy like big hunks of stegasaurus meat, romping across their age, turning on and off electrical charges in the computer, the way the T-Rex must have once terrorized about the primordial jungle. And just like the dinosaurs, those cold-blooded reptiles, the vacuum tubes were doomed for extinction, just too huge and inefficient. They would perish in the early 50s after Bell Labs in 1947 came up with this —"

"Shit. You got it," I said, admittedly impressed upon seeing the twisted little wiry contraption. Since I've known her, Angelica spoke about the original Bell Labs' transistor, but now she possessed it. Of course, she could have re-created the prototype transistor: it was just a few pieces of gold foil, a turned paper clip and a primitive hunk of semiconductor. But, I know Angelica, so I knew the thing was real.

"Don't even ask me how I got it," Angelica positively glowed. The visual impact of the display was beautifully absurd, these mammoth imposing vacuum tubes pushed aside by the flimsy, rinky-dink transistor, the thing looked like it was twisted together by some kindergartner with chewing gum and foil Yodel wrappers.

"How. good does that look juxtaposed against the largest collection of vacuum tubes in the world?" she boasted. And still further down the hall stood the earliest uses of the transistors. Next to every specimen, every craft, every work of art hung a placard, which at first seemed pretentious but soon grew on me. Ultimately, the placards gave these artifacts legitimacy, dignity, gravity, history and authority. Each started much like the one in front of me now: "The Tokyo Telecommunication Engineering Association (now SONY) in 1955 mass-produced the first transistorized pocket radio..." You get the idea. "You've done it," I proclaimed to a satisfied Angelica, "You've made your collection important just by the way you've presented it."

I figured right about now was the best chance to broach the subject of the Sanyo. When I did, Angelica frowned and turned guarded. She said she didn't think she owned any Sanyos from the period. Fortunately, Carmen started speaking, which improved matters. By the time Carmen got to how she lost the clock radio and how long it had sat on her night table we were standing right in front of a Sanyo model.

"That's it!" Carmen proclaimed excitedly. "My God you have it!" Angelica appeared sheepish and ashamed. The object of their mutual interest hardly seemed worth either of these reactions. I cased over the clock, a really early digital model. You couldn't even figure out the time if you didn't look at it straight on. The numbers were in primitive block lettering for the machine couldn't do diagonals, even for the 7, not to mention the fact that the radio was all static. The cheesy lights miraculously worked, although they were not nearly as visible, clean and bright as any digitals since the 80s.

"This is a piece of crap," I muttered under my breath. I'm glad I restrained my opinion, since right after Carmen gave Angelica a whole history of this digital clock and explained how it was one of the first of is kind and how her fiancee Mike Barnett knew she wanted that radio badly, even more than an ankle bracelet, a very popular gift back then.

"You have to understand how much this clock means to me. It was Christmas Eve of 1978 when I waited for my fiancee to come over. I waited all night and tried to call him, but nobody answered and then I had a really bad feeling. So I drove toward his house, and there on the side of the road was his wrecked Guardian, Mike's body already on the stretcher. The ambulance workers were moving slowly. 'What happened to him? Is he dead?' I asked them. They didn't answer, the cowards. He was dead. I cried on the road's shoulder and then got into his Guardian. On the front seat was a present, with this green wrapping paper and this lavender bow, only Michael would pick such weird colors. I knew the gift had to be for me. You know what the card read? 'Now when you wake up every morning you can think of me.' So how do you think I felt when I opened up that Sanyo clock radio?

"Night after night without him, I looked at that clock. I read its words across, 'Snooze, Sleep Off, Real Time, Alarm, Slow, Fast, Time Set, Sleep, Off, On, Function, Auto Buzzer, FM, AM Band, Min./Max Volume.' I memorized the words on back: Date Code 101278, the number 30445035, Sanyo Model No. RM

5100, *Cabinet is high impact molded plastic with walnut grain appearance*; Power Supply AC 120V 60HZ 7W, Sanyo Electric Co. LTD; *Design certified for compliance with F.C.C. Rules Part 15. Made in China.* And do you know what made me cry every time I read it? The warning on the back. It read — *Caution: To prevent electric shock, do not remove cover. No user-serviceable parts inside. Refer servicing to qualified service personnel.* I can't explain it, but I always thought the warning was from Mike, like he was looking out for me. It sounds stupid, but all those years Mike has been dead, his final gift has been with me, ticking on.

"How many digital clock radios you know last twenty years? None even last ten. That Sanyo has been our time together. It's bad enough with the Dangus attack I lost three months of e-mails from my children off my hard drive. Three months of my life vanished and I can't get that back. Please don't let me lose this too."

Angelica was getting weepy. "Alright, O.K. I understand. You can take it home with you." As she spoke those magnanimous words of self sacrifice, I know a gaping hole opened in the museum and in Angelica's heart. I remember one late night when Angelica told me the way she collected obsessively even as a young girl. Around the time of her first communion, the Catholic priests first started handing parishioners the Eucharists rather than dropping them on the tongue. "You know every week for an entire year," she had confessed with a strange combination of pride and shame, "I carefully pocketed the host." She showed how she faked putting the wafer onto her tongue, a magician's slight of hand. "It took all my resources to explain one Sunday morning to my mother why I had 47 hosts in my jewelry box."

As Angelica pulled the plug on the Sanyo and passed it to Carmen, I found myself simultaneously head-over-heels in love with both women, impassioned and generous they were. This would be a love story if I were capable of attending to a single woman for a sustained period. However, none of us remained weepy for long after Carmen lifted the Sanyo and examined its belly. "Hey, Date Code 101278, serial number 30445035, Sanyo Model No. RM 5100. You've got *my* radio."

"Do I? That's bizarre."

"Not really. When did you get it?"

"A few days ago."

Angry, but trying to maintain some semblance of composure, Carmen asked, "Do you work with Dangus or something?"

"No. Don't be ridiculous. I work for nobody."

"Well, do you know Dangus?"

"I know people who know Dangus. I'll tell you this just once: I am only interested in Dangus as far as I am interested in anyone else — for his things, for his collections, for what he's worth."

I think Carmen wanted to say more, but she must have been too overwhelmed by reuniting with her clock radio to add anything else. As we left the Tesla Institute to a weakly waving Angelica, all Carmen would say to me was, "Hurry up. The faster we get home, the faster I can plug this in and the faster I can resume my life."

"Is that all it takes for you?"

"Yes."

"I wish an appliance could do the same for me."

"You have to spend the time with it, you have to establish a history."

I fondled my Intrafacer, grew comforted and drove on...

Channel 96:
A Transfusion for the Intrafacer

I have less hair on my body than at any time since I came out of the womb. I know because I stand naked in front of the mirror, wounded, old and depressed. I don't know why I feel compelled to tell you, but baring my soul appears to be a timely thing to do.

While a couple cops on the Dangus stake-out circled in front of my house, Dolly came by this afternoon, purring around on the last fumes of a Hedonism high. Frisky and intrusive, she groped right for my shorts, first along my pocket grabbing my mouse, but instead of heading front and center, stopped and fondled, find an erectable along the inseam.

"Hey, what's that doing there?"

"Just happy to see you." I wasn't really happy to see Dolly. Actually, I was scared, and my penis wasn't erect; in fact, it was like a turtle's head upon sight of a crocodile. Yet how could I explain that she was rubbing Satan's finger, which was very responsive to the stimulus considering it was dead. Last night, I hooked it to my mouse, like it was a rabbit's foot or a St. Christopher's Medal or something. That she couldn't distinguish Satan's finger from my penis did nothing to build my confidence, but the knowledge thankfully didn't distract me from pretending to be aroused. Just when I thought she would straddle the finger, Dolly completely lost interest in me: the Hedonism had faded.

She grew bitchy and distant and soon I grew very comfortable with her presence. "I know how you feel," I said.

"Then will you get me some more."

I told Dolly I wouldn't get her some more, that I had gotten her too much. I told Dolly that she was the closest female counterpart to me that I've ever met, and I told her to let the Hedonism go and to hold me and that I would help her get through it — that I had been there, that I have tasted being addicted to these things and I knew she must stop. She must stop. And I drew her close and whispered in her ear that I would be there for her. And she wept in my arms. And then I took a moist towelette, wiped away the thick layers of mascara and saw a sad, ugly woman. And I kissed her sadness, her ugliness. I think she liked that.

But I wasn't Hedonism. So I was no use to her. She pushed, turned, and thrashed. As I struggled to contain her, I caught myself in the mirror (that's when I first noticed how incredibly little hair I had left). I wanted to help Dolly. And when I looked at Dolly in that mirror, I knew I was looking at myself. She couldn't help herself; she needed to be wired. She needed to hooked; she couldn't be disconnected.

"Did you hear that?" she asked.

"I hear nothing."

"So you hear that too. I can't live with nothing. It's just too sad. I need the chatter in my head."

"I'll put on the TV and the stereo," I volunteered.

"It's not enough. It used to be enough, but not any more."

"I know what you mean."

Dolly poked and pulled at her ears as if trying to clear them for sound. They grew red and ripe. "I need it now and you're going to get it for me," she threatened, drawing closer, pushing me back on my heels. Then she pulled a switchblade from her imitation alligator purse. She didn't threaten my person; instead she sticks the knife right into the scuzzy port of my Intrafacer. "You get it, or you *get* it, understand?"

Either way, I didn't want to get it, so I deftly turned my Intrafacer away from the blade as she awkwardly slashed at me. "You don't want to do this. You're letting this synth drug take over your life." I said many other things, many other clichés heard on public service announcements, on television docudramas, and even many years ago in high school assemblies. And yet she continued to attack the Intrafacer, ripping off my shirt and lunging. I used my entire body to protect my equipment and she pressed into me, softly slicing my forearm.

Dolly grew more desperate and I grew more defensive. She beat me but could not get to my Intrafacer; she did not know how much of myself I would give to protect it. She was determined to find out, however...

No more ticky-tack bladework from Dolly, she frantically sliced into my chest. Shit that hurt, hot and stinging. I clutched my bosom as the blood started to flow out of me, I'm only grateful that she didn't catch the nipple. Looking remorseful, Dolly too touched my wound. When she got a handful of blood, she smiled and went back at my Intrafacer. Like some warrior in front of an old idol, Dolly rubs the blood into the orifices of my hard drive, into those openings for CDs and disks.

"Noooooooooo!" I screamed and thrashed away from her, the hard drive whacking her dead on in the right nostril from the fast turn.

"Fuck!" she screams, both hands over her face. She is weeping and hollering behind her hands, and soon I realize she is also bleeding. I want to comfort her, but I am too scared. I was right to be scared for when she pulled her hand away from her nose, a gusher of red poured out which she pooled in her hands.

Standing stunned, I watched her charge at me with the blood and proceed to goop the viscous, sticky mess into my hard drive.

"Nooooooo!" I screamed again, now fully understanding what was happening, understanding Dolly was drowning my Intrafacer to death, understanding, as I heard the hard drive just stop breathing, that there would be no way to bring it to life again. Either this sudden realization or the loss of blood from the chest wound sent me dropping to the floor.

I was yelling and crying, she was yelling and crying, together we made too much noise for the stakeout police officers to ignore — even though neither of us were Dangus.

Dolly still held the knife. "Help me," she pleaded, but I had no more room in my heart for mercy.

I looked at the officers, "I'm ready to press charges. Lock the bitch up."

Channel 97:
The Electronic Integration

If last night I degenerated into a quivering, crumbling stool pigeon, then today I have arisen as Lord of my Manor. Before now, I had been afraid to wield the full power of the universal remote in my Smart House, but hitting rock bottom with nothing to lose, I brandish my scepter. Controlling my world, I soon grow confident that with enough practice and clean sight lines, I will be able to turn the entire block on and off, and after that who knows.

I have not been so mesmerized since I was first transfixed clicking the prototype remote at Prometheus Labs nearly a year ago. After a short period of time, I become a quickdraw artist, a real gunslinger, turning on multiple appliances simultaneously, or fine tuning one, adjusting another, and switching off still another all with one push of a button. Everything I had done in the past year prepared me to master this remote. My fingers now completely digital, I roll across the buttons like a Mercedes on the Autobahn. I am the Necromancer and I wave my wand across America, along Route 80; I am the new Manifest Destiny, and I point my new age gun across the plains...

But not so fast Technoman.

Have you forgotten that wild Indian Paddy Dangus? How could I? Sphere barely has a cerebrum, but he has enough wits about him to call me every day with the question. Do I even have to tell you what he asks me? "Has Dangus come yet?" And when I tell him no, he replies, "So you still have the remote then?" No, I fucking threw it into the Great South Bay, O.K. And even if Sphere didn't call, Dangus has become too much of a media icon for me to pretend he doesn't exist. The more dire his situation gets, as the police put on the pressure — they've been to my house twice a day, and I'm sure they're still on a 24-hour stakeout (you'd think my masterful remote could shut off their bugs and surveillance cameras) — the more legendary Dangus becomes. Turn on the radio, the T.V., shit he's not merely national, but fully international.

So I am now master and I am hunted. I feel like the president for Christ's sake. Something must be done. Just how desperate am I? Desperate enough to seek him out in Wyandanch. Get that? A pale mother-fucker like me, still carrying around the Intrafacer, dead and all (how could I just consign it to the scrapyard? Anyway, I thought the blood all over the thing made me look tough), brandishing a few electronic devices of comfort, with more hardware on me than most print shops, wandering along Straight Path, dropping by the all-night market and gas station asking about Dangus. That's right, the same man who couldn't even handle Dolly — although, go ahead, you try to handle Dolly when she is raging like that. Lucky for me, the citizenry of Wyandanch had been so harassed by the police in the past few days that they were willing to leave me in one piece; I can't say I deserved as much, since I had trouble believing my own story: the story goes that I wanted to give Dangus a chance to tell his tale to the world and to offer him enough *Herald* money to get him out of the country fast and comfortably.

Of course, no one told me a thing. Feeling terribly out of place, I had trouble connecting with anyone there. The crazier I behaved, the more everyone on the street knew it was merely an act. Finally, some guy named Kenny with his big arms, tight dreadlocks and a nasty stickpin in his tongue threw me up against my Smart Car. While he ostensibly threatened my person, what really made me tense was the menacing glare he gave my Intrafacer and my car, like he wanted to shoot them both right between the eyes. (How could he know my Intrafacer was already dead? Who walks around with one of those after all?)

"What are you asking so many questions for, G? Why don't you get the fuck out of here before I hurt you." I got in the car. He signaled me to glide the window down, subtly hinting that he'd smash it in if I didn't consent. "This is not the place for you, man. Give me your mouse, man."

"What?"

"Your mouse."

"Why?"

"Just give me your fucking mouse before I bust up your machine." I gave him the mouse, with Satan's finger hanging off it and all.

"What the fuck is this?" touching the finger.

"Oh that. Too hard to explain."

Kenny studied it. "You are one weird motherfucker."

He took out a pen and starting writing savagely on the top panel of the mouse, no, correct that, he dug in so deeply that he carved into the plastic. I felt the small urge well up in me to say, "Hey buddy, you're defacing my private property," an urge which I repressed. A few seconds later Kenny returned my mouse.

"Talk to me on my e-mail address only. And if the police get a hold of this, I'm coming after you." I wanted to say to Kenny that he didn't help matters by making the evidence permanent on what is essentially a part of my person — I just hope the police don't do a full body search.

As I drove back home, I cursed myself over the stupidity of the entire journey. I had no more chance connecting with the brothers of Wyandanch than I did making love to an unaltered woman; you can't connect with what you ignored, or pretended didn't exist all these years. Yet on e-mail, we might just be able to find a common thread of fiber optic. On the street no, but on the web, perhaps.

I wired Kenny, gave my address, made all types of assurances about payment and confidentiality for both him and Dangus, and waited. Within an hour, my underused home computer REX (for Rapid EXamination) clanged. Like the Intrafacer, REX had been behaving pretty temperamentally lately. But I think REX now grew painfully aware what had happened to my Intrafacer. So, REX had become my best buddy. I guess he figured his own preservation was directly connected to my ability to keep Dangus from coming after us.

Kenny's e-mail read:

Hear this and hear this once, and destroy this after you read it. Dangus doesn't want your money, he doesn't want to tell his story, he doesn't want to talk to you. He wants the remote you have, and if you have any mind behind that hard drive of yours, I'd give it to him.

I mailed back:

I know you don't want to talk to me, but I have just three more questions and I promise never to disturb you again. Did you speak to Dangus? Isn't he wounded pretty badly? Is he coming after me?

Kenny replied only three words, not even warnings or threats:

Yes. Yes. Yes.

So Dangus and I finally want the same thing. For the first time since I became aware of Dangus, I could see him in my dead monitor. He was out there somewhere with the other universal remote. My reflection and my shadow, he stands out on Main Street of cyberspace, his weapon in hand, waiting for me to step out from behind my screen and draw.

Channel 98:
Dribblers

I have been imitating originality for almost a year (much harder than imitating the things I'm accustomed to imitating, mind you), and what do I have to show for it?

1) Hair loss.

2) A dead Intrafacer.

3) An accrued debt of $127,000, despite ruthless fundraising drives, creative refinancing, and unjustifiable corporate sponsorship.

4) An unwarranted and unsolicited relationship with the police.

5) An offspring spiraling off into dementia.

6) A cardiovascular system that makes the Long Island Expressway look comparatively clear and functional.

6A) A wardrobe transferable to opening acts for Atlantic City nightclubs.

7) A universal remote.

So, it's been a very good year, though I can't see myself clamoring for renewal. I search for something else. Whenever in the past I wallowed in this type of crossroad crises, I have stretched out for the remote control and clicked months away, never keeping a channel on for too long, just enough to forget about what I should be thinking about. And now with the Universal Remote? Just try getting it out of my clutches, Mother Fucker. While you're at it, try getting the dead Intrafacer off me... I kick your ass. Better yet, I'll call the cops.

And can you believe it? The cops have left the stakeout. "Hey, where are you guys going? I like having you around now." Even though at first I hated their presence, I can't tell you how incredibly safe and secure I now feel having somebody spy on me all the time. What can go wrong when someone is always there to verify and validate your existence? They mumbled something, so I repeated with great openness and warmth, "Why you leaving?" They told me that they didn't think I was a potential target anymore, that Dangus was dying in some Wyandanch crack house, and that every spare man on the force would be needed to flush him out of hiding.

So I said, "Hey man, have you forgotten this?" I brandished the Universal Remote, and just as a reminder, gave them a digital and electronic display of sound and light and motion only normally witnessed at Fourth of July festivities.

"Nice tricks, but they are getting old," said one officer as he walked out the door.

How old? Old enough for Angelica to come by soliciting. "Next month SONY is introducing a new Universal Remote, a remote that, if the advance buzz is at all accurate, will blow the Prometheus Labs model away."

"So, what do you want from me?"

"Why don't you give me your prototype. If you give it to me, you won't have to worry about Dangus because he's not going to bother with something out of circulation. To you, it will soon just be another obsolete instrument gathering dust in your house. To me, it will be a valuable museum acquisition... a grand link in the mighty chain of diode evolution."

As I stared into my blank monitor, she saw I was unmoved. She decided to try another tack, proposing an entire wing dedicated to my year as Technoman. "You've already bequeathed much of your gadgetry and my Dad has almost all of your files from your hard drive, thank God for that considering your Intrafacer tragedy, by the way what are you planning to do with that Intrafacer, it doesn't work, does it? Well let me know when you are going to remove it, I understand how these things can take time to get over... Anyway, the Universal Remote can be the crown jewel of the wing. I would have preferred that it was never used: what could be a more beautiful and perfect piece of equipment ·than one rendered obsolete before it's ever implemented? Like one of those coins from the Franklin Mint. I've got this new ten-inch thick, impenetrable, shatter-proof polyurethane case to display it in."

I didn't want to say no; instead, I pointed the remote around the house, so the foundation rumbled and shattered. "I guess it's still a little early for you," she answered. "When you are at a point like yours, sooner or later you are going to come to the conclusion you need to get rid of your excess baggage. And when you get to that point, remember I'm there for you." Before she left, she lifted my monitor and kissed me sweetly. I nearly dropped my remote, for I hadn't expected the bizarre gesture of humanity.

I pulled my monitor back down. The Intrafacer had started to stink real bad. No matter how many times I cleaned it — and boy did I ever clean that carcass, no funeral director did so with more care — I could not get my blood out of the deep recesses of the hard drive. Yesterday, Zach dropped by and tried to cheer me up, telling me about all the updated, new and improved Intrafacer models, but I had already decided I would not get a new one after I finally relinquished this one.

After about ten trips today around the channels — time can only be measured for me in these clicks and flashes — Zach came by again. He too cared. He had seen too many melodramas in his young life to not understand his role here.

"Dad, it's time to let go."

"I know son."

"Can you take it off?"

"I'm a little weak."

"I'll help you then."

With the stitches on my chest, Zach had to be especially gingerly in removing the hard drive. He took a knife and cut the chords attaching the apparatus to my person and the dead drive clattered to the floor. Both of us winced and tried to catch the resin box before it fell, not that it mattered what happened to it now. While he removed my monitor, I detached the mouse from Satan's finger — no need trying to explain that little artifact to my boy. He stared into my eyes like he saw me for the first time after a long trip.

Both of us exhausted, I passed the Universal Remote to Zach and he became the first to operate the instrument other than me. Zach seemed surprised by my generosity. Strangely, he was only briefly engrossed by the magical handful of sorcery. He clicked channels furiously, God what a gunslinger my boy is, yet behaved guiltily and awkwardly throughout. How guiltily and awkwardly? Well during a commercial for Scott's Turfbuilder, he pointed at the man in the golf shirt mowing the lawn, and asked, "Can you show me how to do that?"

I laughed. Both of us knew he was trying too hard. After a few moments of silence, Zach zapped his way around to the NBA finals. We watched the game for much longer than either of us are accustomed, for the shooting occurred at a frantic pace, the speedy little point guards pushing the ball up and down the floor.

As one of those point guards made a deft move to drive down the lane, Zach offered, "Sure would like to learn how to do that."

This time I bit: "That's a crossover dribble. I can show you that."

"Would you?"

"Sure, next time I'm over."

"Can we go over now. I'm feeling a little antsy."

"Alright." And we drove to the house, headed in the garage and found a ball that Alice had picked up at Sunoco when she bought a tank-full of UltraPremium gasoline. I showed him how to dribble with the left hand and how to protect the ball and how to have court vision and how to bounce pass and how to push the ball up the court or, in this case, up the development streets. Magically, as with the whiffle ball, kids came out of their houses and we were all soon in front of the hoop at the neighbor's house with enough participants for a four-on-four. I played the fun neighborhood dad and was slowly figuring out I was much better at this role than as Technoman.

As my boy learned the crossover dribble, it dawned on me that I could become a Suburban Dad for an entire year merely by declaring myself such in a column. I could play the role so many play daily. They would not read it for its originality, but for its familiarity. And I... I think now I can safely say, I could learn to live with familiarity, since I know, and you now know too, that I am merely imitating it.

And as the game developed, Zach performed an absolutely miraculous impression of the play-by-play man announcing the NBA finals. He seemed like a real son to me and I seemed like a real father. I only wish my Intrafacer was still alive to record this moment.

Channel 99:
Waiting for the Corpse

Even when we first started moving the boxes back into her little cottage on Fire Island, both Little Augie and I had our eyes out on the ocean. We waited for something to wash ashore and, as we started to unpack the kitchen boxes, Little Augie spoke nervously.

"The worst of it is that I think he is visiting me in my dreams."

"He hasn't done that before. What would make you think he's doing that now?"

"Because every night I see him as Father Jeremiah, terminally ill in the oncology ward. In my dream, I come see to him during all the visiting hours. I want to leave, but the stupid nurses let me stay over the designated time. I'm stuck making small talk with a dying devil."

"Sounds like a ball of laughs."

"What's worse, he never initiates any of the conversations. I've got to keep talking and asking questions and complimenting. God it's exhausting."

"I could imagine."

"And that's not the worst of it. As I keep talking to him, I gradually remember, right smack in the middle of the dream, how he got in this terminal condition in the first place."

"Was he contaminated at a nuclear power plant?"

"No, nothing like that at all. I found the son of a bitch here on the beach at Fire Island like all the other Satans, only this one was not dead."

"What did he just walk out of the water?"

"No, he was lying on the shore, like he should be dead, but the bastard was still breathing, you know wheezing and coughing up blood and mucous like he would die any moment. Only he didn't die. And so I took him to the hospital."

"Why didn't you just let him die on the shore or burn him like all the other Satans?"

"Now how could I do that? That would be inhuman, after all."

"Need I remind you we are talking about Satan here."

"Still. I am not here to kill. So when he gets into the emergency room, they stabilize him and the next thing I know he's in ICU on life support. The worst of it, they can't put him on Medicare, so I have to pay his medical bills, and, of course, they won't let me put him on my insurance, the bastards."

"That sucks."

"You bet your ass it sucks. It makes perfect sense, his refusing to croak, wearing me down, corroding my soul."

"I doubt he'd do such a thing," I suggested. "If he did it to you now, he won't be able to give you that as a torture in hell."

"What are you talking about? Why wouldn't he be able to do it in hell?"

"I don't think Satan would repeat himself. He'll have something new."

"If I've learned anything in his life, it is that Hell will offer nothing new. That would be heaven. Hell is all reruns, and particularly bad ones at that."

What do you say after that? "Good thing it's only a dream."

"Yeah, good thing." We worked for hours moving everything in, with one eye always on the ocean, waiting for a body to come in. And you know how it is, if you wait long enough for something, it is bound happen, so of course some undefinable form did make its way to the beach, and of course, we lost interest in our duties and fast.

The late afternoon fog rolled in, so the figure was misty and shrouded. It rested on a sand bar about a hundred feet from the shore. Pushed in by the oncoming high tide, it was soon washed over by the green salty waters that crept up toward Little Augie's beach house. For longer than either of us would have expected, we tried to puzzle out the figure from the safety of the cottage. She passed the binoculars to me: "Do you think it's him?"

I saw a fuzzy, waterlogged blob. "Can't tell." What I could tell though, whatever it was, the sucker was moving — that I could see, even through the layer of pea soup that obscured our vision — flopping and twisting, in the throes of a life and death struggle. I'm sure Little Augie had seen that through the binoculars too. We made our way to the shore, but the tide kept rushing in on us, lifting up across the sand, creating first a creek, then a stream and finally a river between us and the figure. Like two searchers wandering, we peered out into the gloom, straining our eyes to identify the figure, instead only being able to identify the movement — it was breathing and flailing, like it had to do backflips to get in the necessary air.

If you have ever been out on the ocean off the beaches of Long Island in June, you know how fucking cold it is. The water is maybe sixty degrees (my pecker puts it more at fifty-eight). Yet still, we had to go, so I held Augie's hand and we waded out, moaning worst at those intervals when we hit first the toes, then the crotch and finally the nipples. I buoyed Little Augie's shrunken frame to keep her from going under.   We silently considered what kind of colds and sickness would afflict us from this short crossing and thanked the geological contours that the water receded before it reached our faces.

As we stepped onto the sand bar, I pulled Little Augie close and said, "Before we get there, I want you to promise me now, if it's Satan, we don't agree to life support."

"Sounds nice, but pulling the plug on Satan is not as easy as it sounds."

I was going to argue with her, but the hypothetical nature of the discussion made pursuit of the debate ridiculous. Even when we were on the sand bar, we couldn't identify the figure, the mist and the twilight mucking up the visibility so severely. Our imaginations were getting the better of us, for the ocean winds and sea lappings were the stuff of haunted nightmares and piratical sneers. And when nature's dark forces abated, we manufactured our own suspense and mystery. Shit, is this how you underlings of the world live, with no intrafacer or remote control about your person? How could you be sane? I would tell you more, but the pressure became so great in my skull that I made a conscious decision to not think any further until I could make out the figure.

The wizened old Little Augie identified it first. "Thank God!" she exclaimed.

"Yeah."

It was not Satan. It was not human. It was a fish. No, it was a mammal. Sprays of warm mist piffed from its spout. "It's a baby whale."

"Thank God."

"It's dying too."

"Thank God." What a relief! I no longer shivered and the color was returning to Little Augie. A heaving of snot bubbled from the calf's spout as I cautiously drew closer. He almost stunk as bad as Satan with his rotting, fishy exhalations. I wanted to turn away, but his sharp little eye out of the side of the huge head caught mine. It would not let me turn away without attention. Now that we finally reached him, the calf flailed much less, his lower and upper jaws quivered just enough for me to detect a slight overbite. When he arched, the calf revealed some stubbly hair on his pocked underside, a boy's scraggly beard. On his right side, small pink little lice lifted their mandibles, weakly threatening. They too seemed to be dying as they climbed over barnacles looking for a healthy piece of flesh to chew into.

The left side was much darker and cleaner, less diseased. The left eye continued to stare at me, only occasionally squinting toward its demise. I dropped my hand on the clean side and stroked his skin. It was a thick, slimy inner tube and the more I rubbed the more he moved as if he were playing with me. Naturally, I grew scared of something that could play even while it was dying. Little Augie too rubbed the calf.

"There's nothing we can do for him," she said. What a relief to have this woman of science assure me. "We must let nature take its course."

By the time we left, the whale was almost dead. We knew it wouldn't survive the night. Back at the house, we each needed a few towels and a long time in front of the fire to drive the chill away. When Little Augie looked fully revived, I asked her, "And if Satan's body washes ashore?"

She now turned calm and philosophical. "There are worse things I could do with my life than burn up the devil's body every day."

We drank plenty of hot cocoa and stared at the fire. By the time I hung her pictures, midnight had passed and the clearing air paved the way for tropical breezes. Even with the ridiculously huge, illuminated full moon, the stars fought for spots in the sky and Little Augie, tasting the salt of the warming summer waves, did not know whether to look up or look out. Either way, she wouldn't sleep tonight. I could have, even should have, stayed with her, but I left.

In the distance, laughter from pleasure craft whistled and echoed about our ears as they hooked in and out of the Great South Bay. I could hear them long after I lost sight of Little Augie who I imagine was now standing at the shore, shivering, unable to spread her frail arms to the ocean, awaiting the dawn.

Channel 100:
The 7 Synthetic Voyages of Technoman
Part VII: Dangus Kong

I rise up the high speed elevator until I land on the eighty-sixth floor. I emerge at the city's sky and slide past the gift shop. Shuffling by the tourists, who with their cameras take pictures of me as well as the city, I find Dad out on the Observation Deck. He is in the final years of his employment at the Empire State Building back in the 70s, yet anachronistically I am wearing my Intrafacer and scads of other hardware. While I have come from far away to meet him here, Dad merely elevates himself a few floors.

Wounded and weak, Mom and Dave Miller stand to the south, looking out at the Statue of Liberty and Ellis Island. Giving me the nod, Dad turns to them and hands each a remote. They hold their instruments and point out, lighting Lady Liberty's torch. Both of them are soothed, not completely healed mind you, but for the first time in their memory, the pain seems bearable. Dad now looks at me and pulls from his jacket this huge gadget — it is the Universal Remote. He hands it to me with a wan grave smile, like he is passing me his liver.

I accept the gift and can't get my fingers on the buttons fast enough. I press and tap and shoot out signals across the Manhattan skyline. I am not soothed at all by the remote, instead charged like I've never been before, and I aim it out to the world as towers flicker and tremble to my touch. Buildings bend toward me but I must have more and I hurry over to the service elevator. I am no tourist... I know how to get to the one-hundred-and-second floor. Yet before the elevator door closes, some kid slips on. It is Zach.

"How the hell did you get here?"

"I followed you."

"Why?"

"Can I play with the remote?"

"In a few minutes when I am through using it."

The elevator opens up in the ozone layer. I turn on television sets in Staten Island and ignite methane flames out of its mountainous landfill. Zach keeps tugging at my arm, "Daddy, let me open the cages at the Bronx Zoo."

"In a minute."

I fire up the brick ovens of a Nunzio Bakery in Nutley, New Jersey and switch on the landing lights at LaGuardia.

"Can I now, Dad?"

"In a minute."

I need more height and start scaling the peak of the Empire State Building, toward its mighty antenna. Only a few feet up, I can already increase the sonar of a tuna boat out off Montauk Point; a few more steps higher I can beam my signal out into the ocean's deep caverns. Sharks and moray eels vibrate.

"Cool, Dad, it's been more than a minute."

"Just one more minute."   ·

A few more steps higher and I reach Washington, lasering into the White House, changing the channel on the president's TV from C-Span to cartoons. He chuckles, thinking one of his inner circle has played a little joke on him.

I laugh too, but I am soon past him, climbing higher, my sights set on Disney World. Zach crawls along right by my leg.

"C'mon Dad, Disney World, let me zap Disney World."

"In a minute."

Rising to the halfway point of the antenna and preparing to click, I spot a figure in the haze coming up fast, like a ghostly spider. I can't see his face, but sure as shit know who he is. I try to keep climbing, yet he moves too quickly and is on me in a minute.

"Get away." I say feebly. I try to grip the remote tight, but he has it out of my hands so easily that I am too lost to battle with him. He is still climbing though, right to the top and I give chase, Zach still on my leg. When he reaches the pinnacle, he holds the remote gingerly like its Fay Wray or something, swings on the antenna, and beats his chest in grand aping mockery.

Now I am pissed and I drag my ass up that antenna, scaling like a rock climber. I reach the peak and I reach for Dangus, but he is already going back down, expectorating a laugh that makes even the Twin Towers shiver. He pretends to hit buttons, clowning about with his fingers, intimating that there could be no more infantile and stupid behavior. Bastard manages to hit one button though as he slides down to the one-hundred-and-second floor: the one to light the antenna. I might as well have a halogen bulb up my ass. I sprawl out like a weather vane across the top of the building.

Dangus is out of sight and all is lost.

I want to leap off the building and end this dream, but my Intrafacer gets stuck on the antenna. Even as I jump away, I cannot move. And Zach still clings to my leg. I am attached to the transmitter, and now instead of pointing out and altering the world, I stand helpless as signals sear into and through me. I keep thinking they will merely bounce off, a soft blow, perhaps a bit of jostling. Yet the signals come faster and stronger, the waves transmit via my veins.

I slump over and fall asleep, resigned to my role as a conduit.

Channel 101:
Trying To Lose a Grip

Equipment is flying out of my house like a midnight madness sale. I just waved Angelica farewell as she drove off with my Intrafacer, the last piece of me worth keeping. I don't expect to see her again until I acquire something else worthwhile. No, that's unfair: Angelica actually asked me to move out to the Tesla Institute with her. I laughed and declined, although my less digital circuitry could convince myself that she loves me. After she leaves, I stare up at the ceiling and see Angelica's naked body next to mine like two accessory parts; that and a thousand other visions make a slide show in my head. Three cups of iced coffee fight it out with a handful of Somnoids, the battle did not exhaust or even ease my tossing and blinking as I could neither wake nor sleep beyond three-minute intervals. I convulse in my last throes as Technoman, wishing my eyes would stay closed.

So naturally, on this last night of the full moon, unwilling to let nature take its course, I grip my hand firmly to the remote, my head an insistent thunderstorm, and every time the lightening struck I shudder lost with a swelled tongue blocking my throat. With the universal remote, I compulsively turn on and off my entire home, adjusting its collective volumes, tweaking its speeds, its levels, its entropies, modulating and fine tuning every nuance till each appliance grew indistinguishable from the others.

I don't think Dangus expected me awake when he appeared at 4:30 in the morning. Still, I must have presented myself sufficiently catatonic for him to brazenly show his grotesquely follicled countenance to me, all beard and locks, a cruddy, fishing cap on his head. As he ventures to pry the remote away, I can't make out his face at all. His tugs and pulls on the remote are tremendously compelling.

No luck for Dangus though, because I hold tight like my arm has been hours dead, stiffening around the apparatus. I stare right into his ghostlike visage and spot the bloody wound on his shoulder. I want to believe that he too was dying, but I know he is just living badly like me. He takes a good look at me and laughs, wagging a finger to the mighty remote. From his pocket he pulls out his own remote: it is a cheesy little instrument, a five-and-dimer. Nonetheless, he points it at mine and clicks.

A wicked driving surge shoots up my arm like I had just grabbed hold of live electrical wiring. I drop the remote and shudder. Good thing I am wearing my sneakers.

Dangus's mocking laugh shames me to pick up the remote again. I grab the instrument defiantly, yet I notice it is a little altered. A small grey disc is stuck to its back. Fucking Dangus wasn't trying to take my remote after all; instead, he wanted to convert it. I start to tug on the disc and Dangus laughs harder. I look up and see him standing in the shadows, aiming his primitive little remote at me.

"Arrrguh!" this time the pain is much worse, perhaps because my hand was all over the surge device, a veritable atomic bomb in my palm. The remote falls to the floor though I don't even try to let go of it.

I stand helpless, weaponless, staring at Dangus with all his hair, his shadows and his miserable fishing cap. I can't make out his face. Because he is too much Dangus, I begin to wonder whether this guy is Dangus at all, or just another one his imitators. Beaming out to him an appropriately suspicious look, I fashion he is a mad villain in a James Bond film.

Of course, once I begin envisioning him this way, he transforms himself to small and sad, holding his right hand over his bloody shoulder, the left weakly on that crappy remote. I wait for him to grab the mighty universal prize, but he appears more interested in saying goodbye, like we are best friends of something. He gives me a nod. I want to hand him the remote, but I confess I'm afraid to pick it up. Instead, *he* tosses *me* his barbaric little control and laughs.

Almost instantly Dangus, or whoever he is, seems stronger, even with the oozing wound. I bend down and snatch up my mighty remote. Now I have a remote in each hand, and I use the cruddy one to scrape away at the surge device. He laughs louder, uncontrollably, doubling over from the fit. He lifts his hands as a sign he's had enough, continuing to chuckle as he is leaving my Smart House.

I follow him toward that beat-up white truck, I like a zombie ghoul, still holding the remote toward him, pointing and clicking, trying to adjust him with the rest of the phenomenon in my world.

When he starts the truck — a newer, less dented white truck, obviously stolen from a Dangus wannabe — I start the Smart Car, remote still in hand … How could he know that I followed him only for the purpose of giving him the remote; I decide it is a burden I no longer want. Yet the more I wave it across the windshield, and even as he catches sight of it in his rear view, the faster he drives.

As a gesture either to salute or spite him, I hurl his crappy little remote toward his replacement truck, the instrument naturally falling far short of its mark. I manage to run it over as I continue to pursue. Driving on, I tell myself the visitation is merely an hallucination. Yes, much better, much more fitting for this nonsense not to be happening.

I am able to stay on his tail over the Verrazano Narrows, through Staten Island, even over the Goethals. But somewhere in Jersey, as the factory smoke in the dawn light forms a perverse, inverse rainbow, I lose sight of him. Maybe he selected the service road when I took to the main turnpike.

He seems to be expressly driving away from Long Island, away from suburbia. If so, he damn well better have a full tank of gas and a credit card.

Channel 102:
They Come With Warning Labels

Thank the Lord I got off my ass and started fixing up Alice's house. I very well may have saved Zach's life. An overstatement? You be the judge. I'm out clipping the hedges ("Jungles have fewer vines," claims Alice) and my boy is with me, watching, studying. Then at the third hedge (and I do, by the way, have a gift for trimming — I cut beveled edges that would give an English gardener a stiffy), Zach reaches out his hand toward the electric clipper. I came this close to whacking off a couple of his fingers, but I pulled the machinery away instinctively.

"What the hell are you doing?" I asked.

"Just wanted to see how well it cuts?"

"You almost lost your hand there. Be careful."

Zach laughed a snorting laugh, you know, one I could easily interpret as a scoff. "It's not funny." When he chuckled a bit more, I took drastic action and whipped out from my pocket Satan's finger.

Believe it or not, Zach didn't seem fazed. Funny, the finger still made me shudder, what with its shriveling hair and dried blood and gnarled, fungusy orientation? Jesus, what do you have to keep in your pocket to impress a kid nowadays?

Nor was Zach done. As I tarred the driveway, he rolled about in it giggling, plucking grass blades, tossing them in the air, and then watching them stick to his body. Throughout the performance, I ordered him to stop, warned him of the material's toxicity, and watched him imitate an animated figure from a show I've never viewed.

I don't want to even tell you about the miter saw crisis, when Zach announced he wanted to see his forearm cut at a 45-degree angle. When I told Alice about Zach's behavior, all Alice could reply is, "What do you expect from him? The only time he has ever seen a man use power tools was in a Ninja combat arcade game. He thinks whenever anything bad happens to him, he can just hit the reset button and start again."

That very day, Zach tested this notion on a trip to Home Depot. As we wandered through the outdoor garden section, Zach intentionally let a forklift run over his foot. While I expected to see pie crust where his toes were supposed to be, he soon shook the damage out of him, after an appropriate cartoonish red-faced scream.

"He'll be hospitalized before the day is through," I muttered to myself. Suddenly I understood how necessary it was for me to embark on a new life. How else could I endure the anxiety of constantly thrusting out my protective hands so my boy doesn't bump into the sharp metal corners of the world?

By the time I left Home Depot, laden with supplies, machinery, and home furnishings, I was contemplating trading in my Smart Car for a Minivan. I certainly need one to navigate Zach through this treacherous theme park known as Long Island.

Yes, I suddenly understood.

Zach needed me and I needed a new life. More importantly, I needed a new column.

Could I do it? Perhaps if I could assure myself full-time fatherhood was only a year-long venture and I was merely playing a role? I *could* grow out of my familial squeamishness. What more is there to it than firing up the barbecue, fertilizing the lawn and dropping down ceramic tile in the kitchen? I could begin to heal Alice who has lived Suburbia all alone; now I will comfort her the way the remote control has comforted me. That night Alice wore a totally bourgeois negligee and we made love. Somehow the whole thing was good... very good... even wonderful. I imagine my Saturdays could begin with coaching

Zach's soccer team and end with a marathon visit to the Price Club.

So I roam about the house and the yard, a property secondarily to inhabit, primarily to renovate. If my life had consisted of being faxed, phoned, clanged and beeped, now I will be the one sending my own little messages to the world. I grew up with the whispered prediction, a modest prediction at that, that we'd all be spacemen before we died. Like every other prediction of our generation, it has sort of been realized. I will transform my space. No longer just another hit on a website, I will become simultaneously the master, architect, contractor, subcontractor, builder, plumber, painter, landscaper, electrician, carpenter, and janitor of my center-hall colonial. And for all these roles, Zach will be my apprentice. That should increase his chances of making it to adulthood.

Alice drafted a "Honey-Do" list that could fill five computer screens. Space is not the final frontier: it is the first place a suburban dad can prove his manhood. And with my hedge clipper and weed whacker and leaf blower, I will be armed to the teeth. I can actually feel my hair follicles invigorated.

So if you are heading through Long Island and you see me out in the yard, I'd advise you to get out of the driveway because I'll be out with my squeegee and broom and I'll tar your ass to the blacktop if you're not careful.

I dream of Dangus coming to my home trying to rip out my security system, only to find me there with a nail-gun to his head and a Sawzall to his throat. I see it now, the heroic capture itself captured on home video. Yet Dangus doesn't call. Angelica does; she urges me to donate the Universal Remote to the Tesla Institute. "Hey you've moved out of your Smart House, how useful can it be for you?"

"Useful" was one of those words that at this moment of my life meant everything and nothing to me. Instead of the remote, I offered her Satan's finger. In response, she asked me, relegated to incredulous phone tones, "What the hell am I supposed to do with that?"

I didn't answer her, just merely hung up the phone. I remembered it is the end of June and that, by every right, her father ought to be in some chemistry classroom hacking off his next digit about now. The injustice of it all! I immediately called and offered him Satan's finger. He accepted. I like giving Old Man Miller the finger... such a neat, pat, suburban gesture.

The Universal Remote, however, I did not relinquish, nor could I put it in a glass case, for despite everything the two of us have been through, I couldn't keep my hands off it. I even refuse to remove the surge device: that now must be considered another of the instrument's many accessories.

And in those wee hours of the morning when I am truly alone and desolate and I have emerged with the insight that my life has been a series of sequels spun off from an early whiffle ball game, I reach for the remote and click about, pausing at this current life stage a few extra moments on the home repair shows. I click out into the night across the century with a universal remote already obsolete for this universe, stuck in an old universe that moves just fast enough for me not to notice that nothing is new on TV tonight; instead, I face merely a dazzling, glittering kaleidoscope of reruns.

Channel 103:
SuburboMan? What Kind of a Name Is That?

Pines Tar. A New World Manifesto

As I write this column, our best sources say that Paddy Dangus has surfaced in Nevada. Authorities are uncertain whether he is bent on terrorizing Las Vegas or has set his sights on the National Nuclear Waste Site at Los Adios Canyon. Anyway, Dangus's departure is a reminder that we all need a change periodically.

So with a year under my belt, I announce that I have now officially hung up my Intrafacer and put away my plastic Technoman uniform. I leave technology for as good a reason as I strapped it on. Once I realized how difficult a time I was having breaking free of technology, I knew I must go. Hey, the surface of the earth is soft and impressible by the treads of machines. Technology gives a smooth, comfortable ride, not easy to get off. Yet, I have several more lives I have to live.

If you are already missing Technoman, don't fret. Dangus biographer Dave Miller is coming out with *Hard Driving Man*, an unauthorized biography of my life as Technoman. You can get an advanced copy for the special introductory low price of $27.95.

O.K., now on to new business. The fiscal year is over and so is my tenure as Technoman. I part the Resin Curtain with a new lifestyle and a new manifesto. Now fear not, faithful readers. I won't distress you with unwarranted originality, vision or inspiration. My manifesto embraces comforting familiarities and soothing clichés, since I vow to be true to its subject matter — that of Suburbia.

The Suburban Manifesto

1. I will renovate every inch of my house, whether it needs alteration or not.

2. I will fertilize my lawn with an eight-step process, employing the appropriate spreaders at the appropriate settings.

3. I will only eat food purchased from Price Club or another food warehouse consortium, except of course for those outside visitations to Chucky-Cheese, McDonald's or Nathan's.

4. I will cover every exterior surface of my house and property with Vinyl Siding.

5. I will trim hedges and bushes weekly. I will plant additional bushes to create a more uniform and manicured property.

6. I will take up golf, play weekly, exalt its virtues, its glories, its absolute necessity.

7. I will only support business establishments within shopping malls.

8. I will help coach every junior athletic league that my son joins, and he *will* join leagues, and I will accept nothing less than head coach of the soccer team.

9. I will only make love to women who are card-carrying members of the PTA.

10. I will bring my family on vacation at least once a year to Disney World, twice a year if the Magic Kingdom is celebrating an anniversary.

11. I will spend all remaining discretionary funds on insurance policies, tax shelters, and childhood birthday parties.

12. I will have on-hand and I will use, whenever physically possible, a camcorder at every and all events, big and small, in our lives.

13. I will produce at least one more child to whom I can teach the other twelve tenants of the manifesto.

Yes, I will be nothing less than a soccer coaching, mall shopping, PTA attending, baby making, minivan driving, lawn nurturing, Disney visiting, kitchen tiling, jumbo-pack eating, wallpaper bordering SuburboMan. That right's, SuburboMan. Stupid name, huh? Well no matter, I'll be whom I'll be. Well no matter, I'll be there.

If a short order cook is needed at a pancake breakfast to raise money so that senior citizens can take a trip to factory outlets in Pennsylvania, I'll be there. And if a caller is needed at Family Night Bingo, I'll be there. And if a neighbor's weed whacker gets mangled on a hidden stone, I'll be there to trim away the overgrown edges. And if boxer shorts and creative positioning are needed to make a baby or two, I'll be there. And if Disney World celebrates golf history month as the exclusive promotional preview videos now indicate, I'll be there to play a round with Mickey Mouse. And if the cicadas are particularly bad this year, I'll be there on the phone to LawnMaster setting up extra tree sprayings. And if some eight-year-old soccer punk trips up one of my midfielders, I'll be there to scream at the ref. And if there is a once-in-a-lifetime sale, or sales once-in-a-decade or in-a-year or in-a-season, I'll be there, ready to sign up for a new department store credit card to get an extra ten percent off. And if I find any holes in my life or any holes in the lives of my beloved family and friends, I'll be there with the spackle to plug them up.

Yes, I'll be there, and I'll be here too, writing about my experiences for an entire year. I'd advise you to clear out a bookshelf, so you can start collecting the columns like *National Geographic*.